I0586047

Warlock's Path

The Dragon Wars Saga Volume Three

By Marius H. Visser

DRAKE
PRESS

Copyright © 2022 Marius H. Visser
All rights reserved. No part of this book may be reproduced or
transmitted in any form or by any means, electronic or mechanical,
including photocopying, recording, or by any information storage and
retrieval system, without permission in writing from the copyright
owner.
This is a work of fiction. Names, characters, places and incidents either
are the product of the author's imagination or are used fictitiously, and
any resemblance to any actual persons, living or dead, events, or
locales is entirely coincidental.

Published 2022 by Drake Press

ISBN: 9780645301618 (Paperback)
9780645301601 (Hardback)
9780645092271 (ePub)

NATIONAL
LIBRARY
OF AUSTRALIA

A catalogue record for this
work is available from the
National Library of Australia

Dragon Wars Saga

Daughter Of The Ageian
King's Plight
Warlock's Path

Tales From Kraydenia

Mercury Dagger

Short Stories

Cracked sky
The Call of Jonas Creed

Acknowledgement

To long days, a great wife, and copious amounts of coffee, thank you all.

To my brilliant cover designer, Andrei Bat, thank you for making these covers amazing.

To Floyd Largent, a great editor and friend. This book is a better version, thanks to you.

Foreword

Thank you for picking up Warlock's Path. I really hope you enjoy this novel. If you have a moment, please leave a review on your preferred store as this will allow me the opportunity to write more books such as this. I will really appreciate it. Reviews are especially critical in today's world. Help other fantasy readers and tell them why you enjoyed this book. Thank you!

* Leave a Review here:

http://Amazon.com/review/create-review?&asin=B09Y89F5VD

or scan this:

Want to stay updated with news about my books?

* Join my mailing list at:

https://www.mariushvisser.com/contact

* Like me on Facebook:

https://www.facebook.com/mariushvisserbooks

* Follow me on Twitter:

https://twitter.com/MariusHVisser

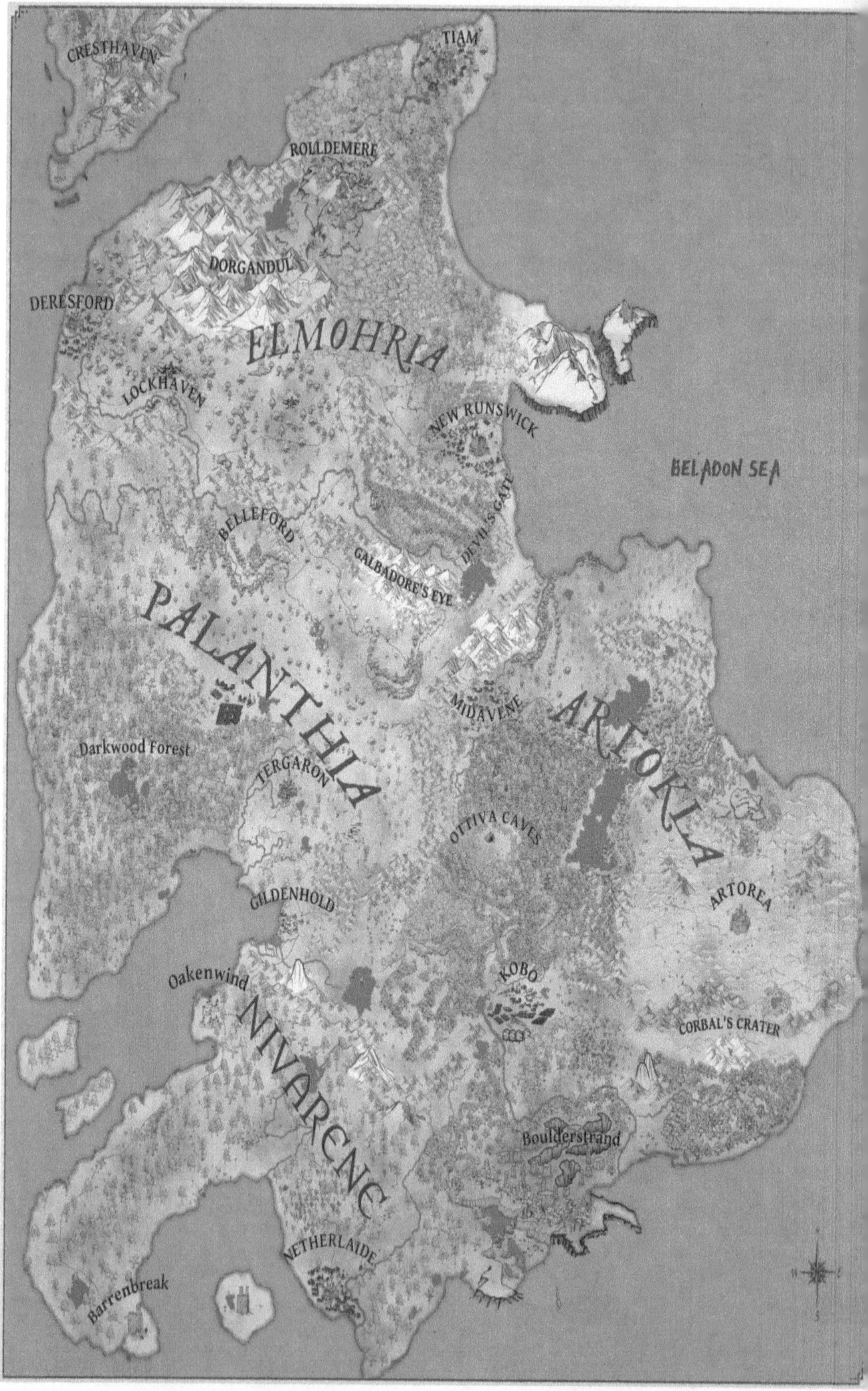
CRESTHAVEN
TIAM
ROLLDEMERE
DORGANDUL
DERESFORD
ELMOHRIA
LOCKHAVEN
NEW RUNSWICK
BELADON SEA
DEVIL'S GATE
BELLEFORD
GALBADORE'S EYE
PALANTHIA
MIDAVENE
ARTOKLA
Darkwood Forest
TERGARON
OTTIVA CAVES
ARTOREA
GILDENHOLD
KOBO
Oakenwind
NIVARENE
CORBAL'S CRATER
Boulderstrand
NETHERLAIDE
Barrenbreak

Chapter One

Sweat dribbled down his forehead, accumulating on his brows to rush down his cheeks and wet his inch-thick black beard. The day's work was finally done. Hadron turned to gaze at the gigantic blocks of granite being readied for the arduous journey back to Oakenwind. The rollers under the blocks creaked and groaned from the weight, and he thought for a moment that they would burst from the pressure applied. Men were drifting off from the quarry and heading back home to rest their bleeding hands. Tomorrow, they would be back to do it again.

'Hadron! Here's your coin for the day.'

Turning to the man, he caught the tossed pouch, pulled out a coin, and bit it. 'Are you keeping a record of my time spent teaching these greenhorns? I should get double what the rest make, Farris.'

'And I should be married to Queen Yalvia, but we can't all have what we want. It's not practical,' said the brooding foreman.

'And how do ya figure that? You ain't got no ties to the royal line, nor are you a prince. Heck, you're not even clean most of the time. I worked for this coin.'

Farris scowled through clenched teeth. 'Now, you listen to me. I don't care what you want or what you're owed. You get what you get. But keep showing initiative, and I'll see to it you always get a spot for the day. How's that?'

A long, deep sigh escaped Hadron before he said, 'Sure thing, Farris. I'll see you tomorrow, you old goat.' His feet burned from the long day's work and constant walking; his toes throbbing with the relentless chafing. *I can still make it back home before dark if I jog. Maybe surprise Veranay with a nice steak tonight. Don't know where she got her appetite from, or where she puts all the food. I'll have to ask her mother when I see her again. Oh, who am I kidding? I can't afford a nice steak. Maybe Yanric can get me some goat meat for cheap, although the bastard won't be happy I'm bothering him after hours. His shop will surely be closed by now.*

Hadron's boot caught on a jutting rock, quickly snapping him out of his thoughts. The ground rushed at him, scattered rocks waiting to draw blood. Arms flailing, eyes wide, he drew in a sharp, deep breath, already feeling the rocks skinning his hands and knees before he righted himself, quickly regaining his footing. 'Phew, that was close. Nearly got my face all scraped up.' A clopping sound from his boot made him stop, and he leaned against a tree to see the sole come away. 'Agh, shit biscuits!' He felt like hitting his head against the tree trunk. Eyes closed, he calmed himself and continued walking, the annoying clopping of his boot his companion for the rest of the journey.

High above, the moon had already proclaimed its dominance in the sky, just waiting for the sun to disappear over the horizon to call out its victory. Yet even with the sun still hovering over the rim of the world, casting its light on the lands, darkness was creeping in on his thoughts. *Now there'll be another stop for tonight. Another hand to fill with coin before I can head home.*

The usually busy streets of the village were quiet already, and Hadron was glad no one stopped to talk with him in his foul mood. Up ahead, to the side of the muddy street, the leerie walked from post to post to light the lanterns and give life to the coming darkness. He turned down a short alley and stopped at a door with the number four carved into the lintel above its frame. Annoyed, he rapped his knuckles on the dark wood. The door swung open, and the old cordwainer smiled at him through his raspy beard. 'Hadron! Good to see you again. Come in, come in,' he said as he moved back from the door, making way for his friend to enter.

Forced to smile, Hadron took the old man's shoulders and said, 'Not tonight, I'm afraid. I have to go by the butcher still and get home for Veranay's birthday.'

The old cordwainer's face lit up, and he said, 'Oh my. How old is she now? They grow up so fast, don't they?'

'She's turning sixteen, Cedoric, and getting more of a handful with every waking day.'

'Ha ha, yes, I believe you there, my friend. Soon she might be married off, though, and will become someone else's burden.'

Hadron chuckled. 'Poor sod.' He removed his boots and handed them over as he continued, 'Can you repair these for me? I'll need them by tomorrow morning before going back to work.'

Cedoric examined the damage to the boot, pulling the leathers apart. 'Yes, I think I can have it ready for you.'

'I'm sorry to have to do this to you, but I have little to spend.' Eyes closed and frowning with humiliation, Hadron felt the old man's hand on his arm and opened his eyes, staring at the thoughtful green eyes behind the spectacles.

'It's okay. I'll use some offcuts and spare materials. Besides, I have nothing else to do tonight. I was just going to rest for a bit.'

'Thank you, Cedoric. It means a lot to me. I promise I'll make it up to you.'

'I tell you what, send Veranay here to learn the trade and help me out from time to time, and we can make this arrangement more often. My old hands are struggling these days. I'm becoming brittle and start bleeding if someone whispers too loudly. You probably had no time to get her something, so just hold on for a moment.' The old man disappeared for a while, with rummaging sounds coming from within his dwelling.

Hadron leaned through the door, glimpsing bright orange flames dancing in the hearth, feeling the warmth spread through the home, and called out, 'Cedoric? Are you okay?'

'Yes, of course,' said the cordwainer as he reappeared, holding a brown leather satchel. 'I've been dabbling in creating more than just shoes, and made this. Please, give it to her. It would mean a lot to me if she were to wear it out and about. This is a gift from you. Not me, you hear?'

Hadron smiled and said, 'You're too good a friend, Cedoric. I'll speak with Veranay. I think she would enjoy learning a new skill. Take care now. I'll see you tomorrow morning.'

Cedoric winked and said, 'Send my greetings to the little she-devil.'

With the door closed, Hadron turned and whispered, 'Now the butcher.' *If I could only make some more coin somehow...but how?* he thought when a bird chirped from a tree to his right, quickly chased away by the lunging of a white cat. 'Nearly got him this time, Binx. If you lost some weight, maybe you could've had him.' The cat turned to him, walking gracefully on the branch before leaping to the ground. A few quick strides and Binx rubbed himself against Hadron's worn pants, trilling and meowing, begging for a scratch. 'Okay, okay. What's all this today? Feeling a bit left out? Where's your mum? You know she doesn't like you running around outside. Come on.' Hadron scooped up the cat, feeling it purr deep in its chest, and walked to a nearby window of an apartment, depositing Binx through the open slit. 'Don't wander off again, or I'm telling on you.'

'Is that darned cat out again?' asked a man swaying back and forth on his porch, trying to grab at the pillar holding up the awning over the balcony.

'I'm afraid he was, Ciril.'

'Missus Machelen must get that little beast under control. If he eats one more of my birds, I'm having cat soup for dinner!'

Annoyed at the drunken lout, Hadron looked away and said, 'Go to bed, Ciril. He won't be bothering you again soon.' He rounded the corner and stopped before the butcher's shop, seeing some lanterns still lit at the back while Yanric was preparing the meat for the next day, salting fresh slabs and hanging them to dry.

'Yanric! You mind opening for me? I know I'm a bit late. Work went on longer than I thought today.' A grunt came from inside the shop, and after a moment of silent staring, Yanric moved closer and unlatched the door. The smell of the spiced and salted meat reached for his nose as the door swung open, and Hadron's stomach churned with hunger. 'Thank you, Yanric. Ooh! What happened to you?' he asked, seeing a purple bruise covering Yanric's right eye.

The stocky butcher whisked away his dirty brown hair and winced as he touched the eye, then said, 'Darn wife of mine's got a mean left hook. Had a little too much of the macho juice and told her off for being so damned needy. She's pretty spry for an old gal. Ha ha.'

Hadron bent over slightly as he chuckled. 'Last time you'll be saying that, I reckon. That's gonna leave a lasting impression.'

Annoyed, Yanric asked, 'What do you want, Hadron?'

'Just came by for some meat. Do you have anything that won't take the clothes from my back?'

The butcher turned and walked down the stairs. 'Wait here. I'll be right back.'

Alone in the little store, Hadron stood with hands resting on the counter, looking at the bloodied knives and cleavers. An image popped into his head of the cleaver cutting effortlessly through bone and flesh, sending chunks flying with every stroke, wondering how easily it could take a hand or a few fingers. A shiver ran down his spine, and he shuddered at the thought.

'You're in luck. Seems I have some chuck steak left over that I really can't keep any longer. Still good to eat for now. You want it? Give me five pieces and we'll call it even.'

'Yes, thank you. Here,' Hadron said as he placed the coins on the counter and waited for the butcher to wrap the meat.

'Be sure to cook it properly.'

Got to get home. It's getting late. 'Thank you, Yanric.' Hadron took the meat with a nod of acknowledgement and made his way down the street, rushing to get home and start a fire. He knew Veranay would soon be home from school, if she wasn't already, complaining about the amount of work they made them do and how annoying it was to learn to sew while the boys could learn swordplay. He stopped before his little home and saw no lanterns lit as yet, then quickly went round back to start a fire. In the dark, he could not see how the little home was falling apart, but at the back of his mind, he knew exactly how the timbers were rotting, the floorboards sagging, bending underfoot, and the cabinets' hinges rusting to break apart at the slightest bit of misuse. There were several leaks in the roof, and with any hard rainfall, buckets would need to be emptied regularly, yet his Veranay never mentioned this, never complained. She didn't need to, and he knew she knew why.

Sparks flew from the iron pyrite, and soon the fire crackled and licked up from the tinder shavings.

'Dad! Are you here?' came a female voice from inside the house.

'Out back! Come and join me.'

Veranay skipped out through the back door and collapsed on a rickety old chair next to the growing fire, sighing loudly. 'How was your day?'

He glanced at her from the corner of his eyes, and said, 'I got off a little later than I wanted to, but it was a good day. Farris won't give me a raise, but he will ensure I have a place on the roster every day as long as I continue to train the new guys.' He knew she was bursting at the seams to talk about her birthday and all the things that annoyed her from school, but he ignored her not-so-silent pleas. 'My boots got damaged on the way back, so I stopped at Cedoric's to get them repaired for tomorrow. He asked if you would want to learn a few new skills and help him out in the shop in your spare time, making shoes and various other items. It's a superb skill to have.'

'Mmm, I'll think about it.' She let out another long sigh.

'If you keep sighing like that, you're gonna fall flat on your face. Now, how about you spice the meat while I ready the grill?' He unwrapped the meat and handed it to her.

'Ah, these look good.' Cocking her head, she continued, 'Did you get them for my birthday?'

'Maybe I just wanted to spoil myself a little,' Hadron said with raised brows.

Veranay flicked the blonde-brown hair out of her face and said, 'Oh, if I wasn't around, you wouldn't eat at all just to save a few coins.'

Hadron frowned at her. 'Run in and get the spice, you cheeky sausage.'

'At least I'm a *pretty* sausage,' she said, skipping back to the door and disappearing into the gloom. A lantern came to life, and soon the faint glow made her shadow dance on the walls. Hadron sat staring at her through the window, then got an idea. The door swung open, and another long sigh escaped her as she plonked down on the chair. From the corner of his eyes, he saw her staring at him with her head tilted to the side, squinting at him with her opal green eyes. 'What is that?' she asked, placing the meat on the grill.

Feigning ignorance, he scowled and said, 'What's what?'

Still squinting, Veranay pursed her lips and pointed to the satchel at his side. 'That.'

'Oh, this?' He turned the satchel around to show it off quickly and said, 'I thought I'd use it for work. What do you think? Looks good, doesn't it?'

'Come on, hand it over.'

'What do you mean, hand it over? It's mine.'

'Nope, way too girly for you. I know Mum isn't around anymore, but that doesn't mean you should take up both roles... Let's have it. We both know where this is heading. Come on, then.' With her hand extended, she waited to take possession of the satchel and snatched it up with glee. 'There, doesn't that feel better, knowing it's where it should be?'

Hadron chuckled and turned the steaks on the grill, sending a sizzle into the air. 'You know, she would be proud of you.'

Veranay's smile faded as she turned her attention away from the satchel and said, 'I hope so. Thanks for this. I love it.' She jumped up and hugged him, squirming with delight.

With a smirk, he said, 'Happy birthday, baby.'

'Do you miss her?'

A quick grunt came from Hadron; he cleared his throat. 'Aye, I do. Now, how about you help me with this meal and tell me all you wanted to say with those long-winded sighs?'

A squeal of delight sounded from her as she stamped her feet repeatedly before mouthing off about everything she'd held in. A stream of words exploded from her so fast, Hadron could barely keep up with what she was saying, then laughed at her excitement and annoyance. Together, they enjoyed the night a little longer before turning in, but Hadron struggled to sleep, and kept tossing and turning in his bed with thoughts of coin running rampant in his head.

* * *

Darkness greeted Hadron with eerie silence and a spine-tingling chill. He stood on the weathered porch and rubbed his eyes repeatedly to wake up, yawned, and set out in the quiet streets, heading for Cedoric's. He walked with no rush, trying to conserve his energy for the hard day's work that lay ahead: moving enormous blocks of granite and hauling them from the quarry. Hundreds would be on their way to the site already, hoping to get a slot on the roster and earn some coin, but he did not have that worry. He rounded the corner to the cordwainer's alley and soon stood before the door, a layer of condensation wetting the dark wood, water running down in streaks to muddy the ground. A few swift knocks, and he heard a muffled call from inside, then waited for the door to open.

The creak was deafening, and as Cedoric shuffled forward, a man leaned out of a window from the second story and shouted, 'Hey! Quiet down there!'

Cedoric barbarously stuck his thumb behind his top teeth and flicked it out to the complaining man. A quick shouting match erupted, and Hadron didn't know what to do except wait for them to finish. 'Oh, bugger off, you wanker, you're making more noise than we ever could.'

'Don't make me come down there and put you in your place!'

'I'd like to see you try, you flat-footed stampcrab!' A few moments of heavenly silence lingered in the air until the man spoke again.

'One day, Cordwainer! One day, you will pay for your insults!' The man vanished, and Hadron sighed with relief that the quiet had returned.

'What was that all about?' he asked, his voice taking on a higher pitch than normal.

'Oh, Cecil doesn't sleep very well, so he always complains about the slightest noise. Don't worry about him. He's harmless. Here, I've repaired them as best I could. They should last you a good deal longer.'

Hadron took the boots and said, 'Thank you, Cedoric. I don't know what I would have done without you. I spoke to Veranay about helping you. She is very excited to learn how you made that wonderful satchel. She loves it dearly. Again, thank you.'

'Oh, stop buttering me up. She'll earn a fair wage and, I'm sure, will soon surpass me in skill. I have no children to pass down my techniques to. It will be an honour to see them live on in her.'

'What about the young apprentice you took on a few years back? What was his name?'

Cedoric nearly choked as he laughed and said, 'Oh, dear. Jannis. What a dolt. Poor boy didn't know his right from his left. It was foolish of me to think I could ever train him.' The old cordwainer looked around. 'Best be on your way or you'll be late, and these need to be worn in some. So you might want to take it easy.' A quick nod, and Hadron set off.

* * *

'Damn! These boots are torturing me today. They're awfully tight. I think I'm gonna have sores all over,' Hadron grumped as he slumped down to the ground and hastily removed the boots, bringing instant relief. He moved his feet and wriggled his toes about, gasping with the satisfaction the cool air brought as it blew through his sweat-covered toes.

'Oh, stop whining so much! You boom like an orphaned child.'

Hadron glowered at the quarryman and replied, 'You should keep focusing on getting that block split, Rangar. We're falling behind schedule, and the next carts should be here any moment to load these new blocks. And make sure they don't have any irregularities, like water rings and spots. We can't be sending poor blocks to the shipping yard. Farris would be livid.'

'Farris can kiss my arse. But yeah, I'll check the blocks. You know I always do. Psh. It's not my first day doing this, you know.'

'I never would have guessed that...'

'That was uncalled for.' Rangar struck his hammer on the chisel one last time, and the block split apart with a mighty clang. 'Come on. I'm doing all the work here.'

A jumble of noises besieged them as hundreds of men were busy cutting, lifting, moving, and shaping the stones. Some were singing in the day's heat, and more were shouting at each other. Working the quarry, Hadron knew, was frustrating and sometimes dangerous. They had lost three people in the last couple of months, and the image of their bodies crushed under the fallen blocks still haunted him. Now, he was very wary of the old crane. Every time he saw someone walk underneath it while it had a load, he wanted to jerk them out of the way and slap them silly. But rarely did people listen.

He saw the crane turn, and heard it shudder with the weight. Hadron quickly slipped his boots on as he said, 'I'll be right back. They're bringing up a new load.' He jumped up and bolted for the edge of the quarry, staring down to see the amount of stone on the platform being hoisted. To the right, Farris was shouting at the treadwheel walker to speed it up. Men were walking below the raised platform, oblivious to the danger above them. A loud groan sounded again and Hadron shouted, 'Move out of the way! Don't stand there! Farris, the weight is too much! Bring it down!'

Suddenly, the treadwheel's axle burst from the machine, sending wooden shards flying with terrible force as it broke out of its cage. The ropes snapped, and the platform dropped, crashing to the innocents below. Workers dived out of its path, and an explosion of white powder and rock filled the area. The treadwheel broke free as the crossbeam crushed its structure, then rolled down the side to disappear in the dust, followed by a crash and screams, the world shuddering from the impact. Unable to see what was happening, Hadron anxiously waited for the dust cloud to dissipate. He ran down the banks, leaping over boulders, skidding on the steep sides. He heard the coughing of men and the screams of another. Fear reached into his chest and squeezed his lungs, suffocating him. The banks turned basically vertical, with a forty-foot drop to the bottom of the quarry. He couldn't run any further.

Quickly looking around, Hadron ran towards the collapsed crane and grabbed the trailing rope from the platform, still connected to the base of the construction, and rappelled down to the bottom. He moved past men who emerged from the dust cloud all covered with rock powder, their faces white, each a mask of horror. He pushed through the carnage of the wreck, helping people down to the ground as he did, then saw the platform. A man was howling next to it, his leg crushed at the knee, torn away completely, with the rest of the limb still stuck under the heavy block. He loosened his belt and strapped it around the man's leg above the knee, pulling it as tight as he could to stop the flow of blood. The victim fell backwards, unconscious. Others joined his side, and several men took the injured man away. Ragged breaths escaped Hadron's mouth, and his bloodied hands shook terribly. 'Get him on a wagon back to the city immediately!'

Hadron got to his feet and stumbled to the fallen treadwheel, where many workers had already gathered, trying to open the caged wheel to get to the two men inside, using their hammers and chisels to break through the mangled construction. He grabbed at a spoke that was ready to break free and pulled with all his might. 'Here! Move this!' he shouted, and three more men jumped in to help him. A loud crack sounded, and the four fell on their behinds. Lying on his back, he saw a man climb out from inside the wheel, his arm broken, the bone protruding through the skin above the wrist. He saw the faces of the surrounding men change from frantic hopefulness to eyes closed, turning away and cursing loudly. A strange sensation came over him. He wanted to jump up and see what was going on, but at the same time, did not want to know; yet he felt compelled to investigate. The other blind crane operator lay with his dull eyes staring up at the sky, a thick metal rod jutting out from his chest, dripping blood on his brown tunic. Men drifted away, knowing there was nothing they could do, while some stayed to extricate the body and send it back to Oakenwind for the awaiting family, if the dead man had any.

In a haze of adrenalin and sadness, Hadron climbed out of the quarry to stand at the ledge, looking away towards where the town should be, when something caught his eye. Squinting, he blinked a couple times before he called, 'Rangar! What do you make of that?' Multiple thick trails of smoke rose over the horizon, creating a dark cloud above that was being swept away to the southwest. Before Rangar could answer him, realisation struck, and he started running. From behind, he heard Rangar alert the men, and soon everyone was running back to town.

* * *

Please let Veranay be safe. Heart racing and lungs wheezing, Hadron sprinted over the rough terrain, his feet burning and aching. He ran, drenched in sweat, ready to collapse from exhaustion, but he needed to get back home. The roar of the flames woke him from his running haze as he went past the first buildings, the heat oppressive and relentless, taking his breath away. A body lay off to the side, bleeding out from an opened throat. Fires blazed everywhere: houses, trees, and buildings licked high. It was difficult to breathe with the smoke filling his lungs, and Hadron coughed constantly. 'Veranay!' he shouted. An older man stumbled out from a burning building half-ablaze and dropped to the ground, rolling to extinguish the flames. Hadron removed his tunic and beat the flames until they died and helped the older man away from the inferno. 'What happened here?'

In pain and asphyxiated, the man coughed, struggling for breath. 'They attacked out of nowhere a little after dawn. Hundreds of men ran in with a beast billowing fire from up high. There was no warning, and nothing we could do. Our guards fell quickly, and the beast...' he coughed again, '...destroyed the bell tower. We could not sound the alarm.'

Men from the quarry ran past them to get to their loved ones, and dread filled him. 'Are they still here?'

'Most left. They've taken a few of our people with them. Threw them in cages like common criminals! But there must be some lingering who can't get enough of the women and ale.' Only now did Hadron recognise the man as the flat-footed stampcrab who had complained this morning.

'Did the cordwainer make it out? He's a dear friend.'

'I don't know, lad. Head to the great hall and see for yourself. They made everyone line up there and killed a few who tried to fight back. I ran back here to save my dog, but... I was too late.' Tears rolled down the man's soot-covered face, his eyes red and his arm and tunic still smouldering.

'I'm sorry about your dog. Stay here. I'm going to the hall to find my daughter.' The man nodded, and Hadron set off. Emotional cries of pain flared up as men found their families cut down in the streets and homes. The bodies became more common the closer he got to the hall. To his right, an armoured man lay bleeding out. He glared down at the hacked-up attacker and thought, *You deserve this, you bastard.* 'Veranay! It's me! Come out!' His stomach churned, and he wanted to vomit, but kept running.

All over, men and women moped about, crying despondently while Hadron shouted, 'Has anyone seen my daughter? Has anyone seen Veranay?' Frantic, he grabbed a woman who stood with eyes wide and unblinking, frozen in place. 'Missus Mavelin, have you seen my Veranay?' Unresponsive, he shook her by the shoulders. 'Missus Mavelin!' But nothing came of it. A constant mumble of incoherent babble streamed from the poor woman's mouth.

'Excuse me, sir,' came a young man's voice from behind him. 'Are you Veranay's father?'

Hadron stared at the young man, guessing he was a little older than his daughter, and pleaded, 'Yes. Have you seen her? Please tell me!' Involuntarily grabbing the boy, he pushed him up against the wall, begging for an answer.

'Oi! Leave that boy alone! They're frightened enough as it is!' yelled a woman from his left. He set the boy down slowly, not averting his gaze until the boy spoke.

'Yes, sir. Unfortunately, I did. We all did...'

Heart racing, ragged breaths, and spotty vision took Hadron by surprise as he hyperventilated, waiting for the boy to continue.

'They threw her in a cage with some other folks.' Hadron was ready to collapse. His legs buckled beneath him, and he grabbed the boy's tunic to steady himself. 'That man over there tried to stop them from taking her, but he was no match for them.'

With great effort, Hadron pulled himself back up and turned to the man the boy had pointed to, seeing only the feet, as a woman lay over him in the street, crying with ear-splitting shrieks. He dragged himself over to the crying woman and dropped to the ground next to her and whispered, 'Yanric?' The woman's head came up and Hadron saw the streaks down her face, her eyes red and her clothes torn. He knew she had endured a terrible morning, yet for him it had started with such promise. He'd woken with hope and joy. Now the day was almost gone, and so was his spirit.

'This is *your* fault!' The woman shrieked. 'My Yanric is dead because of you!' She shoved him again and again, her wailing intensifying even more. Then her fists started pounding into him.

People were staring at them, all knowing it wasn't really his fault, but everyone understood what was taking place. Grief is a terrible thing. Hadron took the beating, letting her expel her anger unto him, and slowly wrapped his arms around her, sobbing as he spoke. 'I'm so sorry, Kanah.' Her pounding fists softened as he brought her near, replaced by fierce sobbing and shakes.

After a little more time, she stared up at him with her brown eyes and said, 'I gave him a blue eye, swole his face up and caused him not to see on his right. If I hadn't done that, he might have seen the bastard swinging his sword down.'

Clenching on his teeth, Hadron abruptly closed his eyes to stop his tears from rushing out again and said, 'No. It wasn't your fault. There were too many men. Their forces would have simply overwhelmed him, and besides, Yanric was no hardened soldier. But he was a damned good man for trying. I will not forget his sacrifice.' Unable to hold it in any longer, tears streamed down his face, tickling his cheeks. 'Forgive me, Kanah, but I have to go after them and try to get her back. Do you know which direction they went?'

'I heard them say their cages were full. They were heading north to Tergaron.' Her face hardened suddenly, her voice growing cold. 'Kill as many as you can. Do you have a weapon?'

Surprised by her change in demeanour, Hadron stammered, 'Uh, no. I, I don't.'

'Quick then, come with me.' Kanah leaned down to kiss her Yanric one last time, and then hurried down the street to their little home, with Hadron close behind.

*   *   *

The door to the butcher's shop hung ajar on one hinge, having popped out the bottom. Hadron lifted the door and placed it back in the hinge socket, but saw the short metal rod had been bent and didn't want to go down completely. 'The blacksmith will need to straighten it for you. I'm sorry.'

'I'm afraid he's also dead. That's not important right now. Come.'

Hadron saw the struggle that had taken place inside. *Soldiers must have burst through the door, and Yanric fought them off.* They stepped over an assortment of broken containers, dryers, and scattered meat. Flies buzzed around the expensive dishes in a frenzy to get their fill, but Kanah did not care about that right now. At the back, around the counter, another armoured soldier lay with the cleaver buried deep in his chest. Hadron struggled to avert his gaze, and shook himself to continue when he heard Kanah rummaging through a room at the very end of the corridor.

A deep groan sounded from the woman as she pulled an old chest — a faded and rusted metal tree symbol spreading over the lid — closer and unlatched the lock. 'This belonged to my father. Maybe it can help you get your Veranay back before it's too late.' She pulled an axe with a thick haft out, and then another.

'Aren't they supposed to be longer?' he asked with raised brows. Kanah glanced at him, then turned the haft-ends to each other. Then only did Hadron see the metal design at the ends as she pushed the two together and locked them in place with a twist.

'It is for storage only. Don't be daft and try to fight with them like this. You would only take off your own leg, or disembowel yourself. When you need to use them, take them apart and give it a good shake, like this.' Kanah pulled them apart and snapped the axe in a shake, dropping an extension from the haft, and twisted the poles to lock it in place. 'Now you can use it. Or you could use it in its shortened form for close combat. Pretty versatile. My father loved them.'

'Thank you, Kanah. I'm sure they'll help me a lot.' Hadron took the axes and clumsily stood with the weapon until she sighed and gave him a back holster.

'My father got these made while he was a lieutenant in the Netherlaide heavy infantry, and after his death, it was passed on to me, his oldest. I'm sure he would have wanted it to go to a son, but I was all he had. Maybe now it can do some good again. There's an entire set of armour in here.' She started rummaging through the chest.

'It's okay, Kanah. I don't like the idea of armour. It's too hot and will slow me down.'

'Your funeral, but at least take the chain mail vest.'

Hadron donned the vest over his tunic and nodded his thanks before leaving her in the uncomfortable silence to start her grieving.

* * *

Hadron adjusted his pack, feeling the poorly stored items poking him in the back while he ran. In a rush to get going, he had raced back home and thrown in items he thought would aid him in his travels, not thinking it through properly. The weight, the necessity... Now he was paying for it. Unable to keep the bad thoughts out of his head, he wondered what they were doing to her and the rest of the caged folk. *What do they want with her? To sell as a slave? Or for sex? I need to run faster...*

He picked up the pace, hoping he would reach them in time. *I wish I had a horse, or that I knew how to fight. What am I doing?*

The light was growing dim, and Hadron struggled to see the lay of the land, the ruts and the rocks jumping out at him like striking vipers. He moved the dagger sheath further to his left and winced when he pressed on the bruise it had created on his abdomen. *I'm coming, baby-girl. Daddy's coming...*

Chapter Two

A realm of fire and brimstone surrounded him, the toxic smell harsh and suffocating. Garidan felt the hairs on his arms singe from the flames, yet it did not touch his skin. A beast's roar sounded from behind. He snapped his head around to see, but a raggedy, torn blindfold covered his eyes, giving him glimpses of a large four-legged hound with short, bristling hair and a muscular body. A voice snaked into his mind, sensually caressing his thoughts, and though he could not understand the language, his body reacted to its seductive nature.

A woman's laughter, twisted and vile, came from his left. 'Who's there?' he shouted, but no one answered. He wanted to remove the blindfold, but his hands were chained. Powerful fingers tore his tunic from his body, stripping him naked. 'What's going on? Let me go! What do you want from me?' Filthy hands massaged his arms and chest; he could feel the dirt and gravel stuck on the palms as they glided over his skin, then pain lanced through him while sharp nails bore into him, tearing out strips of skin. He clenched his teeth at the pain, writhing beneath a weight that settled on him. 'Damn you to the depths of the abyss!' A hand fondled his privates, stroking him over and over. His body responded, although his mind fought with everything it had. 'No! Stop this!'

A sudden undeniable and irrevocable wet heat applied pressure on his prick. Garidan resisted and fought, but there was a certain enjoyment to the act. 'Get off me!' Through the tears in the blindfold, he glimpsed a woman in rags, her breasts bare while she dripped cold sweat on top of him.

'Do you really want that?' came her voice.

'Why can't I see your face? Show me your face!' The woman shifted, veered quickly, and above him was Ladriana, her fiery red hair soaked with sweat. 'My love! How?'

'Is this better?'

'What?'

'We can pretend, you and I. If she is what you want.'

'What is this foul magic? Get off me!'

'All I want from you is a promise, and this will stop.'

More than just his head was about to explode. He could not contain himself for much longer. 'What do you want from me?'

'I want you to promise that when I call, you will answer.' The woman veered again, her auburn hair now complementing the tusks that sprouted from her mouth, and he flinched at their sight. She veered again, becoming beautifully delicate, her milky skin glowing radiantly. Before long, she was tanned and strong, gripping his back with great power as she rhythmically moved her body.

'Agh! Let me go!' Garidan pulled at the chains, shaking them violently, but he could not break free. An evilly seductive laughter sounded before the speed of her motion increased. 'No! Stop this! Please. I am married.'

'Oh, I will have my prize. I will break you.'

A terrible rush of pleasure exploded from his body, and the echoing laughter trailed away. Suddenly, the weight was gone.

A rude but blissful chirp woke Garidan from his delirious slumber, and he regretted it instantly as nausea and pain burrowed into his skull. He opened his eyes and shooed away the goldcrest picking at the ground to get some tiny insects or spiders. With a flap of its wings, it quickly made it to the cave's mouth and settled on a branch high in a tree. Garidan grunted and vomited. 'Thank you, little bird, for waking me from that nightmare. You are truly my saviour.' He spat out some more chunks of the vile taste before rising and nearly collapsed from weakness. A woman shouted at someone in the background, the sound drilling through his mind to his very core, but he ignored it as best he could. His head throbbed and pulsed with every move he made. Unsteadily making his way to the outside to be greeted by the warmth of the sun, Garidan breathed deep the fresh air while he took in the area. To the far east, the brown-grey landscape faded into a light green, becoming darker the further it got from Mount Aga. Small stands of trees became more frequent, and he saw movement in the distance and knew more animals roamed the area. *Water breeds life.* He couldn't help but wonder why the people of Norvaldmire hadn't moved closer to where there still was some water and trees for shade.

Again he heard the shouts, and listened without turning. 'We have to go back for Arundhàbu! He would've gone back for you!'

Borka grunted and said, 'No, he wouldn't have. But that does not matter. What matters is that you are safe. He would not want you in any more harm's way. If he is dead, he died to protect you! Don't dishonour that!'

A voice whispered from Garidan's left. 'For a while there, we thought we'd lose you.'

'You're not so lucky, Tulvar,' he panted. 'I still have some fight in me. What happened? I can't remember anything after coming out of Mount Aga.'

'Yes,' Tulvar said, rubbing his thinning grey beard, 'You were quite out of it when they brought you to Abijiya. She, uh...' Tulvar paused for a time, considering what the worth would be of telling Garidan all she had done, then said, 'Well, she saw you were bitten by a small stretagor you crushed on your back. Must have been during a struggle. Looks like she succeeded in drawing the poison from you.'

Garidan cleared his throat and fiddled with his collar. The frayed hems irritated his neck. 'Where are we?'

Tulvar gestured towards the greener lands, and said, 'We're heading to Velafrey. The Cabinet has put a bounty on all our heads for discovering their little secret.'

'No, this can't be. Please tell me you jest.' Eyes wide and clutching his stomach, Garidan pleaded with Tulvar.

'I'm sorry, I couldn't have foreseen this. We'll have to find another way to help your world, as well as ours.'

Garidan collapsed to sit on a boulder and closed his eyes, knowing his stay had been extended yet again. *I hope you're safe, Ladriana. Forgive me for leaving you alone for so long.* 'What's up with them?' Garidan asked with a gesture of the thumb.

'Arundhàbu sacrificed himself to save us. We don't know if he made it or not.'

'Oh, no,' Garidan mumbled as he closed his eye, his forehead wrinkled with creases. He turned to Naghita, watching her plead with the Tark gladiator to go back for her husband. His throat burned, and his stomach was unsettled. 'Do you have any water?'

Tulvar whistled to get Raegel's attention and gestured for the water while the Ageian cleared the camp. 'Not much, but here. You must be thirsty.'

'Thank you.' Warm water flowed down his throat, tasting like iron and dirt, but he didn't care. The sudden rush of liquids was too much for his stomach to handle, and Garidan quickly found himself hunched over, vomiting to the side of the boulder the most foul of liquids. The bile splattered back up to his pants and tunic.

Tulvar jerked away not to get any of the bile on him, and saw the commotion had pulled the attention of Naghita and Borka from their bickering. Now the two approached. He turned back to Garidan with raised brows and said, 'There is some hope, though. The stone Balamuth you found in the volcano was not stone at all. It is an actual Balamuth! A terrible cold spreads from it — an ice dragon, perhaps? It might be the one to save not only your world, but ours as well.'

Spitting the last few chunks of vomit from his mouth, Garidan said, 'What? That's incredible news!' He saw the man's unwillingness to celebrate, and asked, 'Why does it seem like there's a "but" coming?'

Tulvar picked up a stone and threw it from the cave. 'We don't know how to get it bonded, or even where to start looking. I have some ideas. But it will involve breaking into the Library of Cabinet in Velafrey to get to the old archives.'

Out of breath, Garidan thought for a moment while the Tarks drew near and asked, 'Tulvar, are there any more of the monoliths in this Velafrey? Preferably in working order?'

'Yes, but it is highly guarded.'

A heavy, solid hand slapped Garidan on the back, nearly knocking the wind from his lungs. 'You're awake! I didn't think you would make it, but glad you did,' growled Borka, grinning with his one gleaming tusk.

Trying to regain control after the coughing fit from the blow to the back, Garidan saw Naghita through teary eyes, her arms crossed before her chest. 'And you. Naghita? Are you glad? Or were you rooting for the spider?' She shook her head and walked away from them to join Raegel. 'Hey, Naghita.' He waited for her to look back at him. 'Arun is a tough bastard. I'm sure he's fine. We'll get him back, I promise, but Borka is right. Don't let his sacrifice be for naught.'

The look she gave him shook him to the core, but she did not reply. There was no need.

* * *

'Arundhàbu saved both of us, you know. Barehanded, he took on a stroaros and won. It was like the Arundhàbu of old. The one I knew a long time ago.' Borka guided the horses down the steep slope, every so often glancing back over his shoulder at Garidan. The wagon rocked slightly as they rode over a rock, and Garidan grimaced. His body ached all over with every stretch or knock, but he was slowly showing signs of gaining his strength as the days progressed.

'That is an incredible feat. I've seen these creatures in action, and I don't want to fight one again.'

'I *did* injure it first, and badly so. In fact, I don't think he would have won if I weren't there. Plunged my poleaxe deep into its side. Now that I think about it, it was a smallish stroaros, maybe a pup even.'

Garidan chuckled and shook his head. 'Come on, Borka, you can't be this insecure. You went from admiring him to humiliating him in less time than it takes to finish an ale.'

A grunt sounded from the front of the wagon, and Borka said, 'Then you drink like a girl! Okay, fine! It was a terrifying beast. Nearly shat myself when it shook me like I was nothing but a toy or a piece of meat. Is that what you want to hear?'

'Borka, no.' Garidan never thought he would see the gladiator as a sensitive Tark, but he knew everyone had that something they were insecure about. 'I didn't mean it like that. I know you're a great fighter an—'

'Don't waste your breath on him. The coward would rather see us all dead than go back to fight for any of us. You better watch your back, human, 'cause he surely doesn't have it.' Naghita and Borka glared at each other with deathly stares as she rode past on the big brown horse. The brooding gladiator ground his teeth, but kept quiet.

With Naghita out of earshot, riding up front next to Tulvar and Raegel, Garidan said, 'Don't worry about her; she'll come around. You did the right thing.' For the first time since Garidan came to this world, he saw green grass sprouting up in spots, getting denser with a wild array of brightly coloured flowers. Raegel whistled from the front horse and waved to them, signalling to stop. Garidan blinked and rubbed his eyes with his palms, unable to believe them as a small lake shimmered behind the stand of trees. It was the first proper body of water he had seen here that was bigger than a wagon, and this one was nearly the size of the temple back home.

Borka couldn't pull on the reins fast enough for Garidan, who jumped from the moving cart, momentum flopping him to the ground, although his weak muscles tried their best to keep him on his feet. Terribly thirsty, he ignored the looks of disgust he received from the rest of his allies. He lay sprawled and covered with mud a mere few feet from the bank, virtually tasting the water in the air. On his hands and knees, he crawled into the pond and dipped his head into the cool water, sucking gulps of the liquid down his throat before coming up for air. A dreadful burning sensation ripped through his hand from the hacked-off finger, and he wanted to scream and yank it from the pond, but forced himself to keep it under for some time, feeling it grow numb. Footsteps drew closer, sloshing through the mud, while he scooped more of the cool liquid up to pour down his throat, and heard Borka on his right.

'You humans aren't very hardy, are you? Pretty fragile... I think even the Ageians are of hardier stock.'

Tulvar chimed in from his left, 'They must be used to more in their world. More water, more food, more—'

'Dragons...' interrupted Garidan, 'We also have more dragons. Yet, here I am, still helping you, and not *my* world. So shut up and let me drink.'

They left him in peace and replenished their canteens, drinking their fill.

Raegel, as usual, was standing apart from the group, keeping watch, when the slightest ripple on the water's surface caught his attention. He narrowed his eyes to focus on what he saw. Borka had moved away, content with the amount he'd gathered. Tulvar was near the wagon, rummaging through his pack, and Naghita was leaning against her horse, paying them no attention. 'Garidan! Get away from the water!' Raegel shouted.

'Leave me be, Raegel! I'm as dried up as an old Thenesian renegade.'

Quick footsteps drew near, followed by the hiss of a blade being drawn from its scabbard. The water exploded before Garidan, flashing gigantic teeth and reptilian eyes, lunging up to snatch him by the head. Yanked back, he heard the terrifying snap of the jaws a few inches from his face. He screamed and tried to retreat, but slipped in the mud. A frightful smell came from the beast as it bore down on him — when a sword sank into the creature's head. It thrashed about with the blade in its skull, flinging Raegel around and, with a powerful roll on the ground, dislodged the Ageian and the weapon. Raegel fell with a splash into the pond, and more ripples on the water moved his way. He swam for solid ground, kicking and slapping water fervently to get to the shore.

Borka and Naghita had run in at the first sign of danger, and were now standing between the bleeding crocodile and its prey, making threatening sounds while waving their arms about to scare it off. But it only got angrier, its roars and hisses drawing in more of the beasts. The huge reptiles slithered from the water and crept up the banks, hissing and roaring at them, forcing them back from the water's edge. Garidan stumbled back. *How could I have been this careless?* Aware that they did not have the upper hand on land, the beasts retreated into the now-murky lake.

Garidan collapsed on his back and said, 'I hate this place!'

'Where's Raegel?' shouted Naghita. In the confusion, they had forgotten about the Ageian, now nowhere to be seen. The water's surface seemed calmer than ever, and nowhere on the banks could they see any sign of him. 'Raegel!' she shouted again, joined in by the others, also shouting and searching. 'Raegel, show yourself, dammit!'

Tulvar ran knee deep into the water and plucked a leather waterskin from the surface, quickly turning for dry land. The shock on his face was clear as day when he hoisted it up and said, 'It's my boy's...' Tears rolled over his cheeks and he sagged to the ground, clutching the waterskin to his chest, and let out a scream. Borka closed his eyes and shook his head, unable to say anything.

Naghita spun around and marched to Garidan, grabbing him by the throat and lifting him into the air. 'This is your fault! If you had listened, he would still be alive! You will be the death of us all!' She squeezed her powerful hands, feeling his soft skin want to tear.

In his weakened state, Garidan was no match for her. 'Naghita, no! Stop this!' Borka grabbed her from behind and tore her hands from Garidan's throat, holding her firmly as she thrashed about.

'We're all going to die with him here! Let me go, you mongrel!'

The water exploded again, this time upward as Raegel breached the surface. Borka spun around and grabbed his poleaxe as he ran into the water and shouted, 'Raegel, here! Give me your hand!'

Ripples on the water snaked towards them and vanished. Borka brought down the poleaxe into the water over and over, hoping it would scare them off, as Naghita ran past and dived into the water without a second thought and swam for the splashing Ageian. Coughing and spitting copious amounts of water from his lungs, Raegel was dragged from the lake, struggling for breath as he leaked red. Borka swung the poleaxe down again, and felt it bite into the thick skin of a crocodile. He dragged the weapon free, swinging it sideways as the beast lurched from the water, severing a piece of its upper jaw, and the animal retreated, hissing its anger. He ran from the lake with the brief respite, and joined the coughing Ageian on the bank. Blood streamed from a bite on Raegel's leg below the knee, the large gashes and holes a permanent reminder not to stray too close to the water's edge. Tulvar hurried over with another tunic he had in his pack, tearing it to wrap the leg and stop the bleeding while Naghita held Raegel down.

'Hold still! We need to bandage the wounds!' shouted Naghita.

Garidan sat watching from a distance, unable to pull his gaze from the screaming Ageian. He knew he would only be in the way if he tried to help, but he hadn't felt so weak, so utterly useless, since the murder of his family when he was a little boy.

Borka joined his side to lean up against the wagon. 'Do you still think she'll come around? If she does, I hope it's before she kills one of us. Come with me. Let's find him a crutch from one of these branches. He'll be needing it for a while.'

Without a word, Garidan followed the big gladiator, trying his best to think of solutions to their problems, but his mind felt foggy and heavy. Every time he thought he had something, it would slip out of his head or change into another thought, becoming gibberish and useless. He could not even feel anger, even for himself. All he wanted to do was sleep. 'Something's wrong with me, Borka. I couldn't move, and I didn't want to listen to Raegel. That's not me. Naghita's right about one thing. If I don't get myself together, one of you might pay the price for it.'

'Thirst is a terrible thing, human. Your body will do what it must in order to stay alive. You will get better. Here,' Borka said, and handed the poleaxe to Garidan. 'Get us some firewood. I doubt we will travel any further today with his injuries. We will make camp away from the water and give Raegel tonight to heal. I will get him a crutch.'

*   *   *

Wrapped in a blanket, Garidan stared at Raegel from around the fire with his deep-sunken eyes, harsh purple rings shrouding the sockets. He wanted to say something, but was ashamed. There was silence in the group. No one felt like talking, especially to one another. Everyone sat in the fire's warmth, reliving the decisions made in the last few days, their minds adrift and far away. Borka was trying his hand at whittling, taking lessons from Garidan while they rested, carving little pieces from branches to keep his mind occupied. The constant scraping on the wood was driving Naghita insane, but she had kept her rants to a minimum. A brief cry of pain sounded as the knife slipped from the piece of wood and punctured the Tark's hand, followed by a stream of curses Garidan didn't understand. 'Hey, Borka, guide with your thumb. Don't push with your cutting hand. What are you carving?'

The Tark's face lit up, and he grinned. 'A starfish. I have seen them in the harbour.' He showed them his carving, and Naghita burst out laughing.

'That looks like a crippled dogras. Poor thing. Put it out of its misery and throw it in the fire.' Harsh and forced laughter boomed from the woman.

'Don't listen to her. Just keep working at it. You're doing fine.'

Borka sheathed his knife and put away the wood, grinding his teeth. He swung away, not making eye contact.

Raegel leaned back against the wagon while he rested on a rock and closed his eyes. He stretched out his leg slowly, then said, 'Garidan, you need to stop blaming yourself for all the things that have gone wrong. I can see how it weighs on you. It's not your fault I got bitten by the beast. I should have—'

'But it *is* his fault. Why do all of you keep protecting him?' Naghita chimed in. 'I don't understand.'

'I guess we have learned that blaming everyone except ourselves

27

rarely yields any merit.' Raegel opened his eyes and saw her glaring at him. 'Say what you will, Naghita, but you have a role to play as much as any of us. Yes, he should have listened to me, but I failed to understand the pain he was going through. He is not used to our way of living, and he has no one here except us. How would you have fared if the roles were reversed?'

'But it's not—'

'You said Arundhàbu spoke of him as your salvation. Why do you keep referring to him as your damnation?' She was about to speak when Raegel continued, 'You do not have to answer me, but I think you need to answer yourself.'

'Will you children quiet down? I'm trying to sleep over here,' Tulvar muttered as he turned around and growled something under his breath.

'Hey, where's the human?' asked Borka, coming up to take a breath after stoking the fire, his face glowing orange.

Raegel leaned forward and saw that the boulder where the ghostly figure had been sitting, cradling its legs, was now empty. 'Dammit. Borka?'

'Yeah, I'll go look for him,' the gladiator said with a glare at Naghita.

'Don't look at me like that. If the guilt is eating at him, it's his problem.'

The grey-black contours of the landscape and the trees blended together in a jumble of misshapen figures as Borka walked and scanned for the human. 'Garidan? You here?' His eyes took some time to adjust to the dark, even with a full moon up high. *Where could he have gone so fast? And how can he see?*

A rustling sound came from his right. 'Garidan? It's me, Borka. Where are you?' There was nothing, just leaves and branches scraping against each other. He turned left.

'Borka?'

The big Tark jumped at the sudden appearance of the man, who looked as if Death himself had scratched Garidan's name into his board, the pale visage in the poor moonlight exaggerating the black holes where his eyes were supposed to be. Borka grabbed his chest, heart racing, his mouth dry and muscles tense. 'I should feed you to those kruckogans for scaring me like that!'

'That's a strange name. Where I'm from, they're called crocodiles, although they're not as big. What are you doing following me?'

'We were worried, is all. You're not in the best shape, you know. You shouldn't be wandering around out here alone. What if a stroaros is hunting in the area?'

'Then I suspect I would be its next meal. Besides, it would be better for all of you if I just left. Went back to my world and forgot all this foolishness. Who was I kidding, trying to pull this off?'

'And what?' asked the Tark, gesturing with his arms questioningly. 'Leave us and your world to the fates that await them? The man I fought in The Gauntlet had a drive, a fire burning within that I could not quench. He was ready to forge a new path for both our worlds, and he would let no one stop him.' Borka poked his finger in Garidan's chest. 'But that's fine. Go on back to your shag, your friends, and tell them you're a failure. That they didn't mean enough for you to fight harder.'

'Stop poking me!'

'Oh yeah? What are you going to do? You failure!' He poked Garidan again. 'Huh?'

'I said stop it!'

Again, the thick-fingered Tark shoved him back. 'Make me!'

Before he could land another shove, Garidan grabbed a handful of the long, black braids draped around Borka's gigantic shoulders and yanked. The headbutt came out of nowhere, and blood spilled from Borka's nose. Both men staggered back dazedly and Garidan sagged to his knees, shaking his head to get his focus back. A shout of anger left the Tark as he rushed in and picked Garidan up by the throat, pinning him against a tree. Borka drew his massive knife and sank the blade deep into the bole next to Garidan's head, grunting and breathing deeply to calm down. Their gazes locked, and Borka said, 'Pathetic...but it's a start.'

Garidan collapsed to the ground with the sudden weight of his body back on his knees. He regained his footing and said, 'I need a weapon. I've lost my knives and sword.'

'If you still have some fight in you, get that knife out of the tree and you can have it. It's all I have other than the poleaxe.' Borka turned away and stomped off back towards the camp and said, 'Don't come back to camp without it.' The walk back felt quicker than he remembered it, and upon his nearing, he saw Raegel glance at him.

'We thought we heard some shouting. Where's Garidan?'

Borka lay down next to the flames and said, 'He needs to make a choice. We will see in the morning what that choice is.' Raegel was still talking, but he did not listen. He closed his eyes, and sleep took him almost instantly. Borka had never had a problem with sleeping in loud places. Once he put his mind to it, all he needed to do was close his eyes. It was a wonderful feeling, drifting away, the surrounding sounds merging with his dreams. And in those dreams, there was no Naghita with her snide remarks. It was only him and his clan brothers, the brothers who always fought next to him, living for the hunt.

The scent of wet grass woke them early in the morning as the sun reached for the peaks behind them. Steam rose from the grass-patched ground, and birds chirped all around. Borka yawned with eyes closed, then looked around, stretching his muscles. Garidan was nowhere to be seen. Dejected, he sighed and shook his head.

A low whistle grabbed his attention to where Raegel stood, and he cocked his head towards the wagon as they locked gazes. He rose and walked closer. Soft snores sounded out, and Borka grinned when he saw the human curled up on the wagon's bed between the packs and gear, sleeping soundly while he clutched the Tark's big knife. 'Are you well, Raegel? You seem pasty.'

A wheeze flowed from Raegel's mouth as he breathed. 'I will be fine. Let's get going.'

* * *

The day had been quiet, with few travellers on the road and fewer problems, but Raegel was having a hard time staying on the horse with his leg dangling down, pumping blood to the bandaged holes. It throbbed constantly, shooting pains down the leg to his foot and burning like fire. He had gradually been getting worse as the day progressed, fidgeting constantly with the wound.

Annoyed with the constant mumbling and scratching, Tulvar twisted in the saddle to snap at his son, but cursed as he saw him slumped backwards, drenched in sweat and his face grey. 'Raegel?' The Ageian barely opened his eyes. 'I know this look. His wounds are infected. Give me one of those wafers and find me some maggots!'

Naghita reined in alongside the pair, knitted brows riding her forehead. 'I have forgotten how dangerous wounds are in the woods.' She broke a pain killer wafer in four and slipped it into Raegel's mouth. 'He will need to get to a healer if he wants to keep his leg. How far are we to this Velafrey?'

Tulvar glanced around and said, 'I reckon a three-or-four-day ride to the city. But first we have to get through Manga Canyon.'

Garidan shouted from the wagon bed, 'I'm strong enough to ride — let's swap places. He needs to rest his leg.'

They tussled with the stubborn Ageian, who insisted that he was fine and kicked at them weakly when they approached to pull him down, making the horse skittish and afraid.

Tulvar clung to the mane, too afraid to let go of the mare and help them, rather continuing to shout over his shoulder. 'Raegel, stop this madness! You need to get down!'

This would be a comical scene, were it not for the seriousness of the matter, thought Garidan, moving in with raised hands as the horse threatened to buck and rear. He stared deep into the mare's eyes, whispering soothingly, calming the animal until he was near enough to grab the reins.

'Enough!' Borka blared and walked up to the horse. He grabbed Raegel's kicking foot and yanked him from the horse, threw him over his broad shoulders, and carried him to the wagon. 'You are wasting time. We need to go.'

Raegel surrendered to the strength of the Tark and calmed in his grasp. 'Fine, just spare me my dignity! Put me down.'

Garidan mounted the horse, patting the mare on the neck, and they set off again. Wind rushed over his face, and he breathed deep, embracing the elements. The sun burned away all thoughts of despair, the rhythmic bounce on the back of the horse invigorating him, making him feel alive. The will to survive is sometimes the best medicine, bringing back one's energy with hope. *Ladriana, please keep hope alive. Do not lose it like I almost did.* He leaned forward and spoke against the rushing wind to Tulvar, who lay forward on the horse's neck. 'Don't lean too far. You'll unbalance the animal, cause it to throw us.' Tulvar sat back up and Garidan continued, 'Why do the people of Norvaldmire not move to where there's water, greenery?'

'Many *have* left to seek new homes, but the Cabinet deemed Norvaldmire too strategically important to abandon completely. Now that we know that the drought is spreading, it does not matter where they go. It will come for them regardless, unless we can stop these wyrms from feeding on the world.'

'You mentioned some canyon. What's so special about it? Can't we just go around it?'

'It runs from north to south, coast to coast. It is gigantic, and there is only one way to cross it, at its narrowest to the far south. Definitely the best way to avoid the canyon, but it will take us a long time to go that route. We can also go down and run along the canyon where it opens up to the forests of Velafrey, but it will be a treacherous journey, for there live brigands in those mountains that plunder all who come near, and it's not any shorter than the previous option. We have sent many raiding parties to disband and capture them, but they keep coming back. The last is to go down the canyon and back up on the eastern side at Maligan's Pass. Probably the better of the options, but many have died slipping from the path. We unfortunately can't go the long way. My boy needs a healer.'

Garidan sighed and whispered, 'Sounds charming. We're not really in fighting shape either.' He ran the scenarios over in his head, thinking of the best way to approach this problem while they pushed their mounts towards the canyon, knowing they would need to decide soon to alter course if that was needed. For now, he kept thinking.

* * *

The vista before them stretched out far and wide, the flat plains broken by the sheer drops of the canyon and the mountainous ridges sticking out from within. Naghita went to her knee and gathered a handful of dirt while she took in the view, letting the deep red sand run from her hand to be swept away by the wind. She chewed on a dried piece of volan they had trapped and killed the previous day, letting some of it fester in the sun to get the needed maggots now swarming Raegel's wounds, feasting on his dead tissue, and said, 'What do you think, human? Are we going to make it through?'

Garidan had struggled to eat the adorable, woolly creature. He watched Naghita tear off another strip and turned away, thinking of how terrified it had been. Nearly the size of a pig with a stubby snout and sharp little claws, it displayed its ferocity as best it could, but Naghita had severed its head swiftly. They needed the food, but he could not forget those enormous eyes and droopy ears, or the knowledge they harboured of what was to come. Surprised that Naghita asked for his opinion at all, he stood weighing their options. 'I have regained my strength. I'm ready to fight, but Borka won't be much help while he steers the wagon. Raegel is getting worse; he will be no help at all. And Tulvar...well, he's Tulvar. And then there's nothing stopping the bandits from chasing us down if we make it through.'

'Your point?'

'We'll be quickly outnumbered, and I'm sure they will have eyes on the roads leading in and out, so there will be traps waiting for us. What they are, I can't say.'

She turned back to the canyon and took another bite. 'This is a dumb idea. We should go around.'

'Yeah, but thanks to me, we don't have the time,' Garidan whispered. He didn't think he said it loud enough that she could have heard, but he saw her staring at him from the corner of her eye and quickly continued, 'We ride hard. You at the front, me at the rear. Hopefully, we can keep them from the wagon for a while. Do you have the Balamuth in a safe place?'

Undoing her jacket, she pointed to the sphere tucked away on the inside. 'Take Raegel's sword. You can't do anything with that knife.'

Garidan swiped at a fly buzzing around his face and cleared his throat. 'I, uh... If anyone could have made it out of that battle, it would be Arun. He's probably on his way to us as we speak.'

She said nothing for a while. 'Be ready for anything. We are their only hope. Let's go.'

Garidan looked to the sky and thought, *It's going to be a long day, hopefully.* He leapt on the horse and they waited for Tulvar to get on the wagon. 'Tulvar, uncover everything on the wagon so any eyes following us can see we have nothing worth stealing. Maybe, just maybe, they will let us pass with our limbs intact.'

'Splendid idea, Garidan,' said Tulvar as he removed the sheet covering the packs.

They began at a slow trot down the steep road, steadily gaining pace as they neared the bottom.

Chapter Three

Eyes and lungs burning, Arundhàbu's hand trembled while he stroked the silvery black hair of Abijiya, waiting patiently for her to breathe her last breath. He calmly spoke to the shaman lying in his lap, knowing no one was pursuing them. 'We will see you beyond the gates. What you did here today was a brave and selfless thing. I thank you for your sacrifice, old one. Rest easy, knowing your daughter is safe.'

Ragged breaths escaped her before she coughed up some blood. He turned her on her side to let the liquids run out, and turned her back.

'Who...are you...calling old?' She grinned briefly and reached for his face, stroking the thick tusk. 'Tell her...I'm sorry. Do not...go...through life...bitter.'

Her head dropped back, and a terribly long exhale left her. Arundhàbu rose and neatly folded her arms to rest on her chest, covering the big stab wound. Down in the tunnel, with Abijiya lying still, he searched through the debris of her ruined clay hut and found a yellow flower amid the rubble. He placed it on her chest and lowered himself to rest his forehead against hers, and said, 'Go, find peace with your gods,' then stood and walked down the tunnel.

* * *

The wyrms had collapsed the earth they had fought on, leaving them far below the surface with no way out. For the first day, he'd tried climbing the vertical sides, but the earth crumbled with each handhold, sending Arundhàbu to plummet down onto his back multiple times. Failing this, he then carried the shaman until she could go no further, and waited for her to die. It had now been at least a few days since Abijiya's death, and he still kept walking, hoping to be led closer to the surface, where he could get out and find something other than insects to eat or suck the juice from.

The last drops of water fell from the squeezed and twisted waterskin, evaporating as it touched his tongue and bringing scant relief. The bloody run-off from a deep cut across his face ran into his eye, and Arundhàbu blinked, squeezing his left eyelids shut, then dabbed at the wound with a torn sleeve. His spit was dry, and the dust didn't help so deep in the tunnels. Now, without his breather, it would only get worse. He stumbled forth, struggling within the darkness, feeling his way through. *How am I going to tell Naghita her mother is dead? That I couldn't save her as well? Those last words she spoke to me... What did she mean by them?* The thought of leaving Abijiya unburied gnawed at him. It was not their way to leave a Tark behind with no proper burial, but he had no choice.

Thinking back to the battle, he saw those bladelike legs scything the air and killing with ease as they tore through the ranks of the Ageian soldiers. Their armour stood no chance, their weapons even less. And then there were those giant mouths, able to devour anything in their paths. He had fought against the few soldiers who made it through Abijiya's barrier, stopping them from going after his wife and the rest of the group, but soon the wyrms turned their attention on them all. It was a storm of roars and screams, the world crumbling beneath their very feet. He struck the blacksmith's hammer to his left, where a soldier stood, only to see him vanish with an explosion of teeth that ripped the earth apart and threw him from his feet. A scream sounded from the cliff edge, and he saw Abijiya lifted on the point of a sword, burying her thumb deep in the soldier's eye socket. 'Abijiya!' He ran to her side, sliding past a swishing blade, and swung his hammer, snapping a soldier's leg in two.

Abijiya slid from the sword, clutching her chest in pain as the blacksmith grabbed the soldier at the back of the head and crushed his face on the rocks next to the bleeding shaman. The world was in disarray all around them. He picked her up and ran for higher ground near the hut, when the ground beneath them gave way, erupting with more bladed legs and sending them plummeting into the tunnel far below. He listened to the screams from above as he fell and was, for a moment, glad that he was down in the tunnel. It wasn't until his vision filled with blood that he realised a leg had nearly decapitated him. The wyrms retreated, shaking the earth as they burrowed new tunnels, destroying the world from within.

Arundhàbu shook his head, ridding himself of the memory and stared into the dark abyss, the bowels of the earth, where monstrous wyrms lingered and roamed. He took a deep breath and lay his hand back on the side of the tunnel, using his bruised fingers to guide him further. Fear touched him for a moment, thinking he might head back to Mount Aga if he kept following the tunnels, the last place he wanted to be right now; but at least there, he knew how to get back out to the surface.

* * *

'What took you so damn long to come and get me?' Khanaseri asked, leaning back against the rock wall with his arms crossed.

'Why did you let yourself get captured? The Khanaseri I knew wouldn't have allowed that,' stated Ganda'har, basking in the early morning sun. 'Besides, we tried earlier, but you weren't in your cage. So don't blame us.'

'It's not as if I had a choice. I was a prisoner. And I didn't let myself get captured... I closed that damned rift before it destroyed our world, and the magic nearly consumed me. I'm amazed I'm still breathing.' Khanaseri moved to stand next to the captain and whispered, 'Why don't you want to talk about Blanka? What happened?'

Ganda'har stood instantly and turned to walk away, but Khanaseri grabbed his arm. 'You can't keep ignoring this. Tell me what you know.'

The captain glared at the warlock, then shied away and said, 'You really want to know what happened to him...? His sacrifice was too great to bear. I stopped him from killing himself. Saw him build their burial mounds and stand before a dragon to be burned alive. I tried convincing him to join my side to get you back...' Ganda'har flipped the table and shouted, '...but there was no life left in him! That coward is taking the easy way out!'

'What?' Khanaseri stood back, stunned by what he'd heard. 'And you left him like that?'

'What was I supposed to do? Babysit him, or save your sorry arse? I chose you.'

Kneading his face, Khanaseri demanded, 'Tell me where he is.'

'Corbal's Crater. Do you want me to take you?'

'No, give me a horse and I'll find my way. What are you going to do?'

'We'll keep on taking down the patrols. They've been sending out larger numbers to raid villages and towns to get more people who can touch the Source. So far, we've been lucky enough to stop them, but it's getting harder. We could use your help.'

'And you'll have it, but I have to take care of this. What we need is an army big enough to stand against them, but I don't know where we would find that. Tergaron and Artokla have been sacked. They're both licking their wounds. As I see it, they'll head for Deresford, then New Runswick, and everything in between.'

They heard footsteps coming from the bush, and turned to see a big man slowly draw near with the aid of crutches, his eyes set sternly with a furrowed brow. Khanaseri crossed his arms and asked, 'Can we help you, stranger?' But the man did not answer, keeping his focus on Ganda'har.

From their backs, Anavi mumbled, 'Magnus?'

Only then did Ganda'har recognise the man with his crutches as the barkeep of Kobo's inn. An enormous fist crashed into his ribs and another rocked his head back, knocking out a tooth and spurting blood down his chin. 'That's for lying to me!'

'Magnus, no!' she shouted, but he ignored her.

Khanaseri stood back with a grin on his face, remembering the beating he'd received from Untara a while back when he walked into their camp. How Ganda'har had stood back to watch and enjoy the arse-kicking. Magnus used the crutch to reach out and yank Ganda'har's feet from under him, and rained down blow after blow with the crutch.

The captain grabbed the wooden crutch and tore it from the big man's hand, sending him to the ground in his injured state. A cry of pain sounded from the man, and Anavi quickly intervened, stepping in before Ganda'har with arms raised.

'Please stop. He's just angry.'

Ganda'har spat blood to the ground and felt the gap in his mouth where a tooth used to be, then said, 'And I told you he would be!'

Anavi rushed to Magnus' side and helped the big man up from the ground. Ganda'har turned to Khanaseri and whispered, 'That cripple packs a punch! I think the dragon in me nearly shat himself.'

'Yeah, I saw,' the warlock chuckled.

'Aye, I can hear youse, and youse can be glad that was my left hand! If it was my right, I woulda taken yer fuckin' head!' Magnus brought up his injured right hand, stretching it open before closing it again. He turned to Anavi and pleaded, 'Why d'ya leave me, love?'

Anavi stumbled over her words, forgetting what she wanted to say. 'I, uhm... Where did... How did you... Why are you here? Have you been eating?' She pulled at the loose-fitting clothes around his stomach and frowned at him.

'They came back, burned down the inn and a lot o' homes. Some died fighting them and many ran off into the forest, but I took Lexi and snuck out back like a coward. There were too many of 'em, and I'm pretty useless at the moment.'

Anavi cursed and briefly spun away from him, trying to hide her anger. She knew what The Flying Squirrel meant to Magnus, and now it was gone, thanks to them. 'I'm sorry, my love. It's our fault. We set some prisoners free from their camp, and I fear this was retaliation.'

'Dammit! Shoulda seen it coming. Forgive me, Magnus. For lying about Anavi and this,' said Ganda'har, and sat back down to nurse his jaw. 'You're welcome to tag along with us, but there will be a few scraps. Obviously, you don't have to join in, but you can cook us a meal or so. This bunch don't know what they're doing with food and I remember your steak. It's the best I've had in a long while. How did you find us, anyway? We've been moving around to keep the patrols guessing.'

'I had no idea where to look, but one night, camped in the forest, I was readyin' a fire when three wolves wandered close, growling and baring their fangs, ready to make a meal outta ol' Magnus. Thought I was dead for sure when they attacked. Kept them at bay with the crutch as best I could, but it wouldn't have lasted long. Then my saviour jumped from the bush and attacked them. While they tussled on the ground, I hit another over the head with the crutch and it bolted, followed closely by the other two. Bogar saved me and led me here, keepin' me company the entire way.'

'Is that where you disappeared to, Bogar?' Anavi said with a smile when she saw the pale wolf saunter closer from the trees. 'What do you have there in your mouth?'

The wolf dropped the dead rabbit before Magnus' feet and lay down, staring at them with his ice-blue eyes.

'Yeah, he's been doing that too. Bringing me food to cook for us. Never thought I'd say it, but I love this guy.' Magnus grunted and chuckled, then patted the wolf on the head. 'That's a good boy.' He turned to Anavi and said, 'I tethered Lexi to a branch just beyond the trees. I think she's even angrier at you than I am.'

Anavi smiled and nodded her thanks.

'Hey, Magnus,' interrupted Ganda'har, 'a few magi, healers, and the sort stayed behind to fight against these bastards. I'm sure one of them will be more than happy to speed up your healing. Speak to Vanesh first. She's pretty good.'

Anavi had her arms around the barkeep's waist, assisting him a little as he hopped on the one leg and readied the crutch. Her voice trailed away and disappeared with them down the cave. 'You haven't been eating enough. Just look how loose...'

Ganda'har watched them leave and whispered, 'I can't imagine that woman with any man. Yet I just witnessed it with my own eyes.'

'She reminds me a little of Beuneth. The same fire burns in her eyes,' replied Khanaseri.

'Aye, indeed. Will you come back to us?'

'Yes, of course. And believe me, so will Blanka. But first I have to get Flintlock from Artokla.'

'If he still lives...'

* * *

Hood drawn over his head, Ackelar unlatched the window and snuck into the room, carefully placing his feet so as not to make a sound. Guards patrolled the museum's halls, and they had the authority to be judge and jury, to kill on sight — a frightening aspect. But he needed to get the Declaration of Deeds and Titles of the royal bloodlines going back generations to the founders of Beltokko, the old Elmohria. The room was dark, and the faintest sounds travelled far in the stillness. Surrounded by shiny artefacts and devices on display, he struggled to maintain his focus on the objective, his mind already reaching for the riches so close by. It had been a long time since he'd gone on an undertaking such as this; he had forgotten the exhilaration it brought, the challenges and the prospects of danger.

On the far side of the hall, a guard walked up the stairs, a lantern swinging gently from his grip, casting hideous shadows from the swords and shields on display. Ackelar quickly took cover behind a replica of the old royal mantle worn by the first kings of Beltokko and waited for the guard to pass by. The man's footsteps drummed on the wooden floor, then down the steps on the other end. Ackelar released a long, steady breath and moved up along the wall to the back, where waited a thick glass tomb with the thick scroll fortified inside. Leaning in to see into the corners of the box, he spied the fragile vials filled with a dark substance, ready to break with the tampering of the thick glass tomb. He had seen those vials before and knew what they did. Once broken, a poison spread fast, and any caught in the vicinity would have their songs sung before the sun rose.

Sweating under the hood, he wiped his face with the back of his arm and unfolded the lock pick pouch. He removed a long, delicate, thin-bladed knife, unfolded the blade even further, and worked it carefully into the slight groove beneath the glass lid, taking care not to lift it too high. Halfway to the trigger rope, the blade bending precariously under its own weight as was its flimsy nature, he heard more footsteps coming his way. He could not yank it out, nor was there time to remove it with care. Anxious, Ackelar removed his belt buckle and hooked it over the thin blade handle, keeping it balanced while he snuck away to hide. *I'm rusty... This shouldn't take this long. When I get back home, I need to practise more and stop fluffing pillows.*

The guard turned into the room, lifting the lantern up high to see further down at the back, and said, 'Hello? Anyone here?'

Ackelar watched the belt buckle shift slightly, making the blade wobble and tap gently against the glass, but the noise drilled into his mind as a vociferous commotion.

'Hey, who's there? Come out!' the guard drew his blade and made his way deeper to investigate the disturbance. The light reached further and further until he saw the glass tomb with the balanced blade hanging from the top, tapping away at the lid. Shocked, the guard turned and yelled, 'Ala—'

A hard kick to the stomach pitched him forward, and he dropped the sword in a clangour to the floor. Ackelar swiped his legs from under him and restrained the man with his arm wrapped around the man's throat from the back, then dragged him away from the room's entrance. Kicking and hitting backwards with little force, the man succumbed to the pressure on his neck and passed out.

Ackelar dashed back to the glass vault, working the thin, long blade as he heard voices shout in alarm. He felt suddenly hot, flustered, and whispered to himself, 'Come on! You can do it... Little to the left, a little more.' The blade shied away, and he had to draw it back. 'Blasted shite! Come on! Steady! Steady!' Frustrated and annoyed, he willed the blade closer, hearing the footsteps draw ever nearer as they ran up the stairs. They were so close now. Finally, the curved tip of the blade rested on the tripwire and he cut the rope with a long-winded sigh of relief. Hands shaking, he quickly set about picking the lock, feeling his angst getting the better of him to come crawling up his throat. With no more time left, he threw open the glass top, grabbed the scroll, and darted for the window, diving out to roll on the flat roof high above the grim cemetery now on his left, far below. Legs burning and heart racing, a silhouette in the night, he felt the cold metal of an arrow slice into his shoulder from below. The sudden burn nearly made him drop the scroll. It had been a long time since he felt the bite of cold steel; life had become cosy in the orphanage. Luckily for him, it merely grazed him. He grabbed the edge of the roof and dropped to hug the large stone pillars with his legs and arms, sliding down fast to the ground. Dogs barked and searched for his scent, growling not far behind. Into the cemetery he ran, looking back over his shoulder every so often, catching glimpses of his pursuers.

'Where'd he go?' asked one guard to another while they searched the overbearing darkness, finding naught but angels and ghouls on the headstones of the dead, convoluted trees with arms reaching out to snatch their prey, and eerie howls and croaks in the distance. 'I hate this place! It gives me the creeps. Let's get out of here, Baska. He ain't here.'

'Oh, Tellan, stop being such a girl. He couldn't have gone far. Go right, I'll go left. We ain't givin' up yet,' stated Baska. 'Besides, we be in a heap of trouble if we don't find him.'

Their faint lights fought against the settling fog, their vision only a few feet from their terrified faces now as a dreadful silence crept in, except for a lone owl hooting from somewhere like a warning to all to stay away and lock themselves in their homes until the sun rose the coming day. The wind died, and the fog lay unmoving. Tellan hoisted his trembling sword, pointing it at eye level before him, his nerves a battlefield of chaos. He walked on the cobbled path, jittering from fear and ready to soil himself. With a trembling hand, he reached out and grabbed hold of the twisted wrought-iron railings, feeling the rust on the surface, then a tingle running up his arm, and saw a gigantic spider making its way to his shoulder. A scream and a bout of slapping and cursing followed. The lantern sailed through the dim night and shattered on the path, extinguishing the light. Tellan suddenly felt like he was not the hunter anymore, but the hunted, stalked from a distance by a fang-bearing predator waiting for the time to strike. A rustling of leaves and twigs snapping made him spin to his right. 'Who's there? Stay away! I have a sword!' Another rustle, and a screech from a cat sounded. Tellan screamed, dropped his sword, and bolted from the graveyard, falling thrice over unmarked graves and ditches.

Baska heard his comrade's screams and cupped his hands over his eyes, squinting to see what was going on. 'Tellan! What's happening?' No answer came. 'Sissy! I'm telling on you!' A clatter of wood came from the right. 'Oh, you think you can scare us off, eh? Tellan might have fallen for that, but I won't.'

'I'm not trying to scare you off,' came a voice riding the deathly still air. 'But he is.'

A deep growl and a hissing roar came from his right near the trees. Baska hoisted the lantern and saw glimmering eyes reflect the light, moving graciously with great speed towards him. 'What the—?' He turned and ran, hearing the roars of the big cat drawing near.

Ackelar chuckled, waiting for the faint glow from the lantern to vanish around the corner, and snapped his fingers. The sound, so sharp, echoed through the graveyard, bouncing off the headstones and the low stone walls. Turning to regard the thief with its shimmering eyes, the big cat jumped and disappeared into the mist. 'I hope the inn is still serving. I could use a drink.'

* * *

Golden and bubbly, the ale ran down his mouth in streaks to his cowl with the large gulps he took. 'Another!'

The barkeep grimaced and poured another, for although he wanted to go to bed, he needed the coin that came with patrons still flushing their wits and dramas down the drain with his golden ale. Ackelar waited for the barkeep to deliver the new mug and tossed him a coin.

This one he would sip more steadily, taking in the flavours and savouring the aftertaste. He unfurled the scroll and started reading, working back to the very beginning. *Interesting; for generations, the Rourke lineage has been in a constant battle with death, every time just surviving with descendants taking over, being murdered or dying suspiciously. Stretching all the way back to... Caryk Rourke, killed by his most trusted warden with his own sword after the birth of his son. And so the pattern continues...*

Dull footsteps sounded through the inn, with a man making his way to the counter, a chain jingling from his belt. He leaned over the thick top as he spoke to the barkeep. Ackelar continued perusing the scroll and studied the lineage before the Rourkes. 'A sole—'

'Pardon me, sir,' came the patronising voice of the man who had spoken to the barkeep only moments ago, now standing before his table with a nasty grin on his square face. His stubby nose was crooked and dented. *He's been in a scrap or two for sure.*

Ackelar looked around and saw patrons swiftly move away from his table, then leaned back in the chair and asked, 'May I help you?'

'Oh, I mightily hope so...sir.'

'I'll do what I can, but I'm not from here, and I run an orphanage back home. So unless you're a big-boned child looking for a home, I don't know how much help I could be.'

'Is that right? Well, it doesn't matter. I was merely hoping you could tell me who this belongs to. I would dearly like to return it to its rightful owner.'

Ackelar watched the big man throw a belt buckle embellished with intricate patterns on the table. He stared at the metal buckle for some time, feeling his body grow cold, then turned it over calmly as if investigating it, seeing his initials etched into the back. An old habit he had formed when he first came to the orphanage and never stopped. 'Nope, sorry, sir. Can't say that I've seen someone with this before. That looks like an ancient piece, though. It might be precious. Have you tried the museum?'

'We going to play it like that, are we?'

'Play it like what — possibly wealthy, sir?'

'How's the gift I gave you? Stings, doesn't it? Be glad I just marked you.' The broad-shouldered man tapped his left arm. 'You can call me Dromus. Come along, we don't have to make a scene.'

Ackelar knew the jig was up and rotated his shoulder, his leathers cut and arm bleeding where the bolt had sliced through. 'And just where exactly are we going?'

'Let's go for a stroll. Put these on.' A set of heavy iron shackles clattered on the table, followed by a black hood.

'I thought we weren't making a scene...'

'Oh... This is not a scene. Not yet, anyway. Get moving.'

Ackelar drummed his finger on the table, considering his options, then sighed and reached for the shackles. The dull clinks of the latches fell into place around his wrists and Dromus pulled the black hood over his head. Guided from the inn, he could at least not witness the disgusted looks he was receiving from the patrons, but the silence was overbearing enough for him to imagine it. Still night out; he breathed in the cool air through the dusty hood and sneezed, then coughed. 'How many heads have been in this hood? Dear god, it reeks in here.'

'A few,' said Dromus calmly, pulling and guiding Ackelar by the shackles around his arms.

'What are you going to do with me?'

A chuckle came from the big man. 'Personally, I'd like to chop off your hands, being a thief and all. But I'd set you free afterwards. It's not up to me, though.'

'Who do you work for?'

'You're unable to shut it, aren't you? Questions like that'll see you end up six feet under.'

'All I'm saying is, you seem like a nice bloke. What are you doing working for murderers?'

Although he could not see Dromus' face, he could hear in his voice the genuineness of his reply. 'I *am* a nice bloke. Who says I don't work for the museum?'

'Do you work for the museum?'

'No, dear god. Can you just imagine? Those guards are all so feeble-minded. Baska actually believed that jaguar was real.'

'Oh, it *was* real. He woulda been cat food if he hadn't run.'

They stopped, and Ackelar could feel Dromus staring at him. 'Mpf. What do you know? Now I feel bad for slitting his throat.'

The cavalier attitude that Dromus personified rattled Ackelar. *This is a madman.* They continued moving again. For some time, they walked in silence, until Dromus opened a gate, the rails screeching loudly. Ackelar could only assume that it was heavy, and probably big.

'No peeking.'

Unsure how he was going to get out of this, Ackelar pleaded, 'Look, just take back the scroll and we can forget all of this. What do you say? I leave Deresford and never return.'

'That will unfortunately not cut it for me. You've seen too much, know too much.'

As they walked, Ackelar had worked free the wire he hid in his sleeve. He knew it was risky, but he could tell when there was more focus on him. The distinct smell of cooked cabbage wafted over his nose as they entered a room with a red-ochre rug — he saw it at his feet as the hood shifted — faintly lit by lanterns hanging from the wall. Shoved down into a chair, he felt bile rise in his throat and wanted to vomit. *Be calm, Ackelar, you have been in worse situations. Although this is pretty bad. Shouldn't have got yourself caught. Too late now for berating yourself. Come on, think. How are you going to get out of this?*

Rough hands drew the hood quickly and the sudden light blinded him, making it impossible to see the person standing before him. 'We have a lot to talk about,' came a man's eerily grating voice. 'It seems we can both benefit from what I offer.'

* * *

Parched, Arundhàbu scooped the wet mud into a torn piece of clothing and tied the ends together, squeezing it from the top down. His head throbbed with every breath he took, the pain pulsating to the back of his neck. Slow and steady, drops of dirty water appeared, pushing through his shirt. It was a slow process, but while he sucked on the scummy water, he laughed, knowing it to be a worthwhile one, giving him the strength he needed to continue. Time was irrelevant down in the tunnels. It was impossible to know how long he had been down there for, and he'd barely slept all the while. Step by step, he continued onward, hoping to find an opening to the surface. His eyes had adjusted to the darkness, but still could not see clearly, the annoyance driving him to anger and frustration when he tripped over a root or a corpse, which had happened a few times now. *Who would've thought that meeting the human would send me to the bowels of the world, to drink mud and suck dry the bones of all the insects I can lay my hands on?* Arundhàbu leaned with his palm against the wet mud-wall, and sank to his elbow, drawling curses at the situation. He pulled his arm out and wiped his hand on his tunic, muttering morosely under his breath. Tired beyond reason, he slowly took a step back, and the ground disappeared beneath him. It gave way like a landslide, and he screamed bloody murder as he fell, roots and stones scraping and bumping him all the way down. He tried to grab hold of something, anything, but everything rushed by too fast.

'What's happening?' he yelled before crashing into a gigantic root, knocking the wind from him and flipping him over on his head. The momentum spun him again and again until he spilled out at the bottom of the slide onto a slick floor of mud, rocks, and crystals of a deep blue. Reflections of blue fire danced on the walls from thousands of the gigantic crystals, and a tremendous heat washed over him. He struggled to get up and saw the molten lava coursing as wide as a river a few feet away, funnelling the heat over an enormous chrysalis suspended from the ceiling. Low moans reverberated through the room, shaking the crystals and causing a shimmer throughout. Arundhàbu grabbed hold of a stalagmite twice his size and clung to it while the groan sounded, holding on as the room shook. 'What in the world is this?' he whispered, and carefully approached, but felt the heat become too intense, his hair singeing and leaving behind a foul odour.

With his hand covering his eyes, he spied something in the distant corner of the room and investigated, keeping to the cooler pockets. Skin burning profusely, he felt blisters forming on his arms and legs, but he needed to see what was happening here. He jumped from behind one pillar to the next, keeping away from the direct heat of the magma, and especially the crystals amplifying the heat. A gigantic pile of moulted skin lay before him, the head distinct and unnerving. He glanced up at the chrysalis in the distance as realisation dawned on him, hearing the deep moans and groans coming from within. Amplified heat funnelled directly into the cocoon, spurring forth the metamorphosis taking place. From behind the pillars, he glimpsed the movement inside the chrysalis and pondered what to do. *Should I leave it? How long will it be before it is reborn? Tulvar would have loved to witness this, although he would have long since died of this blasted heat.*

The cocoon shook with the movement inside, then split open at its top, a hoarse roar bellowing from the creature to celebrate its freedom. Powerful legs tore the chrysalis husk from the inside, its gigantic eyes glimmering red from the magma beneath. It burst forth, searching for an escape from the dark room, and spied the collapsed section where Arundhàbu had slid out, then leapt closer, briefly flapping its enormous wings before hitting the ground, scattering dust, rocks, and magma all over. The chamber shook violently as it crashed into the hole, forcing it wider with its body, and crawled upward. The blacksmith ran for the exit and jumped up, grabbing hold of the thing's spiked back leg, cutting open his hand and chest in the process.

There was no time to worry about that. This was his way out.

Thrown around, he bounced up and down, side to side, being cut further by the spikes. They were moving fast, rapidly ascending, and suddenly the earth exploded with light, blinding him. The jarring ride and bright light accosted him harshly, and he released his grip on the creature's leg to plummet through the air and fall onto the hard soil of the surface. His back ached and his mind swam with what just happened, and the knock it took. Arundhàbu coughed and slowly rolled over, pushing on his hands and knees to rise from the ground. He stared after the creature flying away in the distance, watching until he couldn't see the red spots on the black wings anymore.

'Now, what should I make of that? And where am I?' A few

mountains rose to his right, and a flat plain with shrubs and a stand of trees beckoned to his left. The soil seemed undisturbed, mostly, except for the recent hole made by the creature. For a while, he walked, ensuring the sun was at his back in the late hour of the day, yet he didn't know how long he would need to walk.

* * *

They barrelled down what was barely a road, pushing the horses hard as nightfall crept in, taking with it the ease of manoeuvring the wagon and horses over the deceitful terrain. Garidan sliced his blade across the arm of a brigand on horseback, cutting deep. The bandit dropped his mace and cursed loudly, falling back to get his arm fixed up. Another was on his right, looking like a mongrel mix of Ageian and Tark, his tusks skewed upward and more delicate than the average Tark's. 'Human! To your right! Blasted Tarogs!' shouted Naghita over her shoulder, before swinging around to cut off another horseman headed for the wagon.

'I see him. Take care of those two. I'll join you soon.' Arrows and slingshot pellets zinged past them, thudding into the wagon timbers. 'Get down, Tulvar!' Garidan shouted. The old khaliq dropped to the bed of the wagon, holding on to the bouncing Raegel.

Tulvar flailed about, and shouted over his shoulder, 'Can you keep this wagon still?'

'Sure! Just let me...' Borka replied mockingly before crushing another Tarog's nose, throwing him to the back of the wagon to roll over the khaliq and off in a cloud of dust.

Garidan hadn't seen the brigand fall, and ran over him with the horse, trampling his legs while fighting with the Tarog next to him on horseback, kicking and throwing punches at full gallop. Only when he heard the horrible crunch beneath them did he notice the dust cloud of the rolling man behind him.

'The way out is up ahead on the left!' Naghita roared. 'Argh! Two more coming from the right! These bastards don't give up, do they?' A bolt sliced past her on the right and she spun the horse around, heading straight for the attacker, and let fly her dagger, burying it in the man's chest. *Damn, that was a good throw,* she thought. Retrieving her dagger, she took the reins of the abandoned animal and set off, catching up with Garidan at the rear.

Borka fought with another brigand while holding the reins, trying to steer with one hand and defend with another while Tulvar cowered in the corner, keeping out of the fight. Raegel weakly grabbed at the man's leg, but was easily shaken off, getting a boot to the head for his troubles. 'Tulvar! Up front! Now! Grab the reins!' shouted the gladiator.

'I don't know how!'

'Figure it out!' He handed the reins over and leapt onto the bed of the wagon, knocking the attacker back. They grappled and threw punches at each other while Tulvar screamed in angst from the front seat, holding on to the reins for dear life. The horses didn't want to obey, biting and snapping at anything that got too close, even each other. They veered to the right, straying from the path, and bounced over ruts, nearly throwing the gladiator and the attacker off the wagon. Borka shrieked, 'Steer with your hips! Not your arms! Do not pull constantly, just...' In their stumble, he grabbed the attacker from behind, locking his arm around the man's throat, squeezing hard, '...when they need to turn. Turn back left!'

Eyes wide and nerves destroyed, Tulvar tried his best to move the reins with care, not to yank on them and send the beasts reeling. A horseman came alongside the wagon, slicing his sword left and right at Borka. They headed for the ramp to get out, and Tulvar pulled on the right rein, forcing the attacker to stop before hitting the canyon wall. The wheel bounced off the cliff-side, lifting it slightly, but kept rolling as it came down on the hard ground, creaking and groaning from the abuse. 'You're doing well! Keep going—'

Sudden silence followed, and Tulvar heard Borka drop to the wagon's floor, a smoothed round rock used as a slingshot pellet rolling around next to him. 'Yah! Yah!' Tulvar shouted and whipped the reins, eking out more speed to get them out of the canyon without delay. Meanwhile, Garidan closed in from the back and swung his sword at another brigand, cutting the man's leather jerkin above the elbow but missing the arm. Curses streamed from the Tarog before he retaliated with his horseman's pick, landing a blow to Garidan's arm, nearly breaking it. Sword arm numb, Garidan wasn't sure how he held on to the blade anymore. He parried another blow from the pick, glancing it off the back of his horse. The beast neighed in pain, its buttock dipping slightly before continuing up the slope. Another blow came, and he parried it with the sword, extended his reach, and smacked the man in his face with the pommel of his blade. The attacker pitched backwards off his horse, disappearing as they reached the level plains again.

They bolted for the mountains and the pass that awaited them. The horses were tired and lathered with sweat; the constant running was not doing them any good.

Naghita quickly caught up with the wagon, galloping alongside while Garidan remained at the rear, constantly looking over his shoulder at the remaining two brigands, who were following on their horses but not drawing near. After a while, the silhouetted pair gave up and swung back around. 'They've given up! We've made it! Rest the horses!' Garidan shouted. Slowing to a stop, they gathered themselves and he asked, 'Is everyone okay?'

'I'm fine,' said Naghita.

'I surmise Borka is not well,' came Tulvar's trembling voice. 'I, uh... I think he got hit with a slingshot pellet. Who knew they could be so dangerous?'

A groan sounded from the wagon, and the big Tark slowly rose, clutching his head. 'Did we make it?'

Grinning, Garidan said, 'We sure did. Are you okay? I've seen a man's skull split by a slingshot pellet.'

'Wasn't a direct hit, luckily. It bounced from the wagon's bench. I'll be fine, although this egg on my forehead will be here for a while.' He glanced at the khaliq and nodded. 'You did a fine job steering these beasts under duress.'

Tulvar nervously chuckled and brought up his hand to show the gladiator that it was shaking feverishly with adrenalin and fear.

'We have to keep going; we can't stay close to the canyon and give them an opportunity to strike during the night while our guard is down.' Naghita moved closer with the horse she led and continued, 'Tulvar, you need to ride on your own from now on. I need Garidan free from your burden, and the wagon is struggling with the three of you.'

Dear gods, what will I have to do next? Join in the fights? The khaliq wanted to ask, but kept quiet and struggled to get on the horse.

Garidan dismounted and hurried over, helping the khaliq up and said, 'Don't worry, it's easier than it looks. You'll learn quickly.' Tulvar nodded dumbly and stared down, for the first time realising how high up he was. It hadn't bothered him when someone else was with him on the horse, controlling the animal, but now, all alone, he felt like fainting. Seeing the fear in the man's eyes, Garidan fastened one end of a rope to the reins and the other end to his saddle. 'You're not completely alone. I've got you.'

Naghita rolled her eyes and said, 'Stop babying him. You are not his mother, although I think you are more female than me.'

Chapter Four

Piercing shrieks split the sky as three dragons glided over the burning village, celebrating yet another victory over mankind, leaving only ash and bone in their wake. Ragian watched a juniper-green dragon settle to the ground and veer from a distance, annoyed with the arrogant new Kingsguard. Khellar had stepped forth a few days prior, proclaiming his desire to be bonded, taking the chance to be judged by the Balamuths and the dragons they harboured — to be joined forever or torn to pieces. The young dragon Asagar had accepted him. Fully bonded and vengeful, they now soared the skies, one's anger fuelling the other's hatred. Khellar's promotion from lieutenant to the rank of Kingsguard made the men more than bitter, but none would show their true feelings to the newly bonded, for there was nothing they could do. He had been a pompous arse since the day he joined, always trying to show how much better he was than anyone else, but he would never have made the run to Vault and won. When the King announced that anyone could now volunteer for the bonding, he had raised his hand. The men now laughed at his terrible jokes, feigning interest in his stories and hating every moment of it.

But not Ragian.

Soldiers marched around, looting and locking up anyone their mages gestured to as Ragian stormed up to the cocky Kingsguard and gripped him by the throat, slamming him against the wall of a smouldering home. 'What do you think you're doing? Your orders were to frighten the villagers, keep the guards from picking up their weapons.'

Khellar broke free of Ragian's grip and shoved him back, glancing around at the stares they were receiving from the surrounding soldiers. To their left lay a woman crying in the road and covered in soot. She stretched out her burnt arm, and reached for her destroyed home a few feet away on the other side of the street, smoke drifting from her torn clothes, hair, and arm. He chuckled and said, 'Looks to me like I did just that... Captain. Besides, the king doesn't seem too broken up about it.'

Ragian glimpsed King Turneroth eyeing their argument with interest, and cursed under his breath. He turned his attention back to Khellar and whispered, 'I decide on the tactics, not the king. It's my job to ensure the best outcome. Get out of my sight.' The bonded left without a word, grinning broadly.

Ragian heard the man speak behind him as footfalls neared. 'Your Majesty.'

'Khellar! Congratulations on this marvellous victory!'

'Thank you, my King.'

Ragian hadn't turned around, but knew how smug Khellar must feel, getting the recognition from the king directly after their argument about his tactics. Anger bubbled up, his neck hairs standing on end from the frustration he felt. He slowly turned and bowed. 'My Liege, this is unexpected. I did not think you would be here today. What seems to have brought on your visit so far from your troops? They must be a few days' march away still.'

'Yes, indeed they are, but I wanted to spread my wings for the first time. Stretch the muscles and such. I didn't expect it to be so much effort, to be honest. Belroc is a heavy beast,' the king said, his brows knitted.

If you were a true bonded, you wouldn't be so afflicted. You would be as one, not feeling the other as a burden. But you...my lord...are not a true bonded.

Turneroth sensed his hesitation to speak and interrupted his thoughts. 'Khellar is still young, eager to please. Don't let him get to you for not following your orders to the letter. He got the job done – that's what counts.'

'But at what cost, sir? How many magi did he kill who could've aided our way back home? Countless unnecessary deaths happened today that could've been avoided. I thought we were doing this to get back home, not plunder for the sport of it.'

'Cheer up, Ragian. I have some good news for you.' The king draped his arm around Ragian's neck, gesturing to an unseen world, and continued, 'There I was, lying in bed last night, listening to little Moseroth sleep, when a thought dawned on me. And I must admit that I was very disappointed that *I* had to think of this and not one of my constituents, like you or Bohan. See, I remember the stories of the Elven magic and how powerful they were.' Turneroth guided Ragian with his arm on the man's shoulder, walking through the ruins of the village, sneering at the dying woman on the ground. 'If they still dwell in the forests up north, they could save us a heap of trouble and time. Would you scout ahead and locate them? See where they are, and what defences they have, then report back to me immediately.' Turneroth grinned at the Kingsguard, waiting for an answer.

He knew this was not a request, but an order to get him out of the king's hair. 'Yes, sire. I will leave soon and report back to you.'

'Excellent. Tell me, how many did we get from this village?'

'Only two, sire.'

'Blasted rantallion scum!' The king's calm demeanour changed instantly, his eyes watering and turning red, his head and face twitching with every blink of an eye. He spun around and marched off, shouting back, 'Find those elves!'

'Will do...sire,' Ragian whispered back, glaring at the king from behind.

'Got new orders for us, Kingsguard?' Xare asked as he jogged closer from the right, purposely intruding on whatever Ragian was thinking.

'No, I don't. You're to take orders from Khellar until I return.'

'What? We can't take orders from him. He's an idiot. Look, I enjoy killing as much as the next guy, but what are we doing here? First Caryk vanishes, then you get side-lined. Now we're taking orders from this buffoon. The king is acting stranger and stranger by the day, his moods shifting more than Fen's ale count. Trust me, that's a lot.'

'I, uhm—' Ragian glimpsed Bohan walking closer and said, 'Wish I knew. I have to speak with Bohan. We're doing everything we can to get all of us back home. I'll see you later, Lieutenant.'

* * *

'The king is dead! The king is dead! Do not fall for the lies spread by the red-haired witch! She should not be sitting on the throne just because she might have a male spawn growing in her! She should abdicate, give it over to the council until the child is born!'

Mobs of people crowded the square where they rallied against the queen's pregnancy, riling up the people to the point of civil unrest. Soldiers stormed the square, breaking apart the shouting mobs, dispersing most of them swiftly but for the zealots holding firm to their beliefs. Always ready to play the martyr, seeking violent confrontations to bolster their side's claims, people would flock to their aid against the oppressors. They could hear the shouts of anger all the way up in the castle, getting progressively more violent and barbarous. Ladriana's black gown flitted over the stones, flowers the colour of autumn leaves falling from her breasts through the waistline to vanish forever between the unseen folds. Bemused, she danced her fingers over an ancient tapestry on the wall, following the threaded curves of the blossoming fig tree, its white petalled flowers careening in the winds.

'Milady, we've heard nothing from Ackelar since we confronted him in the orphanage,' said Kehlos, keeping an eye on the happenings in the square from the castle window.

Ladriana did not move away from the tapestry. 'I'm losing the confidence of my people, Kehlos. We can't let that happen. Someone must be behind the motivation of these zealots. I need you to find out who that is. Can you do that for me?'

'I can, milady, but it will probably lead to the same dead end we've been hitting.'

'Maybe we should request Deresford and Tiam to send their troops to us. We have the best fortification of the three. This is where we stand a chance,' Captain Volar said, pacing back and forth until Abe lifted his bony old finger.

'If I may.' He waited until Ladriana nodded and continued, 'With all that's going on, I do not think that will help, Captain. They will not leave their cities defenceless, and you cannot blame them for that. Also, if we let so many in at once, more assassins could sneak in for the kill. We cannot risk it.'

'Do you care to weigh in, Thelanor?' Ladriana asked, her head cocked slightly as she regarded his movement.

Straddling the chair, Thelanor leaned with his muscular arms on the backrest and glanced between those in the room while he chewed on a grass stalk. 'I don't care for the old buzzard's sentiment. The queen will be safe with me by her side. Nothing will harm her.' He dusted his bejewelled hands and plucked the stalk from his mouth. 'I don't think the other cities will come to our aid, though. He's right about that.'

Abe clenched his teeth, working his jaw muscles back and forth in anger. 'I do not know if you ever finished school, Thelanor, but I can see you failed the class in manners.'

'I only have manners for those I respect. You, Headmaster, aren't ranked among those fortunate enough.'

Ladriana gazed at the bickering two and said, 'Do *not* make me regret employing you as my court mage, Thelanor. You will show decorum in my halls, no matter who speaks.'

'If that's your wish, my Queen, it will be so. My apologies, old man,' Thelanor said, and mockingly bowed to the headmaster with a grin.

'Have there been any new sightings of the dragons? Have they moved from the cave at all?'

'No, milady. We have scouts monitoring the area for their movement, and so do the elves and the dwarves. Other than the occasional hunting for food, the male stays by her side during this time of birthing to protect them. We dare not get too close,' said Volar, stepping back to show he was done with his report on the matter.

Her eyes scanned the now-emptied street, the commotion calmed. Ladriana asked, 'Abe, how are things progressing with the school?'

'It is going very well. We have had many students sign up, and some teachers I have personally vetted for the positions required. Although our curriculum and the school are founded based on this dragon threat we face, I have already laid out steps for beyond this crisis for when we are done with this nonsense. For now, we are focusing our training on defensive and offensive, no namby-pamby superfluous spells.'

'Good, thank—'

'Excuse me, Queen Ladriana,' interrupted Abe, his finger raised in the air again. 'I must say that I am more than a little uncomfortable that we are not telling the students *why* they are here. I mean, yes, they will learn magic, but possibly at what cost? Their lives? It doesn't feel right. If we don't tell them why they are really here and they find out — and believe me, they *will* find out eventually — they will feel betrayed and leave, destroying the school's reputation long before it has a chance to succeed.'

'Mpf. You're right, Abe, but not yet. Hold off on telling them. Stretch it out some more. If they see what we're willing to teach them, they might take the news a little better.'

'As you wish, milady.'

'Kehlos, how's the wall coming?' Ladriana ticked off the tasks one by one in her head.

'We've run out of rivets a few times. The blacksmiths are working overtime to get to all the work needed and they have made mistakes, but they rectified each one, and we're making progress. The gates are finally in and construction on the watchtowers has begun, but they're far from finished. The masons complain constantly about everything, and I actually think that's their job now. They just complain and shout at others to get the work done. But it seems to work.' Kehlos chuckled and continued, 'I never thought I would do this as a soldier. It's actually why I became a soldier, to stay away from these kinds of jobs.'

'We all seem to be expanding our skills these days. Captain, have we found the assassin?' Ladriana asked, blinking her burning eyes a few times.

Captain Volar sighed as he saw the bags of sleeplessness underneath her eyes, remembering how youthful she'd looked only a few months ago. Now the stress of office had taken its toll on her physically. 'Not yet, Milady. I have a plan for this, with your blessing, of course. We will have to make a very public announcement.'

All at once, the voices of reason shouted out in unison, 'Are you insane? No! We will not allow it! What are you thinking?'

Captain Volar waited patiently for them to finish their tirade, shouting over each other incoherently. At a pause in the shouting match, he said, 'Are you done? Let me explain. Trust me, this will work.'

* * *

Garidan whistled softly, and his horse slowed to a walk, coming to a stop as they neared a busy street, too busy for horses and a wagon to go unnoticed. It was a very different sight compared to Norvaldmire. The city was beautiful, with high walls and great towers and spires twisting to the heavens. Small buildings and large were complemented by the green parks and the broad river running through the city. They dismounted and tethered the horses to the side of the road.

'How's Raegel doing?' Garidan asked, keeping watch for guards while they kept a low profile, their hoods drawn over their heads to avoid people. Crowds descended on shops and stalls, opening up for the day's work to be done. The street was lined with open doors, while various items were carried out and displayed decoratively on tables to lure browsing customers and ensure an easy sale. Shawls, cookery items, pans, weapons, glasses, wooden furniture, clothing, and food dressed the street side, and he found his mouth watering for some fruits that lay in the baskets. He heard someone vomit behind him and whirled around to see Raegel hunched over, spitting the puke from his mouth into the gutter while leaning against Borka, trying not to stand on his maggot-filled leg. Garidan grimaced and pulled a face at the smell and sight of the leg.

Tulvar leaned in and said, 'He needs help, sooner rather than later.

I know a man who can help; he is not far away. On the far side of this road, two blocks down, there is an old monument in the middle of the road — in honour of all the khaliqs who have served this nation — which we can't miss. His house is the third from the right, an old white and brown residence, if I remember correctly.'

'Good, you and Borka get him to this friend, then meet me and Naghita at the Library of Cabinet.'

Naghita mumbled words Garidan didn't understand, but he construed them as curses by the look on her face. 'Who put you in charge, human?' Naghita clapped her tongue, glaring at him from the corner of her eye.

'I'm not in charge, Naghita,' Garidan responded with his hands up in surrender. 'If you have a better solution for us to take care of business quicker, by all means, take the reins. What would you have us do?'

The moment of silence stretched out, until Naghita slowly crossed her arms and said, 'I will go with your plan for now.' Garidan nodded and turned back to Tulvar, who started giving directions.

'Keep to this road; it will take you to the heart of Velafrey, where lies the Library of Cabinet. The further you go, the higher the buildings will get, with living space becoming cramped and inhospitable. You will see the name of the building carved out of the stone blocks at the front, with gigantic steps leading up to the doors. All Ageians are welcome to enter, but I fear they will have a problem with you two, so don't go in until I get back.'

'Fine show of ruling you Ageians have got going, separating yourselves from the other races like they're unwanted cheese on a platter,' Garidan said, shaking his head.

One brow raised, Naghita sucked on her teeth and said, 'That's the first thing you've said that I agree with.'

'Look, it's not me making these laws,' Tulvar protested. 'The khaliqs in charge here make them, and only a certain few of them. It is their expertise.'

'Expertise?' Naghita stormed. 'Do you really want to say that is the best thing in their eyes for this city? To keep other races oppressed and under their thumb?' She poked him in the chest.

Tulvar retreated a step while he stated, 'Please, Naghita, that's not what I meant, and you know it.'

'Naghita, we don't have time for this. Let them go. We need to stay out of sight, not attract attention to ourselves.'

Borka had his arm around Raegel's waist, carrying him as they made their way across the street with Tulvar next to them, his voice fading away the further they went. 'Will it ever change, Tulvar? Will we ever be allowed...'

Garidan sighed and shook his head, blending in with the crowds as they skulked down the street. He turned to Naghita and said, 'I don't know if I told you this, but back in my world, I'm what they might call one of your Eldarre, a member of the Cabinet. But where I am from, there are no other members, just me and my wife. I'm called a king.'

Harsh laughter sounded, and Naghita stifled the sounds coming from her mouth. 'You? A ruler? Why are you trying this pathetic attempt to make yourself sound important? What's next? Do you want us to bow down to you? Please...' She sucked at her teeth again. 'I'm not a fool.'

'Actually, I ask that no man bow before me, but they don't listen. Doesn't feel right. I'm not lying, Naghita. This is one of the biggest problems we face as well, and I have sworn to bring the people together, not divide them like they do here. You and Arundhàbu will be most welcome in my kingdom.'

'What is this "king-dum"?'

'It is what we call the lands, the area, or region that we rule. There's water aplenty, food grows in abundance, an—'

'Why are you trying to sell this to me?' Naghita snapped.

'Because Arundhàbu wasn't lying to you, and I'd like you to join me when I return.'

'Why haven't you told us until now that you are this king?'

'I was afraid... There was no way of knowing what I would encounter, how the people would react to me. If they knew I was valuable, they could use me to take over my city, but nobody would use a messenger for ransom.'

Naghita nodded, narrowing her eyes as she glanced at him and said, 'You must have an enormous burden on your shoulders, then. I didn't know you had a wife.'

He snickered. 'Yes, a beautiful red-haired woman. You two are alike in some ways. You both are not afraid to get your hands dirty if it's needed. I think you will like her.'

Pulling her face mockingly, Naghita mumbled, 'Does *she* like *you?*'

'I would think so.'

'Then I don't know if I would like her.'

Garidan felt the sting of the words and glanced up to her eyes, only to see her try to hide her smile, then laughed. 'Oh, you two are more alike than you think.' They walked through a big, beautifully maintained garden with all kinds of flowers and small bush-like plants with small red flowers sprouting at the ends of their viny branches. He saw Naghita's face light up with delight at the sight of the different colours.

'These plants... I haven't seen them in such a long time.' She hurried over to a plant with large, angled, deep-purple petals, and cupped it in her hands near her face, drawing in a deep breath. A harsh sneeze erupted from her, and then another. 'That sweet smell. I've forgotten how much it makes you sneeze.'

For a moment, Garidan could not recognise the hard warrior woman. He cocked his head to the side and said, 'We've got to go. I see the Library of Cabinet on the right. Let's get eyes from that building's roof.'

Her blade sang as she pulled it from the sheath and she said, 'Will any eyes do? Or is it specific?'

'What?' Garidan jerked to her, seeing her already moving towards a man with his back turned to them. He lunged for her arm and pushed down on the knife, lowering it out of sight. 'No! That's not what I meant.' He glanced around them. 'I meant, let's keep watch...'

Naghita sheathed her blade with a frown. 'Why didn't you say that, then?'

'Come on.'

* * *

They made their way round the side of the building and into the quiet alley, keeping low and out of sight. Naghita quickly boosted Garidan up to a window on the second floor, where he grabbed the rails and manoeuvred up higher. She sneered at the short human, frustrated at the unending help he needed, before leaping up to grab hold of the rails herself, and feeling the wound on her side pull at the stitches. It still itched and pained her from time to time, but the worst of it was over. She stretched to reach the top and pulled herself over the edge, then turned to look down the four storeys. An infant's cries shrouded the area with an impossible ear-numbing shriek, chasing away all hope of a quiet dispensation. Flat on their stomachs, they peered through the enormous arched windows of the Library of Cabinet across the road and saw the long, vast rooms filled with books and scrolls – a world of knowledge inside. 'How are we going to find anything in that place? It's gigantic,' Garidan huffed, feeling the strain on his hand with the missing digit.

'I don't know, huma—'

'Stop calling me "human"! I have a name,' he snapped, flexing his hand a few times.

'Yeah, but I don't like it.'

'How would you like it if I kept calling you Tark?'

She quizzically looked at him with furrowed brows and stated, 'I am Tark. It would not bother me.'

Annoyed, Garidan grumbled to himself as he turned away, crawling on his elbows to get closer to the edge. *In that building lies the answer to me going home, to finding a way back to my Ladriana. I can feel it pulling me, calling to me.* His breath became rapid, his heart thundering in his chest. *What's happening? Yes, I know you're there!*

A strange voice filled his mind. *I am waiting for you.*

He swung to his left, sure that someone had whispered in his ear, but Naghita frowned at him. 'What is wrong with you?' she asked.

'Nothing... I, uh, just need some sleep. We've been going for the last two days straight with no rest. My mind is slipping.'

'Get yourself together. Here come our friends.'

Flexing his hand a few times, Garidan searched through the crowds in the street and saw Borka and Tulvar make their way closer, and waved at them. Crawling on their hands and knees, he and Naghita retreated from the building's edge and climbed back down, waiting in the alley for the pair to join them. 'What did your friend say? Is Raegel going to be okay?' Garidan asked, dusting his hands against his jerkin.

Tulvar looked around the alley, disgusted to be walking in the filthy corners of the city. Scummy water, smelling of excrement, seeped from a crack in the building, flowing down to a run-off drain at their backs. 'He doesn't know. Too soon to say for sure—'

Cold, filthy water took them by surprise from above, soaking the three men. Tulvar spurted out a steady stream of the grimy water like from a whale's blowhole, while Borka shouted up to the woman in the window. Garidan was completely at a loss for words. Stunned to silence for the moment, Naghita curled over and burst out laughing, nearly falling to the ground as she clutched her stomach.

The woman from the window flung another bucket during their shouting match, drenching the laughing Naghita and bringing her full fury to fruition. Before they could stop her, she had thrown her dagger, the knife missing the Ageian woman by a hair's breadth and sinking into the wooden shutters with a loud clunk. A quick shriek echoed from the woman as she avoided the thrown knife and dived back into her apartment. 'I will *kill* you! Bitch!' Naghita was halfway up to the window by the time the woman leaned back out to close the shutters, holding them firmly against the raging Tark.

'Naghita! Come back down! Don't do this now!' Garidan yelled from the alley, seeing people turn towards them from the main street to investigate the disturbance. 'Naghita!'

'Shut up! I will rip her face off!'

Borka jumped after Naghita and wrestled her from the wall, dragging her along while they dashed away from the street. She ranted and squirmed in his grip, glaring back at the woman in the window.

They ran into a connecting alley, then off to the side again, slowing to a walk when Tulvar said, 'There is an old bathhouse we can go to; it's an ideal place to discuss our business. The owner does not take favourites with race. We will be welcome there.'

They all nodded in agreement. Naghita wrung out a section of her tunic, splashing water on the stones, and stated, 'At least we will get this muck off of us,' then followed the old khaliq down the street, pushing through the throng of Ageians going about their daily lives.

Loud calls from a boy handing out flyers, dogs barking, horses neighing while trotting past, merchants shouting wares, a blacksmith's hammer ringing out in clinks and clanks; the streets had come alive, bustling with bodies and businesses. To their right, a gigantic open compound came into view with hundreds of workers manufacturing brick after brick in a production line, placing them on the ground to dry while huge kilns burned hot over thousands of bricks at the back, drifting smoke up over the area. Garidan couldn't believe what he was seeing, and stood dumbfounded for a time before turning to Tulvar. 'What's this?'

The three of them stopped and turned around. Tulvar sauntered over to Garidan with a grin. 'Have you not seen the art of brickmaking before?'

'I have, but what is that machine?' A colossal device stood to the right with a few workers surrounding it, doing various jobs, while two on either side kept turning a lever, constantly feeding a thick, continuous roll of clay into the machine.

'Oh, that. It's an invention of—'

'Let me guess. One of the khaliqs?'

'Yes indeed. As I recall, he faced a particular problem with rebuilding the Library of Cabinet, actually. It was damaged in a severe storm and when they rebuilt it, they opted for bricks, but the old manual process of brickmaking was taking far too long and it would have taken many months just for the bricks to be made, so he set about designing that machine to speed up the process. We can make ten bricks in the time it used to take to make one.

'The men on this side, near the belt. They have the clay ready and lined up in that thick roll for the machine. Those two men drive the clay through it, where blades are set inside, cutting the clay perfectly to the correct size each time, alleviating the need for the old mould. It saves so much time. You can't see from this angle, but on the other side, the bricks run out on carriers, all cut correctly and ready for stacking on the compound floor.'

'Genius!' Garidan mumbled, and slapped Tulvar on the back before continuing down the street. 'We could really use you in our world for things like this.'

'Stop standing around. We need to get off the streets. People are taking notice of us,' Borka said, drawing his hood further over his face to hide his big tusk.

* * *

A pungent odour lingered in the hall, stinging their nostrils and soliciting some sneezes from Garidan and Tulvar. Even Naghita had screwed up her face a few times, holding back until the feeling waned. Clearing her throat, she shook her head and asked, 'Borka, how does this not affect you in the least?'

The brawny gladiator glanced between them and said, 'I have broken my nose more times than I can count. Guess it just doesn't bother me as much.' By pure instinct, his eyes drifted down her body to the see-through toga she had received to be worn in the bathhouse. A myriad pattern of curls and furls hid some of what was desired to be seen, but was essentially useless.

Naghita flicked his ear and demanded, 'Eyes up here! Any of you look at my breasts again and I will cut off your ears.'

A giggle escaped Tulvar's mouth, trying to hide his embarrassment, and said, 'At least you lot have something to look at. Just look at my flabby skin in this diaper.'

'It's the privilege you have as an elder to not be judged by your body,' stated Garidan, nodding to Tulvar.

'That's only because he doesn't have a body...' laughed Naghita, and Tulvar just shook his head. Steam rose over the large glistening surfaces of the baths, each at least the size of her home back in Norvaldmire and inundated with perfumes, an oily layer drifting at the tops. Naghita could not believe that they were wasting this much water for the pleasure of the people. Where she had to budget and save up to get a bucket of water, here it flowed and splashed, spilling to the ground, and no one cared. Eyes closed, she lowered herself to her neck in the hot, scented bath, and let out a long breath, thinking about Arundhàbu and where he might be. Suddenly aware of the echoes of others lounging in the baths, talking business, she realised how many stared at their group, noting what they were. And what they were was not Ageian. Glaring at each of them, unwilling to break eye contact, she waited for them to move on and continue their conversations.

'This feels so good,' said Garidan, swimming closer to Naghita at the edge of the bath. His unfortunate stature in this world of giants caused him to hold on to the sides, kicking water feverishly. 'Do you mind if we move to a shallower end?'

Borka dunked Garidan's head under the water, grinning broadly. 'He's so short.'

'Cut that out, Borka! Let him up.' Naghita stated with a laugh.

A few gasps, and Garidan blew some water from his nose. 'Not funny, Borka. Remember, I know where you sleep.'

'Agh, only cowards attack while you sleep. Are you a coward?'

'No! Of course not!'

'Stop it!' Tulvar motioned them closer and said, 'The Library of Cabinet is always open, meaning there is always someone on the grounds patrolling. Now, I can get in with minor problems if they have not been alerted of our arrival, but you three definitely cannot. The problem is, I need to get to an area in the Library that is guarded, and identification will be required. Only the high-ranking khaliqs have access to this section, and with me being hunted, I do not think I will have that anymore.'

Garidan shimmied along the edge to get closer and said, 'What about the monolith? Where is that located?'

'Also in the Library, in the same area I need to get to. How do you want to do this?'

'We have to fa—' Garidan slipped and disappeared, the water bubbling from the faint outlines beneath its surface until he exploded up and grabbed the edge, coughing up the scented water, tasting the oils and perfumes. He finally cleared the water from his eyes and glared at the genial three. 'This is ridiculous! Move to the shallow end!'

They laughed and drifted away to where Garidan could reach the bottom. 'That's good. Now where was I? Oh yes, we have to face the fact that not all of us are going to make it into the room. We need only Tulvar and me to get to the monolith and the archives.'

'So you want me and Borka to sacrifice ourselves for you two? Typical.' Naghita crossed her arms with a sneer.

'No, Naghita. This doesn't mean any of us need to get caught, but we *will* need a distraction long enough for us to get in and hopefully out.'

Borka thought for a moment in silence, then grunted and said, 'Then a distraction you shall get. When are we going in?'

'Tonight. Let's get back to the horses and find somewhere to rest before it gets dark.'

'Hold up,' said Naghita. 'What's the plan? Why are you going to the monolith? You're not planning on going back to your world and leaving us behind, are you?'

The thought had crossed Garidan's mind more than once, being tempted to return to his love and leave this foolishness behind. 'No, I'm not. I want to see if I can actually control the monolith for when the time comes.'

* * *

Dark and eerily vacant, the streets of the city called out its loneliness, with most of the good citizens of Velafrey having drifted off to their homes while others schemed and plotted. The corridor creaked underfoot, the wooden floors giving away Tulvar's presence in the building.

'Hello? Who's there?' came a voice from somewhere beyond a stack of books and scrolls still undocumented. An old Ageian woman shuffled out from behind the stack, carrying a load of books she was busy filing, and saw the Ageian walk towards her. Guards filed out from the rows of bookcases, drawing closer and eyeing the khaliq from under the rims of their silver helms, halberds at the ready.

'Good day, madam. Can you point me to Khaliq Yerick Tolben's works?' asked Tulvar, nervously glancing at the surrounding soldiers.

'I'm sorry, those are restricted... Excuse me, what's that noise?' A loud and annoying clangour started up at the front of the building, followed by a sudden blaze erupting, lighting up the courtyard of the Library in a ball of fire and smoke. Her mouth dropped open and her eyes went wide before she screamed. A dance of awkward stepping and apologising occurred when Tulvar moved directly into her path as she ran for the door, knocking into her. 'Get out of my way!' she snapped, and he moved aside, watching her storm from the hall with the guards already out the door, leaving him alone.

'This is going more smoothly than I thought,' whispered Tulvar as he rushed to the back and unlatched a window for Garidan to climb through. They made their way around the stacks of books and through the narrow aisles towards the centre of the hall, where stood a statue of the Eldarre assembly of four Cabinet members on their thrones in a circle, staring outwards. They ran around the monument and down a circular stairway for some time before a locked steel door greeted them.

Exasperated, Garidan swung around and growled, 'What is this? You mentioned nothing about this door.'

Arms in the air, Tulvar stated, 'When I was last here, this didn't exist.'

'Argh! Stand back!' Garidan drew Borka's hunting knife and was ready to bang away when Tulvar tapped him on the shoulder.

'Would these not work better? Grabbed them from that poor woman when she ran into me.'

Garidan turned and saw him hold up a ring of keys jangling against each other. 'Next time, lead with that.' He took the keys and set to finding the correct one. Shouts of anger echoed from the front of the

Library. A loud click sounded, and the lock sprang open in his hands. He glanced back up the stairwell for a moment, and thought, *I hope Borka and Naghita got away safely.* They entered the darkness as the steel door slid open, and he slammed it shut behind them, locking them in. Adrenalin pumping through his veins, Tulvar breathed heavily and rubbed his shaking hands, struggling to light a nearby lantern.

'Let's get started.'

Garidan turned and saw the faintly lit room lined with bookcases filled with works so old, he thought they might fall apart at the mere touch of a finger or the caress of a breath. Scrolls and parchments were in abundance, and at the centre of the room stood the grey monolith, twirling its metal rings over itself on top. His hand automatically reached for the monolith, his thoughts racing deep inside. *I could go home right now, if only I knew I could control it. It's in my grasp...*

'Garidan!'

'What?' He quickly yanked his hand back and shook his head.

'What are you saying? I can't hear through your mumbling.'

'It's nothing,' Garidan said, and pulled out the cloth-covered Balamuth from inside his jerkin, placing it on the table next to the monolith. 'Get searching.' *This place is big enough to fit at least a platoon of soldiers, or maybe Ladriana's new wardrobe... I thought it might be smaller. It's gonna take a while to find what we need.*

'Ah, found it!' Tulvar exclaimed, dusting off a big brown leather-covered book with a symbol on the front resembling the Balamuth now resting on the table.

'What? How did you find it that quickly?'

All confused, Tulvar looked around and said, 'Wait, are you actually angry because I found it that fast?'

'No, of course not...just surprised, is all. What does it say?' Garidan quickly joined Tulvar's side and listened to the old man mumble lines incoherently, flipping through the pages to find what he was looking for.

'Not this. Not this. Nor this. The Balamuth is a construction from the...blah blah blah. Not what I'm looking for... The power generated to create...more interesting nonsense I'm not allowed to read right now...

The ancient dragons were a mighty foe to capture, taking years of practice... We need to come back to that.'

'Years?' What little colour could be seen in the flickering flames all drained from Garidan's face.

'That's what it says, unfortunately. Ah, here it is. In order for the bonding to take place, it must be a mutual agreement between dragon and host. A bonding should never be forced...blah blah blah...for destruction and blah blah blah... As what we have observed, only those strong enough to contain a dragon's essence or spirit will be accepted by the beast if found worthy. In our search to find a suitable host for Yidrog, we connected with the beast by means of magic, but we could unfortunately not hold the connection for long. Three Djak-tas died in the undertaking before we were forced to retreat from the mountain due to the growing restlessness of the wraethers. A section had already collapsed, and it forced us to make our escape through the tunnels, past the stretagor queen's nest.' Tulvar glanced at Garidan and said, 'Fascinating. I never thought of them as a hive, more a mother and its young.'

'Do you know any sorcerer who will help us with this?'

'Here? In Velafrey? No, I'm sorry, I don't. Masters of magic here are fiercely loyal to the Cabinet. They have much less leeway afforded to them than the khaliqs. The slightest inclination of disloyalty will see their heads on the chopping block. We cannot ask any of them. They tend to keep a low profile and stay out of sight.'

'That explains why I haven't seen one.'

'Mmm, indeed.'

Who would be crazy enough to help us with this? Hands on his head, Garidan's thoughts ran wild for what to do next. There was no chance of the Ageians capturing the dragons anymore, and they had no sorcerous allies to count on where they were. Not to mention that they were now trapped in the Library's basement.

They were running out of options fast.

Garidan dropped to a chair standing next to a table heaped with books and scrolls, and grumbled, 'Oh, I'm not sure about this, but... I might know someone who can help. Guess we'll be starting up the monolith after all.'

Tulvar's eyes grew wide with excitement, the constant frown turning to a grin. 'I have waited so long for this moment. Please, wait so I can take notes of the event.'

'Always the scholar, eh?'

'Indubitably.'

Chapter Five

The ringed perimeter of Corbal's Crater stood proud over the desert sands before them, the peaks glistening with the cold snow. Flintlock grunted, pawing at the scorching sands beneath him and shaking his head while he waited for an order from his rider. Khanaseri whipped the reins gently, urging the animal on at a canter over the sand to where the soil hardened to a more clay-like substance towards the crater. From the biggest grey rocks to the smallest white pebbles, stones lay scattered between the few hardy shrubs, bushes, and dead trees. The desert's deficiency in colour brought on a certain wakefulness to the warlock. They climbed the steep slope, following an old, worn-out animal trail until they reached a part of the lower ridges where they could enter the crater without having to scale the very tops and fight the freezing cold.

Along the narrow tear in the mountain they strolled, the warlock's deep green eyes scanning the surroundings while he chewed on a berry and spat out the pip. He kept to the shade of the overhang, enjoying the cool it brought from the harsh desert sun, skirting the grey-brown walls of the crater. Soon, a sea of green welcomed them with large trees and grassy fields below, where stood the mounds Ganda'har had told him about. His heart fluttered and felt as though it had sunk to his feet. He shook his head as he mumbled, 'Oh, Blanka... This is not the way.' They carefully traversed down the side, skirting enormous boulders and fissures in the earth where erosion and earthquakes had done their part well.

A loud shriek sounded in the distance, coming from inside the mountain on the far side, its echoes drifting over the currents flowing in the crater. 'Dreyphus, I assume... Have you killed my friend yet? Are we going to lock horns, you and I?'

Flintlock neighed and snorted, shaking his head happily, delighted to be out of the sun and under the cover of the trees. Khanaseri dismounted to give the animal a break from the weight he carried and led him down towards the mounds, then heard a faint clinking, the sound of a pick hitting solid rock. The closer they got to the piles of rocks, the louder the noise became. 'Can you stop making so much noise? You're disturbing everyone here,' Khanaseri called with the lead in his hand, staring at the back of the mounds.

Blanka poked his head out from behind a stone, covered in dirt and sweat, looking dishevelled and unkempt. 'Khan? Is that really you?' He dropped the loose hammerhead to the ground and wiped his hands on his ragged and torn tunic. Sniffing wildly to clear the mucus running down his nose and beard, he combed his fingers through the mat of hair to clear some of the muck.

'Yes, Blanka, it's me,' Khanaseri said, his face lighting up and spreading his arms for the approaching vagrant. 'What happened to you?' Earlier, Khanaseri had wanted to gut-punch the man for not aiding in his escape; but now, as he stared at him, he was at a loss for words, and waited patiently for his friend to come to him. Knowing there was a dragon nearby, he glanced around for any sign of the beast, then released Flintlock to graze.

Blanka was torn; he was so close to finishing the chamber of his final resting place and could soon join Beuneth in the afterlife, but now his friend beckoned him away from his task. He glanced furtively back and forth between the choices, then climbed down hesitantly from the mound. They embraced as brothers long separated, until Blanka pushed away to look at him with a face covered in dirt and streaked with tears. 'I, uhm... I'm glad you came. Made it, I mean... I'm glad you escaped and came...visited me.'

Khanaseri watched him nervously pick at a scab on his arm, and knew an injury had not caused it; rather, it came to be by Blanka's own persistent need to dig his nails into his skin. The man had become unhinged, causing self-inflicted injuries to make himself feel pain, pain that could help his mind stay away from the loss of Beuneth. The warlock had never seen it until now, but his father had talked about it after his mother could not get over the death of his sister, Ayana, the sister he never knew. All he had from Ayana was the ribbon tied into a bow with a lock of golden hair hanging on the wall in their home. And though he never knew her or met her, he missed her. She was the first-born, supposed to be strong and full of life, but she only got sickness after sickness, until her horrible fate took her away forever and drowned Mother in a sea of self-loathing and angst. *After my birth, she retreated into herself, became lost in thought and wandered where no one else could, deep in the crevices of her fragile mind. Then the cutting started. First her wrists, and up her arms, not deep enough to kill, but deep enough to hurt. Father had been so angry then, screaming and shouting at her for abandoning me. Then one day, she cut too deep and never woke again, never sat in her chair to stare at the setting sun over the sandy dunes of the desert.* 'I wouldn't leave you behind, my friend. Come, let's get you cleaned up and sit down for a hot meal. What I have to say to you might just bring you back to the world.'

Barefoot and twitchy, Blanka felt the thick protective arm of the warlock wrap around his shoulder to lead him away from the site. 'No, no, no, I can't, sorry. Khan. I can't go. I have to—' Blanka stared up at the mounds and continued, face twitching, 'I have to finish...'

The warlock turned to him reassuringly and said, 'We're not going far. I will make us a fire in this clearing where you can see the mounds. Why don't you get us something to eat?'

'I suppose I could make some tomato soup. Searched this entire field one day for them and found a little bush on the other side of the crater. Damned good carrier, though, for its size.'

'Sounds great. I'll be here waiting for you,' Khan replied with a thoughtful smile, and watched his friend drag himself up the side of the crater towards a makeshift tent to collect some items.

* * *

Khanaseri pulled a log near the stacked pieces of timber and sat down, his head hanging low and deep in thought. He considered for a moment not telling Blanka about his son, wondering what worth Blanka could be to the boy in his current state and mood. *It could cause more harm than good.* For a long time, Khanaseri warred with the logs in a locked glare, unblinking and far, far away in his head, seeing so much more than the dead branches and kindling before him. With a snap of the finger, the fire jumped to life, the stare never broken.

'Why'd you use magic?' came Blanka's voice as he drew near. 'You never use magic on things as trivial as starting a fire.'

'Huh? Yeah, I guess. Just not feeling it today.' Khanaseri lifted his head and quickly glanced away again. 'I'm glad to see you've cleaned up some. You had a stench on you. Is that why no one found you after the fight? They couldn't bear getting close to this place.'

'Says the ape with half a face,' Blanka growled while setting the items on a boulder. 'At least I can wash away my stench...'

The warlock chuckled and said, 'I missed this back-and-forth between us. I find it...genuine.' He stared at Blanka and asked, 'Why didn't you go with Ganda'har to help me?'

Caught by surprise, Blanka stopped halfway between sitting and standing for a while, then dropped to the boulder with a resounding sigh. 'I have no excuse, Khan.'

'Ganda'har told me what you planned. I was worried I might be too late already. You know, for a man who wants to kill himself, you sure are taking a long time to do the deed.'

Blanka glared at him, and stated, 'Dreyphus hasn't come out of his lair for a while. So I've kept busy making the mounds and the chamber. Been chipping her name into the headstone.'

'Bunch of shite, if I've ever heard any! You could have drawn a blade over your throat and been done with it. Why haven't you?'

'What do you want from me?' Blanka shouted, and jumped up to stand before the warlock.

'I want to see the fire in you! Snap out of it!' He jumped up and smacked Blanka with his palm across the face, sending the man to the ground, blood dripping from his mouth. 'She is *gone*, man!' As Blanka rose, another hand came down, slapping him to the ground again. 'Stop simmering and bring the heat!' He slapped Blanka again, and picked him up from the ground. 'You're my friend, and I will not leave you!'

Blanka growled, his watery eyes turning red before another palm slapped him across the face. 'Leave me alone!'

'Never! You're better than this! Bring the fire!'

Lights exploded in Blanka's eyes. The warlock was sitting on top of him now, beating him from right to left, left to right, not stopping for a breath, his thick, heavy palm burning the sides of Blanka's face.

Khanaseri picked the man up from the ground and shook him around in the air until his weight suddenly increased, becoming too much for the warlock to bear. He dropped Blanka, seeing the man's eyes turn red with fury. A tremendous heat billowed from Blanka's mouth as scales formed and spread outwards. Khanaseri backed away a few steps, watching a tortured transformation take place, the will of two titans clashing for the body, fighting to be its ruler. Belgarr twisted and turned, shaking violently until a blast of fire erupted into the sky in waves so hot Khanaseri had to take cover behind a tree while holding Flintlock's reins, trying to calm the terrified animal.

'There he is!'

A deafening roar sounded from the dragon, then another and another, as though Belgarr shared the pain of the man, and floundered in the grief.

'Blanka!' shouted the warlock, waving his arms about after tethering Flintlock to a tree. The beast halted its throes and twisted down before the warlock, cracking the boulders and snapping trees with its tail. It scraped the stone surface with its claws, cutting deep grooves into the solid floor while saliva dripped from its trembling maw, sizzling with each contact. 'I know this hurts, Blanka, but listen to me. She left you something precious. Something you need to get back. Do you hear me, Blanka?'

He heard only one word, uttered with a growl: '*Speak.*'

'She was pregnant when she went to prison, Blanka. You're the father of a beautiful boy that I've seen with my own eyes. He looks just like her.'

The dragon shimmered and veered until Blanka stood before him, then collapsed suddenly, his energy sapped from the transformation. Gripping tufts of grass, Blanka sobbed until Khanaseri approached and felt his friend's hand rest on his shoulder. 'Why did she not tell me? Where is he? What's his name?'

'His name is Moseroth, and I don't think she knew about him. Her time spent gaoled broke her mentally. The only way to survive was to forget.'

'Where is he?' Blanka rose, his voice cold and fragile.

'Blanka,' Khanaseri said, arms out, gesturing him to calm down. 'He doesn't know about you. He doesn't even know Turneroth isn't his father.'

'Turneroth has him? He's here, in this time?' Blanka backed away, his mind reeling.

'Yes, and we'll get him back, I promise. But we can't be rash.'

'Rash? I'll show you rash!' Blanka veered, knocking Khanaseri back against a tree and taking off in a powerful gust of wind, swirling dust all over.

Khanaseri jumped up and ran for his horse, mounted, and galloped after the black dragon as it crested the peaks and crashed into the ridge of the crater before disappearing from view, creating an avalanche of boulders storming down the side. Flintlock sped up the animal trail at breakneck speeds, bounding over boulders and ruts in the treacherous ground, snorting heavily while Khanaseri drove his heels into his flanks. 'Blanka! Stop! They'll kill you!' He desperately didn't want to lose sight of Belgarr.

Reaching the tear they came through earlier, Flintlock breathed easier as the ground levelled out for a time, the jagged rock faces flashing by them on either side until they started their descent, skidding and jumping to clear great distances. Khanaseri was afraid his horse might break an ankle, but he was more afraid of losing sight of his friend up above. Adrenalin fuelled, they charged down the slope. The magnificent brown stallion's black mane fluttered in the crosswinds, his muscles bouncing with every landing of his hooves. 'Blanka!'

The black dragon soared across the skies while Flintlock thundered over the desert sand, trying his best to stay with the beast above. 'Yah! Run, Flint, we're losing him!'

The scorching desert sand flew up from thundering hooves. The warlock glanced up to the dragon as it momentarily vanished before the sun, getting blinded by its bright fury, and saw it reappear on the other side between the dark spots obscuring his vision. Blinking his eyes, he tried to focus on the dot in the sky when a rift exploded open right in front of them, swallowing them whole in a scream of anger. He thought back to the last time this had happened, how Beuneth had trapped him on the other end. Enraged, they sailed through the dark. *This time,* he thought, *I will be ready.*

*   *   *

Belgarr heard the shout from below and glimpsed their friend disappearing uncontrollably into the rift. He banked and descended to where the rift had torn a fresh scar in the world, and veered. Blanka ran up to where they had seen it last, feeling only the cold malice of the magic left drifting down, the heat quickly returning to the desert. 'Khan!' Turning round and round, searching for any sign of the warlock, he shouted again, 'Khan? Where are you?'

*   *   *

Fire and lightning enveloped the room, burning precious artefacts while Flintlock stomped and kicked in fear, protecting his rider. Khanaseri leapt from the back of the horse and brought down his axe on the first thing he saw move in the gloomy light. His vision had not yet adjusted to the darkness. Stuttering movements flashed in the fulmination of his anger. An explosive wave rolled out with a thunderous clap, extinguishing the flames and lanterns alike. Chaos and destruction overwhelmed the area as smouldering pieces of parchments and books drifted down. 'Khanaseri! Stop, please!' came a shout from behind a large device. 'We mean you no harm.'

'Come out! Who are you? Why am I here?' Khanaseri pulled his dreaded axe from the timbers of the bookshelf and snapped his fingers, lighting the lantern before readying himself. Through the gloom, Garidan and a tall, silver-haired man crawled out from beneath an overturned shelf, dropping the books to the floor, as banging and shouting sounded from the steel door behind him.

'We have little time. Please listen to us,' Garidan pleaded with the warlock.

'Why? Where have you brought me, and how? I don't recall you being a mage.'

'You're in the world of the Ageians. This,' he gestured to the other man, 'is Tulvar. I came here hoping they could recapture the dragons, but things didn't go as planned. What we found instead was this.' He glanced around and picked up the Balamuth next to the collapsed table, then unfurled the cloth, showing it to the warlock in the cup of his hands.

'Fuckin' Balamuth! Those things caused all this nonsense to start with. What do you want with this?'

'During my time here...' More banging and shouting came from the door. 'Look, it's complicated.'

'Then uncomplicate it! I don't mind having to take a detour when I'm offered free ale, but you've taken me away when my friend needed me most, so this better be good.'

Gritting his teeth, Garidan cursed and said, 'We found something that could save our world against the onslaught of the dragons. The entire reason the Ageians came to our world and captured all the beasts was born of a selfish desire to save their own world. They stole away one of the Balamuths, Yidrog, an ice dragon strong enough to put the fear of god into the Alpha. They needed him and tried everything to find a suitable host, but they failed.'

'You think this Yidrog can take out the Alpha and the rest of the dragons will disperse?' Khanaseri lowered his axe. The door burst open, with guards trying to enter the room. Khanaseri made a sign in the air as he shouted, *Valoush!* A powerful explosive wave threw the guards back through the door, slamming it shut. Garidan rushed over to place a chair against the handle, securing it to buy some time. 'Send me back now! Then get out of this place. They don't seem too happy you're here. I don't have time for foolish errands.' The warlock mounted his anxious horse, rubbing Flintlock's cheek to calm his stomping hooves. *How do I get myself into these positions?* 'What's his problem?' asked the warlock, cocking his head towards the wide-eyed Tulvar.

'He's in shock from your arrival. They haven't seen the monoliths used in a long time.'

'That's how you brought me here, with that rock?' Khanaseri asked with raised brows.

'Yes.'

'Fascinating.'

Sounds came from the old man, sitting on his knees, his hands locked together before the nervous animal, but Khanaseri did not understand the words. 'Please, I beg of you, rider. Let us talk,' interpreted Garidan, 'We need your help. Our world is doomed, yet no one but us really knows the truth of the matter.'

Why do I get myself involved in these things? I have enough on my plate. The warlock sighed, shaking his head, annoyed and frustrated, fearful that Blanka had already reached Turneroth's camp and started his extermination. There was nothing he could do now. It was too late for his friend. He worked his jaw muscles back and forth, feeling his heart drop to his stomach, mourning his friend's potential demise. 'Before I agree to help you, stranger, know that if my friend dies because you took me away to this place, I will come back for you. I need to know what we're up against here.' Again, Garidan translated for the Ageian's benefit.

Tulvar went cold, staring into Khan's green eyes, and stated something, then looked to Garidan, who sighed. 'If my life serves as a sacrifice to your friend but saves countless lives here, I pay it gladly.'

Khanaseri unsheathed his axe from his back and called out to Garidan, 'Stay behind me. Lead Flintlock out of danger and don't let him get hurt. This banging is giving me a headache. It's putting me in a foul mood.'

He roared with pleasure while he swung his axe, taking out the chair bracing the door before Garidan could voice his objections. Guards streamed in one at a time through the narrow doorway. With his free hand, the warlock grabbed the first man's head and crashed it against the wall, leaving a smear of blood as the guard sagged to the ground. Then he reversed his motion and caught a mace between his arm and ribs, headbutting the second's nose to a spray of red. Screams sounded, and the third shoved the reeling guard out of the way to feel his leg break below the knee. He never saw the downward kick coming.

'Agh! All this screaming! Stop with the screaming!' Khanaseri ran up the stairs.

* * *

Naghita paced on the roof, whispering harshly to Borka, 'What is taking them so long? That bastard better not have left us behind. I'm sure that's what the little coward has done. Run off to his shag for us to fix this problem on our own.'

'If they haven't, then they're in big trouble. Whatever they've done has pulled in more guards. I can't see them getting out of there. The stairs are surrounded by at least eight men with crossbows and swords.'

'Too bad, then, it's their funeral,' Naghita stated, and turned to descend from the roof.

'Hold on! You just called him a coward if he ran away. Now you're doing the same? Hypocrite!'

Naghita whirled around and snapped, 'Don't you ever talk to me like that!'

Ignoring the rant that followed, Borka leaned forward over the edge of the building and snapped, 'Something is happening! There's movement. The guards seem nervous, glancing at each other.' A force, loud and powerful, ripped the bows from the guards' hands with a mighty *crack* as a big man ran up the stairs. 'Who in the abyss is that? Someone is attacking the guards. I'm going in to help.' He turned around and found nothing but a vacant rooftop, then glimpsed her silhouette in the darkness, already approaching the chaos. 'Shit on soap!' he shouted, and leapt from the roof, trying to catch up with her.

Her lithe form glided over the boulder on the lawn, then skirted the burnt-out wagon they had used to cause the distraction earlier. She ran through the doors in great haste. A guard flew over her head to crash against the wall behind her, and out of nowhere, a whirlwind of dust sandblasted their skin. The roaring howls of the storm shook the building's foundation, making their footing uneasy, and lifting Naghita from the ground. Borka grabbed her by the wrist, pulling her down with his immense weight until the whirlwind vanished as abruptly as it had appeared.

Guards screamed and shouted in confusion.

Borka grabbed the nearest guard and evaded a sword thrust, knocking out the Ageian's front teeth with a heavy right hook. To his right, Naghita ran on the tops of the bookshelves and leapt on a guard, her knees driving him to the ground in a bone-crunching display of aerobatics. Another rushed at her with a knife, which she reversed and thrust back into the guard's shoulder, then crashed the side of her hand into his jugular. The guard flopped to the ground, gasping for air.

Borka turned to grapple with another guard when he glimpsed the stranger lift two guards by their collars and whisper something to them. When their feet touched the ground, death itself was in their hearts, the fear crippling them to cower away against the wall, cradling their knees with their arms, their faces masks of horror. A hard blow rocked his head, bringing him back to focus on his own fight, feeling the strength of the Ageian guard he wrestled with. The Ageian held steady against the power of the gladiator, but a knee to his chest collapsed him to the ground.

The big stranger spied him and approached, drawing his axe before going into a jog, then a run to leap and crash against Borka's poleaxe, pushing the big gladiator to the ground with his axe blade mere inches from his face. Borka twisted the poleaxe, letting the stranger's axe slip down past his face to hit the floor, the sound ringing sharply in his ears as granite chips struck the side of his face. He swung his immense fist into the stranger's face, hitting solid bone and muscle again and again, but the man did not relent, and instead swung his own down. The fist rocked him back and Borka went limp from the hit, his head in a daze. Naghita jumped on the man's back with her arm around his neck, strangling him from behind while screaming like a possessed witch. The stranger pulled her from his back and threw her against the wall, advancing on her as she slid to the ground.

'Stop! Khanaseri, they're with us!'

The guards lay on the floor writhing in pain, crawling slowly to get out of the building as Garidan appeared with a horse, guiding the animal up the stairs carefully with Tulvar at the back. He ran past the warlock to help Naghita up from the floor and roared, 'We could've used the monolith to take us out of that room! They wouldn't have known where we were!'

Khanaseri sheathed his axe and stated, 'I was going to hurt someone or something. Better it was them and not you. This way, I worked out some of my frustration. Besides, don't you want their attention so they can note this problem you mentioned?'

'Not before we have a plan!'

'Thought I *was* the plan,' said the warlock and reached out his hand to the Tark staring up at him. Borka spat blood to the side and grabbed his hand, moving his jaw back and forth. Khanaseri looked back to Garidan and asked with a cock of the head towards Borka, 'What are they?'

'They're Tark. That is Borka, this is Naghita.'

The warlock tapped on his chest and stretched his name. 'Khaaaaan.'

'We'll have time later to get to know each other. Let's get out of here.'

Tulvar was at the back, taking in the destruction caused, the men lying scattered with severe injuries, though none looked dead. For that, he was glad. The Library was in disarray, books and scrolls lying everywhere, shelves overturned and broken apart. He felt sorry for the woman who had been doing the inventory and mumbled, 'What have we let loose on Velafrey?'

* * *

'There's too many of them. How am I supposed to get her back?' Hadron pulled at the chain mail vest and whipped his long, dirty hair out of his face. Far in the distance, over the declivous field, close to the foot of a hill, he spied the group of soldiers sitting around a few fires to keep warm, the cages standing away from the flame's heat. The sun bounced off the patches of white nestled against the hill, blinding him some and forcing him to look away. He twisted around and sat up, blowing out the cold air so high above sea level with a steady stream of smoke. His hands ached, the skin cracking and bleeding, burning with every move he made. Hadron glanced back, leaning out from behind the tree, and kept his gaze on the cages, wondering in which they kept his Veranay. He rummaged through the pack and pulled a cloak forth, donning it over the chain mail. Kanah's father was not as broad as Hadron; he could feel the chain mail pulling his skin left and right. *I will wait till nightfall.*

* * *

'How many prisoners do we have now?' asked the captain, taking a sip of water from his canteen.

A moment of silence lingered, and the heavily bearded lieutenant said, 'That would be forty, sir. How do we know they can all touch the Source? They seem pretty ordinary to me.'

'We have to trust the mages. They have no reason to give us false information.'

'How many more do we need?'

'I don't know, soldier; rather too many than too few. I don't want to

86

be stuck here forever, missing my girls as they grow up and get married off without me having a say. Their mother already has it in for me. I don't need to give her any more reasons to hate me. You have kids?'

'Aye, a little one. Red hair so bright you can see him coming a mile away, but a strong lad. Got his mother's temper, though.'

The captain chuckled. 'Bit docile, then?'

'Noooo!' said the lieutenant, stretching the word with skewed brows. 'Screams bloody murder for the slightest thing. I fart, he screams. I come home, he screams. I leave, he screams. I take his food, he screams. I give him food, he screams. Swear to god, he turns red in the face, then shits himself. If there wasn't a hole at the bottom, he'd explode from the pressure he builds up during his rants. But he's my little Alvi, named after me Da, Alver.'

The captain grimaced and said, 'Why aren't *you* named after your father?'

'Mother wanted nothing to do with him on account of his drinkin'. Wasn't an evil man, just not fatherly material, as she used to say. So she called me Brenner, after *her* father. Got no problems with it. How about you, sir? How in the heck did you end up with Till?'

A lean soldier with thinning long hair settled on the boulder opposite Brenner and said, 'His mother never wanted children, *Till* she saw his old man's cock. Hahaha.'

'Oi! Watch your mouth, you anorchous bedswerver!' said the captain, and cuffed the man over the head.

'Just jokin', Captain.'

'Take your jokes somewhere else. My folks had a rough life growing up, little money and barely any food, until my father got a job as a tiller for a man on a farm. He worked his fingers to the bone and made something of himself. Got known for his good work. They gave him the nickname Till, and it flowed down to me.'

The fire crackled between them, and Brenner leaned forward to remove a stick with a roasting hare shoved over, taking big bites and blowing out gusts of steam from the hot food. 'Captain, I heard that this is just somewhere forward in time. Does that bother you?'

'What do you mean? Why would it? We're fighting to get back home, that's all.'

'Yes, but think about it. Some of these people could be your great-great-great-grandchildren, or your daughters' for that matter. Heck, you could have killed some of them already and you would never know. It seems wrong somehow.'

Captain Till was quiet for a time, then stated, 'I hadn't thought about it like that. Now I'll probably not get it out of my mind...' He rose and walked to his tent, speaking over his shoulder, 'Brenner, get the first shift of patrols underway. I'll be in my quarters.'

The man opposite Brenner gestured something with his hand and whispered with a big grin, 'Probably gonna get his wax on.'

'You have some serious deficiencies, Marteen. Why do you hound him so? He can make your life miserable.'

'My life's already miserable, or have you forgotten?'

The empty carcass sailed into the flames, sizzling up with a burst of embers drifting to the darkness and over Marteen as he walked away. Brenner thought back to the day the dragons attacked after their release, hearing the screams of the victims down in the street. Two of those were Marteen's wife and child of eight, killed by falling debris from the walls. 'Yeah, I remember.' He dug his fingers into the tight breast pocket, the leathers unwilling to bend in the cold, and produced a tiny red section of a knitted baby blanket. Between his dirty, calloused fingers, he rubbed the material and closed his eyes, thinking of his little boy, Alvi.

A commotion started up to his left near the cages, men shouting and the prisoners crying in terror. Brenner quickly rose to investigate and found three of his soldiers pinning down a man who still tried to swing the short poleaxe in his hands. Face pushed to the ground, the man shouted, 'Let my daughter go! Take me instead!' Shouts came from one cage, the girl screaming at the top of her voice for them to let him go.

Brenner motioned for the soldiers to lift the man up, keeping his gaze on the girl in the cage, the darkness making it hard to see clearly. 'What's your name?'

'Hadron, sir. Please, let my daughter go. Take me instead. She's but a child. Please! Have mercy!'

'Are you even a soldier?'

'Quarry worker. I can work with my hands. I'll do anything.'

The girl shrieked from the cage, 'No, Daddy! Don't hurt him, please!'

'Bring the mage; let him be tested,' said Brenner, doubting a good outcome for the father. Soldiers gathered around, getting antsy as they waited for the mage.

'We should string him up!' shouted the one who was holding him. 'See what he did to me?' The soldier turned his arm and showed the lieutenant a cut above his triceps.

'You'll be fine, soldier. He's no threat to us. I'm not killing a man with his daughter watching.' The soldiers parted and let through a hooded woman, her dark purple lips as black as night. She moved closer to the man and lay her hand upon his chest, moving her head side to side, as if listening to some unspoken words.

Hadron felt the grip on him diminish, and instantly whirled around, cracking the soldier behind him in the face with his elbow. The grip on him vanished. He grabbed the poleaxe and the mage, holding the blade by her throat and backing away from the surprised soldiers, nostrils flaring and eyes wide with adrenalin. 'Let us go! All of us, or I'll kill her!'

Brenner kept his eyes on the mage, saw her shake her head ever so slightly and said, 'Calm down. We can use you, but we can't let her go. Neither of you will be hurt as long as you drop the weapon.'

The soldier on his right rushed in prematurely, startling Hadron terribly, making his hand jerk and cutting the throat of the mage. It all happened so fast, Hadron did not know what was going on. He heard the cries of Veranay, the soldier's roars, and felt the ice-cold blade burning deep in his stomach. The chain links did not hold against the heavy, sharp sword. A deafening scream came from the cage, and those around it dropped to the ground, clutching the sides of their heads.

Hadron stared at her, reaching out his bloodied hands as he

mouthed, *'I'm sorry.'*

The men around him drooped, bleeding from their ears.

* * *

Ganda'har kept watch over the camp, the early morning air crisp and wet on his naked arms, waiting for the sun to peek over the horizon. *It won't be long now; the light has changed already.* He took a drink from a steaming wooden mug and grunted to clear his throat. It had been a peaceful night's sleep, a great deal better than he'd had in a long time. Their numbers had grown over time, having stopped multiple attacks on smaller villages around the area. Most of the people they had taken seemed useless to him: a barbershop owner, a merchant, a vagrant... *How do they have any magic coursing through them? They seem like bedwetters and baby kissers,* he thought. Now they helped where they could, to give thanks to their saviours. The forest was quiet still. So early in the morning no birds chirped yet, though he could see some movement of small furry creatures bounding through the thick vegetation under the trees. *Probably looking for scraps before we all wake.* An interesting creature the size of a plump pumpkin with a long snout and big, round eyes jumped into the clearing, sniffing the air and momentarily looking at the captain, then darted for a fallen piece of bread lying next to the cauldron, scramming back into the thick bush as soon as it grabbed its prize.

'Oh, cock!' The thick gumtree behind him groaned and branches snapped with sudden pressure placed upon it. Timbers fell from up high and Ganda'har took cover, diving out of the way and spilling his warm drink to the ground. Another tree next to it gave way, crashing to the ground a few feet away, and Belgarr settled to the ground in a roar of anger. A stream of curses flowed from the captain while he wiped the burning liquid from his face, then said, 'That was the last cup of broth! What are you doing here? Did you miss your own funeral?'

'You're angry, I get that,' said Blanka as he walked closer. 'You have a right to be... I was in a dark place.'

'Damned right I have. You were an idiot — and a terrible friend, I might add. Where's Khan?'

'That's why I'm here. You probably know he went to Corbel's Crater to talk to me. He told me about my son, that he's being held by Turneroth.'

'Wait, you have a son?' asked the captain, his browse knitted.

'Apparently, yes. I was so angry, so desperate to hold something that came from her, that I took to the sky in a fit of rage to retrieve him. Khan and Flintlock ran behind, trying to catch up and stop me, but something happened.'

Ganda'har's voice grew bitter. 'What do you mean, something happened?'

'I heard a scream and turned to see them vanish through a portal. I hoped he'd come back here, but now that I see the look on your face, I guess I was wrong. He could be anywhere.'

'Why are you worried? He uses portals often enough, and how did you find us?' Ganda'har shook his head as he stared at the empty mug, annoyed that he had spilt the last bits of broth, and walked away from the man. '*Everyone* keeps finding us.'

Blanka jogged quickly to catch up with the captain, who approached the cauldron hanging over the near-dead fire, the smell of burnt-out wood drifting up. 'I know your scent well. But that's not the concern here. He screamed... Khan doesn't scream like that for nothing.'

'I'm sure he's fine, probably just sat on his fruits or something. Would make any man scream.' Ganda'har opened the lid of the cauldron and leaned over to scrape his mug at the bottom, hoping to get some more broth. He pulled the mug back and said, 'Senoc's balls! Are you happy now?' He threw the mug into the forest, his face flushed with anger, when a voice came from his right.

'Sir, is everything a'right?'

'Dammit! That was my only mug! Untara, please go search for the mug.'

'Yessir.'

'Did you not hear the part about them having my son?' Blanka asked with raised brows, shaking his head, when he saw Ganda'har's brows suddenly shoot upward, an explosion of blue fire reflecting in his deep brown eyes. He spun around to witness a gigantic bright blue beam roaring up to the heavens and parting the clouds above, far in the distance over the mountainous horizon to the southwest, disappearing as abruptly as it came. A few moments later, a thunderous clap and roar shook the earth beneath their feet, and Blanka could only wonder how harsh the quake must be at the epicentre of the blast. 'Khan!' He ran to the clearing he had created with his earlier arrival and veered, blowing gusts of air over the camp, lifting some tents, with Ganda'har following close behind. Both dragons raced through the grey sky, feeling the currents push them higher.

Ganda'har swerved closer and spoke to Blanka's mind. '*Are you ready for this? There might be a fight on our hands. We don't know what we're heading into.*'

'*I let him down once. I won't again.*' Over the horizon to the left, the sun peeked out with a marvellous display of colours ranging from yellow to pink, the light-grey clouds turning to burnt-orange as the sun rose higher. The further they flew, the more the sun's rays lashed them with its heat, quickly stripped away by the cool winds so high. Silence accompanied them the rest of the journey.

'*There. I see something on that hill.*' The black dragon banked and turned upside down, swooping down fast with his wings folded in to get more speed. The red dragon took a slower approach, calmly lowering itself with a few flaps of its gigantic wings to settle on the ground after Belgarr veered.

They walked through the ghastly scene, and Blanka mumbled, 'What happened here?' All around them lay human limbs and bodies scattered outwards, burnt beyond recognition, around a great depression in the earth, as though the mountain itself had not been enough for the blast. They approached the remnants of a caged wagon torn open from the inside with terrifying power, guts and blood dripping to the ground from the bent and mangled iron bars, the bed split in three and the earth cracked open to large fissures beneath its original location. Blanka fingered the ice-cold iron bars, shocked at what he was witnessing.

Ganda'har stepped over a body severed at the hips, then another headless one, and bent down. He pulled a small piece of knitted blanket from the man's stiff hand, bloodied, the edges lovingly stitched over so it didn't fray. *A gift of remembrance.* He sighed and tucked it back in the soldier's pocket, then asked, 'What did this? These are definitely Turneroth's men, and I know these cages are warded. So how did whoever was in there cause such devastation?'

Surveying the ground, he spied fresh footprints and whistled to get Blanka's attention. 'There's someone here, or was, not long ago. Short. A group of about twenty.'

Blanka jogged over and looked to the ground as he replied, 'Why short?'

'Look at the strides. They're shorter than the average man's, but the prints are just as big. Dwarves...'

'Dwarves? Why not women? They have shorter strides.'

'But they have smaller feet. Except for Stentor — hers are bigger. Everything is bigger with that woman.' Ganda'har began mumbling at the end, his words drifting off.

'What was that?' asked Blanka with a furrowed brow.

'Oh, nothing. Let's follow the trail. We need to find out what happened here.' Ganda'har hastened up the side of the hill, keeping his eyes on the ground to track the footsteps while Blanka surveyed the surroundings. They ran until the sweat poured from them in the cold, wheezing under the pressure of the little oxygen so high. In their human forms, they found it hard to breathe the thin air, but they did not want to scare away the dwarves in their dragovian forms. Boots crunching over hard earth, he scanned for the prints, crashing through brush, and he thought, *If I didn't know that I could just fly up to see where I am right now, I would be panicking. I would surely be lost.*

He had never seen the Chimna Dwarves' city, never roamed through these mountains before now; there was never any need to. The dwarves never threatened Artokla, nor took any sides against them. He knew not what to expect.

Blanka grabbed him from the back and pulled him in behind a bush with a raised finger over his mouth, then pointed to the top of the hills on their left, where a great plume of red hair bounced over the tops of the vegetation with a shortened spear as its company. The sound of stones scraping over one another came from behind the bush, and Ganda'har sighed loudly. 'Bollocks!'

'Shh! They'll hear you.'

'They already have,' he said, and walked out from around the bush to stare at about fifteen dwarves, weapons drawn and ready to use them. He raised his hands. 'We're not here to cause any problems, I swear.'

'Oh, is that why yer skulking around like thieves?' The dwarf who spoke cocked his head to his right and shouted, 'Ye can come down now, Hasgrem.' The plume suddenly vanished, and moments later the big-haired dwarf came skidding down the hill to line up next to the others, brandishing his spear awkwardly. The dwarf in charge glanced at Hasgrem, then to the two men and said, 'He broke his axe, again, 'n picked up this foolish weapon from the unfortunate folk back the way ye came.'

'I don't know. I'm startin' to like it,' said Hasgrem, waving the weapon around.

The dwarf in charge wiggled the large moustache that flowed over his beard to his chest, groaning softly, then said, 'Not now, Hasgrem.'

Blanka said nothing, leaving the talking up to Ganda'har, who stood moving uncomfortably around with the cold on his bare skin, not having had the time to grab his gear or don his attire. 'We came to see what had caused that carnage. We were worried it might be a friend in trouble.'

'What friends do you have that could do that?' asked the same dwarf.

'The sorcerous kind.'

'Man or woman?'

Ganda'har glanced towards Blanka and said, 'Man. We just want to talk. You can see that we don't have any weapons.'

'I'm sorry, no man here. Best leave this behind ye and head back the way ye came,' stated the dwarf, lowering his axe.

'I'm Ganda'har; this is Blanka. May I ask who turns us away?'

'Yallrick Duskhorn of Chinnai.'

'Well met, Yallrick of Chinnai. Would you spare me some clothing, or would you leave me for dead in this cold? I promise, we're not with those dead men back there. We are, in fact, trying to stop the destruction they sow. They have razed many towns and villages.' Ganda'har rubbed his arms and chest, putting little heat back into them.

'Why should I believe ye? Why should any of us?'

'Because I'm not lying. Look into my eyes. They stole everything from us, destroyed our homes, and killed our friends and loved ones.'

The moment stretched out, and no one moved, an agonising period of stares. Finally, Yallrick gestured for his men to lower their weapons and said, 'We don't know what happened back there. We found only one survivor. Poor thing is so traumatised, she doesn't speak. Just rocks back and forth, her mind twisted with the horror she lived through. Come, we have some spare clothes up top. Ye can see the girl there.'

'Thank you, Yallrick.' They followed the dwarves up the hill for a time to a dugout, cleverly concealed with branches and leaves. Once in its confines, Yallrick turned to his men and said, 'Hasgrem, bring some of yer clothes. They will fit this man best.' The round dwarf spun and ran to another room, ranting that his clothes were being given away, before returning with a black bearskin cloak that would have fitted the dwarf well, though Ganda'har could not wrap it fully around his broad chest. Yallrick glared at the dwarf and stated, 'If ye ate less, then it wouldn't have been a problem.'

'Thank you, Hasgrem. You might have saved my life.'

The dwarf nodded.

Yallrick tore a piece of bread in three, handing each a section, and said, 'If yer thinkin' about pinpointing this location, don't bother. Tomorrow it won't exist.'

They accepted the food graciously, and Ganda'har replied, 'We don't care about the location, Yallrick. You have nothing to fear from us.'

'That right? What's wrong with yer friend? He dumb?' asked another dwarf from the back with arms thick enough to fight a god, and a hammer on his lap. His long white beard, fastened in sections with thick silver rings, hung down his chest to his stomach. He noticed the stares from the two and continued, 'I'm Yantore, Hasgrem's older brother. Don't ask me what he's doing with his hair; trying to fit in with the peacocks of the world, I assume.' Some dwarves laughed and Hasgrem glared at him, feigning the hurt he felt.

'I want to impress Vedala. She likes a dwarf with some hair left, not just a beard to tickle her.' More dwarves burst out laughing, and Yantore jumped up to deck Hasgrem, grappling with his brother while trying to rub his stinking armpit in the dwarf's face.

'That's enough!' shouted Yallrick. The two dwarves stopped their bickering and took their seats at a table.

Ganda'har chuckled and said, 'No, he's not dumb. I just don't think he's ever seen a dwarf. He'll come around.'

Yallrick stared at Blanka, motioned for his men to stand guard, and said, 'Come and see the girl.'

The dugout extended far deeper than Ganda'har expected, with multiple rooms adjoining the main sleeping chamber, short and sturdy beds pushed along the sides of the round room. Wide tunnels, dark and cold, led to other sections that seemed to be made for lookout points. It seemed like such a waste to destroy this dugout, but he understood the logic behind it. They followed Yallrick down the tunnel, and the captain said, 'This is quite impressive. How long does it take you to make this kind of dugout?'

'Trying to blow smoke up me arse, Gandi'har?'

A flicker of irritation flashed across the captain's face. 'It's Ganda'har, and no, I'm not. Most dugouts I've seen usually look like they're falling apart, the walls crumbling for not having the right mixture of clay, the roof too shallow, the rooms too cramped. Here you used tree trunks to strengthen the walls and roof. It's high enough not to walk hunchbacked, even for me, there's ample room in the sleeping quarters, and the airflow is good.'

Yallrick tilted his head to stare out of the corner of his eyes and said, 'Ye'll make me blush if ye don't stop. We dwarves don't go anywhere without our shovels.'

Clearing his throat, Ganda'har watched the dwarf from the back. 'You remind me of an old friend, a good leader.'

'What's his name?'

'Galvos, a good man.'

'Thank ye. I shall remember his name if I stray from the path.' Yallrick made to walk, then turned back to them and continued, 'Blanka, why does the sight of our kind disturb ye so, when to me, ye look stranger than any of us?' Yallrick gestured to the man's tattooed face.

Blanka reached up to his mouth, remembering the day Mother had pinned him down with the help of her magnadons to ink his face as punishment for their behaviour at dinner, feeling that bamboo pen stab into his skin over and over, the black ink running down his chin in streaks. Now a thick black beard covered a lot of that memory. 'Forgive me, Yallrick. The sight of you doesn't disturb me; my mind is just elsewhere.' Yallrick kept staring at him, unblinking, forcing Blanka to continue, 'I recently discovered I have a son. A son who has been stolen from me. I'm thinking about how I'll get him back. It's been occupying my mind.'

Yallrick nodded, pursing his lips, and said, 'That's not how ye want to be told yer a father. I'm sorry, lad. The girl is in there.' He pointed to a room a few feet away and stepped forward. 'She's a fragile flower. I'll go in first, then ye can join, Gandi—'

'Ganda...'

Yallrick spun around, staring at the captain. 'What?'

'Nothing. We'll be gentle with her.'

'Hey, lass,' said Yallrick, moving to kneel before the girl on the bed, 'do ye mind if old Yallrick sits on the bed next to ye? My knees are tired.' He observed her eyes with care, seeing them drift slowly to the spot next to her, and sat down. 'These men wanted to speak with ye.' He saw the sudden fear in her eyes as she gripped the bedding and started whimpering. 'They're friends, my dear. Do not worry, I won't let them hurt ye.' His soothing voice calmed her some, and she quickly wiped the tears streaming from her eyes.

Ganda'har followed Yallrick's lead, lowering himself to his knee before her to whisper, 'It's okay, miss, we only want to know what happened back there. Can you tell us?'

Tears streamed down her face as she sobbed, cradling her blood-soaked dress with her knees pulled close to her chest. 'My Papa, they killed my Papa. Those bastards killed my Papa!' she screamed through a trembling voice, and the earth quaked beneath them.

'Blasted earthquakes are getting worse and worse,' mumbled Yallrick, while Ganda'har and Blanka glanced at each other.

The captain took her hand, stroking it gently as he said, 'It's okay, child, they're all gone now. You had your vengeance. What's your name?'

Her head came up, and the rumbling ceased. Confused, she asked, 'What do you mean? I did nothing. I stood there watching as they stabbed my Papa, a raw and deep hatred raging through me, screaming at them to let him go, but I could do nothing. I wanted to kill them all! But then a bright light blinded me and I fainted... I thought I was dead. When I came to, Yallrick had carried me away from there.'

Again he asked, 'What's your name, child?'

'Veranay.'

Blanka joined the captain's side and said, 'That's a beautiful name, girl. Are you sure you didn't see a man who caused the light?'

'There was no one else.'

'Did someone teach you to use your abilities?'

'What abilities? I was to work for the cordwainer before they attacked our town, but I fear he's also dead. I'm not sure.'

'Not those abilities, dear. Where did you learn to touch the Source?' Blanka asked.

Veranay shook her head, confusedly, furrowing her brows while she glanced between the two men. 'No! No! I'm no sorceress! I never have been.'

Ganda'har thought for a moment with his head lowered, then asked, 'Did you hear them mention anything about where they're headed?'

The girl dipped her head, the faint lines of tears staining her cheeks. 'Some men boasted about how they were going to cut off the elf king's head and celebrate with all the ale of New Runswick as they danced on the corpses that will fund their way home.'

Both men rose, and Ganda'har grimaced. 'I'm sorry for your loss, Veranay; may peace be his journey forward. We'll leave you to grieve. Thank you for answering our questions.'

They walked from the room, and Yallrick jogged to catch up with them. 'What just happened back there?' he asked, pulling Ganda'har around by the arm, his men gazing at the pair. 'What do ye mean she had her vengeance?'

Ganda'har gestured for the dwarf to lower his voice, staring at the open door a few feet from them, where the girl wallowed in her pity. 'She's a mage, Yallrick. She might not have known it, but she is. They've been gathering people who can tap into the Source all over the country. Think about it...that cage was torn open from the inside out, with no one left alive except for her. I think the pain she felt when she saw her father die brought her power into the light. A power well and truly deserving of attention. Oh, and these earthquakes you're so worried about are not really earthquakes. It's her getting anxious or afraid, maybe even a little angry. So I'd be very careful if I were you about what I say around her.'

Yallrick collapsed onto a bed in shock, staring at the faces of his men, worry gripping his mind, fearing her presence could put their lives at risk. Heart pounding, he looked to Ganda'har, his mouth suddenly dry, and mumbled, 'Ye take her with ye. Keep her safe. If ye saw that explosion of magic, then so did whoever's hunting them.'

Shaking his head, Ganda'har retreated with raised hands. 'I can't, Yallrick. I'm fighting this war on all fronts, and where I go, danger is ever-present. They hunt for us constantly. She wouldn't be safe. Take her with you back to Chinnai. Keep her safely tucked away in the mountains until this war is over; I'll come for her then. You have my word.'

For a while, the dwarves looked at each other, until Hasgrem stepped forward and said, 'It's the right thing to do, Yallrick. We can keep her safe.'

'But she will put all of us in danger...'

Yantore rose from his bed, followed by Vedalbore, Skrug and Hestith, the burliest of dwarves, crossing their arms in defiance while Yantore said, 'We are Chimna Dwarves. We do not fear a little danger.'

Yallrick rolled his eyes and said, 'Fine, she can stay.'

Blanka reached out his hand, waiting for Yallrick to grip it, and said, 'Thank you, Yallrick. You are—'

'Yes, yes, doing the right thing... Now get going so we can cover our tracks and get out of here.'

Chapter Six

Hood drawn over his head, Ackelar waited for the guard at the gate to be distracted by a boisterous merchant who cheerfully shouted his wares to everyone, ignoring the pleas of the guard to quiet down. Finally, the guard had had enough of the merchant's bull-headed nature, and left his post to confront the man down the line. Ackelar slipped through the gate, having no eyes on him. *I can't believe they've almost finished the walls. This gate will make our work so much more difficult.*

A soft spray of misty rain washed over his arms, the smell of wet grass and dirt taking his senses away from the stresses he felt. A dagger twirled in his hands, flicking over his thumb and back, the feel of the hilt the only thing real at this very moment. The Baron had him over a barrel; there was little he could do but to follow the man's orders and agree to kill Ladriana. Ackelar never enjoyed going against his word. Now, it seemed, he didn't have a choice. He walked with a certain darkness surrounding him, an air of unapproachability shunting away those that dared saunter close. To his left, he noticed that Elvenandre's gates had been opened already, students walking around with books under their arms, laughing and gossiping with one another on the large, open yards before the sandstone building rising in the distance. 'She actually did it,' he muttered.

'Well, she had good bones,' came a surprising voice from his left.

Ackelar turned to the man and shook his head. 'What?'

'The structure... It has good bones,' said the man, drawing near. 'You may call me Abe, I'm the—'

'Headmaster, yes, I know. Pleasure to meet you.'

'Oh goodness, forgive me. Have we met before? My brain is not what it used to be.'

'No, we haven't. I'm just well-informed.'

'And very inconspicuous,' came the old man's grating voice.

Ackelar chuckled as he noted his wardrobe and replied, 'Black rather suits me, wouldn't you say?'

The old man grinned at him. 'I'm curious. Please indulge an old fool.'

Quiet for a while, Ackelar smiled and stated, 'Old, yes. Fool, I somehow doubt. Go on, I'm listening.'

A grin flashed over Abe's lined face again. 'I'm curious. Is your desire not to be seen by others one born from a predilection, for instance, like stealing, where the need compels it? Or is it because of past experiences? A youthful one perhaps, where you felt nobody ever saw you for who you are? And now, as an adult, you can't but want not to be seen?'

Ackelar chuckled again and mumbled, 'Like I said, I doubt it.'

'That might be the wisest of answers. But I'm not here to trap you. I'm just an old man passing his time during breaks. It gets rather dull sitting in that office all day, making decisions, signing papers and whatnot. Can't complain, I suppose. The youth took the position I wanted, the more exciting one. Court mage...showing off his muscles like an inbred buffoon. Ha. Listen to me wail like an old fool.' Abe turned away and continued, 'I could have taken to the road and left this position, left New Runswick behind, but then I wouldn't have realised how big a fool I really am.'

The smile had vanished from Ackelar's face. 'Why are you telling me this, Abe?'

An unfortunate sigh left Abe, eyes cast down to the grass as he kicked at a patch of weeds and said, 'Because sometimes, we find ourselves amid a problem, and can't seem to find the right path to take or decision to make. If we could only step back a few feet, watch the bigger works at play, then maybe, just maybe, we could make those decisions easier.'

Ackelar shook his head, and asked again, 'But why me?'

'Oh, you looked like an interesting fellow to talk with. Thought I could pass some of my...experience on to you.'

There was no trap. Ackelar observed the roads with great care. No one gave him any heed. 'I have to go, Abe. Thank you for the conversation, I think.'

He walked a few feet before he heard the old man's voice again. 'There's a place for you here at Elvenandre, if you want to learn more about your skills.'

But Ackelar did not reply or turn back. He just kept walking, wondering what the old man truly knew of him, for he definitely knew more than he was saying. Ackelar cursed under his breath, worried that the old man had stalled him for a reason. *What was he trying to accomplish, blabbering on like that? Talking between the lines like he knew what was going on in my head...*

He looked up at the old temple to his right, sullenly walking past with the dagger flicking around his thumb, and drew the hood from his head. *If I don't do what the Baron says, he'll destroy the orphanage, the entire operation, and everything that's been running for thousands of years. How can I let that happen? We've worked too hard for this. The orphanage has saved countless children. I can't risk it.*

Blinking the sun from his eyes, he drew the hood back over his head when a child ran down the street, chased by a big, brown dog with only the right eye, the other stitched up. The poor mutt kept missing the boy in its playful attacks, and Ackelar smiled, realising that the mood in the city had changed since the swearing in of the king and queen. Even with the rumours floating around about the king's death, the city had a new life. There was something to celebrate, to fight for again. It wasn't stagnating; things were happening, taking shape.

Up ahead, he saw the castle's walls come into view, and slipped into the alley to his right. From here on, it would be the back routes, the dark corners, the filthy gutters, and possibly even the sewers until he gained entrance to the courtyard, where he would wait for his opportunity to sneak in unnoticed. A sleepy guard, a late rotation, poor eyesight, or just a lack in their care to do the work right would be all he needed to breach their defences. Ackelar climbed to the roof of a nearby building to get a vantage point and see what was going on, hoping to glimpse the queen through one of the many windows.

* * *

'So, uh. Youse really have one of them dragon creatures inside of ya?' whispered a deep voice. Blanka turned around, his creased forehead glistening with perspiration. 'Youse all right? Looks like ya saw a ghost,' continued Magnus, sitting down on the log Blanka had risen from. Magnus stretched his leg slowly, holding the knee while he bent it back and forth.

'Aye, I do. We've become unified, a single entity. As for the reason why I look like I do, it's worry, I guess. I'm worried Khanaseri is in danger, and we have no clue where he is. Not to mention, I have to steal my son away from an enemy who has countless dragons at their disposal and thousands of soldiers always on the lookout for trouble.'

'Mmm, sounds like yer in a pickle. Have youse considered asking for help?'

He heard a wooden spoon scrape against the sides of a cauldron and turned to look. Some of the men were putting food in their stomachs while others lay around, waiting for the next orders to come in from the captain, who was now soaring high above them, checking for any new patrols near the area. 'I can't ask others to risk their lives for my needs. What happened to your leg?' Blanka asked, seeing the scars running down Magnus' shin to his ankle. An involuntary wince escaped his lips as he thought back to when he lay on that torture table, that hammer coming down, flashing brightly. He shook himself to get rid of the memory.

'I wasn't fast enough. All this blubber,' Magnus shook the flab of his stomach up and down, 'nearly cost me my life and the life of another. This is the first day I'm walking without those blasted crutches... Dear gods, I was healing so well, doin' it naturally, but now with the healer speeding up the process with their magic nonsense, everything feels so tight. Can hardly move my knee. Wish I could heal like youse do.'

'I know the pain you feel, believe me. Back home, they shattered both my legs and ripped Belgarr out of me, tearing my mind and soul in two. I had never wished for death to take me more than I did that day. Took me years to get over my injuries. But yes, now that I'm reunited with Belgarr, he helps with the healing process tremendously.'

'Suddenly I feel a little happier with my injuries...must have been rough on youse.'

'It was.'

'Youse say ya don't want to risk anyone else's life for yer needs. Have youse considered we're all here to fight this bastard? If stealing a kid from under their noses means it'll hurt 'em somehow, don't youse think we'd be happy to do it?'

'It might, Magnus. But I can't ask for that. I can see you're a good man and you mean well, but stay out of it.' Blanka turned and left the camp, determined to do this alone.

* * *

The dagger flicked around Ackelar's thumb, landing perfectly in his hands for another flick; born of impatience, the habitual movement had become second nature. He never could wait for something to happen on its own accord. He constantly needed to push and pull the strings of fate to get the outcome he wanted to ensure his success. *This new court mage follows Ladriana like a puppy on a leash. How can I get rid of this annoyance?* he thought, spying on them from the opposite side of the corridor, staying hidden behind the great stone pillars. *How easy it was to gain access to the castle before the swearing in of the king and queen: the empty halls, the quiet nights, few men roaming. Now, it's always busy with servants, cooks, cleaners, politicians, and guards, so many eyes wandering around, keeping everything on schedule and in order.*

Ackelar waited for a servant to stumble by with a heap of laundry obscuring her view, and sneaked down the long corridor to enter the room next to the one Ladriana had entered, quickly drawing the door closed and shoving a chair up against the handle. He lay his ear flat against the wall, listening to the sounds coming from the other side. Faint voices drifted through the wall, the sounds indistinct, but the pitch perfectly clear. There was no denying the fact that there were more people in that room, but he could not place who they were.

With the darkness chasing the sun to a distant corner of the world, Ackelar risked leaping over the balcony and hanging on to the rails, using them to climb across to the other room. Quiet as a mouse, he climbed over the railing and dropped to the balcony tiles, sneaking closer to the window. He leaned down against the wall, so as not to get noticed. Right above him, an old man's voice rang out, speaking through the window. 'Are you ready for this, Ladriana? If tomorrow goes as planned, we will cement your stay in office for the next few months, but if it goes wrong...'

Another voice sounded, elegant yet stern. He knew the queen's voice well after her visit to his home, and judged her to be tired. Her words drawled. 'Yes, Father Ehrhard, I know what I risk, but I can't sit by idly waiting to be removed from office or murdered, letting this monster win and destroy all we're working towards. New Runswick needs us to take this risk, and even if the people don't know it, they do too.'

The tone of the old man's voice changed to one of resignation. 'So be it. I will have the external party notified of the proceedings tomorrow. It will be a public display. We will have to be ready for an attack, and you, milady, won't be able to move quickly with your enormous belly. You will be vulnerable. Put that back, please, Ladriana. We cannot afford—'

Ladriana sounded drained, her words stretched. 'There's no one here except for us. What danger can there be?'

'Ladriana, please. This is too dangerous.'

'Fine, Ehrhard, I'll put it back.'

'Don't worry, priest. I'm here to protect all of you from these bad people,' came a young man's voice.

Ackelar grinned and thought, *Arrogant little shit, aren't you?* He rose to peek through the slitted window shutters in time to see Ehrhard turn and say to the man, 'You need to concentrate on the spell tomorrow. If you falter during the proceedings and anyone sees...all is lost. Get it through your thick skull that you are *not* here to win favour with the ladies, you ignorant fool! What we do has consequences!' stormed the old priest, harsh breathing accompanying his anger.

'Enough! I'm sure he knows the risks as well, Ehrhard.'

'Sorry, my Queen. This man-child knows well how to anger me. Why did you employ him? He is irksome.'

'Hello? I'm standing right here...' said Thelanor with a shake of his head.

Both the queen and Ehrhard glared at the mage before she said, 'Get some rest, both of you. Thelanor, get Volar to come and see me before the next bell.'

'But milady, I can't leave you alone. It's not safe.'

'Come on. Leave, you bastard,' whispered Ackelar, fearing for a moment that the mage might try to defy her. But both men left the room and closed the door behind them, leaving Ladriana with her face resting in her hands while she sat on the bed. 'Good boy.'

* * *

Overwhelmed by all that was going on, Ladriana had thrown herself into her duties, trying to forget about Garidan for the time being. Her father was doing well, and the city was thriving, except for the occasional outburst of zealots causing havoc in the streets. But there would always be those, no matter what you did for them. For some time, she breathed into her hands, eyes closed and pushing away the surrounding sounds of banging crockery from the downstairs kitchen, horses neighing, and guards talking. Elbows resting on her knees, she rubbed her eyes with her thumbs, pushing the pain from them to have a brief respite from the headache she had endured for the last day and a half, when the bed shifted with unexpected weight.

Ladriana jerked her head up, saw the flash of a blade, and rolled backwards on the bed to avoid the cut aimed at her neck. The pain in her head made it hard to focus on the fast-moving fists and daggers flashing towards her. One wild slash caught her across the arm, spraying blood over the walls as she hammered her fist into the attacker's face. The headache didn't help: her vision blurred, and her ears rang, her head pulsating with the pain, throbbing non-stop; she would need to rely on her instincts. *If I can just get to the corner where I left my bow—*

The side of her face burned and she fell to the left, hitting her head on the floor. She stumbled forward and swung her fist up, cracking the attacker on the chin, then launched herself across the room in a desperate attempt to grab her bow; and when she turned back, there was another man in the room, his dagger buried deep in the attacker's temple. The man wrenched the weapon free and dropped the spasming body to the floor, then drew back his hood.

Ackelar reached out to the shocked queen and said, 'You need to be more careful, Your Majesty. You're at war with a powerful man. Are you well?' he asked, pointing to her stomach.

'Ackelar? Yes, I'm fine. How did you get in here? Moreso, how did he?' she asked, panting while he removed the man's hood.

'He must have followed me into the castle, used my routes as his own until I got close, then hid in the closet, waiting for the time to strike. This is my fault. I should have been more careful, anticipated *his* nature as untrusting.'

'Who? Who are you referring to? Did you find out who's behind all this mess?'

'I believe I did, and you won't believe it.'

She crossed the room and lashed out at the dead man, kicking him over and over before slumping down on the bed again, staring at the pooling blood on her floor. She spat on the body and said, 'I'm a merchant's daughter who was sold as a slave for a debt we owed. I grew up with nothing, and I've done things I couldn't say out loud. Now I've become queen to a desperate kingdom, and my husband is lost to me, through god knows where, trying to find us allies against a dragon army marching to destroy our city... Try me.'

'When you put it like that, I guess you might.' Ackelar scratched his head, pulled a chair closer, and sat down. 'First, I have to warn you: there will be more attempts on your life, and tomorrow seems like a prime opportunity for one to take place. Are you mad, going ahead with this?'

'Don't worry about tomorrow,' Ladriana said offhandedly.

Ackelar leaned forward in the chair. 'What do you... Ah, I see. You've set this up exactly for this reason. To call them out of the shadows. Clever. But I don't think you know what you're up against. Not even I do.' He rose and collected the assassin's weapons, sticking the daggers through his belt, and continued, 'It seems this assassination spree has been continuing for ages, from the time one of Garidan's forefathers usurped the rightful ruler, killing the entire bloodline — or so he thought. A boy survived...sounds familiar, right? When the whelp got older, he took his revenge, over and over and over, passing it on through to the next generation and the next. I think the last wants to finish the job for good, wiping all possible Rourke lines off the face of the earth.'

'Wait, so *we're* the usurpers?'

'Technically, yes. But I doubt it matters anymore. The Rourkes have ruled for generations.'

Ladriana rubbed her palm, an itch coursing through her hand, her voice cold and trembling. 'Who is this man, and where is he?'

'Before I tell you, please promise you won't do anything rash. I need to ensure my children's safety first. They need to be guarded, treated with dignity, and given rooms on the castle compound until all this is behind us.'

Ladriana nodded. 'I'll see to the arrangements.' Her eyes followed him, and she asked, 'What did he promise you for my head?'

A quick grunt, and Ackelar laughed. 'Everything. I could have it all. Total control of New Runswick's underground. Total anonymity to work in the shadows. Funding from the crown for the orphanage beyond anything I would ever require, and a seat at his table during delicate matters.'

Eyes wide, Ladriana whistled and said, 'That's, uhm...substantial. Why didn't you take it? You had me on my knees.'

'Oh, I took it immediately. But I've never been good at following orders while being threatened. Besides, it seems like you really have the city's best interests at heart. He's in Deresford. People call him the Baron.'

* * *

Through the dragon's eyes, Blanka could see the camp clearly in the darkness. He watched the city of Belleford burn as the angry king marched through the streets, shouting his outrage that the city had been abandoned. Its citizens had fled to neighbouring villages long before Turneroth drew close. Now, thousands of men ran through the empty streets, looting what they could while four dragons circled above, waiting for a command from the Alpha to set ablaze more buildings. A large grey tower obscured his view as he saw Turneroth grab a nearby soldier and throw him aside in anger. *Probably a scout that didn't report the city's desertion in time. Those dragons won't attack if they don't see me as Belgarr. I'll need to sneak in. If only I knew where the boy was being kept... I doubt they would let the child wander through the streets. It's too dangerous. They would leave him with a guardian nearby.*

Blanka crawled down the hills to the left, seeing a train of wagons waiting outside the city. No tents were being pitched tonight; they would march on through to the next village or risk the wrath of the king. He ran through the woods and hid behind a tall old gumtree, its bark languishing at its base, concealing himself from the men walking in the gloom around the wagons with their weapons at their side. He wished he had a sword right now, although he wasn't very good with one. *Guess I'll have to make do with what I have,* he thought, and brought up his hand, focusing until it scaled over, with great talons appearing on his fingers. The pain it caused while cutting into his flesh sent a ripple down his spine, the blood running down to pool in his palm. Squeezing his eyes shut, he clenched his teeth and flicked the blood from his hand.

Where would he be? In which wagon would they leave him? The train stretched far into the darkness, with the front-most carts pulled through the city gates. *If I were them, that's where I'd keep the boy; not too far back, not too close to danger.*

He ran in from the side when the guard turned his back, and crawled beneath the third wagon from the front, waiting patiently while a guard moved past. Blanka lay there, listening carefully for a child's voice, until the guard on the other side walked by, then rolled out from beneath the wagon. He snuck up behind the soldier and buried his hand in the man's back, feeling the warmth of the organs surrounding his scaled hand, the pulse of the blood fading as he squeezed the heart, stopping it completely. He dragged the man to a nearby bush and ran to the back of the wagon, flinging open the flap to peer in, seeing only crates of equipment. *Damn!* The sound of boots on gravel sounded close by, and he quickly covered the flap to retreat to the second wagon.

The driver was still on this wagon; he saw the soldier's hat bobbing and turning every so often in the dark, being vigilant of his surroundings. Blanka picked up a stick and threw it against the gate on the opposite side, and the man stood to search for movement. He rushed in from the left and jumped up, dragging the driver to the ground, tearing at his throat in a spray of black, and waited for him to stop gurgling before placing him back on the seat, head slumped over as if sleeping.

'Orthen? What's going on, Orthen?' came a youthful voice from inside the wagon. Blanka's heart beat wildly, his mind racing with how to handle the upcoming situation. He rushed to the back of the wagon and leapt inside, adrenalin pumping hot through his veins, burning him from the inside with Belgarr so close to taking over. Twisting and jerking, his arms and shoulders had a mind of their own. Blanka felt the spines and horns of the beast pushing against the inside of his skull, wanting to rip it open and breathe the night air. Before him woke a young boy cradling a blanket and rubbing his face, his eyes suddenly flaring wide as he realised it was not Orthen in the wagon with him, but a monster with eyes of fire and a hand slick with blood dripping from taloned fingers. Instantly, a scream ripped through the air.

Blanka jumped forward and clasped his bloody hand over the boy's mouth, trying to calm him. 'Quiet down, lad. Shh! I'm not here to hurt you! I'm here to rescue you.'

The boy kicked, screamed, and bit Blanka's hand, drawing blood, wrestling to get out of his grasp. The flap flew open and hands grabbed Blanka's feet, yanking him to the wagon's bed and loosening his grip on the boy. Dragged from the wagon, Blanka hit the ground in a burst of light swimming in his sight, the air rushing from his lungs. He could not veer now; it would attract the dragons and the king, awakening the Alpha. Pain exploded in his side from a barrage of kicks that rained down from the three soldiers standing over him.

More soldiers sprinted down the road from the back of the wagon train to see what was going on, shouting orders to keep watching the treeline for movement — until some of those men abruptly turned on the others, slicing and hacking with their blades, swiftly cutting down those in front of them. A gigantic boulder destroyed two wagons, taking out four men before a blinding white light reached up from the earth to strangle three more. The mage jerked his hands, and two guards dropped to the ground with a crunch, their necks twisted right round.

At the front of the train, someone shouted alarm, and Blanka could hear crazed confusion, with many boots drawing near as he covered his face with his arms. Another kick nearly shattered his elbow, and a blow to the back of his head sent him reeling. Curled up, he waited for them to finish the barrage of attacks...then it halted in screams of pain. Bodies hit the ground next to him before being hauled to his feet. Through the blood dripping down his face, he could see Ganda'har's scowl. 'Move, you fool!'

Blanka protested, fighting with the captain to release his grip. 'We can't leave him! Please! He's right there!'

Hundreds of men ran towards them from the city, and then they heard the roar of a dragon. Ganda'har dragged him from the road, not letting go. 'Not today! We'll come back for him. We have to stay alive! Everyone, run!'

Trees whizzed by, the silhouettes of Ganda'har's men scattered and running for their lives seared into Blanka's mind. *Why are they here? I didn't ask them to be here.* To his right, Untara cursed loudly when an arrow penetrated his leather armour, slicing into his back.

Talgar saw the shaft bouncing at the back of the big man and shouted, 'Untara! How bad is it?'

'Fuckin' peashooters! Will polish it out tomorrow, Tal. No worries now.' Talgar nodded to the big man.

Above them, a dragon descended rapidly, picking up speed towards their location, the fire already burning in its throat. 'Form up!' roared Ganda'har, and his men changed direction to huddle around him. A translucent golden sphere of magic enveloped them just as fire rained down on them, burning the forest to a cinder. Men screamed, unsure if they would survive the encounter. Fires raged all around them like a furnace, yet they stood unscathed, waiting a moment longer before they set off, following the mage as he cleared a path through the raging torrent, whirling his cane before him, creating a tunnel of fire. Unable to follow, Turneroth's men gave up the chase before the blaze.

In the bowels of the fire, they were indiscernible from the blaze that wreaked havoc around them, and even the dragon swooping overhead struggled to find them. They ran the length of the blast until the flames died, keeping low and hidden behind trees and boulders when they emerged on the other side. They waited for the beast to fly over, hearing the air cut by its wings as they cowered behind cover. It turned and hovered in the air only a few feet above the highest treetops, scanning the area carefully for any sign of them, its eyes a lustre of death. Tense moments passed as the fire moved towards them with the aid of the wind, and the mage could do nothing now except wait for the beast to leave, risking death instead of giving away their position.

The dry branches above Talgar burst into flames, and burning debris fell from on high until the tree fully erupted, sending a gigantic ball of fire up in the air with a plume of smoke, forcing Talgar to leap away from it. The sudden eruption caught the dragon's attention, its head jerking in their direction instantly, and it descended into the maelstrom of fire and smoke, forcing the trees apart as it settled. In the midst of the fire, it searched for them, eyes glowing from the reflected blaze. Its roar was intense, deafening to the nearby soldiers, some of whom were so close they could see the veins in the creature's eyes from behind their cover.

Ganda'har stood to the creature's right, gesturing to his men to keep quiet. Hard to do when a burning branch lies on top of you, melting the leather armour you wear around your chest. Talgar lay unmoving as the metal buckle scorched his side. Anxiously waiting, the captain could not put the rest of his men's lives at risk for Talgar; he had to wait. The beast flapped its wings with a powerful thrust, extinguishing some of the flames, and ascended to soar back to Belleford with a piercing cry.

Stentor ran from her cover as soon as it was clear, flipping the dead branch off Talgar and then cutting away the armour straps to remove it from him, burning her hands and cursing angrily, then shouted, 'Flip him!' Ganda'har and Untara gently turned him over to remove the armour, seeing the burnt skin peel away with the buckles melted into the flesh.

Untara coughed and spat soot to the ground, then coughed again and said, 'We need to move, Cap'n. We can't stay here.'

With his elbow covering his mouth, Ganda'har nodded, his eyes watering from the smoke. 'Untara, you and Stentor carry him. Make sure not to touch the wounds, got it?'

'Yessir!' said both of them, and hurried to pick up the lieutenant. The captain smuggled them through the forest, guiding them until they were far from the flames, making sure there were no patrols nearby.

It was all happening so fast. Only moments ago, the night had been a quiet one. Now it was a frenzy of chaos and survival. Blanka watched the two giants carrying Talgar and asked, 'Will he be okay?'

Air exploded from his mouth as his body curled over the captain's fist. He never saw the blow coming. Sagging to the ground, Blanka clutched his stomach, struggling for breath, eyeing the captain as he spat and coughed. Ganda'har helped him to his feet and pushed him up against the tree. 'What were you *thinking?* For months we've struck from the sides, maiming them, making sure we do not get caught or injured, and with your first day back, you nearly get *all* of us killed! I should gut you for this!'

'I didn't want you there! I don't even know why you came!'

'If we hadn't come, you would be dead! You can thank Magnus for telling me what you planned. Has it even occurred to you how painfully they outnumber us? That we need every possible fighter to stand with us?'

'I'm here to get my son back! Nothing more. That's what Beuneth would have wanted, for us to be reunited and far away from any danger, living a normal life.'

Ganda'har dropped him to the ground and stepped away. 'We've *all* lost someone. Do you see us running away from this? I promised we would get your son back to you, and we will, but it won't be easy. The boy doesn't know you. He doesn't even know Turneroth isn't his real father. He won't come willingly, as you saw back there. I sympathise with you, Blanka, you're a friend, but we can't take this head on. We have to be smart.'

The tattooed man adjusted his tunic and rubbed his bruised ribs, saying nothing as he fell in line behind the captain.

*   *   *

The sky felt unwelcoming, with dark grey clouds crawling overhead, and soon a sudden downpour of thick drops serenaded the city, blanketing the streets with a layer of water and muddying the ground. Ladriana listened to the heavy drops hammering the castle's roof, then noticed a steady stream dripping from a truss to a bucket on the floor below, near the stair landing. *That's going to fill up fast if the rain doesn't let up soon,* she thought as Thelanor burst through the front door, gushing water from his clothing and cursing. 'Temple dweller's flat monkey arse! All will work out according to plan, my foot up yo... Oh, Highness, I didn't see you there.'

'Go get Abe. I need him to take over your duty today. Fill him in on the details.'

Thelanor stepped towards the stairs and asked, 'Why, milady? I can handle it.'

'You must be ready for a fight, not focusing on my appearance. We have much to do.' Ladriana swung around and stroked her bulging stomach, mumbling, 'I'll be in my quarters.'

'Of course, milady.' Thelanor turned and left, swearing as the rain pelted down on him.

* * *

The rain had finally stopped, but not its effects, causing people to stumble and fall on the slippery mud and cobbled roads as they made their way to the city square. Big puddles formed on the unevenly tiled square, forcing some to stand ankle deep in the muck, annoying the already agitated mob waiting to relieve the queen of her office.

'Get on with it!' roared a man, quickly stirring up those around him to become a shouting orchestra.

Ehrhard shuffled his rigid body up the stairs and over the platform to stand before the milling crowd, carefully inspecting them before he bellowed, 'Today is not a day for celebration, nor one for causing undue strife in our city! Today we are here to prove once and for all that our Queen, Ladriana Rourke, must not be removed from office because of speculation to the king's fate! Yes, it is true he did not return with Captain Bellof and his crew, but that does not mean he is dead!

'She is with child! As such, the Law of the Unborn precludes her removal! The heir inside her womb *is* your new king until such time that his father returns to us, God willing! In the child's stead, Ladriana will rule until his birth, as per our law! You,' Ehrhard looked over the silenced crowd, 'were given the opportunity to vote for an independent physician to inspect our queen's claims to motherhood.' The old priest leapt forward, pointing at them. 'Much more than any queen has allowed in the past. She didn't have to agree to this! It shows how much you can trust her — and I say shame on you! Rue the day you need her help!'

Kehlos stepped forward and whispered in Ehrhard's ear, calming the old man. 'Yes, fine.' The priest gestured on his left to an approaching man with spectacles and a comb-over hiding the sunspots on his pate. 'Here he is, your physician of choice, Belikane Rouge.' The crowds cheered and shouted, clapping hands to welcome the gangly physician to the stage.

Belikane waved to the crowd with a grin, his shirt sleeves tugging up further towards his elbows with every shake and wave of the arm. His hoarse, old voice rang out once the crowd quieted. 'Good day, citizens. Thank you for your vote of confidence in my ability and integrity. If there is any misdeed here, I will find it, rest assured. The truth shall be spoken plainly.' He turned to Ehrhard and continued, 'Is the queen ready for her examination?'

As he spoke, the royal carriage arrived to the right of the square, with Captain Volar riding behind an entourage of soldiers that quickly dispersed to take up positions all around the square.

'It seems so,' mumbled Ehrhard, then signalled to the guards. Two men hurried over to the embellished chair — the red-cushioned back and seat emblazoned with golden linings and symbols — to move it closer to the centre of the stage.

Thelanor stepped from the carriage first, followed by Ladriana and Abe at the rear. Captain Volar dismounted and followed them up the steps, nervously searching the rooftops for any movement that was not his archers, keeping watch over the men and women who leaned from their windows, the children hanging over the railings and dogs barking in the streets. This was his plan, and he feared for it to go wrong. There was, after all, only so much he himself could do. With so many moving parts, anything could happen, and it would take only one person to mess up the entire plan.

The crowd gasped in wonder, seeing how big she had got, for they hadn't seen her publicly since the news of the king's demise spread through the city. Belikane chuckled with a grin and outstretched hand towards the queen, watching her over the rims of his glasses as he said, 'She certainly seems with child. Let's have a closer look, shall we?'

'By all means, Belikane,' said Ladriana, taking her seat in the cushioned chair with the physician's helping hand. She unbuttoned her dress over her stomach, and Belikane gently opened it to display her plump body to all in the square. The physician lay over her, pressing his ear to her skin, gesturing all to be silent.

Volar glanced at Abe and saw the concentration on the man's face, then turned back to the crowd. His heart drummed in his chest, watching the old physician's serious face until the man rose with a smile to the crowd.

'There *is* a heartbeat!'

'We want more proof!' shouted a woman from the window. 'Do the proper test!'

Sighing, Belikane went to his knees before her and cleared his throat, pursing his lips as he asked, 'May I?'

Captain Volar stepped forward, but was quickly halted by Ladriana's upright forefinger. 'It's all right, Captain, just hold up a blanket for me. We brought a few in the carriage. I thought they might want this.'

Growling, Volar swung around and shouted to a nearby guard to bring the blankets, waiting for the man to run back with them in hand.

'You are most gracious, my Queen. I can assure you, my hands are clean,' replied Belikane, and soon men stood around them with raised blankets. He opened her dress and examined her cervix.

Ladriana endured a long and uncomfortable examination, grunting softly when it became too much to bear, glancing over her shoulder to Abe now and then. The pressure relieved and Belikane rose, waiting for her to button up and adjust her dress before dropping the blankets. He turned to the crowd, a delight in his voice. 'I bring good tidings. Our Queen is with child!'

'What's the sex?!' came a shout from the square.

Abe quickly looked up and shook his head discreetly at Ladriana, who paled. 'Surely we can't tell the sex yet. It is too early—'

'Well...' Belikane weighed his response and continued, 'yes, it *is* early, and having my Queen piss in barley and wheat bags will take far too long to please them, but there is another way that's pretty accurate.

118

It won't take but a moment and it doesn't hurt, I promise.' He rummaged through his bag of tools and withdrew a gold pendant suspended on a string.

Ladriana saw the scowl on Abe's face before he mouthed another chant. There wasn't much she could do except hope that Abe would fix this.

Belikane hovered the pendant above her stomach, waiting for it to move. It suddenly jerked to the left, then to the right, before hanging abnormally still, and the physician frowned. 'Strange. Haven't seen that before.' He tried again, this time watching it swing back and forth. He put the pendant away and stated, 'The test is inconclusive, my friends. It is like the queen said. It is too early to tell.' The physician spun around, smiling at Ladriana, and suddenly pitched forward, screaming in pain as an arrow struck his back, clearly aimed for Ladriana's head. 'Run, my Queen!' he shouted, and fell to the ground, squirming in pain. Volar leapt forward with his shield in front of the queen as the crowd shouted and screamed, scramming to get out of the square when another arrow broke against Volar's shield.

Thelanor rushed forward and shouted, 'There! On that rooftop!' His chants bounced off the walls of the building while the people fled for their lives. Guards ran after the figure, who leapt from one building to the next, loosing arrow after arrow at them to get away, until the roof dragged the assassin down with her next footfall, as if it were quicksand. With her unable to move, the guards quickly caught up with Nivea and hauled her from the sludge before it solidified again. Pumping his fist into the air, Thelanor shouted, 'Yes! That's how it's done!' He turned to Ehrhard and continued, 'I told you not to worry.'

Ehrhard wagged his finger at the man. 'You should've had a shield up before her at all times! If Belikane hadn't been there, she would be dead!'

Men escorted the injured physician away while Ladriana stormed to the carriage.

Thelanor shook his head, jumped down from the stage, and ran to catch up with the queen, closing the carriage door behind them as the horses stamped their feet to pull the heavy wagon towards the castle. *Never good enough... I caught the assassin, didn't I?*

A deluge of screams and shouts livened the square, with most of the castle guards still running around, searching for more assassins, while only a handful jogged a distance behind the carriage back to the compound. The horses could feel the tension in the air, their eyes wide and hooves stamping, biting their bits in angst as Ladriana threw open the little door of the carriage and jumped out, furious and relieved. Thelanor was calling her name, but she did not care.

This was still a win, she told herself. *We can question this assassin and find out everything we need to.* Adrenalin pumping, she rushed through the door and scowled when Thelanor grabbed her arm to pull her around. 'Highness, we should interrogate the prisoner immediately.'

Ladriana glanced past him to the soldiers jogging towards the castle. Her eyes grew wild as both gigantic solid oak doors swung closed with a loud crash, the latches falling into place with no human contact. Doors all over the castle banged closed with a terrible shudder, and Thelanor unsheathed his sword. 'Stay behind me!'

They ran to the front door and Thelanor hammered on the wood, pulling with all his might, but nothing budged. Screaming and shouting, they called for the guards outside to break through as an assassin leapt from the second floor, launching a barrage of blows with his mace, all parried by Thelanor's sword. The warlock slammed his palm against the killer's chest, a wave of power throwing the man back against the wall.

Ladriana gasped. 'There's an exit in the kitchen!' He nodded and was about to run up the stairs past the water-filled bucket when another man appeared at the top. 'Not there, this way!'

They dashed left instead with Ladriana in the lead — she knowing the castle better than Thelanor — and entered the kitchen, slipping and sliding on a crimson river streaming from three of her kitchen staff. Ladriana's tough nature took over; she would mourn Eva, Gunthar, and Bella later, give them a proper burial. A knife sailed over her head, ringing steel as Thelanor parried the thrown blade. 'Fuck you!' she shouted as she grabbed a cleaver from the kitchen counter and hurled it back, sinking the blade between the woman's breasts, and kneed her in the face at full sprint, cracking her head open. They jumped over the body and reached the exit from the kitchen, hearing guards shout and hammer against the doors, trying to break it down. It only occurred to her then that while they had thought they were the ones laying the trap, a trap was being laid for them. *Ackelar was right. We shouldn't have underestimated the Baron.*

A shout came from where they had entered the kitchen, and Thelanor grabbed the attacker as he rounded the corner, driving the man's head into the solid door frame. He bashed the man's head with his muscular forearms, driving his elbow into the man's face until he lay unmoving. 'We can't stay here. Let's move! One of them must be a mage. He must be the one locking the doors! We find *him* and we can get out.'

'Sounds easy...' Ladriana jested, and ran from the kitchen towards the back hall, where they would find a stairway leading up. 'Let's get my bow!'

They ran down the corridor, jumping over the bodies of more staff members before entering the hall — immediately regretting their decision, as three assassins waited for them there. Thelanor handed her his broadsword and unclipped his dagger sheath. He shouted to the waiting men, 'Why are you doing this?'

The man in the middle glanced at the woman on his left and the man on his right, then said, 'You don't have to die here today, Thelanor. We didn't come for you. Leave now, so we can finish this.'

Considering his options, Thelanor licked his lips and peered at Ladriana. 'No, Thelanor, don't you dare!' demanded the queen.

Standing back as he winked at her, he swung around and blasted a wave of fire from his hands, scorching the man on the right as the other two lunged forward. Ladriana jumped into the fray, knocking back the woman with the hilt of the blade. *Ah, that stings, eh?* The assassin staggered back and drew her dagger as well, slicing down with her sword in one hand and stabbing with the dagger in the other. Fast and fluent, the assassin danced with the weapons, doing a pirouette and reversing the blade, swinging her sword and stabbing the dagger. Ladriana retreated step by step, losing ground against the better fighter, parrying for her life, until the dagger sailed through her defences and sank into her stomach. An evil, maniacal laughter rang out from the assassin as she twisted the blade with delight.

'Ladriana!' Thelanor shouted from beneath the other assassin, fighting for his life with a dagger against a sword.

'You're dead, bitch!' sneered the assassin, licking the blood on the cut above her lip.

Ladriana staggered back, the knife slipping from her stomach, along with a few feathers floating up through her dress. Confused, the assassin looked down at her blade and saw no blood, then felt her nose break from the queen's headbutt. Using the hilt of the blade, Ladriana bashed it into the assassin's face over and over, shattering bone and teeth. Screaming at the top of her voice, she swung the sword and decapitated the assassin, breathing heavily while she staggered back, covered in blood from the arterial spray, watching the body fall back. 'No, *you're* dead, bitch!'

'A little help here!' Thelanor lay under the assassin — the invader's sword being pushed down — and quickly losing the fight. He felt the blade bite into his skin, cutting deeper, then tried to cast a spell, but could not focus with the pain. Screaming as the blade drove deeper still, he feared for the end...until Ladriana relieved the assassin of his right arm. The assassin jumped up in a fit of rage, lunging at her when she brought down the sword again, and was relieved of his other limb as well. Thelanor leapt up and drove his dagger through the unarmed man's skull from the back, shouting in anger. 'Argh!' He panted heavily and glanced under his shirt. 'Thank you, milady. We have to find this mage assassin.'

They ran up the stairs and down the corridor, round a corner, and into a horde of more assassins. 'Shit, turn back!'

Ladriana swung around and saw more attackers behind them. They were trapped, and her protector was tiring.

Thelanor jumped to meet the first attackers, unleashing a wave of energy to throw some of them back. Ladriana swung her blade left and right, parrying and slicing, but they were overwhelmed, and the assassins knew it.

Chapter Seven

'This is becoming really aggravating, really fast! I can't understand a word you say!' Khanaseri shouted at Tulvar, annoyed that they'd had to run away like scared dogs from the Ageian soldiers to hide in an abandoned and dilapidated old home in the poorest district of the city, South Phigut. The entire city was on alert, brimming with guards and soldiers, searching for the criminals who had destroyed the Library and injured many of its guards. Doors were being hammered on and people dragged from their homes; another restless night awaited the citizens of Velafrey. Angry shouts from soldiers flowed through the city, reaching their ears where they cowered in the dark house, its roof barely still aloft, with gaping holes in the walls and broken trusses. Moss-covered and wet, the walls reeked of rotten plants and skunk.

Garidan had complained that he was getting a headache from the foul smell, and at first, Khanaseri had dismissed it as being weakness. Now the warlock was beginning to agree with him, wiping his stinging eyes and covering his nose while he stared up at the skies, unable to believe he was seeing a machine float overhead, men searching the streets from its belly, the sound of its engines drumming out any possibility of sleep.

'He said we need to communicate with you. I can't keep translating everything. I'm inclined to agree with Tulvar, but how?' Garidan said, and moved closer.

Khanaseri scowled and stated, 'I'm a quick study. You will teach me as much of their language as possible tonight. Tomorrow, we must start whatever we plan.'

'It looks like they're giving up on the search for us. The helvedron is moving away,' said Borka, peering through a gigantic crack in the wall.

'Good, then I can finally get some sleep,' mumbled Naghita from a rickety chair.

The warlock glanced back at Garidan and said, 'Before we do all this, I need to see this ice dragon, so I know you're not bullshitting me. If this is the dragon to take on the Alpha, I want to find the host now so I can rest easy.'

Garidan relayed the message to the rest of the confused group.

Borka opened his pack and took out the cloth-wrapped sphere, placing it on the wet, cracked floorboards, and stepped away to take a seat next to Naghita. She constantly scanned the warlock up and down with her eyes, arms crossed, gauging him.

'I have some theories, but what does your book say?' Khanaseri asked, with a nod to Tulvar, which Garidan relayed.

With a big, wide grin, the old khaliq flipped through the pages to get to the section he wanted and read, pausing now and then for Garidan to catch up with the translation. 'We had three chances, with three masters of magic, or one chance to combine all their power. We chose the latter. Using an incantation of contact to communicate with the beast, such as we've used with many other animals successfully, they reached out to it. But upon its acceptance, the masters froze from the inside out and collapsed to the floor, convulsing, their organs iced.' Tulvar stopped smiling and closed the book listlessly. 'Maybe we should hold off with this?'

Borka and Naghita glanced at each other, waiting for the warlock to answer.

Khanaseri lowered his axe from his shoulder and took the Balamuth. 'Ice dragon, eh? Does it say anywhere that they touched the sphere?'

Tulvar scanned through the page, then the next. 'Not that I can see.'

For a while, Khanaseri stared at the sphere. *How is it that I get pulled into things like this all the time? I know what I have to do, but I'm damned well not looking forward to it.* Removing his glove, he was reaching out to the Balamuth with his bare hands when Garidan shouted from the side, rushing in to stop him. 'Don't touch it!'

'I know what I'm doing. I've seen how they react. The only time the beasts are free from their cages is when they're bonding or latching on to a vessel. When I grab hold of this sphere, you count to five, then rip it from my hands. Do you understand?'

'I do.'

'Okay. Stand back.' He reached for the Balamuth, chanting loudly until his fingers brushed the cold sphere. Instantaneously, his back arched impossibly as he roared in pain, his arms ripped open by unseen talons, stretching up towards his shoulders and neck, his arms turning cold. Garidan was screaming next to him, though he could not hear. He fell to the floor, writhing; but still he chanted, and the world vanished from his sight to be replaced by one of freezing white powder. He trudged through the thick snow, snapping thin, frozen branches of small saplings with the brush of his arms and legs. Above him, a gigantic beast circled and banked towards him, racing at incredible speeds. He tried to run, but the thick, deep snow made it near-impossible. Khanaseri turned to face the beast, seeing the maw stretch open, and a liquid rush from it so cold it instantly froze anything it touched. Eyes on the beast, shouting at the top of his voice, he felt the cold hit his chest; then utter darkness enveloped him.

Khanaseri stepped forth into the void, knowing his feet should make sounds with every step, yet heard nothing. It was imperceptible. He walked, yet he knew not on what. 'Hello? Can anyone hear me?' He ran and ran, but nothing changed. The empty darkness stretched on forever, with nothing changing shape or colour, although he could feel the air change from a tranquil atmosphere of peace to one of tension. The hairs on his arms became erect, a shiver running down his spine. His body sensed the magic in the air, warning him of danger. 'I'm not here to cause any problems.'

This is fairly annoying, he thought. Up ahead, he spied a plant growing from the darkness he walked on, blossoming to display its yellow flowers tinged white on the edges. Khanaseri bent down and held a bud in his hand, then said, 'What is this? A test?'

A chuckle came from behind, and he spun around to see a man with yellow catlike eyes standing a few feet away, wispy white hair flowing down over his shoulders.

'If it *is* a test, then it's cruel. I've been trapped in here for a very long time, and all I have is these flowers sprouting whenever and wherever they please. But always only one of them at a time. It's so very cumbersome. You, on the other hand, are something totally new; go figure...' The man tapped his jewelled hand against his arm, the wide, delicately crafted silver rings scraping over each other, and his head cocked to the side, studying the warlock for a time. 'How did you get in here?'

Khanaseri rose and crossed his arms. 'Where is *here*?'

'Wish I knew. Last thing I remember was bleeding out back in Kraydenia.' The man turned around and shouted, 'Is this another one of your tricks, ya old bastard?'

'Who are you talking to?' asked the warlock, following the gaze of the man up into the darkness.

'My captor. Wily old goat. Answer me — how did you get here?'

A harsh sound, like that of glass shattering, deafened them with a constant ring. They gripped their ears and fell to the ground, seeing the darkness crack like a shattered mirror, fields of light pouring through until it vanished completely.

Coming to in a blaze of pain, his arms blackened as if they were set on fire and ripped open by the dragon himself, Khanaseri unleashed a hail of screams and watched the Balamuth roll away, slick with his blood, on the splintered floor while Garidan used whatever he could find to bandage his shredded arms. Khanaseri pushed him away and fell to his knees, shaking with pain. 'I'll be fine. Kraydenia...can you send me there with that device?'

Ready to burst with excitement, Tulvar reached out to grab him by the shoulders, wanting to know what happened, but immediately backed away at the stare he received. 'Did it really work? Did you see the host? Do you know where to go?' He looked back over his shoulder at Garidan.

'Yeah, I guess. One thing I don't understand is, he said he was dead.'

Confusion was apparent on Tulvar's face as he mumbled the word, 'Dead?'

'Go figure. I've got to find out what happened.' Khanaseri lay down on the wet timber floor, keeping his arms away from any piece of clothing, and mumbled, 'Maybe we will need another day...' then he chanted.

'I know the place you seek; I have seen it on a map, but I cannot promise I will succeed. It is far from our home,' Garidan said, covering the bloody Balamuth while Borka and Naghita stood perplexed, unsure of what to do.

*　*　*

The guards shouted and hammered on the castle door with axe and sword, but they could not get through the solid, magically reinforced entrance. Some men climbed the walls and loosed arrows through the windows, hoping to take out a few of the assassins. 'They're surrounded! We need to do something fast,' shouted a soldier from the wall.

'Bring the battering ram!' shouted another. A whirlwind of confusion and chaos followed, with soldiers running every which way. Captain Volar and a host of soldiers were at the front door swinging their axes, chipping away slowly at the solid structure, while on the far side near the kitchen entrance, Kehlos led twelve men carrying a gigantic log with a metal tip to the door. They screamed and charged, bouncing back with the force of the hit, confused that the door could take the beating. 'Charge!' Kehlos shouted, and the men ran forward again, bracing for the impact. Over and over, they charged at the door, barely moving it on its hinges.

Singer sent arrow after arrow through a window, downing as many assassins as he could from the west wall, and shouted, 'I need more men at the next window!' He watched a man run at Thelanor and loosed his string, seeing the shaft bury itself in the assassin's neck.

Abe and Ehrhard hurried through the gates with mouths agape, watching the proceedings take place, horrified at what was transpiring in the castle. The old priest shouted to a nearby soldier, 'What's going on?'

'A trap, sir! The whole thing was a trap. Thelanor and the queen are fighting for their lives, and we can't make entry!'

Abe scowled and ran up the stairs to the front door, pulling the soldiers away as he shouted, 'Step aside! Step aside, all of you! Captain! Move! Move away! All of you!'

The soldiers waited for an answer from Volar while the pair glared at each other. The captain moved away quickly and roared, 'You heard him, move away!' *Dear Kelcai, please spare our queen!*

Abe sliced his finger with a knife and drew a symbol on the wall next to the door. 'If these are sealed, let's create new ones, eh?' He made a movement with his arms as if drawing symbols in the air, and the earth beneath the castle quaked, rippling all around and under the castle, throwing men from their feet. Heavy groans and creaks sounded as the castle walls cracked and tore fissures wide enough to squeeze through, until the door and wall exploded inward with a powerful blast. The stones hurtled into the castle, snapping necks and crushing limbs from the assassins who waited to attack them. Abe stepped through the dust cloud and uttered words in a tongue unknown, drawing forth a darkness into the castle that made men whimper and flee. Dark and deafening sorcery tore through the halls, rampaging like black riders on black steeds with black weapons extended, slicing and killing remorselessly with scythes and swords. A roving red-black ball illuminated the air above Abe's hands, flashing out tendrils of malice, ripping into the assassins, burning and dismembering with extreme prejudice. Abe floated from the ground, rising steadily towards the second floor where the maelstrom was at its worst. A powerful wind lifted men from the floor, hurling them to their deaths down below. Abe finally settled on the floor, his toes scraping the boards beneath — the power pulling him forward — and looked around, his eyes darkened to night, the veins on his neck and face pulsing with a draw of black. *I am death...* They heard him say. *I am he who comes to take you away forever...*

The terrified assassin before Abe leapt at him with a raised sword, to be drowned by a sudden blackness that rushed over him, coveting his breath, restricting his air. Abe glared at the man and moved his hands, tearing the assassin in half with ease. The remaining assassins wanted to flee from this dreadful power, but did not get far before Volar and his men cut them down. Abe followed his senses, searching for the mage assassin, drifting through the corridors, the world shifting and jerking around him unnaturally.

He paused before a door and slowly turned his head, silvery hair drifting up as if it were riding the currents of the seas. The door burst open like fearful screams in the night, and he entered the room, wood fragments dangling in the air, suspended in time. Moments later, a scream of terror followed, then silence; and all returned to normal. Volar came up the stairs two steps at a time and dropped his sword next to Ladriana, kneeling by her side where she leaned up against the wall, screaming and crying in great angst.

'My Queen! Are you hurt?!' he shouted, seeing fear radiate from her eyes, her body bloodstained and paralysed from it. Examining her wounds, he helped her up and dragged her away from the horrific scene surrounding them, following her head as she gazed down the corridor where Abe walked from the room, back to normal, but sadder somehow. He saw the old sorcerer mumble words, and looked down to see Ladriana fast asleep. More men streamed past to help Thelanor, breaking his view of Abe; and when they passed, the old wizard was gone. *What? Where'd he go?* Volar shook his head, then carried his queen down the hall to another room and kicked open the door, laying her down on the soft bed, shouting, 'We need a healer in here now! One we can trust!' *Can we trust anyone in this fucking city anymore?*

Ehrhard stumbled into the room, drawing a sign of protection over his chest, and said, 'Kelcai have mercy! Bring light and peace back to this kingdom! Volar, I will stay with her. You go to your men. I'm sure there's much to be done.'

'Aye, and questions that demand answers. What in the damnation was that back there? I ain't seen nothing like that before in my life! Scared the living shit out of me. Excuse my language, priest.'

'Don't be too harsh with Abe. He did what he needed to protect our queen.'

Volar nodded and left the room, shouting, 'Where's the healer? You! Is Thelanor going to...' The voice faded away while Ehrhard spoke soothingly to Ladriana, caressing her cheek.

* * *

Bursting through the door, Volar stormed into the headmaster's office, nearly knocking over a glass display case with many little artefacts within.

'Careful with that!' boomed Abe's voice from behind the desk, and Volar grabbed the teetering case, steadying it before letting go. Then, sword in hand, Volar roared, 'What was that back there?'

Abe glanced up while busily packing things in a suitcase and asked, 'Are you here to use that, Captain?'

Volar huffed, then looked at the sword in his trembling hand and replied, 'I don't know. Maybe. It depends. Who are you? I've never seen power like that before...and it scares me.'

'Ah. Yet you rush in here to confront it? The true definition of bravery: to confront something, even if it paralyses you with fear. One cannot be brave if one isn't afraid.' Abe continued packing. 'There are some out there I know of who can put me to shame, friend. This I promise you.' He paused for a moment and mumbled, 'Like Valdrin Ocon...'

'What are you doing? Stop that and look at me!'

Abe's shoulders slumped, his head dropping before he rubbed his eyes and lowered the vial in his hands to the desk. 'I won't be a problem for long, Captain. Please, Volar. You owe me this much after I saved your queen. Let me go, and you will never see me again. Say you couldn't find me, that I vanished. I'll be on the road before the next bell.'

Volar lowered his sword and pointed to Abe's nose. 'What happened? You're bleeding.'

Abe cursed and grabbed a cloth from the desk, holding it over his nose as the blood streamed out. 'It happens. The human body isn't made to sustain such forces. That's why I never use them like back there.'

'Who are you really? Why would someone as powerful as you want to become a court mage?' Volar settled into the chair before the big, fancy desk, eyeing the man.

The sorcerer dropped into the heavy chair and said, 'My full name, Captain, is Abelor Ventrix, former head of The Eternal Conclave of Andore: a union of sorcerous advisers that has spanned the generations of our world, ensuring the safety and longevity of our nation and its people. That is, until one lord died in a questionable accident, staged to make us look like the perpetrators. But I swear, we knew nothing of his death or what had happened to him. The other lords did not want to hear us. They banished the conclave and hunted us to the ends of the world, murdering those they caught. We were eight in the beginning...now only three remain that I know of. I fled to the far eastern shores and made my way here on a ship, becoming a vagabond. I foolishly thought, when I saw the advertisement for the court mage position, that I might have a place again, a home. Guess I was wrong.' The chair creaked as Volar rocked back and forth, pushing his sword tip into the wooden floor to balance himself. 'Don't do that! We've worked too hard to get this place like it is for you to fumble through your thoughts by destroying the floors.'

Volar quickly picked up the weapon and sheathed it. 'Apologies, Abe. Not for just the floor, but also the accusation. I'm sorry to hear of your troubles. Look, don't go yet. You might not need to. And we could definitely use you in a scrap.'

'That's very kind, my friend, but I can't stay in a place where everyone is afraid of me. I can already see how they stare at me with contempt and hatred. They fear the unknown.'

'But you're not unknown, just new. Let me speak to the queen. I'm sure she would want to thank you for coming to their rescue.'

'She will have nightmares for days to come, but it will fade in time. That's why I put her into a deep sleep, one where she could not dream. Tell her I'm sorry.'

'I've got to go. This office gives me the creeps,' Volar said as he looked around the room. Heaps of books lay piled on top of each other on tables and desks, skulls of apes with large fangs lined from juvenile to adult on a shelf of the bookcase. The tapestry on the right came alive, the seas rolling back and forth with the black ship fighting to stay upright, and the strangest lectern holding a thick leather-bound book adjusted its height when the reader approached the tentacled flower stand. The captain rose, eyeing a grey timber dresser filled with magical items he could not fathom, and all the devices displayed on the back wall stand, guarded by portraits that seemed centuries old. 'We will speak of this tomorrow. Don't go anywhere before then.'

Abe waited for the captain to leave the room, then sighed and dropped his head to the desk with a groan.

* * *

Freshly bloomed flowers of yellow and red spread far and wide over the tundra. Arundhàbu felt it in his legs that he climbed constantly, although the gradient was imperceptible. After days of wandering the desert-like region, the blisters on his arms and legs were finally healing, bursting with a foul-smelling liquid streaming down as he gazed upon the lands as they used to be and snickered with a grin. *I never thought I would see this again. This must be The Old Country. I must be getting close to Velafrey.* His feet burned, the constant chafing rubbing the skin raw, and he knew not how far he still had to go. He felt the earth level out, and in the distance saw mountainous peaks jutting from far below where he stood, with a sharp drop off to reach the canyon floor. *Why does nothing get easier? More problems, more battles, more things to make life more difficult.* He shook his head and shuffled on, to be stopped by the canyon that opened up before him.

To his left, he spied stairs cut into the side of the rock face, the sandstone cracking and breaking apart at precarious angles. Roots and vines crawled across the surfaces, forcing the blocks to crack and split, a green ivy growing deep within. Arundhàbu was lightheaded, the world shifting before him as he stumbled forward, lamenting over the hunger he felt, his stomach growling within, eating itself and growing smaller with every breath of air he took. He felt himself wasting away, and wished he had taken the time to catch something to eat earlier. But he needed to hurry, to catch up with Naghita. He shimmied down the edge on his stomach, holding on to the thick roots, reaching with the tips of his toes for the first whole step not yet broken by erosion and time.

The winds tore at his frame, threatening to pull him to his death far below on the boulder-strewn valley floor. Being as big as he was didn't help. He lowered himself closer to the next steps, feeling each one with his foot before putting his full weight on it. A loud howl pushed him teetering on the edge, and a mighty crack rumbled through the stone. He suddenly dangled in the air and large pieces of rock bouldered down the side, bouncing off the rock face to the ground, where they smashed to pieces. He'd grabbed hold of the roots, the enemy that was causing this treacherous climb now his saviour. *Shit! That was too close. Got to be more careful.*

By the time he reached the bottom, the sun was disappearing. So far down in the canyon, it was already dark, though he could see the rays of the sun still lighting up the mountain peaks and the far away rock face where he would need to climb out. *Fuck! Having had to climb down in the light was scary. Now I have to climb up in the dark? Great...* His hands were used to hard labour, but the rough rocks had torn his skin open, leaving them cracked and bleeding. A stiff wind blew through the cracks of the canyon, his burnt arms sensitive to the cold, causing goosebumps to appear as he walked. *I'd have to skirt these mountains, not take any unnecessary risks. Better get to it. I need to be out of here by morning.* He glanced around in the dim light. *Something feels off in this place.*

Gravel and rock mixed in with the soft powdery sands, the red dust snaking over grey boulders. Puddles of old standing water, smelling foul with green algae drifting over their tops, moss and lichen spreading from their sides, lay in patches over the sands. *How did Naghita get through here with the wagon? I hope they're okay. Maybe there was another way down and out I'm not aware of,* he thought. With the setting of the sun, he could see a glow emanating from his right, accompanied by the sound of men laughing and shouting. He walked in their direction, fearful that bandits had captured his wife and the rest. If there's one he knew about his wife, it's that she wouldn't have gone down easily. She would have fought to the bitter end, and so would the rest of them.

Taking cover behind some boulders, he blended in with the shadows and unsheathed his hammer, stamping from shadow to shadow, drawing near the cave of the mocking, laughing men. *What is that?* he wondered, seeing four Tarogs huddled around a fire, poking and hitting something they had strung over the flames, its squeals echoing from the cave walls. Stealthily placing his footsteps, avoiding any brush or loose gravel, Arundhàbu moved closer, getting a better view of the animal, then gasped. *Oh dear...*

Bows rested against the walls of the cave, axes slung loosely in sheaths around their waists. *They won't be quick enough to get to the bows, I'll make sure of that.* He stepped out of the dark with his hammer hanging down to the ground, the old metal reflecting the fire, and cleared his throat, drawing their attention. The four spun around, the nearest to the wall eyeing the bows just out of reach, and the blacksmith said, 'I wouldn't do that.' Raising his left hand, he stated, 'I'm not here to steal from you, and I have nothing you'd want to steal either. But I would appreciate it if you could give me that critter and let us be on our way.'

The four brigands: one bald, wearing no shirt or shoes with small, skewed tusks, the next plagued by a skin disease crusting his face over in scabs, the third's mouth was askew with only one tusk, as if someone had beaten him terribly in the face, breaking his jaw in multiple places, glanced around at one another, then to the last on the right, unsure. People never dared to enter their dwelling without protection, let alone confront them. The last one to the right stepped forward, wearing a fancy white fedora he must have taken by force from a very unwilling female of Velafrey, and said, 'You got balls comin' in here. But not for long.' The Tarog unsheathed his knife.

'With that hat, you have no balls, so why don't you put down that tickler and do what I ask?' The bandit to the left, with the small, skewed tusks, ran for the bow, and Arundhàbu hurled the hammer while Fedora charged at him. He saw the skewed-tusked bandit collapse on the floor with the hammer embedded in his skull, and dodged a vicious swing from the knife-wielding castrated culprit. The other two marauders ran in with their axes. The one-tusked thug received an elbow to the face, knocking him back on his arse, stunned. Then, a harsh blow from Fedora to Arundhàbu's ribs made him curl, but he wouldn't give them the satisfaction of showing just how much it hurt.

The scab-faced brigand came at him, and Arundhàbu brought his left arm up defensively, letting the fist slip by to glance off his chin, quickly locking his right arm over the attacker's wrist and snapping it down. A loud crack sounded as the bones shattered just below the elbow, followed by a shout of agony. A quick flash of metal appeared in the corner of his eye, and he spun the limp attacker when an axe swung in from his left. The thud of the axe sinking into the Tarog's chest made him think of back home, chopping new stopping blocks for his worktable, getting ready for a new project. Eyes wide with disbelief, the scab-faced thief dropped to the ground, yanking the haft from Fedora's hands, who screamed and dropped next to him, apologising for his part in his death.

Arundhàbu walked up to the stunned bandit struggling to rise and hammered down with his fist, knocking him out cold again, two teeth bouncing on the cave floor amidst splatters of blood. He retrieved his hammer, working it free from the skull of the bald thug, and looked at the last Tarog still kneeling by his dead friend, the fedora now on the ground next to them. 'I told you to give me the critter. You better stay there and keep quiet unless you want to lie next to him. Got that?'

A cry of rage escaped the bandit as he charged Arundhàbu with his axe, blinded by fury and swinging the weapon he'd yanked from his dead friend's chest. The blacksmith spun past the scything blade and hammered the back of his fist into the bandit's face, feeling the Tarog's jaw snap under the blow and dropping the thief to the ground again. Jaw hanging slack to one side, the bandit whimpered on the ground, begging for his life with teary eyes, when a deafening roar sounded from further down the cave. Arundhàbu's head came up, and he took in the cave quickly. *Shit! I've been in one of these before.* He ran over and grabbed the juvenile wyrm fastened with thick ropes to a piece of timber, holding it a distance from him while he ran, its short legs scything at his chest and its round red mouth constantly moving, wanting to feed. He shouted over his shoulder to the crying thief on the floor, 'You can deal with that!'

The gigantic wyrm burst through the earth, roaring its anger down the tunnel.

Arrows swished past his face from more thieves coming round the mountain. Arundhàbu scrambled to his right, to where the thieves' horses stood, tethered to the rock face with iron rings hammered deep. *If horses can get down here, there must be a way back out,* he thought. Shouts from the thieves continued until the beast erupted from the tunnel, charging at the bandits while Arundhàbu rode for the exit, struggling to hold the wyrmlet whilst galloping at full speed. It was heavier than he'd thought it would be. He opened one saddlebag and stuck the end of the timber to the corner, holding the other end up high with his left and riding with his right. Carnage voiced its presence in the canyon as he found the path leading out, pushing the horse hard to gain distance over the riled wyrm. The screams faded as he crested the rise, replaced by the stamping of the horse's hooves. *I'm coming, Naghita, and this wyrm will give us the answers we need. I can feel it.*

* * *

'No, put more emphasis on the rrr's. Roll them out and make your speech guttural. Work the words like this: "Koère mana op-Raga!"' Garidan said for the umpteenth time, annoyed with giving lessons through the night while Naghita and Borka slept soundly on the wet floor, snoring and farting as Tulvar sat in the corner, anxiously observing the streets through the cracks in the wall.

Khanaseri sat up, cursing the pain from his arms as they healed with his focus. Learning the new language was causing it to take much longer. 'Enough of this for now. I know what I need, more or less. These wyrms, you say they feed on the volcano's source? And it doesn't burn?'

'Yes, I saw it and I still can't believe it. But yes.'

'Come, the sun will rise soon. Best we get back into that room with that device of yours, so you can send me back. The quicker I can find this host, the quicker this world and ours have a chance of surviving all this. Do you really think Yidrog can kill these so-called wraethers?'

Tulvar turned, rubbing his red-ringed, baggy eyes as he approached, comically lifting his knees up high to stretch his legs, and said, 'It stands to reason, because they search for constant warmth, that cold must be their natural weakness. We can only speculate about this theory. We have not been able to test it given the resources we have.'

'It's time, then, for me to leave,' said Khanaseri, climbing to his feet. He sauntered towards the door, swung it open, and saw the outline of a fist barrelling towards his face. The impact was staggering; all his senses reeled. A fragile bag exploded over his face, and his nostrils sucked up a fine powder with the scent of lavender and horse piss. The floor rushed closer, and the last things he heard were the others' shouts of panic and anger. *Tulvar, you were supposed to be watching the street...*

* * *

The smell of wet dirt woke the warlock, his eyes blinking repeatedly as he tried to focus, the dust irritating his nose. A mighty sneeze erupted from him, his body jerking and throwing him upright to sit flat on his arse. His head was groggy, as if he had been sleeping for a very long time, but the sun was barely shining through the top windows in the wall before him. It brought back those dreadful memories of the assassins; he remembered the cold of that steel slab under him, the searing hot branding iron melting his skin. Khanaseri shook his head to expel the memories from his thoughts and looked around. *Strewn dirt over a polished black slate floor. They are expecting blood... They are getting ready to execute us.* The wall before him was a mural of rulers: four together, holding up the world in their palms. To his left, more pillars were visible in a line running along the hall, with glimpses of murmuring crowds seated in rows beyond. To his right, he could see the foot of stairs leading up to a dais.

Ears ringing loudly, he struggled to hear the muffled sounds from his right and found he was tied to a pillar with chains. The weight of the iron obstructed his breathing, the heavy links unwilling to move with his heaving chest. 'Can someone turn me so I can see what's going on?' he shouted, then heard footsteps echo in his direction. A heavily clad guard with shiny boots and a nasty grin appeared, looking him up and down before smacking Khanaseri in the face. The warlock spat some blood to the floor and mumbled, 'You hit like a girl!' Another fist split his brow open.

'Enough!' came a shout from the right, and the officer stopped to turn around and face the voice. 'Bring him around. We would like to engage in conversation with this human.' The officer gestured another over and took hold of the chains, spinning him around with great effort with the other's help.

Khanaseri winced and frowned, the chains chafing his injured arms. He glared up at the officer and whispered to the Ageian in Tarkean, 'I'll beat you bloody with the wet ends of your torn-off arms if you touch me just once more.' The warlock grinned as he saw those words sink in.

The officer finally moved out of the way, revealing the same four rulers as in the mural, now sitting on high-backed chairs, from left to right, each with a lavish robe of velvet in blue, gold, silver, and black. Before the stairs, on their knees, were Garidan, Tulvar, and Naghita, and to the far pillar on his right they had fastened Borka, the same as him.

'We are the Eldarre, the rulers of this nation. What is your part in all this, human? Why are you here with these traitors?' The one second from left spoke first.

Khanaseri looked around dumbly, then to Garidan, who watched him over his shoulder, and shrugged.

Garidan turned back to the four and said, 'Excuse my interruption, Eldarre of Magnificence, I have only taught him some of the Tarkean language. I fear he does not understand. Do you want me to translate?'

A long silence reigned in the hall before the Eldarre continued in Tarkean, 'That will not be necessary. I am learned enough to speak the foul tongue.' He repeated his previous question and waited for Khanaseri to answer.

'I have only just met them, your rulership of Eldariness—' The crowd gasped and quickly fell silent with the gesture of an Eldarre.

'Eldarre of Magnificence!' shouted the officer.

'Oh, yes, of course. Apologies. They have requested my help against these creatures. I have no reason to doubt them.'

'And the destruction of so many books and scrolls in the Library of Cabinet? The injuries of so many of our men, caused by you! We have first-hand accounts from those men that you were the one that injured them,' stated the Eldarre on the far right.

His eyes darted to the Ageian. 'I was confused. Didn't know where I was until they explained everything to me. They had nothing to do with the attacks. They tried to stop me. But I know I killed no one. Maybe hurt their pride some, but that's as bad as it got.'

The Eldarre on the far left stood and spoke for the first time. 'That does not concern us, but some of my fellow Eldarre want your heads for spreading propaganda that could hurt this nation.' He turned to the three on their knees. 'Khaliq Tulvar. I have known you for a very long time. Explain yourself.'

The khaliq looked up through his bruised eye, the injury puffing up his face, and asked, 'May I stand, Eldarre of Magnificence? I can't think straight with my knees hurting like this.' He received a curt nod from the Ageian and rose. Tulvar raced through the thoughts in his mind, thinking of the best way for them to move forward, even if it meant not telling the entire truth. He knew what he was about to say would not sit well with Naghita and Borka, but they couldn't do anything if they were dead. 'I have been working on the solutions for growing plants and vegetation in the drying Abru Noxel, your Excellencies. This led me to the discovery of how rapidly the drought was spreading, getting worse by the day.'

'Yes, we all know the explosion of the grand tree caused this. We have been working towards a solution for years.'

'Only it wasn't, your Graces. The tree, I mean.'

A loud murmur arose from the crowd, and someone shouted: 'Heresy!'

'Silence!' said the Eldarre in the blue robe, and waited for them to quiet. 'What are you speaking of?'

'We discovered the true cause of the change in climate, the one that Khaliq Yerick Tolben was painfully aware of. Rest his damned soul.'

'He's a hero!' shouted a woman from the crowd, stirring up the mob once more until the Eldarre brought up his hand, quieting them again.

Tulvar waited for her to fall silent, then said, 'He genetically mutated creatures to ensure Mount Aga would never again kill the thousands of people it once had, and we all applaud his efforts. But what he didn't account for was his creation's unyielding thirst. A thirst that would drain the world of its energy, deplete its reserves of water, and cause rain to cease forever.'

The crowd screamed over his words and the demands from the Eldarre to keep quiet, but Tulvar shouted louder than all. 'They feed on the warmth of the earth, slowly killing it from the inside; and soon, it will spread to Velafrey if we do not stop it!'

'I said quiet!' All the Eldarre were up now, standing a few feet from their chairs, glaring at everyone in the hall. 'Continue, Tulvar.'

'Thank you, your Grace. It is our belief that Khaliq Yerrick Tolben worked alone on a solution for this problem, but he couldn't find any, so he caused the explosion of the grand tree and blamed that for the world's slow demise.' Tulvar glanced over to his right and saw the stares he received from his fellow captives and begged them with his eyes to listen.

Garidan closed his slack mouth. *I see what you're doing, Tulvar.* 'It is true, your Excellencies. We never wanted to cause civil unrest in the lands. We only wanted to find the solution to your world's problem. Khaliq Yerrick Tolben was alone in his efforts to hide this truth. I saw these creatures devouring the earth, but we might have found the solution. That is why I brought that man here.' He pointed to Khanaseri. 'With his help, I believe we can fix this problem if you let us.'

There was silence again in the hall, the confusion clear on the crowd's faces, then Khanaseri said, 'You, on the right with your black dress, why haven't you said anything? From what I've heard about how things work here, I find it highly unlikely that none of you knew what this Khaliq Yerrick Tolben was up to. No, one of you must have been in on it.'

The crowd gasped again, a roar of voices drumming against the hall's walls. Garidan and Tulvar shook their heads in disapproval.

The black-robed Eldarre rose. 'You dare accuse me of this crime? They've told us this fairy-tale about these creatures destroying our world, talking of conspiracies, cover-ups, and traitorous affairs. I think they have entertained us enough for one day! Let's put it to a vote. I say it's to the gallows with them!'

The blue-robed Eldarre ruffled his magnificent gown, straightening the creases the chair had caused, and said, 'A little overly hasty, Eldarre Vendegrut, but I have to agree, you give no evidence to any of your claims! I concur, to th—'

'Wait! In my pack! The one on the right!' shouted Borka. 'We have the Balamuth Yerrick Tolben used to study in the mountain. That is proof that we aren't lying!'

'Hold a moment, Fontayne.' Eldarre Vendegrut gestured for an officer to take out the contents and bring it closer. The officer walked up the stairs and rummaged through the pack, pulling out trinkets and little wooden statuettes, a knife, and the sphere covered in a rag. He placed the Balamuth on the dais and unwrapped it before the crowd, which instantly erupted into a booming cacophony of voices.

Eldarre Fontayne jumped up and shouted, 'Silence! This proves nothing! It doesn't prove these wyrms are really destroying the world, it doesn't prove Yerrick Tolben was behind this, and it surely doesn't prove that any of us were involved! Off to the gallows with you lot!' Officers moved forward, unsheathing their swords with militant precision. The crowd cheered for the outcome, until they heard the black-robed Eldarre mutter something and fell silent, waiting for him to repeat what he said.

'Did you say something, Eldarre Vendegrut?' mumbled one of the others.

'I said, they never mentioned the creature responsible...'

The prisoners' heads came up in realisation and Naghita shouted, 'How did you know it was wyrms, Eldarre Fontayne?' A murmur started between the people while Fontayne twisted and turned coolly to his fellow Eldarre.

'What else could it have been? It was a guess. Let's be done with it and send them to the gallows! Give the people what they want!' But few in the crowd voiced their agreements with the Eldarre ruler.

'Enough of this!' stormed Khanaseri as he rose from the pillar, dropping the chains to the ground and smirking with the shock it caused.

Fontayne huddled behind his chair and shouted, 'They are escaping! Put them down!'

The officer with the nasty grin charged at the warlock, swinging his sword down. To his mind he had been in striking distance, but now drifted further away, the world spinning around him, faster and faster, pillars, murals, and walls flashing by before he was hurled through the hall's window. His cries faded until he hit the ground in a crash, shouting in anger and pain on the other side of the wall. Khanaseri looked at the stunned faces and stated, 'I'm a warlock. Those chains would—'

The building shook from a loud crash. Terrified screams rolled over the city, waves of the sounds riding the winds from afar. The earth beneath them quaked and shuddered, the building groaning as the ground pushed up, forming long running mounds. 'Get the Eldarre out of here, now!' someone shouted. Officers obeyed his command, grabbing the Eldarre and rushing out of the hall with an entourage of guards as a wyrm burst through the floor, snaking its head side to side in a roar of anger. Brick, stone, and mortar flew everywhere, crushing limbs and heads where they fell. People scattered, running from the hall as Khanaseri dived to his chained friends, chanting to break their bonds.

The creature bore down on Borka, ripping half the pillar away in its mouth and causing a section of the roof to collapse. 'Run!'

* * *

A thick puff of smoke lingered over the coach, trailing it as he drew closer to the city gate, marshalled and patrolled by many men, all casting suspicious gazes at everyone who wished to pass. Abe lowered his broad-brimmed hat and stowed his old sword under the seat, hoping that having no visible weapons would get him through without an interrogation. *I don't know why I carry this thing with me...sentimental reasons, I suppose. It's not like I have the arm strength to swing it properly.*

'Halt!' shouted a man with a glass eye floating around aimlessly, his working one fixed hard on the old wizard. 'Where are you off to, Headmaster Abe? The queen does not want anyone roaming outside the city for no reason.'

'Er... I have her blessing, of course, soldier. I am heading south to see the damage caused by this army of dragons, to better understand what our defence should be if they come through here.'

The silent stare he received from the soldier felt like a lifetime of judgement.

'Do you have your papers with you for when you return? I don't want to see you thrown in the dungeons over a silly mistake.'

'Yes, yes, of course I do.' Abe rummaged through his pocket and produced a parchment with his letter of office as headmaster and chuckled. 'Thought I had lost it for a moment.'

The guard did not find it funny. He stepped aside and stated, 'Have a safe journey, Headmaster,' then shouted to the guards on the far side, 'Let him through!'

Abe tipped his hat to the soldier and whipped the reins gently. The coach crept forward, passing the long line of men and women still trying to gain entry through the new gate. He had heard of the abandonment of Belleford, and assumed most would be families from that city seeking refuge. People who left everything behind and had nothing but the clothes on their backs. Guilt-ridden for leaving them in this position, he glanced away from them. Abe was never good at leaving things unfinished, but this had been a pipedream.

He was almost through when he heard shouts from the back, underlain by thundering hooves. 'Stop that wagon!'

I can make it... I can ram them with the horse and be free of them. They wouldn't stop me now, he thought, gripping the reins tighter, feeling the leather pull around his hand. Soldiers were storming in from all sides to cut him off, people shouting and scurrying away, not wanting to be caught in a fight. Abe sighed and dropped the reins, and the coach came to a rolling stop. *So close.* 'Captain Volar... Just let me go.' He didn't need to turn around. He recognised the man's voice.

The horse neighed, stamping its feet as the captain drew near. 'You gave me your word you would wait!'

'I'm sorry, Captain.' A host of horses galloped down the street behind a carriage he knew to be the queen's. 'You woke her? Are you mad?'

'Wasn't me, my friend. Ehrhard had his hand in it.'

Abe climbed down from the coach, herded by a picket of soldiers, which he ignored as he walked towards the approaching carriage. 'Might as well get this over with.' The horses' hooves clopped on the cobbled road until the driver reined in before them and a voice came from inside.

'Abe, join me. You too, Volar. You, get his wagon back to the stables.'

'Yes, my Queen!' shouted the glass-eyed officer, surprised to have the queen here at the gates after the ordeal she'd gone through.

Captain Volar dismounted and waited for the older man to join him, holding the door open, face devoid of any emotion. The carriage leaned to one side as they pulled themselves up and entered the small space, closing the door behind them. Without a word, the carriage turned and headed back to the castle, the train of soldiers following close behind.

Ladriana's breath had caught in her throat when she stared into Abe's eyes, now so gentle, so soft, and apologetic. The fear she'd felt the last time she had seen him was surreal, something she did not expect, especially not from him. But here she was, frightened all over again, clutching a dagger, its sheath encrusted with gems, flowing gold, and silver.

'I told you to let her rest. Just look at her. She's petrified,' stormed Abe.

'And I told you—' began Captain Volar.

'I, er...' her voice broke, her thoughts stammering. 'I'm not scared!' It came out louder than she intended. Both men fell silent, heads lowered as if berated by their mother, and she stowed the dagger. 'Abe, the good captain over here has told me your story. I am very surprised you thought I would have you imprisoned for what you did. You saved me and Thelanor. Why on earth would I punish you for that?'

'Forgive me—'

'Wait! Let me finish. They grievously wounded Thelanor in the attack; he needs time to heal. Say what you will about him — he is arrogant, annoying, frustrating, a downright pain in everyone's arse, and don't get me started with how he swings his hair to catch the girls' eyes. It infuriates me to such a degree that I feel like chewing my own wrists to die a painful death, knowing it would be better than walking next to him through this city...' She breathed hard, eyes closed. *Oh, that felt good.* 'But he fought with every fibre in his body to protect me. He has requested to be removed from his position as court mage, and I believe he wants to become your apprentice. Now, with a vacant seat available for the taking, I want you to step up to the position, be by my side during these trying times. What say you?'

Abe turned to Volar, stunned, and saw the smile on the man's face. 'Milady... I must say, I am shocked at this. Thank you, I accept, naturally. First, I would like to apologise. I never wanted to frighten you as I did. Second, Thelanor's bravery was never in question, my Queen. It was merely his lack of respect. But I'm afraid I can't take him as an apprentice. He is much too old. I will, however, naturally guide him as I will the others of the school.'

'Are you saying you would like to do both? Be court mage and headmaster?'

Abe stammered a bit, his voice coarse and strained. 'I, uh, er...yes. Well, there won't always be a war and people trying to kill you. I will have spare time.'

Ladriana smiled, bringing back some of the radiance on her face. 'It's done, then. Thank you, Abe.'

Captain Volar lurched forward and planted his arms around the old man with an embrace, hugging him like a brother. 'I told you I would speak with the queen.'

The life being squeezed from him, Abe patted the captain's back to let go and said, 'Yes, you did indeed, my friend.'

Chapter Eight

'Naghita!' came a shout from the hall's entrance, and her heart jumped in her chest.

'Arun?' She wanted to run to him, hug him, and smack him in the face. Be angry and love him, but first they had to take care of the wyrm as it rampaged over them. 'Here, Arun!' she shouted back.

The wyrm rushed to the dais at speed and suddenly careened to the right from a blow, its head whipping back and forth in a spray of green. Khanaseri had gathered his axe, the blade shining blue as he chanted, wildly swinging it at the beast and baiting it away. 'It wants the Balamuth! Borka, grab it and run! I'll hold it off. Naghita, get Tulvar out of here! Garidan, to me! We need to distract and kill it!'

Arundhàbu ran into the hall, fighting against the mob of frightened citizens as they pushed to flee from the beast, and shouted, 'We need to capture it!' Reaching Naghita's side as she escorted Tulvar out, he grinned lovingly and said, 'I will see you soon. Take care of him.'

The wyrm barrelled towards the warlock, its grinding teeth shattering the black slate floor as Khanaseri leapt away and brought down the axe, cracking its hard outer shell. He jumped back and cursed, his hands trembling from the blow. Arms wrapped in tattered bandages, he could not fully use his strength.

Borka lunged for the sphere and wrapped it in the rag, running and leaping over bodies and debris to get out of the hall as more soldiers converged on the beast, wildly slashing their swords and spears, while others loosed their arrows from a distance — but nothing penetrated its armour. Garidan grabbed a fallen officer's sword and sliced at one of the scything legs, chopping off the last third of the limb with surprising ease. The wyrm squealed in pain, swiping the dismembered limb at Garidan while keeping its focus on the warlock at the front. 'Dear Kelcai, only a few hundred more to go,' Garidan muttered.

Arundhàbu leapt over Garidan's head, throwing himself at the beast and climbing up on its back to get to the front. The blacksmith was past the point of being surprised, not caring how another human could make it to their world. Too many strange things have occurred of late. Nothing would surprise him anymore, even if Abijiya was to rise from the grave. He needed to reach the man, and this was the best way not to get killed in the trying. He gripped in between the hard outer shells of the creature and pulled away his hands in disgust; a slimy liquid covered his glove, excreted from the wyrm, making it slippery to hold on to. Inch by foul-smelling inch, he climbed the beast, its stench making his eyes water the closer he got to its maw, now almost directly beneath him. The man below struck at the beast with his glowing axe, magically pushing it back, a wave of sorcery forcing it to cower away. The blacksmith unsheathed his knife and plunged it into a glistening black eye and leapt off, rolling into the warlock as the beast thrashed about, trying to remove the blade. 'We have to capture it!'

Khanaseri looked to the Tark and nodded. 'Keep it busy, then!'

'We have to lure it outside. I have something it wants. Give me a count of ten, then bring the bastard.' Arundhàbu ran to the right of the thrashing wyrm and heard his blade clatter to the ground. He grabbed the slimy knife up before continuing. *I'll take that.*

Garidan received a menacing blow to the chest and was flung up against the wall. Slow to react, his legs buckled beneath him and he staggered, just in time for a bladelike leg to punch a hole into the wall above his head. He swung the blade and severed another limb. 'Their joints are weak! Cut the legs!' Guards followed with slicing and stabbing until the beast suddenly lifted into the air and was thrown through the entrance wall, raining brick and mortar down. *What the hell?* he thought, and spied the warlock collapsing to his knees, a buzzing chant still coming from the man. 'Khan!' He rushed over and helped the warlock up, draping the heavy man's arm around his neck and hobbled to get out of the hall where Arundhàbu stood in the clearing with a juvenile wyrm on a piece of timber, knife pressed hard against its fragile armour, the big wraether circling them.

'He's in trouble. I need to get the spell ready to capture it. You go help him in the meantime,' said Khanaseri, and set off at a run, drawing a circle around them in the sand with his axe.

Eyes locked in a contest of wits, five to two, Arundhàbu flicked the knife up and cut the juvenile, a green liquid oozing from the screaming critter. The wyrm flinched and grunted its displeasure, spraying slime all over the blacksmith. Garidan circled with the sword, gauging the beast's intent, and saw it charge towards the blacksmith, who stood his ground, shouting back to the roaring creature and lifted the juvenile. At the very last moment, it changed course and lurched at Garidan instead. He rolled back on the ground, swishing the blade back and forth, parrying the bladed legs, and shouted, 'Anytime now, warlock!'

Arundhàbu jumped in front of Garidan, staving off the attack by threatening the juvenile. 'As soon as you trap him, you need to make it scorching hot! It needs to be in extreme heat. Can you do that?' shouted Arundhàbu, and saw the warlock complete the circle around them and nod.

'You will need to move fast not to get caught in the heat,' Khanaseri replied, then chanted, moving his hands back and forth, constructing a cage in his mind while delivering the words to build it. A wall of magic exploded from him to form a barrier behind the beast, followed by another and another and another. Those close to him were flung away as the power built, a tremendous force pushing at everything.

It felt like walking on solid air, the magical floor impenetrable above and below. Arundhàbu saw it needed only two more walls to finish the cage and shouted, 'Run, Garidan!' They retreated to where the last wall would be placed, keeping the beast at bay, and the blacksmith swung the piece of timber, throwing the screaming juvenile into the other corner of the cage. The wraether raced for her wyrmlet, and the last wall fell into place as Garidan and Arundhàbu dived out, running to put some distance between them just in case. The shimmering translucent walls glowed, getting brighter and hotter with every breath, the heat radiating far and wide from the cage. People took cover and hid from the waves of heat, afraid of getting scorched as a house caught fire to its right, billowing smoke into the air. More soon caught fire, and Ageians everywhere ran with buckets to extinguish the blazes, but they did not dare go near the cage.

Inside the inferno, Arundhàbu saw what he assumed was mother and child huddled together, blissful in the extreme heat; the anger subsided. *Come on. Come on.* 'Yes! Look! They are cocooning!'

'Remarkable,' shouted Tulvar on his right. 'They needed more heat to complete their cycle! To finish the metamorphosis! Genius! How long will this construction last?'

They ran to the warlock when they saw him vomit and collapse, his eyes darkened by the use of the Source.

'I'll be fine,' Khanaseri croaked. 'I need to rest. It'll last a couple of days, but we will need to bolster it again. Do you have any magi in this world who could help? I'm drained.'

Tulvar stood and said, 'Yes, we do. I'm sure the Eldarre will be more open to listening after they just witnessed.' He strode off to the Eldarre cowering behind a line of soldiers, far from the danger, their faces a torrent of horror and disbelief. Officers glanced to each other, flicking their blades back and forth between the warlock, wyrm, and approaching khaliq, spreading their arms to protect the Eldarre.

'Stay back from the Excellencies and bow before their presence!' one shouted, flicking his sword towards Tulvar. Hands raised, the old man stopped and carefully went to his knees before them when the black-robed Eldarre pushed the officers out of the way and stepped forward.

Vendegrut looked around at the frightened people holding their sobbing children and loved ones, and his eyes lingered down the path of destruction the wyrm had caused. It had destroyed homes, roads, and monuments in its frenzy, with dozens of bodies scattered across the ruins, waiting for someone to claim them. 'Rise, Khaliq Tulvar. You and your men are free to go for now. We owe you a debt of gratitude for stopping this creature. We will have deliberations tonight and discuss this tomorrow.'

'You do not have the authority alone to let them go. This must be a united decision! And I say it is heresy! They must die!' stormed Eldarre Fontayne, quickly silenced by the glares of the other Eldarre.

The black-robed Eldarre turned to his equal and slapped him across the face, his jewelled hand slicing open the Eldarre's cheek, stunning those around them to complete silence. 'No, I alone do not have the authority, and that is why we three speak as one, but *you* do not have a say any more. Guards, take him away.' A moment of awkward standing around and staring at each other occurred, the officers waiting for the first to make their move when Vendegrut saw their hesitation and shouted, 'Now!' waving his hands for them to seize Fontayne.

'You cannot do this!' Fontayne shouted as they dragged him away, reeling in their grasp.

'Thank you, your Excellencies. My friend over there is requesting aid from the masters of magic. He believes that with their help, we can fix this problem once and for all. He alone is not strong enough.'

The Eldarre bowed in acknowledgement, and the one dressed in gold whispered, his voice strained and coarse, 'We will discuss this tomorrow.'

Tulvar bowed again as they moved away, then walked to his friends huddled around Arundhàbu, celebrating his return.

* * *

The sun was high, but the winds were cold, the forest quiet, and the nearby babbling brook relaxed his thundering heart. Ragian had a terrible itch in the centre of his back between the shoulder blades, making it impossible to reach with his stiff arms. He worked his right shoulder, trying to loosen it up to reach the area, but the old injury he'd sustained long before becoming a Kingsguard opposed his efforts. He spied a broken branch from a willow at the right height and turned his back to it, rubbing feverishly with eyes closed, the hook of the branch finding the perfect spot. Blissfully, he continued rubbing up and down until a snap of a twig drew his attention. He spun around and dropped to the forest floor, keeping low as he searched for what or who drew near. *Khellar, you will not sneak up on me. I will have your heart in my hands before midday.*

Leaves still rustled on a tree to his right, but it could have been the wind; he saw no movement. For the last few days, he had forgotten about war, forgotten about his duties to the king, to give reports on the elves and their location. He had been watching them from afar, putting to rest any hopes he had of ever seeing Alyssa again. His heart ached and his mood was bitter, but he couldn't bring himself to draw his blade against more innocents for Turneroth's benefit.

Another snap, this time right behind him. *I got you now, Khellar, you arrogant bastard!* Ragian whirled around, his hand scaling over, sharp-taloned claws extending to cut deep into the chest of his attacker. It happened so fast... Eyes of fire, his breath causing steam to rise, he realised it was no man, but an elf girl, young and nosy. Their eyes locked for a lifetime, her big, gleaming eyes tearing up as she reached up and touched her chest, blood seeping over her little hands. 'No, no, no no no!' He grabbed her as she collapsed, seeing the fear in her pale blue eyes reflecting him as he ran through the forest, screaming for help.

The village wasn't far now; he could see the first buildings of Rolldemere peeking out of the greenery, the streets becoming livelier with elves spinning around to stare at him. Elven warriors charged down the hill on horseback with swords and spears while more ran down carrying great shields. They quickly surrounded Ragian and forced him to a stop. 'Please!' he shouted. 'She needs help! Something attacked her in the forest.'

'Put her down! Step away from the child!' shouted an elf wearing grand armour with a white-winged helmet, before dismounting his horse. Elves were converging on them from everywhere, shouting in their language and pushing him out of the way. He heard the little girl gurgle blood, her arm reaching out to a man pushing through the mob. 'Papa, Haleth!'

'Make way! Make way!' shouted the uniformed elf while forcing a path for the sobbing father, who carried the girl to a spiralled staircase leading up a tree to a wooden home. Ragian staggered back until he felt the point of a spear pressed firmly against his spine, and for the briefest of moments considered lunging back to be skewered — to get what he deserved, and see his heart pumping on the end of the spear. He dropped to the ground instead, a pitiful mess, heaving and panting with his hands in his hair.

Murmurs and whispers rose as the soldiers quietly dispersed the mob, moving them back to their business while glaring at the human. It wasn't long, or so Ragian perceived it, before the uniformed elf walked from the home up high and pushed himself over the railing, using the branches to descend, then dropped the last few feet to the ground without a sound. 'I am Valheim, son of the elf king! Tell me what happened in the forest, human!'

Ragian couldn't bring himself to look at the elf. 'It happened so fast... One moment she was standing and the next she was on the ground, bleeding from her chest. I ran as fast as I could.' *Forgive me, Alyssa. I'm weak.* He turned his face up to the elf. 'Will she survive?'

'She is fighting, but it's a severe wound. What attacked her?'

I happened to her. Me, a killer of children... Ragian shook his head, and whispered, 'Misfortune.'

'What was that?' asked Valheim, leaning closer to hear.

'Nothing. I didn't see.'

Valheim turned to his men and said, 'Volin, Scenthis, Yalia, you three scour the forest for any signs of bears or big cats. If one is this close to Rolldemere, we should drive it off. For now, no children are allowed out unattended. Spread the word.' The three bounded down the road Ragian had come in on, their strides long, and swiftly vanished into the woods. 'Where are you from?' asked Valheim. 'And what were you doing in our forest?'

What was that city's name again? Shit! 'I wanted to see the elves, is all.'

Valheim grabbed him by the collar and lifted him from the ground. 'Did Queen Ladriana send you?'

'Yes! She did. She feared for your lives and tasked me to report back to her if anything bad happened,' lied Ragian.

Valheim shook his head. 'She is relentless. Amalar and Yontis, you two escort him back to the borders of the forest. I'm sure he can find his way further. You, human, tell your queen we will be fine.' The two who grabbed his arms were big for elves, burly but quick, their long, dark hair smoothly folded behind their pointed ears.

Ragian grabbed at Valheim's uniform as they dragged him away and begged, 'Please, can I stay? Just until she's better, or darkness takes her. Mhaelenal Shaua be with her on her journey.'

Valheim swung around and glared at him. 'Wait! Let him go. How do you know this name?'

'My mother...she loved your people. She told me your stories. I don't know how she came by them, but now, here, I feel her again.'

'Amalar, take him to the quarters high in the Evertree. Get him some food and show him where to bathe. He reeks. My father will want to meet him soon.' He turned and whispered, 'And berate me for letting him stay.'

'Thank you, Valheim. You will not regret this. Thank you.'

I already regret it, human, thought Valheim.

* * *

King Turneroth walked the camp, intent on snapping necks, fists balled up. 'Where is that fucking Ragian?' Men slunk away to avoid being caught in the path of his fury. 'That was not a rhetorical question! And where is Khellar? He should have been back by now!'

'Ragian has not yet returned, my lord. And we do not know where Khellar is. There was a bright flash a few days ago to the southeast, and he took off. Probably to impress you, my lord, by bringing back a prize,' said a man busy shaving, using a small shard of mirror propped against his pack on a table.

The king turned to him and stormed closer, confronting the man. 'What's your name?'

'Lieutenant Xare, sire,' he said, jumping up to salute the king, his face lathered in animal fat.

'All these pathetic excuses.' Turneroth gazed around, seeing virtually no one in the vicinity. 'Everyone flees my presence in fear today; why not you?'

'Mother said I fell on my head as a child, sire. Must have a damaged noggin. Can't help myself sometimes.' Xare still stood at attention, waiting to be excused, but it never came.

'Come, soldier. You will be the next volunteer to be bonded. I'm losing my Kingsguard like swatted flies, and we cannot afford that,' the king said as he turned about and started walking away, expecting the lieutenant to fall in behind him.

'But I don't want to volunteer, sire.'

The king stopped and turned. 'Yes, you do, and you want to do it now. I need four new Kingsguard, so round up the men and get my volunteers! I want you front and centre of the line. Don't make me look for you. Got that?'

Xare's hand had drifted down, and he quickly saluted again. 'Yes, sir.'

Turneroth mumbled a stream of curses. It annoyed him that he did not have his Second to send around on errands, having to do them himself, finding it tedious and a waste of time to hunt for the people he was after. *One is a traitor, the other a coward, and the new one an idiot. Can't I find decent help these days?* Mud covered his boots, and he sweated like a pig in the humidity, yet his mood lightened as he glimpsed a skulking little figure creeping deviously towards him. Walking beneath a great tree, he snapped off a thin branch the length of his arm and stuck it through his belt.

A shrill voice shouted from his right, 'On guard, ye scallywag!' A flimsy stick drummed against the side of his stomach.

Turneroth jumped around, drawing his stick sword with one eye forced closed, and shouted, 'Ye'll never get me treasure, ye gold-lovin' mongrel! It's all mine!'

Moseroth dived to his left, tucking the stick neatly under him as he rolled and got to his feet. 'Be it the rum that spills or me blood, we shall have it!' They charged each other with their fiercest battle cries, swords held high. The clatter of the wood resonated and soldiers walked out of their tents to witness the fierce battle. The pair circled one other, and little Moseroth feinted a swing to his right. Turneroth waited for him to change his hands back and get into his stance. Then the strike fell on the king's leg, paining him slightly, but he didn't mind. He fell into the muck, his death throes exaggerated and dramatised.

'Ye has bested me! What would this cruel world be without me gold and grog?'

Moseroth watched the king play out his death, grinning wide with hands cupped over his mouth, and shouted, 'You're not really dead, Papa! I'll share it with you!'

Turneroth jumped up to the applause of the nearby soldiers, his heart a little less heavy for the first time today. He scooped up the little boy and marched towards the cages and the fire-breathing beasts keeping guard. Ever since the last escape, he'd had four dragons keep watch of the prisoners, not wanting another escape to occur. 'You've got so big and heavy since we started this journey, my boy. Where have you been hiding all the food?' The boy giggled and said some nonsensical words he strung together, waiting for a reply from the king. Turneroth frowned. 'I've told you before, Mose, don't talk like a fool. It's one thing to play a scene like back there. But don't be a fool.'

The little boy looked down ashamedly and said, 'Yes, Papa. Will we go home soon? I miss Yelganoth. Why couldn't he come with us?'

The king's heart suddenly felt heavy, his mood turning foul again. The chances that Yelgan still lived were highly unlikely, with Caryk playing the usurper. He knew he would leave no one alive. 'Yelgan has a very important future. He needs to be king one day.' The words, spoken out loud, hurt him deeply.

'Will I ever be one? To rule over the lands as a fair and just king, like you, Papa?' Moseroth swished the stick in the air, nearly knocking

Turneroth on the head.

'Maybe one day, my boy. Maybe one day.' He knew it was a lie, but what harm could it do? 'But I think you might have an even grander future than to play king and sit in your castle one day, waiting to grow old and die behind the walls you've built. No, I see an adventurer in the making. One who will travel the world and see things most men never dreamed of seeing.'

'You really think so?' the boy asked, beaming.

'I know so!' He lowered the boy as they neared the cages, watching the dragons guarding the prisoners. The beasts slept mostly, but only a man wishing death upon himself would dare wander into their midst. Their sensitive hearing and keen sense of smell would make it a foolish endeavour indeed. As if feeling the attention of the Alpha on them, the beasts woke. Their slitted eyes flashed open and narrowed their gazes on them, and Moseroth's breath caught in his throat next to him. A soft, cold little hand, grimy and wet, probably with snot, reached into Turneroth's palm and clutched it tightly.

'Will they hurt us? They frighten me.'

'As long as I stand, they dare not harm you, my boy. But don't go hitting them with your sword... You run along now. I've got work to do. We'll talk later.' His head pained him again, the slow throbbing behind his eyes getting louder with every breath. Little Moseroth scurried away over the mud-trodden area, swinging his stick as he charged a man walking up to the king.

'Oh, Mossie, you need to be studying the works of the grand archmage, not playing soldier. Your father has entrusted me to oversee your studies, and you are not helping me win his favour!' Bohan chided the boy.

Moseroth shoved the stick into the mud and stamped his feet, standing like it was his hand on the hilt of a blade. 'But those books are so boring, and they make little sense. Can I play a little longer, then study tonight?'

The impertinence of the young was a growing pain he knew every parent went through. They lacked the understanding that you meant only to empower them for their future, to give them the knowledge to become more, more than their parents' miserable selves. The mage glanced to see if the king was listening. There was no evidence that he was, not a twitch or a glance or a move of the head to hear better, but he knew Turneroth heard every whisper. 'Dear boy, the longer you put it off, the longer it takes to finish. You can play a little longer, but tomorrow, you will study twice as long, agreed?'

The boy stood with his hands on the stick, peeling the bark from it with his nails, contemplating the contract, and said, 'Agreed.' Moseroth knew he could get out of tomorrow's studying some other way. The contract was always meant to be broken; he just needed to find the loopholes. He ran off before Bohan could change his mind.

The mage watched the boy run away as fast as possible, out of fear of being called back, when he heard the king speak.

'Kids should be kids first, then adults. Why do you pester him with all these books? You know he will find a way out of the lessons tomorrow. I indulged your request to teach the boy, but I have seen nothing of value that he has learned. For your sake, I hope you know what you're doing.'

'I know he will try to get out of our agreement tomorrow somehow, and even in this, there is a skill to be taught. The art of being cunning is one that books can't forge. It is something that has to be moulded, worked on over time. For this, it is acceptable. He needs to be ready for the world outside of this kingdom; I am sure you would want him to have all the tools when the time comes to step out of your shadow.'

'Uh-em,' Turneroth wiped his mouth after a bit of spittle flew out and said, 'Of course I do.' His voice turned sorrowful as he continued, 'Bohan, how many more magi do we need? Would the elves be enough to send us home?'

The mage took a deep breath to release a great, long-suffered sigh. 'I wish I could tell you they would be, sire. But we are in uncharted territory. Without the great pit's power to bolster our efforts, I am unsure. We do not know how many they have who can touch the Source, or how much they can attain.'

'Uh-em.' Turneroth cleared his throat again and turned back to the cages to see the many men, women, and children pressed together in them, barely able to sit and rest their feet, some sleeping on top of each other. 'It is a terrible thing I'm doing, but it has to be done to take us back. We don't belong here.'

'Yes, sire. We understand. The kingdom comes first.'

* * *

The mountain covered much of Chinnai, safeguarding its location from prying eyes. The group of dwarves had returned a few days back, leading the haunted girl past the deluge of onlookers who stopped what they were doing to stare at them. Nervous under the scrutinising eyes, Veranay reached out to Yallrick, grabbing a handful of clothing before pulling herself close to him. Already taller than the dwarf, she could not hide behind him completely, but his warmth and presence made her feel safe.

'All right, all right! Go 'bout yer business and stop gawking at the girl like ye've never seen one before.' Yallrick shook his head at them, then whispered over his shoulder, 'Sorry, girl, this is most unusual for them. We don't bring strangers into the city. They won't cause ye any harm.'

She released his jerkin and gave him a little room to move again, fighting the fluttering heartbeats to calm herself as they walked past homes cleverly carved into the side of the mountain. Thousands of rooms and tunnels forming a maze, she was sure, ran deep into the earth's crust. Dwarves carrying picks and buckets came from the tunnels, all sweaty and covered in soot and dirt. From a home to the right in the distance, she saw a dwarf rise from a chair with a scowl, the cropped-up hair and fuller bosom making it obvious she was female. Yet Veranay wasn't sure until she saw the baby suckling at the tit from a sling around her waist and back. Yallrick's face beamed, and he stretched his arms to her.

'Ah! There she is. Just look at my beautiful girls!'

It was the ugliest baby Veranay had ever seen. The head was too big for the pudgy body, the face uncharacteristically hairy, with thick, red, bushy brows, and she was sure she had seen a moustache forming on the poor thing.

'Where've ye been, Yallrick Duskhorn? Ye should've been back days ago. Instead, ye leave us fending off this mob of salty bootlickers! Ye can't leave this fine thing alone, ye know!' She gestured up and down from her feet to her head, face set in a permanent scowl.

'Yorel, my beauty, if these men know what's good for them, they'll stay well clear of ye.' He embraced her, forcing her reluctance aside so she put her arms around him as well. Yallrick lowered his head to the little one and tickled her with his large beard for a moment before turning to Veranay and saying, 'Yorel, meet Veranay. Veranay, this is my lovely wife, Yorel, and daughter, Roveliah Duskhorn.'

Not forgetting her manners, Veranay curtsied and whispered, 'Nice to meet you both.'

'Dear girl, she's just skin and bone! When last did she eat?' Yorel didn't wait for an answer and glared at Yallrick. 'Come in, girl, we can feed ye some proper food. Not the slop they forced ye to eat on their patrols.'

Veranay couldn't help but wonder what world she had stumbled upon. She had been a young girl ready to take on the world, and now she was living with dwarves in a mountain far from home, with no family and no idea what was going on or what her future held. She felt completely lost and utterly alone, the bitterness in her heart painful with the loss of her father, the only man she had ever loved. Lip quivering already with this slight show of affection from Yorel, Veranay didn't want to speak any more, fearing that she would burst into tears to sob uncontrollably, and merely nodded.

The dwarves had been very kind to her, but she knew some were deliberating and arguing with Yallrick over the decision to bring her back to the city, though behind closed doors, so she could not hear. The notion that she could bring them danger seemed so foreign to her, that she somehow had the power to touch the Source, the power to manipulate energies and create from nothing.

Over the next few days, she had become accustomed to the city. She had walked the great forges where all the metal works took place, watching the molten iron running along funnels to their moulds through a field of mazes as dozens of dwarves hammered on their pieces, shaping them to become whatever they desired: weapons, armour, cutlery, crockery, belt buckles, buttons, art pieces, and so much more. Fascinated by the way they bent the metal to their will, she wanted to learn more, do something with her hands to rid herself of the frustration she felt, of the thought that she was merely a burden to everyone around her, and picked up a blacksmith's hammer that was leaning against an anvil. A dwarf rushed over when he saw her struggling to lift the tool, and caught it in time before it fell on her foot. His solid, long red moustache ran past his face, dirty and filled with metal shavings, his rough and scraggly beard streaked with grey and his eyes covered by the large goggles skirting his button nose, wriggling constantly from the irritation of the metal shavings.

'Ye have to be more careful, girl, this hammer will take a toe as it has in the past. Mean old thing... I call her Sanguine on account of the spray she makes when you miss your mark...'

Veranay sulked and said, 'Apologies, master dwarf. I will leave you to your work. I only wanted to do something, to not feel so useless.'

He looked at her through those dark goggles, knowing her story, as it had spread throughout Chinnai. Some grunting sounds came from his throat before he spoke. 'Here, take this one.' He held out a smaller hammer, waiting for her to take it, and led her to a forge at the back with a smaller table and anvil, handing her a spare apron. 'My name is Hurst, but ye can call me Pappy.'

'He be the father we never wanted!' shouted another dwarf, lifting his goggles to show his big grin through the mask of muck.

'Shut it, Vergo! Or I'll make ye work with Sanguine for a month! Now, where was I? Oh yes. We use this for the kids to learn and practise. It's a much better beginning point, my dear. What ye say we make ye a wee knife to keep for protection?'

Her face gleamed, her smile broadening as she nodded, delighted to have something to do. Pappy took an old piece of iron that was meant for a sword — but a youngster had messed up the blade — and shoved it into the firepit. 'Lesson has started, lass. Best be working the blower to keep the heat, otherwise yer metal will be worthless.'

For the rest of the day, Pappy guided her, helping her hold the hot iron while she hammered it, folding the blade over itself again and again, flattening it and forming the edge and long, curved tip. Sweat streamed down her, sticking her clothes to her skin all over her body, and her arms burned from fatigue, but at least her mind was not in a dark place anymore. She was seeing some light at the end of all this. Back and forth, the knife went into the firepits to heat it up and get hammered, then cooled in oil and beeswax, tempering the blade. It was a long and hard day's work with many failures and successes, and by the end she had the blade ready for the haft to be placed.

'What are we going to use for the handle, Pappy?' she asked, excited to see the final product.

He tapped his finger on his hidden chin through the thick beard and said, 'I've got an idea. Ye said yer Da worked in a quarry, right?' Veranay nodded. 'Hold this,' he said and jogged away to return a few moments later with gemstones in a variety of sizes and colours. She had never seen the likes and was amazed, wondering their worth, then pointed to the blue-and-brown opal.

'Oh, a fine choice indeed. Ye've done all ye can for now, lass, and 'tis late. Come back in the morning, and I'll have it done for ye. Okay? Go get some rest, and tell Yallrick I think he made the right choice. He'll know what I mean.'

A little disappointed she would not get the knife today, Veranay bowed slightly with a curt nod and pursed lips. 'Thank you, Pappy. Today was a truly great day. You have been a marvellous teacher.' Invigorated with the excitement of the day, she ran for Yallrick's home, and once she reached the exit of the mountain, the cold suddenly knocked her breath away. Inside, near the forge, she had forgotten the cold, and now regretted not having worn the heavy tunic when she ran out into the open. She quickly donned the attire and walked with haste, smiling at those still outside, waving courteously. The further she walked in the gloom, the more her mind pulled at the strings of her sanity again, seeing the soldiers and her father wrestling on the ground, the mage's neck opening up from the axe her father held... Her chest became heavy and strange, tingling inside, the same as it had before she blacked out a few nights back with her father's death. Angst gripped her by the throat, constricting her breathing and making her pulse race. Veranay felt her heart thundering in her head, the veins on her neck throbbing with every beat while her vision threatened to grow dark.

Strong hands gripped her shoulders, and she spun around to see Yallrick.

'Ye're okay, lass, nothing here to hurt ye. Come inside and have a meal, then off to bed with ye.'

Her heart calmed as she looked into his caring green eyes and slipped into the small home. After dinner, sleep came instantly for the first night since all this started, with no nightmares haunting her.

Early the next morning, before the sun even rose, she jumped out of the little bed, eager to get back to work with Pappy, unable to control her excitement. Yorel was already up and making breakfast, chuckling at Veranay's elation when Yallrick appeared from their room, yawning and scratching his head through his wild black hair, looking like a cow had been licking him the whole night long. 'What's all the noise?'

He walked up behind Yorel and squeezed her bottom, making her jump with a start. He chuckled as she spun around and whipped him with the rag she had been using to clean the counter, then settled at the table.

Veranay was anxious, twitching and moving about, ready to head out the door when Yorel stated, 'Nah ah, missy, ye'll eat first, and then ye can go.' An annoyed growl came from the girl until she saw the steaming fresh breads and eggs and bacon on plates arranged on the table. Her stomach suddenly growled back at her, furious at being neglected, and she jumped in, stuffing herself with the delicious food.

Yallrick stared at her, trying to figure out what brought this transformation on, a little disturbed to see her push so much bread, eggs, and bacon into her mouth, worrying when he saw her struggle to chew with the bulging cheeks. 'Slow down, child. There's plenty more. Ye're gonna choke on all that. Spit it out,' he said, observing her with his own bread hovering close to his mouth. A loud, audible swallow came from her that made Yallrick feel the pain in his chest, squirming until she drew a breath.

Licking her fingers clean, she jumped from the chair and ran for the door, saying, 'Thank you for the meal, Missus Yorel. It was delicious!' Then slammed it shut before Yallrick could voice his objections.

'What was that? I've not seen her act this way before,' he asked, turning to Yorel.

'Pappy's been teaching her how to make knives. It's got her all excited, and it keeps the memories of what happened away some. It's good for her. Poor child needs something to keep her mind busy.'

* * *

Pappy laboured over a firepit that was struggling to breathe, pumping the blower to liven it up when Veranay skidded around the corner, nearly crashing into another dwarf and apologising as she snuck away. 'Making friends, I see,' said Pappy mockingly.

'I apologised. Besides, it's your fault that I'm excited. Did you finish it?' she asked, pressing her fingertips together repeatedly.

'I did.' He rummaged in his apron's front pocket and pulled a black leather sheath from it. The sparkling blue-and-brown opal haft stuck out, shaped with four big grooves for a good grip, the butt made of silver. He unclipped the sheath and pulled it free. The shining blade reflected the molten iron from the forges, dancing with the red on the dark walls, and she took hold of it with mouth agape and eyes unblinking. She fingered the symbols around the butt as he continued, 'What do ye say ye help me on some more projects today?'

'It's beautiful! Of course I will! What do these mean?'

'They are dwarvish. This around the hilt is *slësva*, meaning family. The ones on the blade says *häsvagnèr*: Remember.'

She could not believe that this was the very weapon she had forged after the master blacksmith did the finishing touches and polished the blade. The weight was substantial, and she knew she would have to train to use it properly. Holding it with her fingers wrapped around the hilt and her thumb guiding the blade as she swung it, Pappy gestured her to stop.

'Reverse the blade, lass. Let it run up yer arm. Slice and stab, slice and stab. That's it. Enough playing with it; clip it around yer belt and come help me. We need to make a new axe for Hasgrem. It's the second request this month from him for another weapon. I swear, that boy loses more iron than we can mine. Go, bring a new cart in for us.'

She was giddy, tripping along before the dwarf in one place, and threw her arms around Pappy, then dashed from the room to search for a cart of iron.

Over the course of the day, they worked on preparation for the axe and various other items, and she loved it. The last cart of iron she had struggled to bring in was only half. Now she stared at a fully laden cart at the very back of the workplace, and wondered how she would move it. Veranay leaned in and pushed the heavy cart of iron past the hammer-droning dwarves towards the rear forge where Pappy waited, her legs trembling and her stomach growling again. Having eaten not so long ago, with Yorel bringing her some food, she felt as though she could skin a cow and devour it whole already.

She never thought hard labour could make you this hungry, and felt a wave of sympathy flush over her, remembering how hungry her father had been at night-time, yet he always ensured she had enough to eat. She knew now that he had taken less than he wanted to and needed to, realising how it must've felt. How weak he must've got at times. Using her last bits of energy, she pushed the cart near the anvil and collapsed, panting and rolling around, trying to get blood flowing into her limbs, when Pappy kicked her feet and said, 'Come on. The day is done, lass. We'll continue tomorrow with the axe. That bumbleheaded buffoon can wait a little longer. Off ye go before Yorel throttles me.'

'Thank you, Pappy. See you tomorrow!' Veranay ran back to Yallrick's home in the dark, knowing he would be a little upset with her coming in this late again, and dashed out of the mountain, this time remembering her tunic.

The night was quiet; all noise fell away from the forges and the work deep in the mountain. Something felt out of place. She walked and searched the shadows, fearing that *those men* had returned. They had struck with no warning back then, and she had the same feeling as now. Again, powerful hands pulled her around, and she stared at Yallrick; but no caring eyes tonight. Tonight, they were focused, brows pulled into a scowl, his finger over his mouth, gesturing her to be silent. He led her quickly out of the open area to under the mountain, all lanterns extinguished. She didn't like what was happening. It felt too familiar. Yallrick pulled her close, and she saw more dwarves huddled together, all keeping very quiet, weapons ready.

He pointed to the sky and whispered, 'They're searching for us. We canno' stay here and let that thing find Chinnai. You'll need to come with us. We'll protect ye.'

Unsure what *thing* he was referring to, she decided now was not the time for questions and nodded, knowing it was her who was putting them in danger. Summoning all her courage, she asked in a whisper, 'Where do we go?'

He took her by the shoulders and said, 'Darkwood Forest. We know it well. Stay close.'

It was like a punch to the gut; her stomach reeled. She wanted to vomit. *Why does this keep happening to me?* The world spun past her sight, a blur, moving faster than she thought possible, with dwarves readying gear and organising their farewell from their families. She briefly remembered Yallrick leaning his head against Yorel's and kissing the ugly baby; then there was darkness and trees racing by. Every so often they would pause, scan the skies, and run for more cover, keeping away from open areas until they were a good distance from Chinnai.

On a hill, far from their home, all the dwarves embraced one of their own, an older dwarf with a heavy scar across his bald pate, running down and over his dead eye. *He's scary-looking, but then they all are when they're ready to fight,* she thought. They left the dwarf behind and ran from the area as fast as they could.

The sun would rise soon, the black of night slowly turning grey as they reached an old bridge spanning the gorge with the river rushing over sharp boulders far beneath; still, she felt the spray of the water on her skin.

'He has lit the beacon. The beast will see it soon. We have to move quicker!' Veranay remembered one dwarf saying, then more running.

Chapter Nine

'Youse want more coffee? Youse seem tired,' mumbled Magnus as he extended a cup, taking a big swill from his mug and enjoying the warmth it brought into his bones.

Blanka pushed the tasteless porridge around in the bowl, not having much of an appetite to begin with, but he was trying to get back to his old self, not trying to forget Beuneth, but to move on without her. He took another mouthful and regretted it, chewing quickly to swallow the slop. 'Yes, please. I need to get this taste out of my mouth.' The warm drink flowed down his throat and he gargled with it, sloshing it around in his mouth until the bitterness obscured the porridge. 'Dear gods, that stuff is vile. Tastes like he used sand for a spice. Thank you.'

'Hey, don't look at me. I didn't make this morning's batch. ''Twas that big fella, Untara. Poor soul. He tries to help everywhere, but he's just good for one thing, really. He should stick to fighting.'

'Seems he'll stick to more than that.' Blanka pointed to the giant of a man stirring the big pot, and saw Stentor slap him on the arse as she walked by. Untara cussed with a start and shook his fist at her with a grin. 'Loads of *tension* between those two.'

Magnus laughed harshly as he sat down next to the bonded. 'Can youse even imagine what would come from her loins if those two shacked up?'

Blanka snorted with laughter, thinking of the idea of the two giants and their offspring. 'Speaking of giants — and I mean no offence — you've lost so much weight. Here I was thinking *I* wasn't eating enough...'

'The captain wants me to pull my weight,' the barkeep wiggled his nose, the growing moustache irritating him, 'which I literally couldn't do. So I been working out and eating that green shite, fruits and such. Ya know, get back to fighting shape now that my leg is getting better. It's just my hand that still needs healing. Anavi doesn't like it, though, says I don't look like her old bear anymore.'

'Whoa, my friend.' Ganda'har laughed as he approached from the back. 'If that woman hears you talking about her behind her back, she'll make you a mule.'

'What do you want, Ganda'har?' sneered Blanka, keeping his gaze on Untara in his struggles to fend off Stentor. Magnus rose and tried to sneak away when Ganda'har spoke.

'Stay, Magnus.'

The barkeep swung round, shaking his finger at both of them. 'Oh, no! I won't be party to this. Youse two act like a pair o' tits looking for support!'

'He's the bigger, lumpy tit, ya know, the one that always reaches for the knees,' interrupted Blanka, still angry over the unexpected gut punch he'd received from the captain.

'Oh, stop being a little girl, Blanka. What's done is done, and you know you deserved it!' stated Ganda'har.

'Stop it! Weze are supposed to be fighting them, not amongst ourselves. I have half a mind to drag Anavi away from here and go rebuild my inn to leave youse two to kill each other.' Magnus stalked off, mumbling something they couldn't or didn't want to hear.

The thick air between them grew stale with no conversation happening, until Ganda'har swallowed his pride and said, 'I understand you want your kid back. The best time to do this is when they're preoccupied with war, not expecting thieves to steal him away. It might not look it, but I *have* thought about this for a while.'

Blanka fidgeted with his hands uncomfortably and glanced at the captain. 'You have?' he whispered.

'Yes. I think our next move must be for me to go to Artorea and beg the king to send his remaining troops to New Runswick. You need to go to Midavene and do the same, while the rest of the men will follow Magnus and Anavi to the city. We'll meet them at New Runswick and join with their forces. While the battle is being waged, their numbers to safeguard their prisoners and camp will dwindle. The king will have his hands full and the mages will be busy. We'll take a small group into their camp, get some of their clothes and armour to blend in, then head for the child. What do you say?'

One brow raised, Blanka looked at Ganda'har and said, 'This plan might have some chance of success. Thank you, Captain.'

'Good,' Ganda'har clapped him warmly on the shoulder. 'We should leave immediately.'

'What about these elves they're headed to, though? Are we just going to let them be slaughtered?'

Ganda'har lowered his head and kicked a stone. 'I can't see us being of any help to them. We can't help everyone.'

* * *

People walked around the glowing red cage, giving it and the warlock a wide berth, the heat searing if one got a little close. With the Hall of Justice destroyed by the wyrm, the crowd was moving back to the open area before the Library, where the Eldarre would convene again to deliberate on the findings of their investigation. Khanaseri saw an anxious guard moving towards him and chuckled. *Probably given orders to get me to cooperate.* He raised his hands in surrender, to the surprise of the guard, and calmly walked away from the cage, staring at the cocooned wyrm inside. The juvenile had died, its body turned to ash. *The heat must have been too much for it.* He joined Tulvar and the rest at the front — all unchained this time — and spat to the side, clearing the phlegm from his throat, and glanced up to the clear blue sky, wiping the sweat from his face. To his surprise, only three Eldarre were present.

The black-robed Eldarre named Vendegrut stepped forward and

announced, 'We have questioned Eldarre Fontayne about his knowledge regarding these creatures.'

A ripple of shock ran down Tulvar's spine, knowing what it meant to be "questioned." He shook his head to rid the idea from his mind and listened to the Eldarre speak.

'Although he might not have been involved with the original projects, those being so long ago, and cannot be held responsible for the act of treason himself, he covered up the fact that his bloodline, spanning through the ages, had kept this secret for generations. They have marked us for death to spare their names the humiliation of failure. For this, his punishment is death by association. He will walk into the cage to die by the side of their cover up.' The crowd broke into a loud buzz, people talking over each other about this uncharacteristic sentence. Never had an Eldarre been convicted of a crime. 'Citizens of The Old Country, bear witness to the laws at work,' Eldarre Vendegrut gestured to the left, past the crowds, from where they marched the blue-robed Eldarre down the street towards them, shoving him along to fall on his bruised face, skimming the skin from his soft cheeks.

They had done a number on the Eldarre, and it impressed Khanaseri that he had held out to the point where they had taken a few fingers before he squealed.

'He has pleaded with us for the life of his family, calling for their ignorance of this secret. And because of his high office and standing, we have granted him this request. They will not be subject to the punishment of association,' continued Vendegrut.

To the right, Fontayne's wife and children huddled together under the guard of the soldiers, forced to stay out of reach of the approaching husband and father. Khanaseri found it strange that they would go as far as death for a crime committed so long ago, especially that they had considered putting the entire family to death for it.

A long moment of silence followed as Eldarre Vendegrut took a deep breath. The crowd watched as Fontayne reached out to his children and wife in his bloodied state, all of them crying and wanting a final hug goodbye. 'We, as the Cabinet, unanimously declare them free from this trial. They are not to be touched. Guards, stand aside and let them have a moment together.'

As soon as the guards let them go, they rushed into each other's arms, the two young boys sobbing in their father's embrace while the woman held all of them together. For some time, everyone waited in silence under the wailing family, waiting for the end to draw near, and so it did. The Guards pushed in between the embracing family at the gesture of the Eldarre, pulling them apart and forcing Fontayne to walk the short distance to the cage. This was a cruel fate, making one walk to his own demise with the incentive of keeping his family safe.

Fontayne shouted to his wife and children, 'I'm sorry!' walking backwards to the cage, unwilling to avert his gaze from them as the heat boiled his flesh further the closer he got. His clothes burst into flames and still he walked, keeping them in his sight, watching them scream and cry. He vanished in a cloud of billowing smoke as he stepped through the threshold of the cage.

Khanaseri turned to see the remaining Eldarre stand to attention with their arms stretched out, palms open as if inciting a blessing or a prayer for the Ageian. The three Eldarre turned back in unison to Tulvar and said, 'We thank you for your service, Khaliq Tulvar, and for bringing this to our attention. You have requested the masters of magic to aid this man in completing this task, and we give them gladly, although we are unsure they will be of much use. None of them know the other's craft. Do with them as you see fit and report back to us. Good luck, Khaliq. Do not fail us as Yerrick Tolben did. You too, human...' Khanaseri nodded.

Tulvar bowed, followed by the rest of them, and said, 'We will do our best, Magnificence.' The crowds dispersed slowly with the departure of the Eldarre, astonished at what they had witnessed, their mutterings low and hushed, when a tall, gaunt Ageian nervously approached Tulvar. The khaliq smiled at first and said, 'Gorbel! It's good to see you.' Garidan and the three Tarks drew closer, listening in.

'It's always good to see you, my friend. But not today, I fear.' He lay his hand on Tulvar's shoulder and the khaliq's smile disappeared. 'Your man fell into a fever after you brought him in. We fought it with everything we had, and I thought he might just pull through this morning when I saw him. He looked lively enough. I quickly went out for some ingredients I needed to fight the infection, as I was running low; and when I returned, he had stopped breathing. There was nothing I could do. I am sorry for your loss. Was he a close friend of yours?'

Garidan cursed and turned away, knowing Tulvar wouldn't have said it was his son, and heard the khaliq whisper, 'Yes, yes, he was very dear to me. Thank you for trying, Gorbel. Let me know what I owe you, and it will be so. Makes little sense that both of us need to suffer.'

Naghita glared at Garidan, burning holes through him with the fury in her eyes, and stormed off, hearing Arundhàbu shout from behind for her to stop.

Borka lay his hand on Tulvar's back and mumbled, 'Uh... Sorry, Tulvar. He was a good one.'

* * *

Four masked figures stood before the Library of Cabinet, only their mouths left visible, from which the warlock could tell one was female, her slender face and supple red lips revealing her gender. They stood with hands clasped in front of their long blue robes, staring out through the white porcelain under their hoods, their black eyes a stark contrast, giving them a demonic appearance.

'Dear lord, what is this?' Khanaseri asked, shaking his head, exasperated. 'Why do they need to look like something out of a bard's pathetic rhyme? We're not here to win some contest or have a show of fashion! Remove those bloody masks!'

The masters turned to one another, moving stiffly under his scrutinising stare, until Tulvar said, 'They cannot. It is forbidden to show your face if you are Djak-ta.'

'What is Djak-ta?' asked the warlock with a frown.

Garidan shook his head. 'Don't look at me. I've no idea.'

'They,' Tulvar gestured with his open hand, 'are Djak-tas. Masters of magic.'

'Well, that's a stupid fuckin' law,' mumbled the warlock, seeing the Djak-ta unnerved by his lack of respect for the law. He grabbed the nearest Djak-ta and whirled him around to face the bright red cage a distance from them, ignoring the surprise of the rest as they fell back defensively. 'Can you do that? Can you make that happen?' he asked the man. The Djak-ta mumbled words in Ageian, and the warlock angrily shook him. 'Speak Tark! Show me what you can do.'

Borka, Arundhàbu, and Naghita watched from the side, all with grins on their faces, enjoying the shift in dynamic at work. Naghita felt her hatred for the Ageians flourishing as she watched the Djak-ta, his arm bent in the warlock's grasp while he muttered, 'With training...I can. I am a master of manipulation. I can feed whatever I want into people's minds. That is my speciality. Groahn,' the man flinched as his arm bent a little too high with the warlock's frustration before he pointed to the Djak-ta on the far right and continued, 'is the master of imbuing objects with magic. Coralay is the master of potions and speaker of trees. Hannus is the master of energy. Agh!' he shouted as he fell on his face, his porcelain mask shifting to the side to reveal his high cheekbone. He speedily covered his face again before anybody saw him, and rose, dusting his robe with the dignity he had left, and saw the three Tarks laughing.

'So, you're bloody useless! Why is your knowledge so limited?'

'It's the way they work here,' said Garidan, picking something from his teeth. 'It's ridiculous... They won't share their knowledge for fear of being replaced as khaliqs and Djak-tas.'

'So they're expected to learn everything on their own?'

'Or find the knowledge by some other means. Some khaliqs and Djak-ta, I suppose, start sharing their knowledge with their young when they know their time is short, but not all,' said Tulvar, thinking of his failures as a father to Raegel.

Hannus stepped forward and said, 'We have our failings, sir, but w—'

A sudden fist pounded him on the chin, cracking the mask and dropping the Djak-ta on the ground. No one else moved, but Coralay trembled as the warlock approached her.

'Master of energy couldn't stop my fist. What do your trees say about that? I don't have time for this shit! You all will learn how to replicate and master what I have done with that cage or by whatever god you pray, I will cast you into that cage to join the pompous Eldarre Fontayne!' Khanaseri rounded on Tulvar and saw the old man jump. 'I saw... I *fought* with an Ageian Gatekeeper. Where are *those* warriors? He was something to fear, something to respect, and someone you wanted on your side.'

'You actually fought a Gatekeeper?' asked the three standing Djak-ta in unison. Coralay continued, 'We thought they were a myth. Something created for us to aspire to.'

The warlock saw he was getting nowhere with them and growled, 'It seems we're not going anywhere today. Garidan, go study the monolith and ensure you know how to send me back after this. I'm not spending a day longer here than I need to. Got that?' A curt nod and Garidan headed to the Library of Cabinet. 'You three,' he looked to the Tarks, 'Clear your minds and focus on the time you spent in the mountain. Think of nothing else. Once I'm done with these Djak-tas, I want to see what you saw.' Borka and Naghita glanced at Arundhàbu, waiting for his nod before agreeing to the warlock's demands.

Tulvar stood waiting for his job, for his purpose to be laid bare, but nothing came forth. So he took it upon himself to find out, for surely he would be needed. He was, after all, Khaliq Tulvar. He tapped the warlock on his shoulder and asked, 'What should I do?'

Brows bunched in a scowl, Khanaseri turned to him, trying his best to be polite. *It's always good and proper to be polite, my boy,* his father used to say. He remembered the tirades his father would go into if he were impolite. Even on his own deathbed, Galvos Brathos shook his finger at him, spewing up blood as he confronted him to show respect to the king. He calmed his voice and said, 'You are not a fighter. As I understand it, all of this was set in motion because *you* would not sit idly by to see this world die. You have lost your boy and saved the rest of them from the gallows on this journey, and you have organised these

Djak-ta to aid me. Haven't you done enough? Let us take it from here.'

Soft whimpers, like those when you knock your bare toe against a stone, escaped the khaliq. His eyes wandered, staring at the three Tarks lying on the grass with their hands behind their heads, eyes closed, and to the people walking up and down the streets, going about their business. Yet he had nothing to attend to now. 'Exactly. My son is dead, and this plan is now out of my control. I have nothing else to do, and I fear if I don't keep busy, I might just walk to the gallows myself.'

Something in the baggy-eyed khaliq's face made Khan think of Blanka. 'Fine. We need provisions. It will get boiling hot, so we need liquid, lots of it, and food to keep our strength up.' Tulvar's face lit up. 'Naghita! You can go with Tulvar and help him with this task. You never saw the lair, so you're of no use to me with this.'

The Tark woman rose from the grass and sneered at him. 'How'd you know I wasn't in the lair? I never told you.'

'All these questions! Agh! Just do what I ask. If I have to explain everything, we will get nothing done!'

'Oi! No need to talk to her like that,' Arundhàbu said as he neared, and stood towering over the big warlock, being at least a head taller.

Khanaseri gritted his teeth, hearing them screech over each other, and growled, 'Oh, so you wanna roll, do ya?' and unslung his axe. He had been in a foul mood since he woke this morning, losing his temper at the slightest annoyance.

'Stop this!' shouted Tulvar, pushing in between the two, forcing them apart. 'As much as it pains me to say this, the warlock is right; we need to stop asking questions and get on with it.' Pushing at their bulk, Tulvar was concerned for a moment they might end up flattening him instead if they ignored his act of bravado. *What made me do this?*

Khanaseri lowered his axe, then sheathed it before he spoke. 'I will explain what I can, when I can. But not now.' The blacksmith gestured for Naghita to go with Tulvar, then joined the amused Borka back on the grass as the knocked-out Djak-ta rose to his feet unsteadily, and Khanaseri grabbed the man's arm. 'You're okay, fella. Took a bit of a spill. Should be careful where you tread, eh?'

The confused and probably concussed Djak-ta scanned the ground to see why he had fallen, but saw nothing and said, 'Yes, sir. Won't happen again.' He wondered why his jaw hurt so badly.

Khanaseri stalked off to where a goat bleated from behind a fenced-off yard and leapt over, grabbing the animal by the horns as it tried to ram him. A quick scuffle and he pulled the goat over the fence, ignoring the disgusted stares from the citizens walking around him. He carried the fighting goat over his shoulder, wincing every time he scraped his arms against something. 'Hold out your hands. Cup them,' he said to the Djak-ta. He lowered the goat, raised its head, and cut its throat, spilling its blood into the stunned Djak-ta's hands. A small child wailed after seeing the gruesome act, and clung to his mother, who scurried from the area. Khan moved on to the next Djak-ta.

With their hands filled, he dropped the spasming goat to the ground. 'Now, time is scarce and there's a lot to do, so listen up. Arundhàbu, Borka, remember what I said. Think of your time in the mountain, nothing else. And if you feel a sensation like you're being watched or spied upon, ignore it. It's just me prodding your memories.' He saw the two Tarks fight the urge to ask questions, then turned to the Djak-tas and said, 'Let's join them on the grass and relax. Take a deep breath and forget about this world.'

Sitting cross-legged before them, he hummed a chant and shuddered, his head twisting left and right as squeals of pain escaped him, tearing his mind in two. *This is not the way to do magic, Khanaseri...magic bites.* He visualised himself being split, and felt the sundering take place. His voice echoed to the right, and he heard himself ask a question to the left, reaching out to the Tarks through their minds, getting images of the mountain from when they arrived, seeking the entrance. More information flowed into him, while on the other side, he chanted out loud and felt the sticky, warm blood of the goat on his fingers as he stirred it in their hands and pulled the four mages into the training realm.

'Open your eyes.' The four Djak-tas immediately jumped up in surprise, seeing nothing but grey stone and a barren landscape with the warlock before them. Khanaseri rose steadily and said, 'Excuse the scarcity of imagination, but I am a little distracted on the other side trying to work out the mountain. In here, I will train you for whatever I think is going to be needed in the mountain. The first session is focus...'

A whip snapped from his hand, breaking the skin of the Djak-ta whose name he didn't know.

* * *

'Shh! The beast is on our trail, lads. I can feel it searching from above, waiting for us to make a mistake.' A loud growl sounded next to him. Yallrick glanced to his right and glared at Hasgrem, who played the ignorant fool, ignoring the stare completely as if nothing had happened. 'I told ye your stomach would be the death of ye. Better eat something before ye call a challenge to the beast.'

'Yes, sir,' Hasgrem said, and poked through his pockets. He stuffed his cheeks with cheese, messing white crumbs all over his red-brown beard.

'Hasgrem, I love ye like a brother, but please move away from me. We have a lady present.' Veranay lay to his left on her stomach, and giggled with an outstretched hand before the dwarf moved away with hurt in his eyes. He handed her some of the cheese with a smile right in front of Yallrick's face, then crawled away to the far right, joining his brother Yantore and receiving a slap against the head for his behaviour. The two started up again, getting ready to pounce on each other, so Yallrick threw small stones at them, wagging his finger like a disapproving mother. The pair quietly returned their attention to the trees up the ridge, struggling to see through the mist and the dark bark of the crevalorn trees that gave Darkwood Forest its name. 'Come, boys. Let's move deeper into the forest.'

Veranay clutched the dagger's hilt at her side, making sure it hadn't fallen to the wayside. They had been running for the last two days through rain and mud, only stopping for short periods before moving again, always vigilant about what was following. Yantore had told her the day before what this beast was, but she found it hard to imagine seeing this *dragon* in her mind, visualising a flying lizard that breathed fire. She could not see how that was possible, but she could see the fear in the dwarves' eyes. That was something she didn't have to imagine. When it attacked her village, she was inside the school, hunkering down, and never saw it. By the time they dragged her outside and threw her in the cage, the beast was gone, only the aftermath of its destruction left as evidence.

Mist drifted low, covering shrubs, bushes, and saplings with its wet touch. The gentle reminder that nature is always looking after itself, protecting itself from foreign travellers, was clear as it took their sight from them, making it nearly impossible to see which way to go. But the dwarves were not so foreign. They had been part of the forest for a long time, using it as their hunting grounds when food got scarce on the mountains, and they knew it well. A whistle sounded from somewhere, followed by a sinister voice.

'Come out and play, master dwarves. Or just hand over what I want. I don't care for your kind.'

Yallrick turned to Veranay, spinning his axe in his hand, then shook his head and motioned her to hurry past the moss-covered boulders, grey-green lichen growing in places. She noticed what seemed to be the remnants of an old statue of a man holding a sword lying on its side, broken by roots and covered by the moss. She'd never been this far up north and certainly never dreamed of venturing into the Darkwood Forest, knowing only of the tales spun by wives of the forlorn few that did. Breathing deep and fast, it still felt as though no air made it to her lungs, as though the oxygen was stealing her breath instead of gifting it. Two dwarves back, she heard Yantore speak.

'It's only a man. Why are we running from a man? I can take him.'

'You know, I never thought dwarf tasted so sweet. I always reckoned you'd be salty, being so filthy, living with the animals and all,' the voice drifted to them again, followed by a perverse laughter. 'It was kind of you to leave me a snack, even if it was to pull me away from your city.'

Skrug swung around and whispered, 'He ate Yanush? I will strip him of his teeth!' He climbed out of the suspenders crossed over his shoulders, and unsheathed his axe, readying to run at the voice, when Vedalbore grabbed his arm, shaking his head.

'I don't know what he is, but that is no ordinary man. Yanush knew the risks.' Around twenty dwarves crept through the thick mist, heading for the heart of the forest. Vedalbore turned to Yallrick and continued, 'Ya know what lives where we go. Are we really doing this?'

Yallrick eyed him for a while, then said, 'We have no choice. We can't fight that alone.' Everywhere around them, they heard footsteps running over the soil of the forest, seeing glimpses of weapons and armour. 'Orcs! Be ready.' But no one attacked them. The sounds passed by their position and swiftly headed towards the cynical laughter behind them. Standing ready with their backs to each other in a circle, they waited silently until Yallrick said, 'They haven't seen us yet. We have to move fast. We'll not be that lucky for long.'

The clash of steel sounded, followed by a roar that shook the earth and a ball of fire that lit the mist in a glorious veil of orange and red. 'Run, dwarves!' Behind them the footsteps got louder again as orcs retreated, running from what they thought would be an easy meal, that now turned out to be a harrowing ordeal.

Hasgrem gazed left and locked eyes with an orc running for his life only a stride away, an awkward moment for both with his plume of hair waving in the wind. The dwarf swung his axe and saw the head fly from the haft as the wood tore to splinters, ripping through the thin breastplate and sinking into the confused orc's chest. 'Agh! I told Pappy I needed a new axe!' He thought about dropping the haft, then realised he had nothing else and kept it instead. *Better something than nothing, right?* Trees cracked and splintered to their right, with screams of the dying orcs accompanying the shattering trunks.

It was drawing closer.

The forest floor was a treacherous marathon even for dwarves, and the constant bushes and shrubs didn't make it any easier, especially for Veranay, who had fallen many times, skinning her hands and elbows and knees. But she kept running, trusting the dwarves to protect her. *But who will protect them?* she asked herself, suddenly feeling guilty for taking them away from their homes and putting them in so much danger. *Yorel would kill me if something happened to Yallrick. No, they must get home safely, even if that means I don't. As soon as we're out of this mess, they must go home, and I'll give myself over to this creature. No one else will die because of me.*

An orc ran into her, throwing her from her feet and knocking her breath away as she hit the ground. Veranay scrambled for her knife, which lay a few feet away, near to where the orc was rising to his feet, shaking its head dizzily. *Must have knocked its head against a tree.* Its rotten, skewed teeth protruded from its mouth, where a large wound, thick and red, oozed blood over its chest. *No one else will die for me.* Eyes wide and screaming fiercely, she grabbed the dagger and jumped at the orc, plunging the blade into its neck over and over, sobbing and shaking with fear as it collapsed to the ground in shock. Yallrick came to her side and dragged her off the dead orc, shouting, 'We have to go! He's dead, lass!' He held her hand as they ran for their lives, swinging the axe with the other at more orcs now aware of their presence.

Hestith dragged his axe from an orc's neck and limped to catch up with the rest of the dwarves. A cut on his thigh stung horribly where the orc's sword had stabbed through, luckily missing the bone. Arrows zinged by their heads. Aiming for the height of a man, not a dwarf, the orcs were releasing the strings at anything that made a sound. A breath of fire singed Hasgrem's hair, and the dwarf slapped himself on the head to kill the flames before they reached his pate — he couldn't afford to be as bald as his brother. How would he ever mock him again?

'Over there! To the right!' shouted Yallrick, pointing to a path he knew led up a ridge and over a ravine to skirt a cliff, down a narrow path to where they might lose these orcs and dragon in a labyrinth of caves. They ran up the ridge, with Vedalbore helping Hestith at the rear, his arm draped over his friend for support, leaning heavily to his left. They could hear the orcs being slain by the beast, their aggressive nature getting the better of them. The thick mist obscured their view — and them, for now — but they knew that as soon as they reached the top of the ridge, there would be nothing concealing them.

The ground became muddy from the run-off near the ravine after a heavy bout of rain had flooded the area, their boots sinking into the earth, sucking them in and tiring them with the slog up. Veranay was covered in orc blood from the one she'd killed, her face a sheen of terror. She held on to Yallrick's hand, pulled up on the ridge by the powerful dwarf. Above the mist now, she turned to see a tree crash to the ground, disappearing into the fog below, and knew the beast was close. A powerful tail swooshed up and over the trees as it thrashed at the orcs, killing remorselessly to get to the dwarves.

'Quickly, jump over!' shouted Yallrick, drawing near to the ravine. He saw Vedalbore and Hestith struggling closer and cursed, knowing the injured dwarf could not jump the gap filled with rushing water. It would pummel him to death; dwarves did not make for good swimmers. He pointed to Yantore and growled, 'Get her across and make for the cave. I will get Hestith over.' Hestith was pale from pain and exhaustion by the time he reached Yallrick, panting like an old dog that hadn't run for a long time. Yallrick and Vedalbore grabbed the injured dwarf's legs below the buttocks, getting ready to hurl him across. 'Ready, one, two, three...'

Hestith cried out in pain as he flew across, the wound in his thigh bleeding badly after they pushed right on it. He crashed into the other side, slipping down into the rushing water, grasping at tufts of grass and rocks, his fingers digging into the slippery dirt, to no avail. *So this is it,* he thought angrily. *Done in because I couldn't jump or swim.*

A hairy hand grasped his, dragging him up with a loud heave. Skrug was already on the other side, and had jumped when he saw his friend fail to clear the gap. 'Not yet, ye bastard! Not yet! Ye still owe me a chance to beat ye at Gwamie.'

'Even dead, ye'll never beat me. Ya barely know how to hold the cards...' laughed Hestith as he climbed up the side, relieved to be in the arms of his friend.

A sharp pain shot through his neck and he heard Skrug scream, but he knew not for what. His legs were suddenly numb. *I must be more tired than I thought. I'm just glad there's no more pain.* The world shifted as his legs gave way under him, and he tried to grab his friend's arm. *Why are my arms not moving?* he wanted to say, but realised he couldn't speak.

Pushing his hands over Hestith's bleeding throat, Skrug fumbled with the arrow, unsure if he should pull it out. The shaft was still stuck with the bladed tip at the front, Hestith's spine severed instantly.

Yallrick and Vedalbore leapt across and grabbed the screaming dwarf, hauling him away from his friend bleeding out on the ground. Skrug saw the man responsible, standing further down with an orc bow in hand, his face dripping blood with a grin, showing his teeth as he laughed, then followed them, sauntering up the hill.

* * *

'Wake up!' Garidan said, and kicked the warlock's legs. Startled, Khanaseri swallowed his snores and sat up, his eyes puffed up and looking tired. 'The helvedron is on the way. It'll be here soon.'

'Helvedron? Why aren't we using the monolith?' he asked, yawning and stretching his body. The wounds on his arms were turning pink where the scabs were peeling away, giving him the look of a newborn.

'It seems the lightning show you put on when you came through damaged it, and with it being so old, they have no idea how to fix it. Heck, they don't even understand how it's working. Tulvar organised the helvedron for us.'

'Is he okay? I saw him light the pyre last night in the square.'

Garidan turned to the sleeping old man, and said, 'He will be. He stayed there for most of the night on his knees, clutching what was left of the ash until the guards begged him to leave. Up, everyone!'

Naghita groaned when Arundhàbu moved her arm off his head, and turned away from him to continue sleeping. The blacksmith yawned and squeezed her buttock as he said, 'You can try to wake her. I need no more trouble in my marriage.'

The front door crashed against the wood, breaking off the hinges, and fell to the floor, rocking the house. Naghita jumped up, her knife flashing, reflecting the moonlight as she let go of it to thud into the frame next to Borka's head. The gladiator pulled the knife from the frame, with eyes wider than usual. 'Sorry, it slipped from my hand with this blasted wind.' Naghita blinked her eyes and wiped the sleep from them, ignoring the fact that she'd nearly killed Borka, and yawned loudly.

'Are you all ready for this?' Khanaseri asked, waiting for their answer, but none came.

Garidan rose and whispered to him, 'Without the monolith, we will need to make our way as we did the last time, and the last time was not pretty. We all nearly died back then, so it's safe to say they are *not* looking forward to this. None of us are.'

Khanaseri nodded. 'Yeah, I saw what happened when I worked with those two.' He looked at Borka and Arundhàbu. 'Do you think they'll be trouble again?'

'It looks like they've worked out their issues for now. I think they'll be fine. But the mountain may bring back some of the anger they harbour.'

'Yeah, keep an eye on them. We don't need more trouble.' Grabbing the gear Tulvar and Naghita had put together, they slung their packs over their shoulders and made for the square before the Library, walking the eerily quiet neighbourhood of South Phigut. The homes were in disrepair, falling apart at the seams on all corners of the street they walked on, a few stray cats following their moonlit shadows, hoping to get a scrap of food from a generous donor.

The area had been well lit with lanterns already, to guide the helvedron for landing. Khanaseri and Garidan stared at the massive dome-shaped ship while it lowered to the earth. Slowly and steadily it reached for the surface, pushing the large metal feet into the ground as an anchor, holding it in place. Hot air flowed from the loud engines, blades spinning at incredible speeds, generating gusts that whipped their clothes around. Tulvar slapped them on the backs and continued to the ship's door and said, 'Don't worry, she'll get us there.' The khaliq entered the bottom carriage and disappeared from their sight as the three Tarks stopped next to them, eyeing the contraption as well. Although they had seen them flying on numerous occasions, they'd never been in one, and the thought of being trapped up high was not a glorious one for them.

'I would rather ride on the back of a stretagor,' growled Arundhàbu with a grin before starting for the ship, then spun around and continued, 'but there are none around here, so...'

'But there are horses!' shouted Borka angrily, annoyed at Naghita's mocking laughter from next to her husband.

'She's been ignoring you since the news of Raegel's death. What happened?' asked Khanaseri, following the Tarks just out of earshot.

Garidan didn't want to talk about it, and was instantly irritated by the question. He bit on his lip and sighed. 'I was an idiot. It's my fault Raegel is dead.' He saw the warlock didn't like where this was headed and continued, 'I was terribly sick, starving, and had drunk no water for nearly two days when we found a lake. I couldn't help myself and didn't listen to his warnings to stay away from the water's edge. I was just so thirsty... A crocodile lurched out of the water, wanting to grab my head and pull me under, but Raegel leapt in before it. He saved me...and got pulled under instead. By some miracle, he clawed his way back up and away from the beasts, but they had done a number on his leg. He died because of the infection. Because of me... I don't blame her for being angry. I am too.'

'Uh, he sounds like a brave man.'

'He was.' Garidan reached the ship first and pulled himself up by the rails as he stated, 'Braver than me.'

'Oh, stop this pity party. You give yourself too little credit. Few warriors would breach the gap between worlds to find allies. Few would dare to do what you did. There are always casualties in war. I know that doesn't make his death any easier, but it should give you some perspective. You fight for more than just one man. You fight for an entire nation, the world even, and if you fail, there will be many more deaths. Carry him with you in this fight and the next.' The machines groaned even louder while they lifted from the ground, getting higher and higher as they walked into the main sitting area where the rest already had taken their seats, flanked by the four Djak-tas and a section of soldiers sent to accompany them. The warlock looked around at them with raised brows. 'Seems we'll have more company on this trip than we thought.' He took his seat next to an open window, feeling the hot air brush over him as the ground pulled further away. A sense of vertigo made his head reel. *Why does this bother me so? I've flown on the back of a dragon; that didn't bother me. Then again, they have wings...how does this thing even work?*

Chapter Ten

The cave was dark and dreary, but the dwarves did not mind that. They were used to it, after all. What they weren't used to was being hunted in the caves. Slung over Vedalbore's shoulder, Skrug swung back and forth while they ran through the maze, unaware of the danger lurking behind them in peaceful sleep, with a bruised chin where Vedalbore's fist had landed, rocking his head back violently to call for darkness. They had to knock Skrug out to stop him from attacking the man who killed Hestith.

Whimpering at the front and clutching Yallrick's hand, Veranay was utterly afraid, struggling to see in the perpetual darkness of the cave, which resulted in her scraping her boots on the surface in fear of tripping over a rock or rut again. Her hand still burned from the last spill; the small pieces of gravel and rough rock had torn the skin as she stopped her fall. 'Do any of you have a lantern?' asked Yallrick, holding out his hand without looking back. A bit of whispered mumbling echoed through the cave, with someone rummaging through a pack. She could not see but heard the chimney being removed, then the sound of stone hitting stone, sparks flying until the wick jumped to life, chasing away the ominous feeling that so pressed on her with its dark nature. Yallrick took hold of the handle, and it swung by her briefly. *So bright,* she thought for an instant.

They travelled through the chamber for some time, and Veranay noticed the walls had changed, turned from rough and jagged edges to a smooth surface with ancient symbols carved into it. She glided her finger over the surface; it reminded her of the granite blocks her father worked with after they were polished, except these had a glimmer to them. 'What is this?' she asked, pulling Yallrick back.

The men slowed behind her, and Yallrick saw the look in their faces. He wiped his finger over the surface, ridding it of dust and sediment that had accumulated over time, revealing the golden shimmer underneath, shining almost red in the flame's face from the lantern so close. 'A very long time ago, our brother dwarves called this cave home. Mined it for generations before the orcs took over the forest and drove our people out, killing most of them. Some fled the onslaught of the orcs and made it to the Chimna Mountains, where they built Chinnai, as you know it, but our hearts always called this home. With the orcs, they brought in other beasts — beasts best not described, for they are vile and dangerous, and we have come for them to fight the dragon that hunts us. We are here for the manticore. If they still live, then they are beyond those doors.'

She jerked her head up to his and asked, 'Will they not attack us as well?'

'Aye, they might. But I think they will attack the biggest threat first.'

She didn't like the plan, but there was no better one. From behind, she heard Skrug's voice roar angrily. 'Put me down! I will *kill* that bastard!'

'Shh! Quiet, Skrug! That's an order!' shouted Yallrick. 'We will do just that, but let's be smart about it, eh?'

A mighty roar from deeper in the cave shook the ground. The beast was getting closer. 'We have to get those doors open. In there, we stand a chance. Hurry!' Skrug had his suspenders off again, ready for a fight, but followed Yallrick's command and ran after them to the door. 'Yantore, Vedalbore, the release should be to the right if I recall the tales well. There should be a latch to move the stone wall.'

The solid steel door flowed with patterns of gold, and Veranay couldn't help but think of how she and her father had suffered for scraps when all this just sat here.

The two dwarves jogged over with the lantern, breaking old cobwebs and chasing the spiders away from the wall. In between the scattering critters, Vedalbore followed the engravings and reached for a lion's head protruding from the wall, closing his eyes as he pushed his fingers into its mouth. A soft click sounded and a sliver of the wall jumped open, running all the way to the top. Yantore was already at the sliver and stuck the blade of his axe into the thin groove to get a better hold, wiggling it to move the wall further apart. The maniacal laughter sounded not far away now. 'Move it!' said Vedalbore, as he shoved his axe in as well, while the rest of the men stood with weapons ready, covering Veranay behind them.

The wall finally moved away, and Vedalbore and Yantore grabbed the thick chain, pulling it with all their power to move the door.

'Kill the light!' shouted a dwarf from somewhere in front of her. She was unsure who it was. Soon after, the light was dead, and the darkness was so much more oppressive than she remembered it to be. Old air, musty and stale, rushed over them from behind, and they hastened into the unknown. They could hear the footsteps calmly drawing closer, echoing off the golden walls just outside the door. The chamber they entered was vast, filled with piles of bones, and stank profusely, getting worse the deeper they went.

Hasgrem picked up an old axe and shield still attached to the arms that carried them, shaking them off to clatter on the ground. 'Thanks for nothing, Pappy.'

Yantore slapped him over the head and whispered, 'He's so old, he might have made that. And stop making so much noise!'

Gigantic pillars spread out over the chamber as far as they could see in the dark, their sight slowly getting better with time. In the far corner to the left, it looked like there was a second level, with an archway, the corridor stretching beyond their sight to the right.

Cowering behind a pile of old bones, they watched the man step through the door, dusting himself off before walking closer.

His voice bounced off the walls, making it hard to hear. 'I am

Khellar the bonded, Kingsguard to the king of Terenore, and you do not want me against you. I plead with you now. Hand over what I seek, and I will let you go. Don't be foolish. We all know what will happen here today.'

Yallrick had moved to another pile and shouted, 'Oh yeah? What will that be?' He looked to his men and made a few hand signals that Veranay could not make out.

They scattered in various directions, and Vedalbore turned to her as the last dwarf there and whispered, 'Apologies, girl.' He scooped up a heap of bones at the bottom of the pile and said, 'Get in as far as ya can, and don't move. We'll get ya when it's done.'

She eyed him for a bit before swallowing her pride, and wormed her way in under the bones, clutching her nose for the smell as Vedalbore dropped the rest over her. Half a skull lay facing her with its jaw hanging slack, its hollow eye socket staring deep into her while a bony hand caressed her head.

Khellar laughed at the question and stated, 'There will be a slaughter here. None of you will walk out.'

From his right, a dwarf charged out, swinging his axe as he shouted, 'I piss on yer grave, ya beardless wanker!' The blade sliced past Khellar's head and chest as he jumped back, returning with a menacing blow to Skrug's chest, skidding the dwarf over the floor and into a pillar. More dwarves charged out from behind their cover, with Yallrick in the lead. His stomach churned and his fears were answered as the man veered, stamping his massive claws on the ground and shaking the earth with sparks flying from his talons.

The dragon suddenly careened to the left from a heavy impact as a manticore crashed into its side, ripping talons through the dragon's thick scales and lancing with its venomous tail, trying to find a soft spot for the poison to enter. A loud roar reverberated through the chamber from the right, moments before another manticore crashed into the dragon. Twice the size of a male lion, and twice as strong, they flew with leathery wings and a whipping tail, a nasty spike at the end with deadly venom, hunting for a victim. There was nothing pretty about them.

They were ugly beasts, with twisted, snarling snouts and gigantic fangs. Piercing shrieks sounded as they attacked, and the dwarves used this chance, rushing in to chop at the beast. They clambered on it while it was in its throes, avoiding the manticores as best they could. Yallrick was right in his thinking. The only problem was they would still need to fight the one left standing.

Fire exploded from the dragon's mouth as it whipped its head around to burn everything to a cinder while it clawed at the infuriating manticores. A blade bit into the top of its head, spraying blood over the dwarf Skrug. The dragon lurched forward and crashed into the pillars, splitting the columns and throwing the dwarves from him.

Through the holes and gaps of the skeletons, Veranay watched and sobbed for her new friends, knowing so many were getting injured to protect her. The earth quaked with another hit from the dragon, the pillar buckling, and she watched a boulder get dislodged from up high to flatten a dwarf, but could not see who it was. 'No!' she cried, jolting from the shock, the bones moving and tumbling off the pile like an avalanche of the dead. An ear-splitting cry sounded, and in between the flashes of fire, she saw the dragon tear one manticore in half, throwing its writhing body to the ground before clawing at the other while the dwarves loosed short arrow bolts into the beast. She desperately wanted to stop this, but what could she do? She and her new dagger...

Veranay recognised the dwarf clambering on the dragon's neck to its face, using its scales and his dagger for grip. *Skrug is relentless when he's angry; he won't stop until one of them dies,* she thought.

The surviving manticore drove its poisonous tail into the folds under the dragon's front leg, piercing scale and flesh, releasing some of its venom before the dragon lashed out and caught it with its fangs, crushing its wings and tearing the tail off — leaving it to dangle from its chest — with bone-splintering power, casting the body aside. Fire rained down on the furry creature, roasting it alive at their feet. Never had she heard the wailing of a beast such as this, sounding hollow and despairing. Another dwarf was close to the dangling tail and yanked it out, draping the thick muscle under his arm as he moved up towards

Skrug.

All went silent suddenly. The beast stopped spewing fire, darkening the room to where Veranay could not see what was happening. *No! No more dying for me!* She wormed out from under the pile of bones and ran.

'Enough!' roared the dragon, its voice thunderous and coarse. 'Sons of Yamlhieer, I praise you for your courage to stand against me, Asagar, but you cannot win. Lay down your arms and step away from this fight.'

Yallrick stood before the beast defiantly, glaring at it as he stormed, 'Ye should know, Asagar! Yamlhieer fought to the death for his people!'

'In other words, shut it, ye smelly, brain-rotted gutter rat!' shouted Skrug as he drove the stinger of the manticore's thick tail into the eye of the beast, laughing hysterically while holding on to its scaly brow, being shaken around furiously with fire crawling over the ceiling of the chamber, flames rolling over each other as it spread far and wide. A vicious shake sent both dwarf and tail through the air while the poison ran its course, blinding the dragon's one eye, turning it into a shrivelled-up sack, folding in on itself, dull and dead.

'Veranay? Run, girl! Ye shouldn't be here! Don't look back! Run!' shouted Yallrick as all the dwarves ran in again... And fire was their answer.

No! No more dying for me! Veranay rushed forward and held her dagger up to the dragon's gigantic face, shouting to the beast, 'Stop this! Let them go! I am the one you want!' Asagar jerked his head up to glare at her with his lone eye, a rumbling in his throat that mimicked laughter. Hands shaking, eyes wide, Veranay wet herself, the urine running down her legs uncontrollably.

'No! Run, girl! What are ye doing? We have him just where we want him!' shouted Yallrick from beneath the dragon's claws, flattened to the ground and being slowly squeezed to death by the weight of its limb. Dwarves lay scattered, bleeding and burning all around her, and few were left standing.

'So *you* are the prize I am after, girl,' rumbled the beast, rolling its foot over Yallrick's chest, crushing him slowly. The dwarven leader screamed in pain, while the rest were unsure if they should attack. 'Save your friends, or watch them die. What's it going to be?'

No one dies for me any more...

Blood ran out of Yallrick's mouth, deep gashes lining his shoulder while the beast's head hovered before her, dripping fire to the cold floor. The beast pushed down on Yallrick's chest until he couldn't breathe anymore. Veranay could see him gasping for air. 'No!' The dwarves rushed in with weapons raised. Time slowed for her. All around her, she saw the suffering they'd endured. Hasgrem knelt over Yantore's body, screaming as he sobbed. Older Vedalbore had nasty burns covering the left side of his chest and arm, his face a swollen mass, yet he fought on. She did not see Skrug and feared for the worst: that he lay somewhere, dying alone. A trail of blood led to another dwarf, who sat propped up against a pillar some distance away, ragged breaths escaping him as he clutched a wound, heavy and thick across his chest. *No more dying for me...*

She saw her father standing before her again, the sword flashing up while she stood hopelessly trapped in the overcrowded cage, screaming for them to stop. Her blood boiled, her skin rippling with enjoyment as a supernatural force took over, bleeding out of her in pulses of chaotic energy. She focused on the beast, seeing it and it alone. Everything else dropped away into darkness; then a bright light rushed out of her, shaking the earth in waves of power, pulsing through the hall, and forming great cracks in the floor around her. She could hear nothing, her ears bleeding and hurting as the chaos tore from her a legion of hate and hurt. The power consumed her utterly, drawing deep from her well until she had nothing left to give. Cold, hard stone rushed to meet her face, and darkness was born.

* * *

Ragian sat by the large cataract with eyes closed, listening to the rush of water, the power it held as it crashed down on the rocks far below; and for a moment, he wished he were those rocks. He deserved it, didn't he? *Alyssa would not love me if she knew what I have done...*

The spray of water wet his clothes, making his tunic stick to his chest, cooling him down during the increasingly hot day. A soft tug on his wet pants made him blink the water from his eyes, to see a young elf boy with a plate of food standing back so the water did not ruin it. *Who would do this to me? Who would offer me food when I deserve the whip?*

His unintentional scowl made the boy uncomfortable; he could see it in his body language. The nervous glances over his shoulder, looking for backup, the twitching hands and feet, the licking of lips. He softened his scowl, squeezing his eyes shut for a moment, and relaxed. 'Is this for me?' he asked with a smile, pointing to the plate of food, then to his chest.

The boy smiled and handed it over, quickly scrambling away to the safety of his home, where an old elf waved with a pipe in his hand, blowing smoke clouds into the air. He had not expected the elves to be so normal. He honestly didn't know what to expect, though. Aside from the strange nature of living in the trees, there was little that separated them from humans. The folklore of their magical feminine wiles and unsurpassed beauty seemed almost mythical now. Sure, he had seen some of their women that made him look twice, even thrice, but no more so than his Alyssa. Their true beauty, he decided, lay in their language, which flowed with a certain grace from their lips, inviting a certain sexual attention afforded to them. Of course, they didn't know this, because they spoke the same way, but a foreigner, an outsider, struggled to resist their tongue. He waved back to the old elf, bowing slightly to show his gratitude, then stuck a piece of the stew-covered bread in his mouth, enjoying the rich flavours. Their generosity astounded him. Thinking back to his days in Terenore, no one would have looked favourably upon an outsider like this. He couldn't even imagine what would happen if an elf ventured into the city and asked for some food, even if they were ready to pay for it handsomely, with coin in hand. *The pit would have had another victim. That's what would have happened,* he thought.

The peaceful street and soft-spoken elves in the market made his mind wander as he leaned against a great tree, filling his belly with their generosity, until the sound of horses broke his meditation. A squadron of their guards, led by Prince Valheim, thundered past the market to cross over the bridge and pass under the archway, kicking up a cloud of dust in their wake. Scooping the last bits of stew with the bread, he shoved it in his mouth and rinsed the plate in the waterfall's rush before running over to the old elf's home. The old elf wasn't in his chair anymore. He glanced around, then left the plate on the outside table and dashed from the area, running for the woods after Prince Valheim.

The forest had a nasty smell to it today, that of burning wet logs and rotten fish. He would need to run fast to catch up with the horses, and so he did, avoiding flying at all costs. They would see him coming a mile away if he soared over the treetops. The more he ran, the more he heard the distinct metal sound of swords clashing, the chaotic din of battle. Horses neighed and roared, stamping their feet, and he knew they were kicking violently at whoever they were in battle with. *Must be Turneroth's scouts,* he thought. In between the rushing trees swishing past at speed, he saw movement up ahead, the group of elves fighting from their horses, harrying figures on foot.

Ragian dashed over boulders and ran towards them, the smell growing more intense the closer he got; then he saw they were engaged with big hairy orcs, not Turneroth's men. He jumped for an orc that ran up to Valheim's horse from the rear, and tackled it to the ground, wrestling with it to get the sword out of the creature's hands. The orc thundered a right fist into his face and roared, spittle flying into him, leaving a reek that made him want to gag. He rained down punch after punch in return, using his elbows to crush the orc's thick skull, and screamed as the orc latched on to his elbow with its rotten teeth, tearing at his flesh and ripping out a chunk to swallow it with a grin. 'Bastard!' His finger found an eye, and he dug deep.

'Move!' came a shout next to him, and he jumped to his left as a horse's hoof rushed by his head, missing him by mere inches to trample the orc's face. He looked around, bleeding from his nose. At least ten orcs lay dead that he could see, with one horse dying on the ground, its eyes fearful and breathing ragged, confused about why it couldn't get back up. Other elves were standing around the animal, helping one of their own out from under it. It had taken the stab of a sword instead of its rider. A hand suddenly appeared before him, extended to help him up. Valheim pulled him to his feet and spoke as they walked to the horse. 'Thank you. I did not see the one creeping in from behind.'

Ragian nodded, watching the rider of the horse lean over the animal, stroking its neck gently as he spoke to it. 'What's he doing?'

Valheim glanced at him and whispered, 'The horse sacrificed himself for the safety of his rider. He is giving thanks and wishing it a safe journey to the meadows. It is a noble gesture and the least he can do.'

Ragian didn't know why, but this saddened him deeply. He'd had many horses before, and many had died, yet he never took the time to thank them for their service. Valheim stepped away, and he followed the prince.

'Bloody orcs,' said the elf prince. 'They grow bolder by the year, trying to gain a foothold in the forest. We have constant skirmishes, and I fear we will have an outright war with them soon. What are you doing here? It was reckless to attack without a weapon. They could've killed you.'

'I couldn't just stand by. I was worried it might be that dragon army, so I followed you.'

'Come, I will give you a ride back to the village,' said Valheim as he mounted the horse and extended his hand. 'My father will heal your arm. We can't leave that untreated. Those orcs are filthy creatures, a stain on this earth.'

'Yes, I smelled them. What are they? I mean, where did they come from?'

'That is a long and sad story, my friend. One I will not tell you now.' Ragian nodded his understanding, even though it gnawed at him, not getting an answer.

The ride was uncomfortable. With every footfall, the prince pressed on his back and breathed in his neck. The sensation made him squirm, but he clenched his teeth until they reached the Evertree in the village and dismounted, just too glad the ride was a short one. He wasn't sure how much further he could endure. The long walk up to the hall had been quiet, both men unsure of what to say to each other, and rather waited it out in silence. Valheim pushed on the hall's doors and strode through, with Ragian following behind. A strange smelling scent drifted through the rooms, irritating Ragian's nose, and he sneezed.

'Apologies, it's the Phelohrundia we burn. It's supposed to relax you, but some can't stomach it, me included. Come, he must be in his study. I fear the older we get, the more wisdom we seek. You may follow.'

They turned down a corridor from the hall, the wooden floors creaking with their weight as they passed a room on the right, modest with no doors, then another on the left that was scarcely better, which he assumed was the king's sleeping quarters. At the end of the hall, they entered through a door to a chamber that opened up somewhat, with stairs leading to a new level and books all around. Swinging silently in a hammock, reading a thick, red leather-bound book, King Elyon peered out from beyond the material and clambered out, struggling to get out with a chuckle.

Finally out of the contraption, Elyon looked back as though angry and said, 'These infernal things are so comfortable. I just can't help myself. Apologies, Ragian.'

'Please, King Elyon, I don't think I'd have been strong enough to get out of that thing for anyone,' Ragian jested, and cleared his throat when he saw the king's faint smile.

'Father, Ragian got injured in the orc raid protecting me. I assured him you would look at his wound.'

Elyon took hold of Ragian's arm to inspect it, turning it in his hands, then mumbled, 'My son, when are you going to learn to master our gifts? You yourself could have healed him and saved him this time in pain.'

The prince lowered his gaze to the floor and said, 'Yes, Father. I apologise for my ineptitude.'

'Hold still,' demanded Elyon while he lay his hands over the arm, mumbling something under his breath.

The Kingsguard gritted his teeth as heat spread from the elf king, warming his arm drastically. He could feel something drain from his arm and saw it drip into Elyon's hand, a thickened black sludge. Valheim quickly retrieved a rag that covered an old book and handed it to the king, who wiped the sludge from his hand. He folded the rag and handed it back to the prince. 'The filth of the orcs. It would've infected you. Not to worry now, it should be all gone. But you need to rest. You will be tired tonight.'

'Thank you, King Elyon.' Ragian bowed stiffly.

'Excuse me, Ragian, I have matters to attend to. These orcs leave little room for delight these days,' said King Elyon with a curt nod.

'Of course, I understand. I will be in my quarters.' He turned briskly around and headed from the hall.

Once out of earshot, the king grabbed Valheim's arm and said, 'Watch him. There is something strange inside him, something powerful.'

* * *

They breached the dark clouds, and over the horizon loomed the mountain covered with smog, thunder roiling overhead. Arms crossed, Khanaseri watched from the foredeck while they glided closer and descended gradually.

Garidan appeared next to him. 'Here,' he said, handing a breathing apparatus to the warlock, and showed him how to use it. 'The air down there is nearly unbreathable. This will help.'

'Let me guess,' replied the warlock with a sneer, glimpsing the rust stains on the device, 'another item they don't know how to reproduce. I'm amazed these people know how to breed... Knowledge hoarding. Never heard of anything more ridiculous.'

'I agree, but just take it. There's no use in arguing about their way of life. They are what they are. Will the Djak-tas be up to the task?'

They both turned to the four sitting ever so quietly, as they had done since the start of the flight. 'I have given them the knowledge to do what is needed, and they have trained some. They showed promise. Say, how big are those spiders, really?' he asked with a raised brow.

'You saw the wyrm; use your imagination...'

Khanaseri shivered, a ripple running through his body as he shook off the feeling. 'Never did like those eight-legged fiends.'

Garidan chuckled. 'Really? That's what you're afraid of? I didn't—'

'What?'

'Nothing. I just didn't peg you as being afraid of something like spiders.'

The helvedron shook as the legs pushed into the ground, interrupting their conversation and nearly rocking them off their feet, whereupon an officer swung the door open for them to disembark. Khanaseri was the first to step off, taking a deep breath of the ash-ridden air, and winced at the pungent smell even through the breather. 'Keep close and use no magic. We have to conserve our energy for when we reach the wyrms.'

Hoods drawn over their heads to ward off some of the constantly falling ash, they made their way up the mountain, while Naghita jogged ahead to find the trail they'd used before, guiding them over the smouldering terrain. A wide, jagged fissure scored their path, with molten lava flowing a few feet below where they stood, boiling and bubbling, glowing an angry red. One by one they leapt across, following the Tark woman. 'It should be up ahead, near that boulder. Keep your eyes peeled for a narrow opening near to the ground,' shouted Naghita.

They combed the area, looking for the entrance, moving rocks with their feet, thinking it might have been closed by the constant rumblings and tremors. Khanaseri was searching the ground, leaning down near a massive boulder, a wall of old solidified lava on its side, when Arundhàbu walked up to him and asked, 'Why are we here?'

The warlock stopped in his search and stood, confused. 'You're jesting, right?'

'No, I mean... Why do we three Tarks need to be here? What can we offer? You have soldiers, you have the mages. Why us as well?'

'Ah. Garidan told me your wife is of shaman bloodline. He told me what her mother did to pull the wyrms to her. I'm relying on Naghita to do the same. Be the bait, as they say. You and Borka will be by her side, with all the soldiers at your disposal. Once it grows hot enough, the wyrms will calm, as you saw. She knows this. Has she not spoken to you?'

'No, she neglected to mention this to me.' Arundhàbu glared up at his wife, waiting to catch her gaze, and locked stares with her for a moment before she walked away.

'Over here!' shouted a soldier, using the plank he carried to widen the hole, scraping out the earth. One by one, they slithered through the gap to drop stealthily into the musty chamber. Khanaseri squirmed through the hole, feeling for the bottom as he shimmied down, but he couldn't reach and dropped the last bit. He blew dust from his nose and wiped his face, trying to see in the gloomy chamber, but the faint light that shone through the hole, disappeared when the last soldier slid through headfirst — probably thinking it the better method — and dropped to the ground with a loud rattle and clangour coming from his pack.

'Quiet!' demanded Naghita, clutching her side where the wound had healed, the painful memory making the scar itch. 'Be silent! You do not want to wake them.' He quickly stifled the loose items, while all of them silently searched the chamber for any signs of movement. Armed with knowing that these stretagor behaved like a hive mind, they could not afford for any of them to be forewarned of their presence, as the entire cluster would come charging down on them. Thick webs hung from the ceiling, spanning across the room to various points, any of which could alert the spiders if touched. 'This is new,' Naghita whispered to Tulvar, who stared at them with a bewildered gaze, too afraid to say anything back.

Slow and steady, they crawled through the open sections between the webs, carefully placing their bodies. *Not far now until we reach the long bridge. So far, so good,* thought Arundhàbu, keeping his eyes on the walls he knew could crumble at any moment with the arachnids beneath their shells. He could see, past the wide bulk of Borka, the chamber opening up, and he breathed a sigh of relief.

'I'm stuck! Help!' came shouts from a soldier at their back, caught by the web as he bent down to step underneath it. His pack was shaking the thick white strands.

'Stop moving, you fool!' shouted Naghita from the front, already standing on the bridge a distance away. 'Cut him loose! Carefully.' Two soldiers behind the stuck Ageian started getting anxious, pushing and shoving to get by him, when they heard a clicking noise reverberate from the walls. 'No! Stop!' shouted Naghita again in a whisper, but fear grabbed hold of them. Swords in hand, they cut the web and shoved the stuck soldier out of the way, sending him to the ground as the walls behind them burst open with hundreds of gigantic, hairy legs squirming out from the cracks and holes. The soldier on the ground tried to get up, but soon found himself pinned under the belly of a stretagor, fangs bearing down on him. His screams ended swiftly.

'Run!' shouted the warlock, feeling angst as he watched the spiders run along the side of the bridge, trying to cut them off. Arrows flew from the soldier's bows, striking down the smaller arachnids with ease, but the bigger ones were tough, their hides strong and resilient. They fought through the onslaught of spiders, chopping limbs with swords and axes, halberds singing their songs as blue blood sprayed. Two more soldiers perished on the bridge, being dragged from the heights and feasted upon. They hung far down on the spiders' webs, enclosed in silky strands by the ravenous arachnids. Reaching the far side of the bridge, Garidan pressed his hand against the door, watching it grind open on the stone floor and ran through with a big enough gap, then waited for the rest to join him. The door closed with a solid crash, severing the back legs of a spider trying to push through. It flopped on the floor in a craze, dragging its body towards the warlock with fangs dripping venom. Blue light followed the thrown axe, cleaving the spider in half, spilling its guts to the floor.

'Shit! Ugh! Damn spiders!' shouted Khanaseri in disgust. 'How much further?'

'Not long now,' replied Garidan. 'We need to get past the corridor of traps, and then we're at the monolith that will take us to the lair.'

'Traps?'

'Yeah, but we got these to get around them right quick,' Borka said, and pointed to the long planks that some soldiers carried. 'Last time was no fun.'

*　*　*

It didn't take them long to get to the laboratory at all; the planks had worked like a charm. They filed out into the room, waiting for Garidan to make his way to the monolith in the corner while Tulvar strayed, walking around, gawking at every piece of equipment and scrap of parchment, wanting to stuff it all down his pockets to take with him and study back home.

'Are you all ready for this?' Khanaseri asked. 'All of you know what's expected of you now.' He saw the blank stares on their faces, and wasn't sure if it was fear or confusion. 'Blacksmith, you and Borka have command of these soldiers. Protect Naghita with everything you have.' The Ageian soldiers gritted their teeth and sneered at the thought of being commanded by a Tark. 'Do we have a problem, soldier?' Khanaseri asked, seeing one spit at Arundhàbu's feet.

'I don't work for these—'

The wooden cabinet fixed to the back wall crashed to the floor as the soldier slammed into it, his face pressed to the rocky wall by the warlock's big hand.

'I have a real problem with disobedience and a lack of respect. How about you work on both real quick-like?' The rest of the soldiers jumped back, shocked at the man's aggression. 'What do you say?'

'Sorry, sir. It won't happen again.'

'That's better.' Khanaseri shoved the soldier and turned. 'Tulvar, remember. You stay at Garidan's side. Nothing! And I mean, *nothing* can happen to that device. Garidan, you said you could transport it with us. Make sure it's high up somewhere, away from the action.' Garidan nodded. 'Djak-tas...you're with me. Each one of you will create your endpoint to join and form the complete structure. Be sure not to falter with the spell. This world relies on your strength and abilities now.'

'Er, Khan,' whispered Naghita as she stepped forward.

'Yes, dear. You have something to share?' said Khanaseri, ignoring the glare he got from Arundhàbu.

'I'm not sure I can do this. I mean, I'll try, but I can't promise anything. My mother taught me this dance a long time ago, when I was still a child hard of hearing.'

Khanaseri sighed, his hands on his hips as he stared at the ceiling. 'I won't lie to you and tell you something I know very little about, but I can tell you this. Shamans are a powerful element. Where most wait for the gods to speak to them, shamans speak to the gods, bend them to their will. Know who you need to communicate with and be assertive. I... We believe in you.'

She nodded nervously, shaking her hands and legs, cracking her neck. 'Ready.'

Garidan laid his hand against the stone monolith, waiting for the signs on his arm to respond, waiting for the burn to start with the shifting of the letters – and surely it did. Grinding his teeth, he worked through the pain so he could think clearly, then laid the mountain out in his head, pinpointing the location he wanted to send them. The metal rings spun faster and faster, glowing with a bright light as the hum of the device deafened them.

Khanaseri stared into the light through the slits between his fingers, trying to understand how this machine could do what it did. Faint lines appeared, getting clearer, creating an image in the brightness until those lines blurred with the reality of the glowing red rocks and blackened walls...and suddenly there they were. The heat took their breath away, and the height their courage. The soldiers squirmed near the edge, looking down at the wyrms floating in the magma below.

'You chose this spot well, Garidan. It will be hard for them to reach,' said Khanaseri with a smile. Those around him leaned over and vomited. 'Takes some getting used to, this form of travel. It's similar to me creating a portal. The first few times are rough.' The jagged rock-formed ceiling dipped and rose at random, with a few large natural rock pillars running all the way to the bottom. To their left, they could pick their way down carefully, dropping a few feet to reach the next level. Down and down they went, towards the danger lurking at the bottom, creeping closer to the magma pools and gigantic wyrms.

Chapter Eleven

Khanaseri pointed to the Djak-tas' assigned locations and said, 'Remember what I taught you, and you will survive this.'

'Yes, warlock Djak-ta,' they answered in revered unison. 'We will not disappoint you.'

'We'll see about that. Go.' From the shadows of a gigantic column, they waited for the Djak-tas to make their way to their destinations, carefully climbing over the hot, jagged rocks, avoiding the hundreds of wyrms in the lair.

A loud roar from a wyrm on the far side shook the chamber, dislodging boulders from their precarious positions, tumbling them down the walls, splintering them and splashing large splatters of magma onto the boiling pool's banks. Its huge maw created terrible vibrations through the earth, curling its head up as it stretched out like a wolf howling for its pack. More answered the call, lifting their heads in response to the booming roar, sending more shards of rocks falling from up high into the molten pools.

'That one seems in trouble, warlock. Shouldn't we help?' whispered Naghita, and pointed to the edge of the glowing pool on the far left, where Coralay scrambled up the collapsing side. The roars were causing the edges to break apart, widening the pool as boulders and earth caved in. She was on all fours, frantically looking for help as she clawed at the smouldering rocks.

Khanaseri stood, considering the options, seeing the other three reach their positions around the chamber. *There's always one,* he thought. *There're no trees here to help you now...*

'Do something, warlock!' demanded Arundhàbu, stepping forward as he prepared to run to Coralay's aid. Slipping further down, she was only a few feet from the magma now, her boots smouldering from the heat. 'Warlock!'

'Agh! Fine.' He closed his eyes and chanted softly. The earth below her rose steadily, levelling out until she could clamber back up to a flatter section. They could not see her face behind the white porcelain mask, but they knew the relief and angst that was hidden there as she sat cradling her legs, her chest heaving back forth. The warlock locked gazes with Arundhàbu and turned away, shaking his head. 'Naghita, get ready.'

Coralay gathered herself and got to her feet, shaking off her near-death experience, wanting to climb into bed and sob the entire day...but she had a job to do. People were depending on her. She took a deep breath and watched Khanaseri creep towards his goal, while the rest moved away to the left. He grabbed the rocky ledge up high and pulled himself up to a platform, where he disappeared into the darkness as he stepped back into the shadows. Coralay started her chant, glimpsing the other Djak-ta standing with outspread arms, mumbling the words over and over.

Moving swiftly down a broad section of the lair, Naghita felt her confidence slip. 'Husband, I don't know if I can do this,' she whispered.

Arundhàbu turned to Borka and gestured to the soldiers. 'Arrange them. You know better than I all the battle tactics. Like you said, I am a blacksmith, not a soldier, or a gladiator.' Borka nodded and whispered orders to the men, while the blacksmith spoke to Naghita. 'I agree with Khanaseri. You can do this; your mother taught you well.'

She steeled herself and cocked her head left and right, sharp cracks sounding from it before releasing a long breath. Naghita slid the small hand drum around her waist and began her dance, shaking, drumming, trying to focus, but found it awkward and shameful, feeling the stares of the soldiers, feeling their hidden laughter. She felt hot flushes rushing through her body, and it was not because of the magma pools. She stopped, saying, 'I can't. This is stupid!'

'Normally, I would agree with you, but not now. You can do it! You have to!' said Arundhàbu, echoed by the voices of the soldiers and Borka whispering to her.

She sighed and closed her eyes. *Time to strike a bargain with a god...* She moved her feet to a wider stance, her arms swinging around her head and down, her fingers calling out to something far beyond the realm of which the surrounding men could see. The awkward and shameful dance became something to behold. Her mind drifted away, her body becoming a conduit, connecting her to the gods as she drummed and danced. Around her there was a flurry of activity when the closest wraethers swung to her, roaring loudly, but she didn't listen or care about that. She was nearing the god's location, feeling his presence the more she sang. Yet she did not know what was being said. An explosion of new worlds opened up to her, the worlds of the gods and where they dwelled. Hunting for the one she needed, she sped across the realms, a star guided through the cosmos.

'To the right!' shouted Borka, hacking with his poleaxe to chop off a wyrm's leg. Soldiers spread around the oblivious Naghita, guiding her away to keep her safe. They had stirred the hornet's nest... Wyrms from all over the vast chamber were now drawn towards her, getting closer with every heartbeat.

An obscure figure, blurred and vague as if standing behind a dirty pane of glass, appeared to her and her alone. Naghita opened her mouth to speak, the sounds coming out raspy and strange, a voice she did not know in a language she did not understand, yet she felt like she was communicating with the figure. He shifted and reappeared, the bladelike leg of a wraether cutting through him with no effect. Seemingly annoyed at the ignorant creature's lack of respect for intruding on their conversation, the figure turned and uttered a single word, and the wraether staggered back as if dealt a harsh blow, swinging its head from side to side, roaring pains unseen by the soldiers. It crashed into the pool, slowly submerging into the boiling red.

'What do you want from me?' she finally heard and understood. *With his power, we can be rid of them instantly. Why not kill them all?*

'I know you. You are Gheylig Mallus, the god of the animal world.' The figure nodded. 'I plead with you. Kill them all. They are an abomination. A malformed creation that should not be. Be done with it and destroy them all.'

'I cannot and will not intervene. You brought this upon yourselves. It is not for us to repair your mess!'

His voice sounded like a scream in her head. She felt her face contort in unimaginable ways, her mouth dry and tearing the sides open. A soldier to her right rose from the ground, skewered by a wyrm's leg, his lifeless corpse thrown back and forth as the creature kept fighting with him dangling on the leg. 'Then call them! Call these wyrms, these fucking wraethers, so we might deal with them ourselves if you are too much of a coward to do anything.'

His answer was short and stern. 'No.'

'*What?*' Naghita reeled, her confidence fluttering away while the figure waned, his body growing transparent and vague. A flush of angst rocked her like a hammer blow. 'No! Wait! I'll do anything!'

'Take up your mother's burden. We need a conduit to the world. An emissary, if you will.'

'You mean a *plaything?*' Naghita asked, her voice cold.

'Sometimes, I suppose.' The face flickered and turned to the onslaught of the wyrms on the surrounding soldiers, her husband in the mix, brandishing a sword from a fallen soldier. Arundhàbu bled from wounds on his face and legs, standing before her as a protector. More wraethers approached. Soon, they would be overrun. 'Time is running out,' the god mocked. Borka was on his knee, the old injury to his leg forcing him to the ground while he staved off a gigantic scything leg, swinging the poleaxe to clash against its hard armour.

'Fine! You have your plaything. Now call these bastard things!'

Not a word further, and Gheylig Mallus vanished. The earth rumbled and quaked. Naghita turned to the warlock and shouted, 'Get ready! They're coming!' The cage construction was already under way, with the magical cornerstones of the Djak-tas in place. The heat was building, with the outline of red barely visible over the glowing magma. Wyrms burst through the walls of the chamber, dangerously hurling boulders around.

Hannus jumped for his life as a boulder crashed into the earth where he'd stood only moments before, flinging himself over the jagged, scalding rock floor. He grabbed at the rushing sharp edges, getting cut and burnt, and latched on to a solid piece jutting out from the rest, stopping himself from going into the fiery pool. The cornerstone wavered and waned as Hannus lost his focus. He quickly jumped up and grabbed at the magical elements, forcing them back together. Above him, the cage fell apart, the magic crumbling. Veins on his neck bulged incredulously with the effort to take control of the magic in disarray, and he screamed, forcing the structure back into place as a gigantic wyrm bore down on him, its mouth crunching rock when its beady eyes caught sight of him.

Khanaseri reached out to cast another spell, but it happened too fast. The wyrm was on top of the Djak-ta. He took over the construction of the cornerstone as the earth disappeared where Hannus had stood, not even a splatter of blood to mark his former existence. Instantly, the strain of the magic doubled on his shoulders, and for a moment, his knees buckled. *We can't lose any more Djak-ta.* To the right, on the main path, he watched the group of soldiers and the three Tarks retreat, with the hundreds of wyrms coming at them from all directions. He wanted to help them. Wanted to put a barrier around them, but he was at his limit, and he knew it. Had they underestimated the number of wyrms there would be? Maybe. Waves of power coursed from them, the construction nearing its end, building the heat to ridiculous levels above the magma pools. *I'm sorry, I can't save all of you.* So few of the soldiers remained, and the Tarks were tiring.

'To your left!' Arundhàbu shouted before a wraether devoured a soldier and severed the head of another. 'Run!' When he looked up, he stopped, instinctively putting out his arm to protect Naghita, seeing no way out. They were surrounded. 'Agh! Come on! You filthy soil sampler!' Bladelike legs raced over the hard earth and rock towards their prize. Borka swung his poleaxe, snapping legs cleanly from their joints, forcing the front-runners back. Naghita stabbed the softer underbelly with her long knives, spilling the creatures' blue-green blood over herself. Soldiers sliced and stabbed, fighting to the death with the beasts. A moment of reprieve occurred with one wyrm colliding with another, causing an avalanche of falling wyrms.

'Hold out just a little longer!' shouted Khanaseri, seeing them with their backs against each other; only five of them left, and Borka was at his end, his leg folding in under him with every swing of the poleaxe. Seven wyrms stormed them from different angles. Trying his best to cast another spell, the warlock felt his fingers burn with magical malice, turning black at the ends, the darkness spreading as he continued. The cage construction was losing shape without his full focus.

He remembered the lesson Beuneth once gave him.

'*Magic bites!' she said, whirling the whip round herself at blistering speeds. 'Mistreat the Source, and it will punish you. Do not reach beyond your limits!'*

'*How will I know where my limit is?' asked Khanaseri, stroking his long, dark hair out of his face as he leaned on the weapons rack.*

'*Oh, you will know. I think a demonstration is in order.' She walked to a crate with some glass jars, took them out before turning the crate over, placing a few empty jars on the base. Beuneth glided by him with her graceful form, another crate dangling in her hands. She placed the remaining jars on its base and poured water from her canteen in them. 'Stand in the middle...good. Now, I want you to move those empty jars on that crate and stack them on top of each other—'*

'*That's easy,' he interrupted. The whip lashed him on the shoulder, tearing a red gash into his skin with the leather tip. 'Argh! Shit! What was that for?' he asked, rubbing the gash.*

'*Interrupting! I want you to move those empty jars on that crate and stack them on top of each other, while changing the water in these to something else: wax or blood. Doesn't matter.'*

At first, he thought it was going well, moving the first jar on top of the other, while the colour of the water changed slightly to a milky red. Then, stacking the second took a mental bite out of him, making him struggle. The more he fought, the harder it became. Red in the face, he strained at the task, wanting to scream as it felt like his body was being torn in two.

'Enough!' shouted Beuneth.

'No! I can do this!' The more he focused, the more painful it got. He knew he should be able to do it, as if the power was just out of reach, but it was truly out of reach. Blood seeped down his face, his skin and body trying to tear asunder, not knowing which way to go.

A punch to his nose dropped his focus completely, sending his senses into disarray. 'I said enough, you barbaric fool! Look at yourself. Here. Take it.' She handed him a small mirror and laughed at his face while he looked at himself, concerned. His broad face seemed broader, his scalp loose and stretchy, with blood oozing down the tear over his back.

'If I hadn't stopped you, there would be two of you... Well, two smaller versions of you, thank goodness. Magic bites...'

Now here he was, tearing himself apart once again, and there was no one to stop him. *I can do this...* They fought like champions, all of them, not taking no for an answer, and so would he. The cost was high; most would say too high. But this needed to be done. A weight lifted from him, and he saw Coralay straining to take over Hannus' cornerstone, screaming under the pressure. With the momentary respite, his spell took effect, slowing the wyrms down around the group...but it wouldn't be enough.

Suddenly, an explosion of light surrounded the five remaining souls, a beam pulsing up high just before the wyrms collided with them, only to pass straight through to the other side. Again and again the wraethers attacked, their heads going in one way to disappear and re-emerge on the other side in confusion. Khanaseri fell back, grabbing hold of the construction before it was too late. He turned his gaze searchingly to the top of the pit, and in the far left he saw Garidan with his hands on the monolith, blue-white light radiating from his location. *Of course – he has created four doorways around them! We have to hurry; Garidan can't hold them open for long.*

'Let go of one, Coralay, I've got it!' With all his focus on the cage again, it surged in temperature, growing hot to the extreme. The hotter it got, the calmer the wyrms became. The cage construction was complete, linked up between all cornerstones while the Djak-ta made their way back carefully.

Arundhàbu bared his teeth at the wyrms, growling at them in shouts of anger as the doorways around them vanished, getting ready for another attack. But the wyrms turned slowly away, the heat calling for their nature to take over. More and more, the wyrms turned to the cage, crawling to the comfort of beginning their cocooning process. The wyrms headed for the pools, growing slow with the new stage in life drawing closer. While Khanaseri and the Djak-ta finished the spell, the Tarks and the soldiers retreated to the monolith to escape the intense heat.

Strands of web spun from the spinnerets of the wyrms, connecting to the sides and over the pools in the cage, and soon the cocooning started for all. The Djak-tas were dead tired, dropping to the ground to catch their breath, and Khanaseri was in heaps of pain, his blackened hands cracked and bleeding pus from the fissures. They struggled up to the group waiting near the monolith, eager to get away from the incredible heat, and found the Tarks sitting on the ground against the hot wall, sweating profusely while the two remaining Ageian soldiers cradled their legs, their heads low between their knees. Garidan and Tulvar were silent. There was nothing to say. The cave was swelteringly hot. Breathing did not come easily, even with the breather doing its job.

Khanaseri collapsed against the monolith, then to the ground, trying not to use his hands to lower himself. 'Get us out of here, Garidan. That must be all of them.'

'It would be my pleasure.' He reached out to Naghita, waiting for her to take hold, and nodded for the rest to grab on, then placed his hand on the monolith. He had got used to the burning of the letters on his arm, the strange sensation as they crawled over his skin, itching and burning at the same time until they found their new resting places. The light grew bright, and they were gone.

* * *

The wailing old elf's cries resounded throughout Rolldemere in the early hours of the day, waking everyone to a morning of sorrow. Ragian ran outside in his sleepy haze, nearly going over the low railings so high in the trees, and watched Haleth walk from the healer's room, carrying his limp daughter in his arms, the sobbing uncontrollable. They both sank to the floor, their knees weak, and Ragian felt his heart shatter. *What have I done? I'm a monster!* More elves came out to witness, howling for the loss of the youth. He couldn't let this stand. He won't sit idly by for Turneroth to slaughter more innocents. *I'm sorry Alyssa...*

Ragian ran up the tree to the king's hall and pushed upon the doors, stepping in with eyes suddenly darting to him angrily. The king and Valheim jumped up from their seats, drawing their swords as the king shouted, 'What is the meaning of this?'

'Apologies for the intrusion, King Elyon, but you all need to flee from here immediately. I have word on good authority that the Terenoran army is headed here. You cannot withstand their onslaught. It will be an annihilation.'

'This is a day for mourning. Can't you feel the sorrow in the air?' Valheim shouted.

'I'm truly sorry, Prince Valheim, but there will be plenty of mourning if you don't leave this instant. Order the evacuation! Head for New Runswick, immediately!'

'Where are you getting your information? And why wait until now to tell us?' demanded King Elyon.

Ragian moved closer, kept at bay by Valheim's sword waving in his face. 'I know you suspect something of me, and you're right to.' Elyon and Valheim glanced at one another. 'I'm...here to protect you, and we have scant time. Trust me, they *are* coming, and there's nothing you can do!'

'Valheim, lock him up! We don't need his mania today,' roared King Elyon.

A loud but dull whistle sounded, and again, moving fast — a sound

Ragian knew very well. The sound of enormous wings cutting through air at great speeds. 'Shh! Quiet!' he said, pointing up to the sky.

'Don't you shush me!' warned Elyon, but the finger vigorously waved at him to keep quiet. Darkness rolled over Rolldemere, blocking out the sun a wing-beat at a time.

Ragian ran outside and searched the sky, but it had passed over already. A voice in his head called to him. *'He circles. I can feel him.'*

'Who is it, Isaluth? Kingsguard or pure?'

'Kingsguard, yes. Not pure,' came the bestial roar in his head.

'So that hateful Khellar, then?' Ragian wanted to stream a non-stop barrage of curses to the air, but Valheim and Elyon joined him outside, watching the skies.

'No, not Khellar.'

'Then who?'

Isaluth kept quiet then.

'What are you looking for?' demanded King Elyon, eyes glistening with fear.

'I think you know... They have found you. That was a scout, which means *they* are not far behind.'

Valheim swung his arms around. 'What are you two talking about?'

King Elyon stood with mouth agape and pointed to the rising sun. 'That, my boy. We're talking about that.' The beast flew before the sun, banking so the spread of its wings blocked the rays, then turned towards them.

Valheim's heart jumped into his throat, his stomach suddenly loose. Fingers snapped before his eyes to pull him back to them. 'Father, we have to get you out of here!'

'That's what I've been saying! Now, order the evacuation to New Runswick. It's your best option!' exclaimed Ragian. 'I'll hold them off as long as I can.' Before they could say anything else, Ragian pushed over the railing and leapt from the footbridge up high in the trees to rise with forceful gusts as Isaluth. He hovered for a moment before the stunned pair. Valheim had leapt back with sword drawn, while Elyon kept his stern eyes on the slitted pupils of the beast as he spoke.

'I will order the evacuation, but some will stay to give the rest a fighting chance.'

Isaluth turned his gigantic head to the dragon up high and flapped his wings, pushing the king and Valheim back. With the beast's departure, Elyon turned to Valheim and said, 'Order it. We make for the city of Man.'

'Father, I will stay and fight with the men. I will die with honour for our people!'

The slap was fast and harsh. 'You will do as I say! You are to be ruler when I'm gone. That is where our elves need you – by my side. They will need protection on their travels. We are to give it. Understand?'

'Yes, my King. As you command.'

'Good. There will be a lot of frightened elves down there. Sound the alarm and get them ready to run. We will take the route to the east down the mountain. There will be no stopping until we reach the city.'

'Understood, Father.' Valheim ran down the tree, using the railing to slide down lengths at a time.

* * *

Isaluth glided towards the approaching dragon, the sun blinding him slightly until he neared, then saw the yellow scales of the beast, his sombre mood not doing much to get him ready for a fight. But the beast bore down on him, intent on attacking. For the moment, while he was up in the air, he listened to the trees swaying in the wind, birds chirping, and the bugle of an elk sounding somewhere to his right. It probably knew of Turneroth's approach and was warning the others to run. He felt akin to that elk just then, and wished it well.

They collided in a hail of fire, teeth, and talons, ripping and tearing to kill one another.

The yellow dragon forced Isaluth down, pushing him to the ground to crash through branches and boulders, uprooting and felling the ancient trees of the forest. Bestial roars and hissing plagued the area, shaking the earth with their intensity. They rolled to a stop in a flood of destruction, a long path of destroyed forest in their wake with Isaluth now on top. Talons ripped into his side, and the yellow dragon got out from under him. It paced a distance away, felling another tree with a swipe of its tail, then veered suddenly, changing to its human form, and Isaluth backed away, doing the same. 'Xare? What? How? I thought you would never...'

'I had no say in the matter, thanks to you... Why did you leave? The king is furious!'

'He's no *king*! He's a tormentor. A vile and sadistic piece of shit! I'm just sorry it took me this long to do something about it!'

Xare was a tall man, at least a head taller than Ragian, and a good soldier. He stormed over and swung his fists down, missing the dodging Kingsguard, who hit Xare's midsection with a few punches. He grabbed Ragian by the throat, picked him up, and hurled him into a tree, snapping the trunk with a loud crack. 'Turneroth *forced* me to volunteer for the bond. Me and as many were needed to make up three other Kingsguards. And he will do it again when we die!' Xare spoke the words as he landed blows to Ragian's stomach. 'He...still...has...four...more!'

A thunderous uppercut sneaked past his defences and caught him on the chin. Black dots washed over his sight, blinding him as he staggered and dropped to his knees, swinging slightly and shaking his head. 'Whoa. Didn't think you could hit that hard...'

Ragian spat blood to the side and said, 'I can hit harder. Let's stop this nonsense before one of us gets hurt for real.'

Getting to his feet unsteadily, Xare leaned against a tree to catch his breath and stated, 'You don't understand. You never did. My family is not in the past, tucked away far from his reach. My family is *here!*' He pointed to nowhere in particular. 'The squad that has been with me from the beginning.' Then he pointed to Ragian. 'You are my family! They are in his grasp. In his camp! If I don't do this, none of them will make it home!' He stormed again, using the talons on his fingers to swipe at his friend.

The talons tore Ragian's shirt open as he jumped back, narrowly missing his stomach, and again. He dived away and said, 'Do you think this is easy for me? I'm losing my family, and I know it! We can still stop this! I can help you get them out of camp.' Xare lost his balance and fumbled the last swing, ended up in a problematic position under his friend, who then swung his fist down hard against Xare's shoulder from behind, dislocating it.

'Agh, you mangy fucker! Still fighting dirty, I see!'

'It's a fight, Xare. We're not arm wrestling. And I recall you always being the one to play dirty.'

Xare leaned over, his limp left arm hanging down to the ground. He turned his gaze, scanning the forest, chest heaving with every rasping breath, and stealthily clawed some dirt in his hands. Throwing it in Ragian's eyes, he darted towards a tree at full speed, crashing into it with his shoulder and popping it back into place with a scream of pain. 'Son of a bitch! That hurts!'

Ragian rubbed and wiped his eyes, using the hem of his shirt to get rid of the dirt. 'Did you really just throw sand in my eyes like a girl? You sure screamed like one.'

'Ha ha...funny. Always were the funny one, you.'

'Let's stop this before one of us really gets hur—' Breath exploded from his mouth as he hit the ground, a shoulder driven deep into his chest. Xare's knee pinned him to the earth as punch after punch rained down, while he defended his face from the continued attack.

Xare grabbed his hands and started punching Ragian in the face with his own fists while he shouted, 'Why are you hitting yourself? Huh? Why are you hitting yourself?'

With raised brows, Ragian brought up his knee fast. Xare's eyes went wide, and he dropped like a stone to the ground, caressing his fruits and rolling around, little squeals escaping his mouth. 'Dirty, dirty man.' He coughed and struggled for air. 'I think...I'm gonna spit up...my sack... Here it comes...' Vomit spilled from his mouth. He stared at it for a moment, then said, 'Just last night's deer... Phew.'

'I told you we should stop before one of us got hurt.'

Still rolling on the ground, Xare flicked up a hand and squealed, 'You did.'

Ragian got up and reached down to pull his old friend up. 'Come on, Xare, stop this. I could feel you pulling your punches. You want this as little as I do.'

The new Kingsguard slapped Ragian's hand away and carefully pushed up against the tree, caressing his privates with a sigh. *Tell that to ol' Slip.* 'What do you want from me, Ragian? If I don't come back with you, they're dead. And that's no joke. Just come back. Say they imprisoned you somehow, and I helped you escape. Or something. Do this, and we all can go home soon.'

'It's not so simple, my friend. I can't let them hurt more innocents. Alyssa would never forgive or love me if I was that guy. I wouldn't be able to live with myself.'

'So you would condemn us to death?'

'I'll do what I feel is right for me.'

Xare approached to stand before Ragian and said, 'There're more Kingsguard. They won't be as forgiving.'

Ragian gripped his friend's arm and pulled him near to embrace him and whispered, 'I will miss you all.'

'I hope we don't meet on the battlefield.'

Ragian gritted his teeth, fighting the urge to cry. 'How far away are they?'

'Not far. I will walk back to give you time. But that's all I can do.'

They separated, and Ragian stated, 'If you make it back home, please tell Alyssa I died with courage, doing the right thing. Protect her from him.' Then he took to the sky, the green dragon Isaluth flying low over the trees back towards Rolldemere.

'Just great,' sighed Xare, watching Isaluth crest the trees, making them swing with the force he generated. He brought up his hand and extended his finger, the talon growing until he was satisfied. He steeled himself, shaking himself to bolster his courage, and ripped the talon across his chest, tearing shirt, skin and flesh. Blood sprayed from the wound, and for a heartbeat, Xare was concerned he'd cut too deep. 'That's definitely gonna leave a mark,' he muttered.

* * *

Elves ran from the village with belongings spilling from their arms, a chosen few laying traps and ambushes for those enemies brave enough to enter first. Isaluth watched from afar, seeing the Elven warriors in their silver-and-white battle attire take up positions on the highest buildings, readying their bows for their final conflict, saying their last prayers.

A few hundred feet from the main bridge, Turneroth's army prepared to run over the ancient structure, waiting for the order to charge in. He searched the sky, seeing no other dragons or Kingsguard in the air yet, although he knew them to be close. Voices drifted over the valley, their war chants coming and going with the change in the winds. *This will be quick...*

Isaluth was gliding over the trees, scanning the area where King Elyon and Prince Valheim led the elves down into the valley away from prying eyes, when the first cries of battle rang out. Valheim glared back at him from atop his horse. He could see the anger and frustration on the elf's face for being forced to abandon his people, to leave them fighting alone, dying alone, with no leader to guide them.

Near to Rolldemere, Turneroth's men advanced, marching over the bridge with sword and shields locked to form a wall. A mighty explosion rocked the valley, the cracking of the percussive blasts ripping the bridge apart, bodies and limbs flying in a disturbing display of defiance. The train of elves stopped to glance up at the collapsing bridge, wanting to cry, but they were not allowed. The slightest sounds could give away their position.

Isaluth saw one of Turneroth's scouts in the valley close to the retreating elves turn and run back to base. 'No, no. *He cannot make it back, or the entire army will head straight for them,*' said Ragian to the beast's mind, and they dived, breathing deep before setting fire to the area, scorching the scout, waiting for the burning man to realise he was already dead and drop in the midst of the blaze; and sure enough, the scout's knees gave way after a few more feet.

The collapsed bridge did not hold Turneroth's men back for long. They rushed sturdy, long ladders to the front line and placed them across the dropped section even as the dead were being carried away. Great groans sounded as fire brought down the first wooden buildings to crash on the ground, killing more attackers, shaking the hills. By then, Ragian stood on the high paths in the Evertree, unwilling to kill his own people but wanting to defend the elves. He watched as arrow after arrow struck down men he knew, some he didn't, and some he considered friends. The fire spread, blazing up the buildings where some elves were fighting from, forcing them to jump. A brief skirmish took place, and the elves lay on the ground, bleeding out.

Ragian had seen enough. He knew this once-peaceful and beautiful village would be destroyed before long. There was nothing he could do. It was indeed a sombre day, one of widespread loss and mourning. He took to the sky, sneaking away to the back, trailing the elves to ensure they were not being followed.

Midday, the sun glared from up high and the distance between the elves and Turneroth's men grew. By now, they would have figured out that the elves weren't there. He thought he could hear the angry growls of the king, but that was just in his head. Turneroth's scouts would get a proper lashing now, until Xare told the king he was to blame for their escape.

* * *

Turneroth walked over the ladders with care, taking out a handkerchief to cover his nose from the stench of the burnt bodies. With eyes red as glowing coals from lack of sleep and the stresses of leadership, he glanced at the four elves they'd caught, the rest of their brethren lying dead at their feet. Pushed down on their knees, they held their heads high with pride, the elves would not be broken. Turneroth commended their honour with a dip of his head and turned to one of his men, asking, 'Where are the rest of them?'

An officer jumped up from his work, saluting excessively, and pointed to a home with smoke drifting from its chimney. 'The men heard voices coming from that building, sire.'

Turneroth was past anger and thought, *Another village that we find abandoned. Ragian, you bastard!* Through the rubble on the path, he made his way past the officers standing around and saw they were about to breach the home, and lifted his hand. 'Stop! I will enter alone.'

The soldiers were riled up, antsy, begging for a fight, their faces twitching and strained. He casually climbed the four steps to the balcony, testing the wood underfoot, feeling the slight give with each step he took. *They might rot,* he thought. *Homes are always more maintenance than they're worth, aren't they? There's always something that needs fixing. The balcony floor, the roof, the trusses and beams, all so susceptible to the elements...* He neared the blue-painted door and softly knocked twice.

'You are going to come in whether or not I say so,' came a voice from inside.

'True,' mumbled the king, and pushed on the door, hearing it creak on the hinges. *More maintenance, more fixing. What manner of fool would build out here in the forest, where all the bugs and critters can burrow into the logs, eat them from the inside out?* He pushed his hands through the growing crack. 'I mean you no harm. Will you attack me?'

Silence lingered, then: 'I have no weapons.' The voice sounded angry and hurt.

Turneroth peeked into the home, then gradually entered, staring at the back of a hunchbacked elf labouring over a table with a large, delicate purple chiffon cloth draped over the side, covering something. Turneroth walked around the table and saw the wrinkles on the old elf's forehead, feeling a sense of urgency wash over him with how the elf tucked the sides of the chiffon under the item it covered. The old elf was crying, gentle sobs that came unabated, hands shaking while he fixed the last of the material and pinned it together with a silver and gold broach formed in the shape of a swan.

The child's body beneath the fabric was undeniable. 'I am sorry for your loss.'

'Says the man who just murdered how many of us?'

'I wasn't the one who struck the first blow. I merely defended.'

The old elf nodded. 'Actions are always justifiable in the end, even if you kill a child. My little Eirela was struck down a few days ago by a foreigner like you. He swore it was an animal, but Eirela told me it was him. That it was an accident. She crept up on him, thinking he was an elf, wanting to scare him...'

Turneroth took a pin from his shoulder, formed of iron and set in a dragon's head, and pinned it beneath the swan. 'This was meant to be for my boy, but I fear he's lost to me now. Maybe it will serve your Eirela better.'

Haleth turned to Turneroth and bowed slightly. 'It is in our children that we lose ourselves. I know you search for the others, but you won't find them here. You won't catch them now. They go to the city to flee from you.'

'Thank you. Forgive my intrusion on your day of mourning.' Turneroth left the home and was greeted by many soldiers waiting to go in. 'No one enters this home! We go to New Runswick. Xare! Where is he?'

From the collapsed bridge, the red-headed Kingsguard jogged closer, clutching the slash across his chest as he said, 'Here, sire. I was waiting for you to exit the home. It seems Ragian has deserted us. He's taken up arms with the enemy.'

'He left you alive?'

'Yes, sire. We were friends once. He's a better fighter than I remember.'

'It seems the fun starts now, Xare. Send out a hunting party. The elves make for New Runswick. The rest of the company will join them before the city wall. No killing before the mages inspect them. Capture them. Got it?'

'It will be done, sire.'

Chapter Twelve

The glass-eyed officer, Fenrick Blemmel, scribbled away on his important document, filling in the information of a tall, couth gentleman with a thin, pencil moustache and a bespoke purple gambeson deserving of a king, stitched by the finest tailor to exaggerate his features. The high boots, new and shiny, were specked with dust on the toes and sides. 'You say you're here to see who, exactly?' Fenrick asked, leaning in to hear the man's soft voice.

'The merchant, Roahn Nuka.'

'Right, right. And your name?'

'Ebron, good sir...'

'So it's business?'

'Very much so.'

Fenrick stopped his spinning eye and wiped it with his sleeve, leaving a smear of pus on his arm. Ebron nearly gagged and glanced away, covering his mouth with his fingers. 'Dear me, man. Use a handkerchief.'

Fenrick cracked a smile. 'Maybe on my other eye.' The smiled dropped away. 'What do you bring into the city?' A loud noise started up from the wall and Fenrick shouted, 'Oi! Can't you see I'm busy? Quiet down.' He turned back to Ebron. 'Sorry, continue.'

Ebron started again, and was cut off by the officer as a rhythmic tune built its way down the road, but Fenrick could see nothing over the rise. 'What is that?'

A man shouted from the wall, drawing Fenrick's attention. 'Dwarves, sir!'

The officer turned his gaze back to the road and saw that the tops of their heads were now visible, swinging side to side with their jaunty tune. It wasn't long before he saw their stocky forms, and behind them, oxen pulling two carts loaded with equipment covered with white tarps. They sang with grins from ear to ear, swinging their fists with cheer, ignoring the confused and disgusted looks they received from those in line or working outside the walls. 'What is this?'

Archers from the wall immediately nocked their arrows, trained them over the group. 'Halt!' shouted Fenrick as he pushed Ebron aside and made his way closer. He looked up at the archers, feeling the sun's warmth on his face, then back to the group. 'State your business!'

The leading dwarf ruffled his rust-coloured beard and tipped his digger hat with a slight nod. He glanced up at the wall, seeing the glint of metal through the slits. 'Is this how you welcome those invited by the queen?'

'State your name!'

'Dorgal!' came a happy shout from behind Fenrick, causing the officer to spin on his heels, face flushed with anger. Kehlos jogged past the officer and looked back at the wall. 'It's okay, lower your weapons! They come with the express permission of the queen. Let them through. Excuse me, people, make way. This is a very important delivery.'

Fenrick stamped his feet in anger and shouted, 'They must be made to wait in line like the rest of the good folk here! Just like dwarves, to be given a handout!'

'Oh, there's no need for that, laddie,' began Bleak, the frown setting deep lines across his forehead.

'Watch yourself, Blemmel! Or do you want to spend the day explaining to the queen why you insult her guests so?' Kehlos asked, pointing his finger at the man.

Red in the face, Fenrick boiled from within. He was the one in charge here, no one else. He had the power to say who went and who stayed, not some soldier he didn't even know the name of. *Everyone is throwing the queen's name around to get what they want. I'm sick of it!* 'Your name, soldier? It will take but a moment!' Fenrick grabbed his clipboard and flipped to a new page, dunking his reed pen into the ink and splashing it over Ebron's attire.

'Argh! You imbecile! You've ruined my clothes!' stormed the man. 'I hope you make enough to get this fixed, or I will have your hands!'

Fenrick grabbed a rag and dabbed at the dark stains flowing down the gambeson. 'Forgive me, sir. I'm sure it will wash out. No, wait!' he shouted after Kehlos and the dwarves as they pushed by, a train of apologetic faces floating past, unstoppable. The last dwarf to walk by tossed him a lemon. As he caught it, he heard something race from the dwarf's mouth. 'Sorrylad, yagottousethatrightquick, otherwise we'llsingsongsforyerefamily. Rubitdownpropernow. Yeknow Ihadaweeladonce. Notmine, buthesureasheckthoughthewas, keptcominbacktooformore—'

'Odus, leave the poor man. Can't you see? He doesn't understand a word you say,' demanded Dorgal from the front.

The snub-nosed Odus sighed and lay his broad hand on Fenrick's shoulder. 'Goolucklad.' Then set off at a run to catch up with the rest. 'Waitformeyadwarftossers.'

Fenrick stood with a howling crowd, angry at the double standards, especially in favour of the dwarves, and eyed the lemon in his hands. *Oh heck, might as well give it a try.* 'Do you mind, sir? I will take the gambeson and get it cleaned for you. My sincerest apologies.' The shouting crowd was driving him mad. He glanced over his shoulder and shouted, 'Shut it! You'll get your turn!'

* * *

'Mighty fine to see you too, Kehlos,' said Dorgal. 'Say, I heard from a little birdie that there'd been an attempt on Ladriana's life. What happened? Did they catch the bastard?'

'Aye, they nearly got to her. We know now who's responsible. His time's running out.'

226

'But he's still out there...' grimaced the dwarf.

'That doesn't sound ideal,' countered Bleak, leaning closer to hear what was going on.

Kehlos looked back at them and replied, 'No. It's not ideal. But please don't bring this up with the queen. She's stressed enough with all that's going on.'

'Sure thing, lad. Damned fine woman, that. Would hate if something happened to her.'

Kehlos looked around as they made their way up the road to the castle, and felt ashamed of the citizens of New Runswick. The stares and ghastly remarks whispered and mumbled along the way went mostly ignored, but he felt the sting of their effects. People stopped in the middle of their conversations or what they were busy with to glare at them, some openly shouting their disgust.

'Go home, you gutter gnomes! You're dirtyin' our streets!' one shouted, emptying a filthy bucket of brown water near the end of an alley to run in a stream down the road.

'Things will never change, will they?' Dorgal asked with a sigh. 'We come to aid the world of man in a time of crisis, and this is how we're greeted... It's disgraceful.'

'We should go home, Dorg. It ain't safe for us here. Twenty dwarves in a city full of haters,' came a voice from amongst the dwarves.

Dorgal knew who it was and didn't need to turn around. Only one dwarf ever called him that. 'Yer right, Grimmel. We leave as soon as we can.'

'Working on these issues with the people has got away from the queen after the attempts on her life. Yes, multiple. But she still hopes to fix this. She wouldn't want you to leave so soon. People are just afraid of what they don't know.'

'Mmm, I get that, Kehlos. But men have always been warmongers. Kill first, worry about diplomacy later, 'specially when resources get scarce. What makes you think she'll change anything? As much as we adore her, I think this is beyond her reach.'

'You underestimate her. Look, just come up and speak with her. I know she would like to see you.' The crowded streets had a reek to them. Too many were living in close quarters. Some slept on the streets, their few belongings scattered in their little corners of seclusion. Kehlos saw the dwarves' eyes wander. 'I know, it's not a pretty sight at the moment. Most of these are refugees from Belleford, fleeing the enemy's approach. We don't have enough accommodations for all of them.'

A little girl, covered with filth, her blonde hair turned brown with grime, sat with vacant eyes holding her teddy bear on a blanket near the castle gates, her mind lost to the hardship she had endured. Kehlos stopped and turned when a big dwarf stepped out from the train to head over to the girl. Ink lined the hard, broad face of the dwarf, snaking down to disappear under a long black beard, separated into multiple threads by silver rings. His eyes glistened with moisture, and he cleared his throat as he neared.

'Galiban, back in line!' worried Dorgal, seeing the stares from the nearby crowd.

'Won't be but a moment, Dorgal. Don't get your knickers in a twist.' Guards from the gate started forward, but Kehlos abruptly halted them. It did not matter to Galiban what they did; he was going to the girl. With a soft groan, he planted himself before her, cross-legged with his hands on his thighs. 'The wee fella... He gots a name?'

It took some time for the girl to realise that someone was actually speaking with her. Sad brown eyes turned to him, and the smallest voice said, 'Sir Balin Tole.' She gripped the bear tighter, his one leg nearly torn off, hanging by a thread.

'Oh deary me, lass. It seems Sir Balin Tole has been through the wars and back. Ye mind if I fix him for ye? We dwarves always carry a needle and thread. Never know when ye might need them, eh?' He reached out, waiting for her to respond.

The girl looked around at the unfamiliar faces, searching for someone she knew, but saw none. It was truly her choice. She slowly handed over Sir Balin Tole and said, 'Don't take him from me, please.' A crowd had gathered now, watching the dwarf closely.

'Oh, I would never.' Galiban pulled a small kit from his pocket with a curved needle and thread already attached, then put on a pair of glasses and glanced around. He leaned forward and whispered, 'Me eyes are not what they used to be...' Carefully stitching the leg back into place, he tied the thread and bit it off. 'Here ye go, girl. Sir Balin Tole has a few years left in him now. Every bit a fine warrior. What's yer name, girl?'

'Millie Tole,' came her squeaky voice.

'Oh, what a beautiful name. Where's your folks, Millie?'

She shied away, clutching the bear. 'Papa stepped on a snake when we left home. Got really sick.' Her eyes widened as she expressed herself. 'He told me and Mommy to wait for him here. But he hasn't yet come. Mommy is looking for work.'

Dorgal dropped back down the line to Odus and whispered a few words to the dwarf. It wasn't long before the rambling dwarf walked up to Galiban and handed him an item covered with a white cloth. 'Thank ye, brother.' He turned back to the girl. 'Here, now, don't eat it all at once. And share some with your ma. Got it?'

Head bouncing up and down, she took the item with both hands and carefully opened one flap, smelling the rich aroma of the cheese bread. Millie tore a piece off and stuffed it in her mouth, chewing while the dwarf grinned at her.

Galiban reached behind his thick neck and unlatched the silver necklace, handing it to her. 'Keep this safe now, you hear? Yer mommy can get plenty of food for this.'

Dorgal walked up to her and knelt, taking off a golden bracelet from his arm. 'Here, girl. Be wise with it.' Then Bleak stepped up and put down another bracelet on the blanket. Before long, the other dwarves followed suit, each leaving something of value for her. As young as she was, she knew these represented wealth. She knew she would eat for a few days. She just didn't know how much value they had, and being all silver or gold, it was a lot.

'Why don't you spread the wealth, you dirty dwarves!' shouted a gangly man from the front of the crowd.

'Close yer ears, Millie. Galiban needs to talk to the crowd and it ain't for young girls to hear.' He rose from the blanket, struggling to get the blood flowing to his legs after sitting cross-legged for so long, and turned to the crowd eyeing all the loot on the little girl's blanket. He fixed his eyes on the gangly man as he spoke in an ice-cold tone, 'Any of ye coin-hungry fuckers think of messing with this here girl or the gifts we gave her, and ye'll see the business end of me axe on yer throat! Let this be a warning to ye. Galiban Roch will come for ye.'

A woman pushed through the mob and burst out crying as she flopped on the ground, clasping her hand over her mouth to stifle the sounds. She crept to the girl, who turned and smiled, holding up the trinkets as she said, 'Look, Mommy.' Spit and snot flowed from the woman while she grabbed hold of Galiban's shoes, kissing them fervently.

Uncomfortable with this, Galiban quickly pulled her up and said, 'Miss, ye take care of yer Millie now. Go on. There's no need for this.' She jumped forward and embraced the dwarf, holding him tight with shivers pulsing through her. 'There, there. Okay. It's all going to be okay.' He eventually got her off him and joined the rest of his companions, but the woman was not yet done showing her gratitude. She ran to each dwarf and embraced them, putting a smile on all their faces.

Kehlos walked to a gate guard standing close and ordered, 'Vehera, you make sure nothing happens to this mother and child, got that? Watch them, day and night if you have to, and make sure nobody steals from them.'

'But, sir, my wife—' Kehlos threw him a look that silenced him instantly. 'Yes, sir.'

The train continued on through the gates to stand before the steps of the castle, the oxen tired of hauling the heavy load, bellowing their discontent.

Dorgal eyed Galiban and asked, 'What was that back there?'

'I reached out, showed them we're not as bad as they think.'

'Yeah, sure, and the whole axe waving and cursing at them? Definitely reached me...'

'Got a little emotional. Won't happen again, Dorgal.'

'See it doesn't. As much as I'd like to, we can't help every soul in this city. We dwarves are cursed... We're born givers. It's all we do when we see someone in trouble, we give, be it food, gold, a home, a fight.'

'What happened to the castle?' asked Bleak, leaning over Dorgal's shoulder. The stones had been put back in place, but the mortar had not yet set, making it look out of place.

'It happened during the last attack on the queen. It was utter chaos.'

The door swung open, and guards escorted them in. A high staircase greeted them with a chandelier that lay broken on the floor. Men and women were busy cleaning up the mess, sweeping the floor, and picking up debris. 'It was not a priority to clean this all up. No company was expected. Excuse the appearance,' mumbled Kehlos as they walked in.

The dwarves gawked at the castle, marvelling at its size, although they weren't too impressed with the build quality. Bleak glided his finger along the wooden rail running up the stairs and sneered. 'No one takes pride in their work anymore. These aren't even smoothed out. Get nasty splinters in the delicate hands of these running around here.'

'Bleak, we're not here for that...'

'Sorry. The walls look crooked, too.'

'Bleak!'

'Sorry. Just sayin'.'

They walked down a long corridor to reach a room at the far end, reinforced and heavy. They could almost not hear the knock on the solid structure. Kehlos stood back and said, 'It's me, milady. I bring Dorgal Dammelsfiere and his host of dwarves.' Loud latches fell away on the other side. The dwarves glanced at one another suspiciously until the door swung open, then stood tall with sudden smiles on their faces.

'Lady Ladriana! What a pleasure,' said Dorgal aloud, going in for a hug when he noticed her stomach and gently continued, leaning to the side, careful not to press too hard.

'Oh, stop that, Dorgal. I'm no flowerpot! Come in here, my friends! All of you! I'm so glad you're here.'

'Oh deary, seems you've put on some weight. Ha ha,' mocked Dorgal.

She slapped him on the arm. 'Come in, come in! There's room aplenty.'

They entered the room and were greeted by an old man bowing stiffly, and a man whom Dorgal could see had done hard labour for a long time, his leathery skin blotched with sunspots, his eyes constantly darting around to look for trouble.

Ladriana sat on the couch next to the leathery-skinned man and said, 'This is my father, Roahn, and this is Ehrhard.' She gestured back to the dwarves. 'This is Dorgal Dammelsfiere, leader of the dwarves. Where is Rochar? Did he stay behind again? I swear he'll stress himself to death, that one.'

'Aye,' muttered Dorgal, nodding to the two gentlemen. 'Are you okay, Lady Ladriana? You seem...a tad too cheery.'

'Oh yes, I'm perfectly fine!' Her head lolled, her eyes searching for him, swimming until she found him. 'Stop moving around so much, you're giving me a headache.'

Ehrhard crept closer and leaned in to whisper in Dorgal's ear, 'My apologies, master dwarf. I gave her a sedative to help her sleep. She has been up for days. The last attack stirred a fear in her that does not want to let go. She fights sleep with every fibre of her body.'

'Oh, dear. Leave it with me. I know what to do.'

'You do?' asked Ehrhard, brows raised.

'Aye, trust me.' Dorgal whispered something into Bleak's ear, who relayed the message with some worry on his face.

'Close the door, Kehlos.' When the locks fell into place, the dwarves swarmed her, grabbing feet and arms, holding her down while she screamed at the top of her voice.

'Let me go! Dorgal, what are you doing? Ehrhard,' she glared at him, but he shied away. 'Kehlos, I command you to get them off me!' But he turned away. 'Father! Surely you—'

The tears in his eyes dropped to the couch as he looked away. 'I'm sorry, my dear. If they can help, we have to let them try,' Roahn said.

Dorgal ran his hand down her neck, feeling the tension in her muscles as she wiggled and wormed to get out of their grasp. 'It's an old Elven method, taught to me by King Elyon himself a long, long time ago. Those elves and their tricks, ya know? Always have something to try.' He worked his fingers down her neck to her left breast, stopping just above it and pressing firmly while messaging the muscle. He ran his other hand down her head, applying pressure at the back of her ear, mumbling in the Elven tongue as he did so. Riled up and fuming, shaking the dwarves to let her go, her eyes soon became heavy and her body relaxed. A few moments later, she was asleep.

Stunned, everyone turned to the dwarf, shocked at how easy Dorgal made it look. The dwarves carefully placed her legs on the couch and all of them retreated from the room to let her sleep. Once outside, Kehlos said, 'That was amazing, Dorgal. Please stay until she wakes. We have rooms ready for you all. There's food in the hall, and ale being brought in. She knows how much you like to eat.'

Dorgal turned to his men, seeing their mouths water at the mention of food. *Oh, we are too predictable... Send us to battle for a table of food and mouthful of mead...* 'Sure, I guess we could stay until then.'

'Excellent,' announced Ehrhard, and scurried off, calling over his shoulder, 'Master dwarf, I will meet you all in the hall soon. I have questions!'

Kehlos grinned and said, 'Come, I will show you the way. You must be tired after the journey.'

* * *

Behind closed doors, the three Eldarre rested their feet against the warm brazier, the fire burning happily within, its flames licking away time and stress. Smoke funnelled out through the chimney stack above, drifting away in the night sky to obscure the stars above the House of Eldarre. It was a rare thing to see the Eldarre in a social gathering, but they had just murdered one of their own, a man they respected and thought above reproach. How wrong they had been...

Their world's problems were never the result of some natural phenomenon. *They* were to blame for all the hardship. *They* had failed in their duty as Eldarre, and failure was not something looked upon with pride. 'We are all in agreement, then? This is not something we could have foreseen or stopped?' Benamene and Yaltus did not turn to Vendegrut's stare, but both nodded their heads in silence. The shadows cast by the flames made their eyes seem sunken and dark, their usually clean-shaven faces revealing stubble on their chins. 'Good. Let's not speak of it again.'

The doors swung open and their heads came up as four armed guards escorted the warlock and Garidan into the room. 'Thank you, you may leave us,' said Yaltus to the guards, motioning for the two foreigners to join them. Two cushioned chairs stood a short distance from the brazier, close enough to get some of the heat, but far enough not to be within reach of the Eldarre too quickly. Not that they expected any trouble.

Garidan sat down gradually, glancing at each Eldarre. Not so long ago, these three were ready to send them to the gallows. 'You called for us, Eldarre of Magnificence?'

Still standing behind the chair, Khanaseri interrupted, 'Can we make this quick? I need to get going.'

'You are not one to show respect easily, are you?' asked Vendegrut, lying back with his hands on his lap.

'Just because I don't show it doesn't mean I don't have it. But in this case, I guess you're right.' Garidan felt his heart jump, and he shook his head, listening to the warlock continue, 'I can't come to terms with your backwards way of living. The constant need to hoard what you know, hoping to hold certain positions. It infuriates me.'

'How dare you insult us?' shouted Benamene, his silvery robes shimmering red in the dance of the flames as he jumped from his chair.

Vendegrut thrust out a hand, quieting his colleague, and said, 'You've done us a great service, for which we are forever grateful, but please, let's be civil here. Tulvar mentioned the problems in your world and the reason you came here, Garidan. But unfortunately, we lost the art of dragon capture a long time ago, during the subjugation wars with the Tarks, when the last of the Gatekeepers fell to their swords. The little knowledge we have left on record is useless without those that know how to interpret it. So there is no help we can give you there—'

'For once, I must agree with my friend here. That is utter bullshit! We risked our lives for this world, hoping for your support in return, but it seems—'

'Careful, Garidan... Before you finish that sentence, I wasn't finished with mine.' Vendegrut knew he had little to bargain with. 'We want you to stay until whatever hatches from those cocoons—'

'What?' began Garidan.

'In return, we'll send a host of ten thousand soldiers with you. We only ask that you stay until the end to make sure all is finished.'

The warlock shook his head and said, 'I can't stay.'

'No, you can't,' agreed Garidan. 'But I will. We barely have twenty thousand soldiers, and another ten thousand gives us a fighting chance. We can't stand against Turneroth's army otherwise. Even without the dragons, they outnumber us at least three to one.'

The Eldarre grinned at each other, and Yaltus said, 'We thank you both. The soldiers will be at your disposal when the time comes.'

Khanaseri turned to leave when Benamene spoke, his voice thick and loud. 'The Djak-ta speak highly of your skill. They have never seen the like. We have stories of Djak-ta possessing the power you wield, but none have come close in the last hundred years. If ever you wander with no apparent direction, you will be welcome here to instruct our people and break the cycle that you hate so much.'

Khanaseri tapped his finger on the back of the chair, eyeing the Eldarre. He nodded and said, 'Maybe one day. I've fought with one of your Gatekeepers. He was a great warrior. Garidan, let's go. Eldarriness...' He tipped his head and left them, waiting by the door for Garidan, who bowed respectfully before retreating from the room.

The Eldarre returned to their silent gathering as the two men left. Guards closed the door behind them, the stone door grinding deep grooves into the basalt floor. Khanaseri stared down the cold corridor at the confusing array of doors lining the sides. He turned to a guard and said, 'Oi. Which way? I don't want to be stuck here forever.'

The guard sneered at having to listen to the Tarkean tongue and replied in Ageian, gesturing with his hand, 'Follow me.'

Once outside, they made their way to the Library of Cabinet's lawn a few blocks away, where Garidan had deposited the monolith on their return from Mount Aga, burning a great black circle into the earth around the device. Red light glowed from the cage to their right, brightening the area and making it possible to see the creature within moving slowly, forming something new. 'Ain't that a sight?' asked Arundhàbu as he stepped from the shadows.

'You really thought you could leave without saying goodbye?' came a woman's voice as Borka, Naghita, and Tulvar emerged from the darkness as well.

The warlock stopped and smiled. 'I didn't think that I'd made any friends here. I wasn't the best of guests. That said, I'm gonna miss your ugly mugs. I would be honoured to fight beside any of you.'

'And we you,' the blacksmith said and gripped the warlock's arm above the hand crusted with blackened skin, seeing the scabs formed over the wounds.

Garidan smiled contemptuously and said, 'And I'm staying a while longer, it seems. Are you ready, Khan?'

'I am.' Khanaseri jumped up onto Flintlock's back and walked him closer to the monolith. He glared at Garidan. 'Don't send me to some godawful place, ya hear?'

'Wouldn't dream of it...'

Letters crawled over his skin, the sensation becoming something he was looking forward to, something he wanted to do more often. He had yet to tap into the full power of the monolith, but this little taste he was getting pulled at him, wanted more from him. Garidan concentrated on the destination, trying to remember the port they had once sailed to in the bay of the golden city, remembering its beauty as it glistened in the rising sun; the waves lapping their ship's hull and the deep blue waters with the dolphins swimming next to them, guiding them. Sandy beaches and white foamy waves crashed together on the strand. Beyond the shore stood blackwood trees with small yellow flowers drifting to the ground, covering the earth at their feet.

The metal structure whistled noisily, the rings spinning crazily over themselves. It almost looked like it was standing still, not moving at all, but the whirling was unmistakable. Khanaseri stood before the device, realising how much less malignant it was than when he created a portal. *Would it be possible to create a more stable version if I knew more?* he wondered, but there was no one to teach him. The portal opened up to him. He looked back to the waiting group and waved before Flintlock passed through to disappear, the portal snapping shut behind him.

* * *

The faint smell of Lilly Pilly and sweetened rose oil hung in the room, chasing away the musky odour of the old wooden furniture. Ladriana opened her eyes. Her head was heavy and her mind dull; she struggled to construct a coherent thought. A glass of water rested on the side table, a ring of condensation gathering around it on the dark wood. Moving her mouth up and down, feeling the dryness as her tongue stuck to her palate, she picked up the glass and drank deeply, feeling the cool water moisten her insides.

'Ah, ye're awake,' came a gruff voice from the far side of the room.

She gently shook her head, the throbbing easing as she rubbed her eyes. 'Dorgal? That you? I remember seeing you earlier, but good heavens, I've no idea what happened.'

'We, uh...we helped you get some sleep. Ye were acting strange, and Ehrhard told us ye hadn't been sleeping. Ye've been drooling on your pillows for a day and a half. Time to get up, lass,' came the voice, followed by footsteps towards the bed. He poked his head around the divider and smiled. 'Me and the boys will head back today, now that ye're up. I have delivered the finest swords, bows, axes, hammers, halberds, and spears, as promised. It took some convincing for the smiths to make the spears. A dwarf will be a dwarf... Captain Volar seems very pleased with them.'

Her head was groggy and slow, but it was functioning, at least.

'Thank you, Dorgal. Of course, I understand. This is not your fight.'

He felt the stab of those words, and his smile disappeared. 'The boys are down in the hall eatin' all yer food. I better go stop them before ye have a shortage or, knowing them, they destroy half yer hall and put it back together again the way they like it. 'Twas nice seeing you again.'

The words left a bitter taste in her mouth. She wanted to stop him, but the door had already closed. 'Superb tact, Ladriana, just wonderful,' she moaned. 'Maybe next time you can throw some burning coals in his eyes for good measure. You know, just in case he didn't pick up that you're being a twat.' The world spun as she got up. *Too little sleep, too much sleep... Nothing is ever good for you... Better get myself cleaned up.* 'Vehera! You on duty today?' she shouted.

'Yes ma'am, sorry milady. What's wrong with me? And Panthos. Do you require anything?' came the muffled voice from behind the door.

'Get me Abe. I'm riding out with the dwarves to the gates.'

'At once, milady.'

* * *

'Wait! Master Dorgal!' Ladriana called as they raced down the road through the gates of New Runswick. Ahead of them, the two wagons loaded with sombre dwarves came to a halt. Their faces brightened at the sight of her. Most jumped up to be at eye level of the woman on her brown mare, but some still managed to fall short.

'She looks a wee bit pale, Dorg. Ye sure she be fine?' asked Grimmel, running his fingers through his knotted beard, tugging the stubborn strands.

'I'll be fine, Grimmel,' said Ladriana with a smirk. 'Some sun, and I will be back to my old self.' She reined in the walking horse and dismounted. Abe's horse trotted closer, and he dismounted as well, followed by ten armed guards in full metal armour, their visors drawn over their faces and ready for anything. The sun was high, warming her open arms, and the wind soft, flicking her long, red hair up behind her.

Dorgal hopped off the front of the leading wagon and walked closer. 'Would ye look at that? The wizard made it to ye. Nice to see ye again,

Abe.'

'I'm honoured you remember my name, master Dorgal,' said Abe with a deep bow.

'What's with this master nonsense? I ain't nobody's master. Ye call me Dorgal. That's all.' Abe tipped his head again, with a wry smile to the dwarf.

'Ye feelin' any better than this morning, lass? Ya sure look it.'

'I do, thanks to you.' Ladriana coughed shyly and glanced away, looking at their surroundings. To their right, a vineyard green and ready for harvest – the dark grapes plump and beautiful – spread far and wide. Beyond the vineyard lay fields of various vegetables: pumpkin, tomato, cucumber, radishes, and many more. 'I apologise for my snap this morning. It wasn't fair.'

'No, it wasn't. But I forgave ye already on account of all that's going on.' Shouts from the wall, frantic and alarming, sounded in the distance. Everyone turned to the screams of alarm, seeing men run on the wall readying weapons, but they were not sure why. Men pointed to over the rise on the bluff far away and the queue outside the city stormed through the gates, stampeding Fenrick and the other guards who tried to keep order, but failed miserably. They had no choice but to jump out of the rushing mob's way if they didn't want to get trampled.

'Come, milady, we need to get back to the castle for your safety,' said Abe, his face serious, his brows rising. The dwarves had already unsheathed their axes and hammers, readying themselves. The guards circled the queen, looking around for threats while forcing her horse back to the gates. Ladriana mounted and struggled to keep the mare calm, the horses becoming skittish, yanking on the reins with eyes wide and ears flicking up and down.

A cacophony of thunderous roars sounded from afar, turning their stomachs upside down. An icy chill gripped Ladriana as she saw men, women, and children running over the bluff, jumping from the low cliff to roll in dust clouds down the side. The sound of metal rang out at the back, and they knew they were fighting for their lives. 'Elves! They are in trouble!' shouted Dorgal. A green explosion of magic erupted over them in the distance, electrifying the sky and the few clouds forming above.

Ladriana pushed her mount through the protective circle of guards, sitting awkwardly on the galloping mare with her enormous stomach, her legs forced apart and her knees protruding wide from the horse's flanks. Without them seeing, Ladriana had grabbed the sword hilt of the guard she pushed aside, unsheathing the weapon as she continued. Abe raced his mount after her with the guards in tow, the dwarves behind, the wagons following.

Dorgal lashed the oxen to pick up the pace, but they were slow beasts not fit for fighting. He cursed as the rest pulled away from them, leaving them in their dust. More horses raced past them, and he shouted, 'Grab yerselves a ride, boys!' Dwarves leapt from the wagon, nearly causing more chaos as the horses buckled under the sudden extra weight of the dwarves jumping on their backs. Riders cursed angrily, wanting to throw the dwarves from their horses, but they were steadfast. 'Just ride! Ladriana is in trouble!'

Elven warriors on horseback now appeared over the ridge, fighting with other men, hacking and slashing to prevent them from getting to the fleeing elves coming down in droves. Ladriana saw King Elyon and Valheim at the back, beside their men in the confrontation, as two dragons clashed above, the collision shaking the earth beneath and their roars shattering the perception of safety for anyone near New Runswick. Then she was in the fray, slashing down at an attacker who had lost his horse, cutting his chest wide open. She pushed her mount past the fleeing elves and shouted, 'Run for the gates!' dodging a blow from a warrior with an axe; his reach too short, hers just perfect. Her blade sang and slit his throat, tumbling him from the horse.

The armoured guards drew closer, protecting their queen from the onslaught of men. Abe slowed his mount and glared at a dragon up high, seeing it turn to them. 'Don't do this. Turn away, live and be free!' he pleaded with the beast, but it was deep under the spell of the Alpha and unreachable. A thick bolt of lightning arced from up high in the clouds, coursing through the beast and searing it with loud, thunderous cracks. 'Leave now!'

It turned and fled, trailing smoke through the sky.

Dorgal jumped from his hitched horse, chopping down with his axe and burying it in an attacker's skull, splitting the man's metal helmet and head. Short arrow bolts flew, sinking into horses and men, toppling them for the dwarves to jump on. Blood sprayed as Odus rammed his hammer through a man's head, shouting nonsensical babble, the words coming too fast to understand. Men and dwarves were on the ground, fighting side by side to save the elves. It was a violent clash, fast and brutal.

Valheim was at his father's side, defending him as they retreated, when Ladriana rode up to them and shouted, 'Make for the city's gates!' Warrior elves on horseback grabbed their fleeing citizens from the ground, galloping at full speed to the city while the rest fought on.

A wall of flames erupted from one dragon, slowing the approach of the attackers, giving the elves a much-needed break before two other dragons tore into it, the jumble of reptilian bodies crashing into the side of the ridge in a hail of rocks and grey dust. The two attacking dragons slashed and bit deep into the other, blood spurting from the allied beast in streams and shrieks. Elyon closed his eyes and whispered to the listening world, feeling it respond to his pleas. Strong vines shot out of the ground, wrapping around one enemy dragon, constricting it enough for Isaluth to break free and bury its fangs into the throat of the other dragon, tearing chunks from the beast. Isaluth streamed fire over the dragon, and staggered away from the char-grilled beast as both collapsed to the ground, surrounded by pooling blood and shuddering with pain.

The constricted dragon had just broken free from the vines and lunged for Isaluth when a red blur severed its head swiftly, its gigantic skull crashing to the ground moments before its body tumbled after. Another roar sounded from the left, and a charcoal dragon flew low, scooping up the attacking men and their horses in its giant claws, slicing off their limbs and crushing their bodies, taking them high into the air to drop them to their deaths. Confusion and chaos were the course of the day.

The last of the attacking dragons turned and fled, the Terenorans broken and running scared. The day was theirs. Elyon could barely hang on to the reins anymore, his left arm hanging limp with blood pouring to the ground down the white mare's thigh. He dropped from his horse and staggered through the smoke of the burning fields towards the last place he saw the dragon Isaluth. Valheim pulled at his robes, but Elyon shrugged him off.

'Father.'

Soldiers had surrounded the fallen beast, throwing spears while it writhed and tried to stand. Elyon stumbled closer and shouted, 'Stop! He is with us! Stop this! Did you not see that he saved us?'

Ladriana lifted her hand, and the soldiers ceased. Isaluth veered, its pained cries soft and groaning until the man's voice took over.

'What sorcery is this?' Ladriana shouted and staggered back, wanting to lift her hand again for her men to attack, but Elyon quickly intervened.

'No! Trust me.' They approached with caution. Thick, dark blood pumped from Ragian's neck, his hands pushing aimlessly at the grievous wounds, affecting nothing. Eyes wide, more of the red spilled from his mouth, a gurgling cry forcing air out. Elyon and Valheim rushed to Ragian's side.

'It's true, I saw it,' came another's voice from the smoke. All the soldiers jumped to him with weapons ready. Ganda'har strode closer, glancing between Ladriana and her soldiers. 'I'm on your side. Relax.'

'Why should we believe you?' asked Ladriana, as Dorgal joined her side, a streak of red covering his face.

'Because I saved his...' Ganda'har stated, pointing to the struggling Ragian. 'At least, I tried to.' He knelt by Ragian's side and took hold of the man's hand and whispered, 'You must be Ragian. Khanaseri told me about you. I had my doubts, but he was convinced that you're a good man. Today you proved him right.' Ganda'har saw the fear in the man's eyes while the elf king prayed next to him. He knew this was a futile attempt, but said nothing.

Ragian's grip was growing weak, his strength fading fast. He tried to speak, but the words didn't want to form, and mere sobbing echoes left

him. Ragian tried again, the words coming sparsely, 'Stop...him...
He...c-can't—' Ragian was afraid, not of dying, but for his wife's safety.
Turneroth could *not* make it back to his time. *I'm sorry, Alyssa...*

His eyes turned dull, and Ganda'har tapped the elf king on the
shoulder. 'He's gone. I'm sorry.'

Elyon sagged to the ground, pressing his knees into the dirt, head
dropping. 'He fought off three dragons, killing two to protect us. You
are right, warrior, he *was* a good man. Deeply flawed, and burdened
with the weight of wrongdoing and sin. He made mistakes, but he
atoned for them today. We elves will remember him.'

'King Elyon, let's not linger here for them to regroup and come at
us with a stronger force. We need to get behind the walls,' stated
Ladriana, stunned at what she had observed in this skirmish. Dragon
and man becoming one; the thought of it made her shiver. Although
she knew of the legend, to see it was something else.

A loud roar sounded and everyone jumped around, watching the
charcoal dragon settle to the ground and veer, a golden refulgence
swirling around him into a misty spray. Blanka approached and tipped
his head to her and said, 'I believe we're even now. We have much to
discuss.'

Ladriana's mind raced as she thought back to the fight with the
Desert Dogs, feeling like it was ages ago now. 'You! How? What? You
jumped...with her...'

The memory nearly brought tears to his eyes. 'Yes. Now I'm back.'

'Where is that bitch, anyway? I swear if I find her—'

Ganda'har jumped up, hearing her speak, and glanced at Blanka.

'Dead. She's dead.' He walked away from the queen, leaving her
speechless next to the dwarf.

'Shit...' she whispered, shying away. 'I'm sorry,' Ladriana yelled after
him, but he did not stop.

'I ain't gonna pretend I know what's goin' on here,' mumbled
Dorgal. 'But it sure beats a day on the wagon.'

Ladriana turned to her men and said, 'Take them to the healers.
Did we lose anyone?'

An armoured officer lifted his visor. 'No, milady. Minor injuries, but we all survived.'

'I best be goin', lass. If they're here, our home is in danger.' Dorgal looked around and gestured his men closer.

'You can't leave, master dwarf,' said Ganda'har, lifting Ragian to his shoulder.

'And why the bloody hell not?' asked Dorgal, his voice cold, bloodied axe hanging from his hand.

'Turneroth's army is everywhere. You're cut off from the mountains. They won't pester your kin, but they *will* kill everything that looks like a threat. And you, master dwarf, look like a threat to me.'

'What is it today with this master nonsense?'

'You say they won't pester his kin. Why is that?' the queen asked. 'What do you know?'

'I'm Captain Ganda'har from Artokla. We've been hunting them from the beginning, and we know what they want. The rift they created to get to this time was chaotic, feeding on this world, and soon it would have destroyed everything. So we closed it, but now they're stuck here. They search for magic users, anyone who can touch the Source to draw power from it. They intend to sacrifice all of them if that's what it takes to get back to their time. Back from *when* they came, they pulled power from the magical pit in their city, Terenore, to bolster their mages, but that's no longer an option. The spell they cast depleted its energy. Besides, wherever he goes, there will be more bloodshed. Better we stop him here, now. They've taken men, women, and children for this murderous purpose. Not to mention the possibility that opening another portal like that could cause the destruction of our world.'

'Gods. So the very thing we sought for our protection, opening the school of magic, is why they're here... You made it to us. Can't we flee from them?' Ladriana asked.

'Yes, but wherever you go, they'll follow, causing more destruction along the way. He has dragons patrolling the skies, scouts everywhere. There's no escaping him. My men will be here in a couple of days, and we've sent word to Midavene and Artokla, but we don't know if they will come. Artokla is licking its wounds and Midavene seemed...how should I put this...*disinterested.*'

Dorgal listened carefully and sheathed his axe. 'So our options are to run home, be outnumbered, and probably die — or stay here and probably die. I don't like those odds; it feels a little one-sided,' he bobbed and weaved his head, 'ya know, on the dying side.'

They walked back to the dwarves' wagons to lay Ragian's body on the bed of one, and Ganda'har said, 'Yallrick Duskhorn sends his regards. We ran into them a while back.'

Bleak's face lit up. 'What about cousin Bullie? Did you see him? Tallest dwarf there ever was, I swear. Stands a head taller than me.'

'Everyone stands a head taller than you, Bleak. I'm surprised old Duskhorn still breathes. He's a good dwarf.' Dorgal turned to his men as they climbed up the wagons. 'What will it be, boys? Ye all heard the captain here. Are we running? Or are we fighting? Either way, I'm dead. Rochar will slit my throat for puttin' ye all in danger. But we all go, or we all stay. We do not separate.'

Galiban stepped forward. 'If it's all the same to you, Dorgal, I'll stay and fight.'

'Aye, me too,' said Bleak.

'Gonnagivethosebastardsagoodthrashin, I'mstayingtoo,' stated Odus.

'Aye, me too,' came another and another. Dorgal felt pride swell in his heart for his people and their courage. 'Are there any among you, my brethren, who wishes to go home and stay out of this fight?' A single hand rose slowly at the back of the wagon, and all the dwarves spun around. 'Speak up, Ghutal.'

The grey-haired dwarf plucked his finger from his ear, shaking the wax to the ground, and shivered with delight. 'I'd like to go home and pluck my dear Bev's feathers one last time. She be right lonely without me. If she finds out I'm fightin' without her, she'll have the forger make a cage for me todger.'

The dwarves broke out laughing, and Odus slapped him on the back. 'There'sareasonwe'vesofewchildren. They'reanightmare.

BecarefulGhut.'

'She might be glad yer gone for longer, Ghutal,' laughed Dorgal. 'Okay, so we agree. We all stay?'

'Aye!' shouted the dwarves in unison.

'If you don't mind, Dorgal, I'll ride with you so I can give Ragian a proper burial,' said Ganda'har.

The dwarves turned to the body, removing their hats in respect, a hum sounding from them, and Dorgal said, 'Aye, lad. We will help.'

Chapter Thirteen

In the dead of night, while the owls hooted and the big cats prowled, a portal opened on the deserted strand. Flintlock emerged warily, his hooves tapping on the rocks while the warlock scanned the area with his hood drawn over his head. Streetlamps burned in the distance, lighting up the seaside city. Khanaseri smiled at the sound of the waves crashing on the strand, their rolling motion entrancing. He shook the reins, and Flintlock started walking towards the city. During the last year since Beuneth's arrival, he had seen more and experienced more than he had his entire life. It felt like a lifetime ago that his father had died in his arms. It felt like another life altogether.

They made their way over the soft sands, and Khanaseri pulled on the reins, listening to the lapping waves, smelling the salty sea. He dismounted and removed his clothes, leaving Flintlock on the cool sands before wading into the sea. The salty waters washed over him, cleaning his wounds and burning his arms and hands like acid was poured onto them, his mind on fire and his soul searching for escape, the pain bringing new feelings to the surface. The water was freezing, sending cold shivers through him while he swam, and Khanaseri wondered at all the various coloured fish that could be swimming around him as company. He took a deep breath and dipped his head into the chilly waters, sinking as he wished it was daylight so he could see them all. He was not sure if there would be time later or even if he would be alive.

They say change is the only constant, but I would add fleeting time to the list. There just never seems to be enough of it these days. Always too little time to spend with loved ones. Too little time to get the job done. Too little time to do what you love before it all goes to shit. He opened his eyes, feeling the sting of the salt, and blinked a few times to get used to it. Vague shapes flashed by him at speed, some small, some large enough to startle, but he remained fixed, staring into the darkness of the waters. Khanaseri reached out to a thick, long shape that slowly floated by, feeling the rough skin of the fish, thinking it should have felt scalier and smoother.

From the depths of the water, the full moon was the only thing visible under the surface, glowing far above. Khanaseri closed his eyes to centre himself, to calm his raging heart and soothe his nerves. No warrior, no matter how strong, can say they haven't felt the sting of too much bloodshed, too much fighting... He opened his eyes and drifted to the top, taking a deep breath as he breached the surface. Flintlock stood in the distance, shaking his head in anger and angst, annoyed at his rider. The warlock could see that he wasn't happy. 'I'm coming, Flint. No need to get edgy with me.' He had been under for so long that Flintlock had got anxious and rose from the sand, neighing, watching the waters for his rider to come back up.

If he thought the water was freezing when he got in, the wind was now chilling him to the bone, his skin pulled tight with goosebumps covering him as he jogged out. He grabbed his clothes and quickly donned them, stopping the wind from blowing through to his core, and let out a soft whistle. Flintlock padded up behind him, playfully shoving from the back and kicking the air, dashing away down the moonlit strand to race at full speed, his mane whipping and shimmering black. 'What are you doing, Flint? What's got into you?' The horse spun in the distance and raced back, kicking up sand as he raced past the warlock, covering him with the stuff. 'Flint! Ya bugger!' Khanaseri wanted to sound angry, but found himself laughing at the crazy horse. 'Come on now, you wild thing, let's get going.' The horse trotted back and followed him up the hill to more solid ground, using the moonlight as a guide down the path towards the city. *Such a good horse.*

He sauntered through the neat and vacant streets, wondering where he would find this person he sought. *There's no better place to gather information than at the inns,* he thought. *They must be able to give me something to work with, somewhere to start.* He looked around while he walked the quiet streets, listening for loud crowds singing songs in drunken camaraderie, or slurred shouts of angry men wanting to brawl. It usually went to one or the other, in his experience.

Small arched bridges, painted white and covered with bird droppings, spanned the dark rivers that flowed through the city, connecting the suburbs all around. On the street he led Flintlock along, he counted ten he could see, until the darkness claimed their existence. He turned down one that was broader than the rest, thinking it to be the main street of the city, and followed it. Around him, the apartments and shops opened up to a big, cobbled circle with benches and plants, walkways and green grass, and in the centre rose a statue of an odd-looking man — or so he thought — with large eyes and ears, older by years and resting his one foot on the head of a snake slithering underfoot, his sword raised up to the sky triumphantly. He neared and read the plaque, '"Dedicated to Melche the Mekkel for his outstanding bravery and honour shown in the face of danger. We salute you for your courage!" He must have been a great man to get his own statue. Strange name, though...'

Khanaseri walked down to the docks, glad to not be cold anymore, his heavy overcoat waving in the winds blowing through the streets, passing two guards on their patrol who looked at him with some suspicion. He tipped his head in greeting and continued on, hoping they would not stop to question him. That rarely ended well for anyone. The guards eyed him as they sauntered past, mumbling to each other, smoke drifting from their mouths as they continued walking. Khanaseri let out a sigh of relief.

He led Flintlock over a rickety wooden deck near the docks that showed some signs of old burning, the black char marks leaving flashes across the half-wooden, half-stone inn called The Hollow. A hitching post stood to the left of the inn against the stone wall, the metal rings shining brightly still. *Must be new. Iron would have rusted by now, being so close to the water,* he thought as he tethered Flintlock to the rings and pushed the feeder closer for the horse to reach. Neighing happily, Flintlock dipped his head into the water and food, flicking his tail at the annoying flies. An old feeling of being spied upon washed over Khanaseri as he pushed on the door of the inn, glancing around while he entered to see a cheerful crowd of patrons enjoying their ale, singing songs and flirting with the girls serving drinks.

He made his way to the back, where an empty table stood, and slumped down to count his coins, eyes drifting to him from the crowd. Something flashed from under the table in the light of the lanterns swinging over his head, catching his eye, and he bent down, retrieving a lost coin. Khanaseri rubbed the filth from it and looked at the detail, seeing an old man's face stamped into the metal. He untethered a small leather pouch from his belt and shook it over the table, cursing as only two coins slid out to drop flat. Glancing around, he cupped his hand over the coins and muttered a few words. When he pulled his hand away, a stack of coins lay before him, all with the man's head stamped into them, and he quickly scraped them back into the pouch.

A girl brushed past and asked, 'What can I get ya?'

'Bring me your cheapest ale and a key to a room for the night.' As she turned to leave, he grabbed her wrist. 'Who here lines their pockets for information?'

'You want to remove your hand or lose it, sir,' said a man as he lowered himself opposite Khanaseri.

The warlock let go of the girl and said to her, 'Just the ale and a room, and a hot bath prepared, thank you.'

This man was not someone most would consider threatening, being bat-eared with a stubby nose curling up over puffy lips, his overly large front teeth pushing out of his mouth. He was not a handsome man, and his thinning hair did not help. But Khanaseri knew better. A man such as this did not rely on his physical appearance to scare people. It was his knowledge-hoarding that gave him the upper hand. The warlock knew, though, there was no knowledge of him in this place.

'I'm Barlow Hill. What do you want to know, and why should I divulge anything to you?'

'I'm looking for a man—'

'There's plenty of men, or boys, if that's what you prefer... Which one, exactly?'

The warlock grimaced, pulled away with annoyance, and said, 'Not like that. Another statement like that, and I'll take my coin elsewhere. Got it?'

The man laughed, his crooked, long teeth making him look like a rat that hadn't chewed on anything for a while. His pale face reddened slightly, but Khanaseri reckoned it was just the lantern lights playing tricks on him; it was gloomy, after all. Barlow raised his hands and whispered in a grating tone, 'Got to poke the bear to see when he'll bite.'

'Don't poke this bear,' the warlock said without humour.

'Fair's fair. Who is it you're after?'

'What will this cost me?'

'How much you got?'

Khanaseri grunted, took out a few coins for lodging, meals, and ale, and emptied the pouch before Barlow. The man's eyes sparkled as he stared at the coin. 'Will that do?'

'Uh... Er... Yeah, uhm, that will do.'

'Good.' The warlock leaned back, his green eyes shining unnaturally in the gloom. 'I'm looking for a dead man, or where he's buried. He had long, white hair and yellow eyes. Those of a cat... Too many strange folk in the world now. I believe he was some kind of sorcerer.'

At his words, those around him went quiet, and Barlow slowly rose from the table. 'Best you take your leave and not mention any of this to anyone.'

'Look into my eyes,' said Khanaseri, his voice icy. 'I will break this place apart to get to you, and if I have to make you tell me what I want to know, the night will turn sour. Who is this man, and where is he?' People shuffled away, and some slipped out of the inn as the air grew tense. His ale sloshed over the mug's rim as the servant girl roughly placed it on the table, throwing the key next to it.

'You two better not start anything in here. Sit down!' she shouted, glaring at them both, then turned to Khanaseri and asked, 'Why do you want this man?'

'It's a long story. Let's just say that I need to pay my respects.'

She sighed and said, 'We don't know what they did with Anukke the Bastard's body, but there *is* one who might know. A farmer on the outskirts of Caldonia, you can't miss it. His is the only farm with goats and no sheep. If anyone knows, it'll be him.'

Barlow Hill scraped the coins from the table into his pockets, making to leave, when Khanaseri grabbed his hand and squeezed it hard, twisting the arm down. He sagged to the ground, a silent scream leaving his open mouth, and mumbled, 'Please, we gave you what you want.'

'You gave me nothing. Give it to the girl. Now.'

Some unscrupulous folks got up from their tables and started shouting at him to let Barlow go, but were too afraid to do anything about it. 'But you got what you wanted,' Barlow whined.

'From the girl, not you. Give it to the girl, or I break your hand.'

Moaning and groaning, Barlow slammed the coins on the table and gasped as Khanaseri let go of his hand, rubbing it while he stumbled from the inn in shame, screaming curses at the big warlock. 'You ain't seen the last of me! Bastard. You'll regret the day you were—' The doors closed before he finished his sentence, and Khanaseri chuckled.

'Go on, take it. I'd much rather pay you than that weasel.'

She slipped the coins into her pocket with a smirk, and walked off to serve other customers while he watched her leave, enjoying the sight from behind, and smiled, thinking of her dimples when she'd smirked. His stomach rumbled as he took a drink, complaining that it hadn't been fed for some time, and he felt the effects almost instantly on his empty gut, burning him within. For some time, he sat there, thinking about Yidrog, and now this Anukke the Bastard, wondering where all this would take them. *Will it cause another avalanche of issues to be resolved?*

Or will this truly be the end?

A thick layer of smoke drifted in the room from all the pipe weed and cigars, irritating his nose, and Khanaseri stood from the table. He called out, 'Hey, girl, send some food up to my room, would ya?'

She nodded and replied, 'Second door to the right.'

He walked up the stairs, exhausted, feeling the old timbers bend under his weight, and couldn't help but feel like those timbers himself, buckling under a heavy load. The corridor was narrow, barely wide enough for two to squeeze past, but he'd been sleeping in that dilapidated house with water dripping on his head and wind rushing through the cracks, so this was the least of his concerns. He slipped into the room and saw the steaming bath in the corner. Khanaseri dropped his gear on the ground and took off his clothes to get in. The water felt good, hot and relaxing. He rested his head back, closing his eyes to drift away, when a knock at the door came. 'Hold on, I'm coming.' He suddenly regretted asking for food to be brought up, wishing he could've just fallen asleep in the tub.

He rushed to the door and grabbed the handle, swinging it open to the bar girl's wide-eyed stare. He had forgotten to clothe himself.

The girl blushed and nearly dropped the tray of food, unable to turn her eyes away from his swinging excellence. Only then did he realise he was naked, and grabbed a piece of clothing from the floor to hold before him as he said, 'Argh! Forgive me, my mind is elsewhere. You can put the food on the bed,' and he quickly got back into the tub.

The girl cleared her throat to grab his attention and nervously mumbled, 'Do uhm...you need a...some help? You know...with your hair?' She shook her head, seeing his bald pate and corrected herself, 'I mean, a massage to the head? It's very relaxing.'

He thought for a moment, and said, 'I need all the help I can get to relax.' He heard her pull a chair closer, its feet scraping over the floor, then her chilly hands dipping through the water to massage his neck and up his head past his ears. 'Do my burns not disgust you?' he asked as she glided her hands over the old marks on his neck and ear, the assassin's symbol still clearly visible.

She ran her finger over the arrowhead, then the sword on the symbol and said, 'No. This only proves how strong you are.'

He felt the water rise, and then her cold flesh against his. Eyes open now, he looked into hers, her dark brown hair loosened to drift over the water's surface. 'I don't even know your name, girl.'

'Nagalia. Now you know...'

* * *

Sun rays as sharp as swords cut through the cracks and holes of the heavy curtains, revealing the dust hovering in the gloomy room. It looked like some god was poking holes into a tin for air. One beam danced over Nagalia's naked rump as she slept, the sheets only covering half of her while Khanaseri got dressed. *Underneath all the layers of clothes, you have a fine body,* he thought, goggling at her feminine form. *What a welcome. I think I like this place.*

She stirred and sucked in a long, lung-full of air as she woke, pushing herself up to search for him through sleepy eyes, wrinkling her nose from the setting dust. Nagalia sneezed lightly, and again, covering her mouth with her hand. *She's got manners, too. Bless her.* She caught sight of him in the room's corner and said, 'You heading out already?'

'I am. Lots to do and little time to do it in. Can't stay around here.' He clasped his bootstraps and picked up the axe and pack from the floor. 'Take care of yourself, Nagalia,' he said before walking to the door and pulling it shut behind him, hearing her groan frustratedly as she dropped back to the bed. He saw in his mind how she rolled her eyes, as she had done a few times during the night over some of his remarks.

'Can I get some carrots, apples, feed for the horse, and food for the journey? Maybe some water and something stronger?' he asked, walking down the stairs and seeing the barkeep cleaning the counter. The stocky man dropped his rag on the counter and walked to the back. Khanaseri waited for the man to return, tapping a coin on the wooden bench. The thought of having abandoned Blanka like he had did not sit right with him, and he hoped his friend was okay, but this needed to be done. After a while, the innkeeper appeared with a few items in a basket and put it on the counter. Khanaseri slid a few coins over with his gloved hand and took the items, slinging the horse feed over his shoulder, and headed out the door.

'Morning, Flint. You ready for a ride down to this Caldonia?'

The horse curled his lip, bubbling gently with excitement as it saw the fresh food. 'Come on, Flint. This is for the journey.' The horse nudged him with his head, begging for a scrap. 'Agh, fine. Here, you can have the carrot.' Flintlock neighed and chomped at the vegetable while Khanaseri loaded the gear into the side bag. He looked up at the window of the inn where his room had been, wishing he had something back home to fight for. Sure, he had his friends, but they all had someone else worth fighting for, and it sure as hell wasn't him. *Who am I kidding? I'm not husband material. Just look at me...all dinged up.* He climbed up and mounted Flintlock to ride away from the inn, weaving through the crowded streets of Millanthross. He was pretty happy for a while, riding in silence, hearing the clip-clop of Flintlock's hooves on the hard ground. The sun was up and the temperature agreeable; green grass and forested areas lay to his right, with more hills to his left.

* * *

Despondent elves sat huddled in the hall, sobbing and holding their loved ones while guards and healers aided them. Ladriana stood at the door, watching them with arms crossed, worrying about what was coming. She felt a man's presence next to her, and she glanced at him. 'Captain Volar. Have you recalled all the troops in the area?'

'I have. If their front runners are here already, the main force won't be far behind.'

'Yes, I gathered that,' she said, rubbing her fake belly. It was getting harder to make it look real as time passed. A strange sensation of a caring nature overwhelmed her, the feeling of being a mother. For a brief moment, she wished it really *was* a baby, and shook her head. 'Get your men and the advisers together. We need to prepare for war. And where is Abe? He needs to make it clear to every single person in his school that they will have to pitch in if they want to survive. I want some kind of protection against those fucking fire-breathing bats. Bring those other two, Captain Ganda'har and Blanka, as well. If they'll fight with us, we need to include them in our plans. Ensure that all citizens unable to wield a weapon, stitch a wound, carry messages, or dig fucking trenches are off the streets. Everyone who can do something *will* do something. The citizens of New Runswick will open their homes to all who don't have a place of safety, by royal decree. We will leave no one in the streets. Make that very clear to them.'

'Yes, milady. What about the dwarves?'

'Have them all join the council. There's no hiding anything from anyone. Get my father up to the castle as well. He needs to lock up his shop for the time being. Force him, if you must. On second thought, I'll take care of that. You're far too busy with the other things on the list.'

Volar nodded and left the hall in a hurry.

At the far end of the hall, King Elyon dragged his feet over the marble floor, with Valheim supporting him, and slumped down on a bench, the exhaustion clear on his face. Ladriana made her way to them, lowering herself to sit next to him. She lay her hand over his in his lap, staring at the disbelief in his eyes, and said, 'Your people are safe for now, King Elyon. But we must be ready for battle, for it will surely come.'

'I had a thousand men when we left Rolldemere. Of those, I don't know how many survived, but I know all who did will fight with you till the end.'

'How's your arm?' she asked, gesturing to the bloodstains on his robe.

'The healer stitched him up. He will be fine,' Valheim said through gritted teeth. 'Where are Dorgal and those dragon men?'

'They're in the other hall, with more of the elves. This room was getting too crowded for so many. We can walk there if you'd like. I need to speak with them as well.' She saw the anger on the elf's face, his fury rising with every breath. 'Follow me.'

The corridors were a jumble of chaos, with men running around helping wounded elves and sorting out food and water and blankets for those who needed them. Gone was the idea of them being elves; now they were survivors. What her men had witnessed from the walls and beyond had changed them, humbled them, their arrogance cast to the winds upon seeing the fire billow from those beasts' gaping maws to melt steel down to worthless scraps.

A hubbub sounded from down the corridor, loud and concerning: men shouting over each other, ready to throw punches. 'I don't care if you can turn into my mother! I won't take orders from ye, ye lizard!'

'I'm not giving you orders, you half-cocked gutter gnome! I'm explaining what the situation is!'

'I'll shave your neck with mine axe and plant my boot up yer a—'

'Enough!' shouted Ladriana, moving to stand between the dwarves and Ganda'har, her guards immediately surrounding them. 'The only boots that will get shoved up anywhere will be mine! And I have a few high heels that will make things *very* uncomfortable for all involved.' The guards glanced at each other, smirking and looking away. 'What's going on here?'

'He insulted us, he did!' said Dorgal, and more dwarves nodded, swinging their fists and pointing fingers, stirring up the hubbub once more.

'I did no such thing!' stated Ganda'har, flicking his arms out to them.

'Quiet!' Her voice bounced off the walls and all fell silent, tamed by her anger. 'One at a time. Ganda'har, what happened?'

'I'm trying to explain to these...' he struggled with the words, 'dwarves, that they should stay behind the walls.'

'He calls us cowards! We're not cowards. Have ye ever seen a dwarf fight, young man? No, because if ye were fighting with one, ye'd be dead! Deceitful bastard!'

'Calm down, Dorgal! I've not seen you this worked up. What are you not telling me, Ganda'har?'

The captain sighed and said, 'I wasn't hiding or deceiving anyone. Fighting them is not the only reason we're here. They have Blanka's boy, and we mean to get him back. Once we get him away, we'll rejoin the fight. Simple as that. We plan on sneaking into their camp while they're attacking New Runswick to take the boy, but now the dwarves want in, but we can't have more noise made.'

'See! Now he's calling us fat-footed dwarves.'

'You *are* dwarves! And those feet are enormous!'

'They are regular!'

'Have you ever seen a dwarf at night?' barked Dorgal.

Ganda'har shook his head. 'What? No—'

'Exactly!' shouted Galiban.

'That doesn't even make sense!' retorted Ganda'har, his arms in the air.

'Wise-arse!' roared another dwarf.

'One more outburst, and I swear I will make you sit in your corners like children!' barked Ladriana.

Valheim pushed through the mob of angry dwarves to join her. 'I have an idea you dwarves would be perfect for, but we'd better get to it quickly.'

* * *

'Hey, Flint, have you ever seen a woman as fine as Nagalia?' Khanaseri asked, lying with his back against the horse's neck, his feet criss-crossed over Flint's rump while eating nuts, throwing the shells next to the road as they walked. Flintlock shook his head and snorted, nearly throwing the warlock, who flailed with arms in the air. 'Hey, there's no need for that. I ain't replacing you, boy. It's just a wishful dream for one day. You know. I'm sure you've had your eye on some filly somewhere on the prairie...' He glanced over his shoulder to look ahead. 'Damn boring road, hardly ever turns. Must be a thief's nightmare, this, they'd spot 'em a mile away. Can you imagine trying to commandeer a wagon on this stretch?' He laughed. 'You'd be waiting days and still get spotted by the most novice of drivers.'

Flintlock neighed.

'When last did we see anyone on this road? Yesterday? Anyway, where was I? Oh yes. I bet you'll find a lady-friend way before me. Have yourself a nice little family, settle down somewhere quiet-like. All while I stumble through life, finding shithole after shithole.'

A storm brewed up ahead from the east, grey clouds rolling in with no love for the high trees, thunderous lightning arcing down, reaching for their tops. The wind picked up, blowing the clouds over them, and soon soaked them with their abundance of water, making Khanaseri a fairly cranky warlock. 'I shouldn't be complaining about the rain, but couldn't it wait until I got to some shelter?' He turned in the saddle and leaned forward, pushing Flintlock to a trot. Off to the left, swinging in the wind a ways down the road and through a stand of trees, lanterns flickered wildly. 'You reckon that's a farm? This damned storm has stolen daylight from us. Wait, are those goats?' Khanaseri squinted and cupped his hands over his eyes, seeing the white blotches jumping all over the farming equipment. 'Is that one on the roof of the barn? How...?'

He dropped from Flintlock's back and took the lead, guiding them through the woods, scraping past the trees to get to a low fence. He looked at the impediment, then to the goat on the barn's roof, and chuckled. 'Lotta good this will do you.' He led Flintlock to a gate and entered the property, sneaking to the barn to dry off. Hay lay heaped in one corner with farming implements to the right: a disc plough, a seed barrow, scythes, rakes, shovels, and plenty of others. Flintlock pulled the reins from the warlock's hand and trotted over to the hay, greedily digging in to fill his stomach.

'Guess we'll wait until the storm passes before we go say hi.' Khanaseri walked around inspecting the barn, and saw a strange latch on the floor near the back. He'd just bent down to investigate it when a swooshing sound sailed over his head, wind rushing over him as splinters flew from a snapped pillar used for support to the thin walls cordoning off various areas. Khanaseri leapt forward as he saw the glint of a weapon being swung down, splintering the wooden flooring where he'd stood. Again, the weapon came down, crashing into the wooden slats set up to house animals, smashing holes through them with ease. On the ground now, he pushed himself back with his hands and feet, the hammer crunching into the floorboards before his crotch, wood chips flying into him. He stared at the colossal hammer with its etched runes being dragged from the floor and hoisted up for another swing.

'Wait!' he shouted, but the hammer kept coming. A swing to the right, and Khanaseri jumped away, evading the blow and drawing his axe. Flintlock neighed loudly, standing on his hind legs, forelegs scything at their attacker. Metal on metal screeched as their weapons collided, sparks flying from the strike. Taller than Khanaseri, their attacker had the upper hand, and he was strong, pushing the warlock back with terrifying force.

'Why? So you can steal Old Bill?' growled the attacker, his voice harsh and unforgiving. The pen's wall took another hit, and as he drew the hammer out, a massive, sharp horn thrust through, collapsing it to the ground. It hit the floor with a loud clatter and a gigantic bull stormed from the pen, eyes red with anger.

'Shit!'

The bull nearly skewered the farmer, scraping its horns against the wooden frame as the man jumped out of its path.

'What would I want with that monster?' Khanaseri shouted while they both circled the bull on opposite ends, watching it decide who it wanted to attack. 'We need to get it back into the pen!'

'Nah, really? Figure that out all by yourself? Yer mother must be so proud.'

Khanaseri shook his head, annoyed at the retort. He made his way to the pen and jumped over the still-standing walls, carefully gauging the animal.

'Yeah, good. You be the bait. I'll get the gate.' The bull scraped its hooves, getting ready to charge. The colossal one-and-a-half-ton beast's black hide rippled with tension and excitement as it bolted off the line, bellowing with rage, and dropped its head, horns flashing past. 'Oh, yer in for it now, boy!'

Khanaseri waited until the very last moment to jump out and over, the horns punching holes through the wooden wall, nearly crashing through. Khanaseri gabbed the horns on the other side, holding on as hard as he could. 'Quick! The gate!' The bull shook its head furiously to break free, hitting the sides of the stall with its broad body, and bellowed, aggressively pulling to be freed.

'Yeah, yeah. Hold on to yer knickers, boy.' The man picked up the wall and drove nails through to secure it in place, taking his time before doing the other side. He stepped back and looked at his handiwork, cocking his head at the skewed wall. 'It'll do for now.'

The bull ripped its horns from Khanaseri's hands and the timbers, turning around in the pen to search for more threats, forcing out the air from its nose and dripping snot to the ground. The warlock sagged to the floor, glad he hadn't been skewered, when powerful hands grabbed his throat, hoisting him into the air. He hit the back wall of the barn, air exploding from his mouth, and stared at the man holding him off the ground, chewing at a dead cigar. Deep lines criss-crossed the man's forehead, his long brown hair lined with streaks of grey, while icy blue eyes stared back at him. The cigar shook in the farmer's mouth as he pointed to the bull and said, 'That ain't Old Bill. Who are you, and what do you want?'

Only now did Khanaseri realise how loud the rain fell on the roof above, and the thought of the goat on top came back to him. He shook the thought from his mind and dropped his axe on the ground, seeing the older man's arms shake. 'You fight like a veteran. I don't have any grief with you. I'm Khanaseri. We can talk, if you put me down.' Khanaseri cocked his head. 'Are you Old Bill?'

The big man chuckled humorously and dropped him. 'Like anyone would want to take me... No, I'm Malachai.' He picked up his hammer and walked away to sit on a bale of hay, waiting for Khanaseri to talk.

'I came in here to dry out from the rain. Wanted to wait for it to pass over before knocking on your door. I got directions to you from a girl in Millanthross. She said you might point me in the direction I need to go—'

'Well, that's easy. You go out this door, carry on until you get to the road, then you turn left or right. I don't give a damn. Is your horse seriously keeping us apart right now? As if you're the victim...'

Khanaseri walked up to Flintlock and took his reins, leading him back to the hay pile while rubbing his neck. 'It's okay, Flint.' He glanced back. 'Do you have some water for him?'

'There's a water trough over there, near the main doors.'

'Thanks, Flint will appreciate it.' He led him to the water trough and left him there. 'I could really use some guidance here. I was told you would know where I could find Anukke's body or bones. It's very important I find them.'

Malachai tilted his head and rose from the bale, pointing his finger at Khanaseri. 'You be very careful with your next words, or your horse might need to step in again. What do you want with that bastard?'

The tension rose instantly. Khanaseri shook his head and sat down, groaning from the never-ending trouble he seemed to find himself in. *I could make up some lie and tell him what he wants to hear. They don't like this Anukke at all.* 'I have come to take him far away from here, across the seas to the land of my people: the desert warriors of Artokla.'

'Are you mad? What are you, like, his cousin or something?'

'What's going on in here? I heard the ruckus all the way to the house,' came a voice from the door.

'Back here, Gwen. All's good. Had a little trouble with Pheistus. He broke out of his pen again. And we have some company, it seems.'

A woman with bouncing curly hair appeared round the corner and stopped at the sight of Khanaseri, who slowly stood.

'Pleased to meet you. I'm Khanaseri. Forgive my intrusion, I was just telling Malachai here that I—'

'He wants to take away Anukke's body,' interrupted Malachai.

'He wants to do what? Is he mad?'

'I asked him that...'

'And?' She looked at Malachai.

'And what? He hasn't answered yet, what with you yappin' away like a bored housewife. I told you to make friends with the neighbours.'

She glared at him, set to punch him straight in the mouth, then composed herself quickly and swung to Khanaseri. 'You hungry?'

'Starving.'

'Now wait a moment, there! You can't be seriously inviting him into our home, where our children sleep. We don't even know him. He could be a murderer, for all we know,' Malachai pleaded before his wife, hands in his hair.

Gwen looked past her broad husband and asked, 'You a murderer? Or a thief? You wish us any harm?'

'No, ma'am,' said Khanaseri, smirking at the deviousness of this woman.

'There you go. Come on. Malachai, set the plates.'

'Dear! Dear! Don't ignore me...' Khanaseri heard the big man's voice as he followed Gwen out of the barn.

The three entered the grey timber home, and Khanaseri relaxed with the warmth it projected. A ticking sound came from a device hanging on the wall in the lounge, where two large couches and a single leather armchair stood before a fireplace. A dining room table was set in the corner with six chairs around it, the plates already stacked on top of each other on one end. Gwen gestured for him to sit at that end and waited for him to comply.

It was awkward being in someone's home. He remembered that they had visited other people when he was a boy, when his father needed to talk business, but he was never invited alone. It felt strange, and he wasn't sure of the etiquette.

As soon as he took his seat, Gwen spun to him and glared into his eyes, her brows furrowed. Suddenly, he understood why Malachai was so gentle around her. Inches from his face, she said, 'Now you're in my house, and you better understand this. I've seen Malachai break men's bones with his bare hands, crush their bodies with that hammer with a single blow, and I promise you: that's nothing compared to what I will do to you if you try anything to harm us. Got that?'

'Yes, ma'am. You won't have any trouble with me.'

'Good. Malachai, plates! I'll make up a room for our guest.' Unwillingly obeying his wife, Malachai set a plate before Khanaseri, mumbling as he did.

The warlock felt awkward, like a young boy again before his father, not knowing what to say when he came home angry from work. He looked at the ticking device and asked, 'What is that?'

Malachai peered up at the device. 'It's a gift from a friend who's as annoying as he is good with his hands. He calls it a time-dial. He actually thinks everyone will have one soon. Ha. It keeps track of time in the day. Don't know why you'd need it. You need only look up at the sky and you know how long the day has left. So unnecessary. Here she comes.' He leaned closer and whispered, 'You will eat your fill, sleep, and leave tomorrow before the sun is up. We won't talk of this Anukke business again.'

Khanaseri leaned forward as well. 'I've been on the back foot since I got here, but be very careful not to misjudge me. I've had my fair share of scraps, believe me. I ain't afraid to break a few bones myself. We *will* talk about my business before I leave.'

A deep growl left Malachai, and he gripped the edge of the table, his knuckles turning white with the pressure, showing great restraint. 'Fine, but not at the table in front of my kids, yeah? Tomorrow we go to the field and you can cry all you want, boy.'

Khanaseri gritted his teeth. 'Just because you're old doesn't make me a boy!'

'Eat your food.' Malachai walked away and slapped him at the back of the head, before sitting at the other end as Gweniviere walked into the room with a smile, a young boy and girl following close behind. It forced Khanaseri to do nothing and take that bit of humiliation, and Malachai enjoyed it, smirking behind his grey-streaked beard. They ate in silence, a constant bit of tension in the air, with little conversation to go around.

Chapter Fourteen

An anxious flutter rippled through Ladriana. Garidan was rumoured dead, assassins were still after her, and a battle they could not win waited on their doorstep, yet she persevered, clinging to the belief that they would survive somehow. Impoverished refugees from neighbouring villages and cities flooded her kingdom, finding shelter in the bosom of New Runswick, hoping their walls could withstand whatever *they* could throw at them. She could not stay out of the streets forever, though, not with all that was going on.

Her breath was icy, even with the sun beaming vigorously. A trembling in her core made her unsteady, her legs wobbling beneath her as the world contorted with every step down to the lobby. She stood with her hand on the doorknob, taking a deep breath, and pushed on the door, stepping out with a show of confidence and defiance. *I will not be afraid.*

'Should I get the carriage ready, milady?' asked Whiley, waddling in through the gates for his shift.

'No, I'll take my horse. This is no time to look weak.' She adjusted the pillows under her clothes, cursing the annoyance they brought, and glanced around to see who took notice. A quick jump, and she pulled herself up. Her stomach caught on the stirrups, tearing a gash at the front of the green velvet gown. She wanted to cry and scream and shout. She wanted to flop on the floor and throw a gigantic tantrum... It all felt like too much for one person to bear. At that moment, she decided it was okay if she didn't come out of this battle alive. She'd give it her all, fight with every drop of strength she had left to save New Runswick and its people, but she didn't want this burden anymore. How could it be expected of her?

'Your Highness, what are you doing out of the castle?' asked a soldier from her right.

'Kehlos, you have impeccable timing, as usual. Get on your horse and join me. We ride for my father's shop, and then to Abe to discuss the strategy with the students. I need to know that we have some kind of defence ready.'

He whistled to the men riding in behind him at a slower pace. 'Stop messing about and fall in.'

'Milady, you look as beautiful as ever,' smirked Brookley, bowing slightly from atop his horse.

'Stop kissing so much arse, Brook,' mumbled Singer as his horse drew near.

'Oi! Some respect. You're speaking to the queen, not some bimbo in the pub.' Kehlos glared at them and swung to Ladriana in his saddle. 'My apologies, milady. They forget their place once they feel too comfortable around people.'

The queen chuckled. 'It's okay, Kehlos. I don't know what he's kissing, 'cause I can barely lift my arse out of the saddle today.' The two soldiers smiled and fell in next to Ladriana, with Kehlos at the lead, walking down the busy streets at a brisk pace. Store owners were busily shutting their doors, boarding up the windows and leaving restless buyers fuming on the sidewalk. An orderly line had been formed through the streets of those unfortunate souls who had lost their homes, waiting to be assigned a place of safe harbour for the battle to come. No unnecessary feet on the streets during the attack; there would be enough confusion and chaos on the day.

Ladriana clenched her teeth and gagged as a terrible stench burnt her nose; her eyes tearing up while she leaned over the saddle. 'What *is* that?' They rode through a lower sector of the city where the streets were muddy, and she recognised the healer's home where Magnus had recovered. To the left, human waste drifted down a river of filth to form a pile shrouded with flies and maggots.

'The city can't take the strain of all those additional folks. Too much shit, too little space, as my Da used to say. Excuse the language, milady. If we don't die from the battle, we'll die from this. People will get sick and soon we'll have a plague on our hands.' Kehlos glowered at the pile, cursing as he saw a drunk woman take a shit next to the pile, using a low wall to hang on to. But who could blame them? They had nowhere else to go.

The gift that keeps on giving, being a ruler of a nation. Who in their right mind would want to do this job? Every time you think you have a handle on things, something new crops up and stirs wood splinters into your porridge. I wish Atwood was still here... How did that old man manage everything for so long? I haven't been here a year, and the treasury is exhausted. Shit's flowing down in such amounts that they'll need to start paying taxes, and I don't know how we'll pay the soldiers for their service. She looked at the three around her and wanted so badly to tell them to leave; that she couldn't pay them...but the city needed them, she needed them.

They came to a stop before her father's modest shop, a grey-painted sign with a gold-leaf border in the window with the name *Nuka Jewellers*. Ladriana dropped from her horse, gazing at the people who gawked at her, and said, 'Stay here and keep them out. I'll be back soon.' While the people waddled through the shit, she walked with her velvet gown stretched over her fake belly. *I will make this right...*

She strode into the shop, searching for her father, and saw nothing but empty display cases, the jewellery all taken out and stored for safekeeping. Voices grew louder the deeper she walked, until she reached the back. Lifting the small client counter, Ladriana passed through and reached a door, spying on a man dressed in fine clothing shouting at her father. Roahn shied away from the man as a finger waved in his face, spittle flying from the angry man. 'Where is my gold? You will pay me everything you owe me! I fronted the business, and I lost everything! You promised me a return!'

Roahn cowered behind his arms, and whimpered, 'You stole from us, causing the failure of the business, and now you want *more?*'

The man grabbed a hammer from a nearby workbench, ready to swing down, when Ladriana grabbed him from the back and hurled him against the wall. The man jumped up and shouted, 'You bitch!'

'Ebron?' she whispered, frowning at him.

Ebron glanced between them and grumbled, 'Who are you?'

'Look closely. You know who I am. Forget the fact that I am queen of this nation.'

'No...no. It can't be.'

'Yes, it is. I've always wondered why the shop didn't make any coin. We sold more and more, yet less came in. You piece of shit! We trusted you!' A hard right hook bounced off Ebron's jaw, snapping his head around, followed by a hard kick to the ribs, pinning him up against the wall. The gown tore further, and the pillow pushed through. Ebron's face lit up with a smirk under her boot. 'Liar! You're not pregnant! You won't be queen for long! Just wait until the word gets out!'

She didn't even try to conceal the pillow. Ladriana lunged at him with her knee extended, crashing into his stomach and curling him over. Her fist came down with a scream and she cracked him on the side of the face, dropping him to the floor with a spray of blood. She felt instantly better. 'Come, Pops. You'll stay in the castle for now. This fool won't bother us again. Kehlos!' She pulled her father from the ground and turned to the soldier dashing into the room with sword drawn. 'Kehlos, meet Ebron. The bastard who stole from us. The monumental piece of shit who saw me and my father sold as slaves.'

'Is that right?' Kehlos grinned as he extended his hand and slipped, cracking the man on his face just as he was about to rise. 'My apologies. The floor is so slippery. What would you have me do with him, milady? Feed him to the wolves?'

Ebron paled. 'You can't do that to me,' he said, spitting blood on the floor.

She thought for a moment and said, 'No. Clean him up and put a sword in his hand. Take him up to the front wall to stand beside the soldiers there. Put him between men you know and trust to keep my secret. If he runs, set the dogs on him. He'll fight for New Runswick to reclaim his freedom. Maybe, just maybe, if he survives that, I'll let him go and pay him a fair wage for his service as a soldier.'

Kehlos chuckled. 'You're in for a wild ride, Ebron. Are you left-handed, or right-handed?' the soldier asked as he forced the man to his feet and out the door.

'Left-handed, why?'

'Just working out where not to put my friends.'

Roahn shuffled over to his workbench and said, 'Let's fix that gown first. We don't want people gawking at the pillow-baby.'

* * *

'King Elyon? What are you doing here?' Ladriana exclaimed as they exited the shop, seeing the elf king approach on horseback with a host of his warriors, and the priest, Ehrhard, following behind, cursing the animal under him with every step. *They look much better than yesterday,* she thought. *Elyon has some colour back in his face.* Although cleaned up, the bloodstains on the elegant blue-white uniform still lingered, made known in the sunlight, but the elf king bore himself with pride, his long dark hair combed back, waving in the winds with a thick braid at the back in between the loose strands. His deep blue eyes pierced hers, and she could not help but look away, her palms suddenly wet.

'Ah, Queen Ladriana, we've found you at last. Ehrhard has been nibbling away at my ears about having to see you regarding the Elven warriors, to talk strategy. So here I am, trying to appease the old one. It seems, though, that the horse did what I couldn't.'

Another elf helped Ehrhard down from the animal with groans of suffering as the old priest rubbed his bony buttocks. 'I swear these beasts were made for torture, nothing else. Hello, my dear,' he said, limping to her with an abrupt smile. 'I've figured it out,' he whispered near to her. Flashing back to King Elyon, he continued, 'Roahn, would you regale King Elyon with your fine works that you've been busy with? I have a personal matter to discuss with the queen. It is a sensitive matter that cannot wait.'

The jeweller's face brightened, unable to think of a more fortuitous arrangement than having his wares shown to the absolute master craftsmen of the world. 'I would be delighted.'

'What is the matter with you, Ehrhard?' the queen demanded. 'Out with it.'

Ehrhard smiled and dragged Ladriana a distance away, and rejoiced, 'I know how to save your seat. I know what must be done!'

She was not sure she wanted to hear the rest of this. Ladriana just wanted to hold out until the battle; then no one would think of her seat, just of survival, and afterwards, she wouldn't care what happened. She could disappear. *If only it were that easy...*

Ehrhard gestured to the elf king with his open hand and smiled. 'He's your answer. It would be the perfect way to keep your seat, as he is a king and nothing will strengthen the coalition between humans and elves more than a marriage. And he is quite the catch. Even I can see that, with my misaligned virtues of human favouritism.' He saw the sadness in her eyes and sighed. 'I know you miss and love Garidan still, my dear. We all do. This is the way you can show him yourself. That you would not let New Runswick down. Fulfil his wishes and unite the races! If you want to see change, this is how it is done!' Ehrhard shook his head, seeing he was not about to make any headway with her. 'At least think about it,' he grumbled, turning around angrily and stomping off past the elves, waving the one away that wanted to assist him back onto the horse. 'I'm walking, thank you. That infernal creature will get no more of me today!'

Ladriana was at a loss for words, feeling weak and fragile, and she hated it. Eyes closed, she stood to collect herself when the gentlest touch to her arms made her jerk. *How did he move so quietly over the mud and rocks?* She stared into Elyon's eyes and was lost in their radiance, afraid to say anything for fear that she would burst into sobs.

'Come, let's walk to the wall. Ehrhard mentioned you wanted to see the wizard. He is waiting for you there.'

'How'd you—'

He smiled caringly. 'I have my own talents.' Holding out his arm, she slipped hers into it, and they walked down the road together, hearing gasps from those trudging by, the usual bows replaced by a flicker of uncertainty and shame and disgust. It did not bother Elyon in the slightest; he held his head high as they made their way to the walls.

Cleverly designed, the walls did not have open stairs running to the top on the outside, but were hidden behind a layer of stonework inside the wall, so any who made it over would need to run out in single file through the doorway at the bottom, making them easy pickings for a few archers lying in wait. They ascended the steps with the host of elves, Brookley, and Singer at their rear, greeting the soldiers who worked to ready armaments for the coming siege. Not having been able to exercise in a long time, Ladriana's thighs were now burning from the climb up the wall, but it felt good.

'Are you well, Ladriana? You seem winded,' frowned Elyon. 'You need only ask and we can return to the castle. In your condition, it is understandable.'

She felt ashamed of the lie she carried, wanting to rip the pillow from her stitched-up gown and let the truth come blundering out. 'No, I'm fine. I need the exercise.' They reached the top and filed out, standing watch over the parapet, listening to the sounds in the air.

'Ah, Queen Ladriana, King Elyon. Glad you made the trip to the wall.'

A dark terror pulled at her stomach as she looked at him, but knew it was still the effects of the magic of that day. She shook her head and acknowledged, 'Abe... Yes, I was feeling holed up in the castle. I needed to stretch my legs. Any news from the students?'

The idea didn't sit well with any of them, but ballistae alone would not be enough to hold off the dragons. The old court mage nodded unhappily, his voice grating as he spoke. 'Yes... I've had the discussion with them, and although a lot of them believe me reprehensible to make them use their gifts in this manner, they have agreed to lend a hand. Those who outright refused, I have sent to the dormitory, not to leave their rooms until this conflict has been resolved. We have three hundred willing to stand by us, and the dwarves have been very helpful in creating focal points for our spell to tack onto.' Abe walked over to the wall behind Ladriana and palmed a shining octagonal prism made of metal with a fiercely sharp point reaching up and twisted into a spiral to look like a claw. 'They are truly master craftsmen. It took them a day to create eight of these, where our blacksmiths just scratched their heads, unable to understand my needs.'

Elyon approached the device fastened to the wall and ran his finger over the curved edge. 'I haven't seen the dwarves craft magical amplifiers in centuries. It must've been an interesting conversation to get Dorgal to agree. The dwarves are famed for their stubbornness. How did you persuade them?'

'I gave them a gift,' gloated Abe from under his dark, bushy brow, smiling.

'Dwarves rarely want more than food and mead. What could you possibly have offered them?' probed Elyon. His eyes narrowed on the wizard.

'A gift they didn't know they wanted,' Abe replied, making it painfully obvious he would say no more on the matter.

Elyon turned back to the parapet overlooking the fields below. 'Queen Ladriana, I believe the best position for us elves is here on the wall. We are the best archers, and have superior bows. We will thin their lines long before they reach the walls. I will stand with Abe to lend my talents and, if need be, defend them to my last breath.'

'I'm sorry, King Elyon. I can't have you in harm's way. We must protect you for the sake of your people,' Ladriana said.

He pierced her armour with his eyes. 'And where will you be? By my side in the halls of your castle, waiting for the end to come? I think not. I can see it in your eyes. You yearn to be the tip of the spear, and I will be right here with you.'

'Uh, milady. I think you better have a look at this,' called the eagle-eyed Singer from the right, pointing to the mountains far to the west. Ladriana's heart sank upon seeing the black mass of enemy soldiers swarming down the side of the mountain from Camp Peliay, knowing the time had come. For a moment, she stood alone on that wall against the approaching horde, unarmed and outnumbered, chilled to the bone. Then she noticed the warmth in her hand, the rubbing of skin on skin, and her mind drifted back, peering down at Elyon's hand firmly clasped around hers.

She might as well. The end was so close now.

* * *

'Look at them... Running around in my city like they own it. Cockroaches!' shouted Turneroth as he lowered the spyglass.

'Sire, the best position for the camp would be to the right over there.' Xare pointed, rubbing the scar across his chest.

'Yes, send one of the Kingsguard to secure the area and report back. You will stay by my side to fulfil my orders. I don't want another Ragian messing up my plans.'

Xare bowed and turned away, seeing the three other Kingsguard making light of the situation, not at all concerned about the lives lost among those who had volunteered before them. Slip had raised his hand after the king forced Xare to volunteer. He would not let his friend go through it alone. *You idiot...you should have never stood up.* He wanted to break the bonding halfway when he saw Slip's eyes bulge from their sockets, but he was restrained by the other Kingsguard already turned. He watched his friend torn open like a tin can, his body smouldering as it boiled from the inside. There was nothing he could do, and he would never stop resenting them for it.

Turneroth gripped his head, squeezing it to relieve some of the throbbing. A constant fire lingered behind his eyes, burning fiercer each day. His men marched down the mountain through the narrow, treacherous path leading to the forest below, a forest he knew well, their black and brown leather armour making them look like thousands of ants scurrying for a scrap left on the floor. Soon, they would start setting up camp.

A storm raged in his head, with Belroc at the centre, burning his humanity out of him. Scales hard as steel slithered forward, the ground quivering with fear. Eyes the colour of hate hovered before him; slitted pupils like blades on fire carved pieces of his life from his mind, while rotted fangs the size of broadswords crunched on his sanity, a snakelike tongue licking the blood from his bones piece by piece. *Malice is his name...* He felt a foreigner in his own skin, a journeyman who hadn't paid the toll with an angry ferryman sitting across from him, rocking the boat aggressively and spitefully while their eyes locked, floating over a river of damned souls. Arms reached up from below the filthy water, threatening to overturn the small craft, those depthless hollow sockets promising a lifetime of torture and suffering for the penitent. *Vengeance is his name...*

A sound, so annoying and grating in his ears, screeched loud, buzzing in his head, and he snapped out his arm, claws extended.

'Papa! It's me! You're hurting me!' Moseroth squirmed in the scaled claws, a talon shaving his chin while he stared into the eyes of something demented.

'I'm not your father, boy! I never was!' Turneroth felt his hands tighten around the soft neck. The king tried to stop himself, but his body had a mind of its own...or, more accurately, the one harbouring inside did.

'Papa!' came the boy's strangled cries, with no respite in sight. Black spots covered his vision, and suddenly Moseroth dropped to the ground, gasping for breath as Turneroth coughed and sneezed, spinning around in a cloud of pink powder, fighting off an endless assault on his senses. The wizard Bohan stood nearby and glared at him, gestured with his head to get back on the wagon. 'Go to your studies! Now!' shrieked the wizard. Scrambling on all fours, the boy slipped and fell twice, looking back at his father, who was still recovering from the settling powder.

The king waved the air in front of his face, dissipating the powder. His eyes returned to their normal self, and he spewed pink phlegm to the ground, drawing a deep breath before spewing some more. 'What happened? Guards!'

'Oh, stop it. It is me, Bohan. Some water to rinse your eyes and you will be fine.'

'Your head will roll, wizard! How dare you?'

'How dare *I*?' he shoved a waterskin into the king's hand and watched as he rinsed his face. 'You nearly murdered your own little boy! Look around you! You will lose the confidence of your people long before you return home with this thing trapped in you. Moseroth fears you now.' Bohan leaned on his cane and walked away from the king, mumbling before he called over his shoulder, 'Remember. If my head rolls, you stay right here...forever.'

The king glanced around him, seeing the worried faces of the soldiers as they strode past, unwilling to make eye contact. *We're going home soon. Then all this can stop. All this will be in the past, forgotten with time.* Silent, he fell in next to his nervously marching men, descending the mountain on foot.

* * *

Mist drifted low over the ground, like a blanket of wool rolling through the fields of the farmlands, covering their feet and hiding the rocks and holes beneath. Malachai loosened his muscles, stretching this way and that before the protruding hammer shaft, keeping Khanaseri in his sight. Far to the right stood the farmhouse they'd walked from in the early hours of the morning. The sun had barely crept over the hills when Malachai dragged him from the room, forcing him out with angry shoves and little patience. Gwen had stood in the lounge, arms crossed and angry, persuading her husband to let this go, but he wouldn't listen. He was as hard-headed as Pheistus, and nearly just as strong. 'Gwen has taught me lots of patience, and the children have quenched my anger loads, but I cannot and will not give you what you want for nothing.'

Khanaseri combed his beard with his fingers and asked, 'What *do* you want?'

'I want you to get on your horse and never come back here.' Malachai shifted with unease suddenly. Those same words he had spoken to a good friend a long time ago; saying them again brought back those hard memories. He remembered watching his friend ride away. *It's been so many years now.* He shook his head. 'You walk, and we don't do this. We *do* this and you don't walk, permanently.'

'You will find I don't break easily,' replied Khanaseri, removing his jacket and placing it on the ground. 'I didn't come here to fight you. I only want Annuke's body.'

Malachai grunted. 'I tell you what. If you can beat me, then I'll tell you; heck, I'll take you there. If not, then you leave and don't come back. Deal?'

'You're looking for a fight?'

'Fight? We can if you want, but I was thinking we could play hugball. A game I invented that is as physical and violent as a skirmish on the battlefield.' He tossed an oval-shaped, leather-skinned ball stuffed with pieces of torn clothing and rags to the warlock and continued, 'You run for those trees over there. If you make it, you get a point. If I stop you, you get nothing and I get the chance to run to those bushes over there for my point. Drop the ball, and I can claim it to score a point if you can't stop me. After each turn, we start from the middle of the field. Get it?'

'Er... I think so.'

'Good. First to ten wins. I have to say that I'm a poor loser, so we might end up fighting anyway.' Malachai stretched his thighs, kicked his knees up one at a time as high as he could, and lowered to the ground, pressing his knuckles through the white mist into the soil, feeling small stones push into his skin.

Khanaseri followed his lead and squatted a few feet away, scanning the field to work out a strategy. The sun was yet to rise high enough to chase the mist from the field. For now, they would rely on their luck.

They stood facing each other, getting ready for the run, their stares unflinching, and Malachai shouted, 'Ready! Set! Go!' Both men blasted off the line, but Malachai reacted quicker and crashed into Khanaseri with his colossal shoulder, driving it into the warlock's chest, bellowing his war-cry out loud. They sailed through the air, with Khanaseri driven backwards in an explosion of air to plunge into the mist and onto the ground. Malachai was quick on his feet, and didn't wait for the warlock, who groaned in agony and struggled for breath as he sat up, caressing his ribs. 'Whew! What a rush!' Malachai yelled as he grabbed the ball from the ground a few feet away and ran to the bushes. 'You need to hold on to the ball. At least try to make it difficult. That's one for me.'

'Stop your yappin' and let's go again. Your ball,' hissed Khanaseri. They reset, lowering before each other glaringly. 'Ready! Set! Go!' Khanaseri jumped up and was immediately blinded as blood sprayed from his nose, his eyes tearing up while he collapsed to the ground on his knees, clutching his face. Malachai had thrown the ball as hard as he could, shattering his nose, then picked it up again and jogged to the bushes where he did his victory dance, waving up to an invisible crowd.

'I can hear their cheers! Can you? We should play this game in gladiators' arenas all over Kraydenia.'

Khanaseri twisted his nose, straightening it with a crunch and a groan. 'Snake tits! Bastard! This is not a fair game.'

'Life's not fair. Deal with it.' The big man sauntered over to the middle of the field. 'You giving up already?'

'Just get ready! Your ball, again. Ready! Set! Go!' The world spun quick and endless, his head hitting the rocks and dirt now visible with the rising sun. Malachai's arm had come out of nowhere, catching him in the throat and hurling him to the ground. 'Fu—'

'Oi!' interrupted Malachai with his hands on his hips. 'Watch your language! There be children in the house. That's three...'

'Blasted, stupid game! Come on, then! I don't have all day! Your ball, again!' In frustration, the warlock hit the ground with his palm and readied for another run. 'Ready! Set! Go!' Malachai came straight at him with a boarish grin, shouting to intimidate Khanaseri. The warlock waited for the big man to draw near and dropped to the ground at the very last, hooking his legs in between the giant's, sending him sprawling to the ground, his face covered in dirt and cuts.

Malachai shook the dust from his face and hair, then stated, 'Finally, you show some backbone. Your ball, no point.' Clouds slowly gathered above, drifting in before the sun, immediately cooling the area. 'Ready! Set! Go!' Khanaseri swerved to the left, then to the right suddenly, spinning on his heel to duck left as Malachai launched himself at the warlock, tearing his tunic and ripping away.

Khanaseri stumbled to the ground but kept running for the trees, crossing the line with the big man on his heels. He spun around with a grin right before the full weight of Malachai landed on his face. 'Get off me, you big ape!' he yelled from beneath the farmer, pushing at the piece of meat on top of him.

'Are you calling me stupid?'

Khanaseri's breath exploded from his mouth with a fist drilled deep into his stomach. He couldn't breathe, and with his last bit of consciousness, he slapped his palms over the big man's ears before fainting.

Malachai staggered back, blood running from his left ear, while a stinging sound accosted him from everywhere. He turned and dropped to the ground on his knees, unable to hear anything, not the birds nor the wind rustling through the trees. His heart sank, worried he might never hear his wife's or children's voices again. A cold sweat bathed him, his pulse racing uncontrollably, and he made to stand, but his balance was lost to him. He saw Khanaseri rise dizzily, shaking off the confusion to stroll to the centre of the field with the ball under his arm. He heard the muffled shouts of the man and stumbled closer, focusing on his mouth to read his lips.

'Ready! Set! Go!' he shouted, and Khanaseri jumped off the line, evading the stumbling Malachai with ease to score another point.

The warlock scored four more points to even the score to five each, before Malachai's hearing returned, along with his balance and a thundering clothesline. Tension was building as Malachai scored a quick two points, storming over Khanaseri and nearly breaking his arm. But the warlock would not relent and came back with a terrifying blow to Malachai's jaw using his elbow, stunning the farmer, causing him to drop the ball. Khanaseri grabbed it up and ran for the trees, but he was too tired to celebrate and merely bent forwards, searching for breath.

'You learn quickly... But I'm still the game's master. You will not win,' mumbled Malachai, spitting blood to drip down his chin and clothes just as big, warm drops fell from up high to bounce in the dust, covering the earth with water. 'Let's see how you fare in the mud!'

It took two points more for Malachai to stop Khanaseri, using all his strength to hoist the warlock into the air above his head and slam him to the ground. The ball rolled away from them and Malachai ran for it, followed by the coughing Khanaseri, who could not keep up. Eight points each. The end was drawing near, and both men were tired, panting like dogs as they slipped and slid to the centre of the muddy field. 'Ready! Set! Go!'

Khanaseri threw the ball over Malachai's head, sprinting to get to it as it rolled close to the trees in the pouring rain, the mud sucking them down with each footstep. Malachai ran next to him, gaining a lead until the warlock grabbed hold of his collar and yanked hard. The farmer's feet kicked in the air before he hit the ground and rolled, giving back the lead.

Khanaseri scooped up the ball in a slide, nearly tripping over the rocks and crossing the trees with celebratory splendour, his smirk annoying Malachai utterly. 'Get back to the centre! The game ain't done yet!' They had not reached the halfway mark yet when Malachai quickly rumbled, 'Ready, set, go!' and launched himself at the warlock, elbowing him hard on the side of the head. The ball bounced away and Malachai was on it fast, running for the bushes before Khanaseri knew what'd happened.

'Last point, boy! And I have the ball. I hope you're ready to pack up and head home,' mocked the big farmer, blowing snot and mud from his nose. Their clothes stuck to them like an octopus to a prey, water sloshing from them. They could barely see through the downpour, never mind hearing anything, yet this was the last point needed and neither of them would forego this opportunity to beat the other, even if it was just for the sake of pride. *No, this had to be finished.*

In the centre of the field they hunched down, fists sinking into the mud with arses up in the air, ready to sprint away and claim the victory. Malachai clutched the slippery ball under his left arm, hoping to use his right as a battering ram against Khanaseri's face. His opponent glared at him, as if reading his thoughts.

Khanaseri waited for a lull in the rain to see better, and also make his opponent nervous, prolonging the start with excruciating patience. He saw the twitches in the big farmer's right hand and waited a little longer. 'Come on, g—'

'Ready, set, go!' he shouted, and Malachai dropped the ball immediately, grabbed Khanaseri's wet tunic, and pulled him closer, swinging a right hook at his face...

* * *

Campfires burned late into the night, with men standing guard at every corner of the camp. They prepared their weapons, a constant scraping sound rolling through camp as soldiers glided their swords and daggers over whetstones while the archers waxed their bowstrings. It was quiet. No one talked. Everyone knew what to do and where to go. For some, this would be their last night alive. For others, it might only be the beginning of their careers, recognised for their valour and courage on the battlefield to be promoted. Bohan walked the campgrounds, calmly pondering what to say when the king would lash out at him for what he'd done. The king had mentioned nothing the entire day following the incident. And to make matters worse, Moseroth had crept into his tent with big, wandering eyes, holding a stuffed bear when the light had faded. He knew then that it wouldn't be long before the king called on him.

He strode with confidence through the site, knowing that whatever happened, he would not die by the king's hand, although he was not so sure about the beast dwelling within. The guards stationed outside the tent bowed slightly and drew open the flap for him to enter, and the one on the right whispered, 'Thank you, sir.'

Bohan halted for a moment, flicking his eyes up to the guard, and nodded, then entered the room. That small comment made the wizard feel good. *Be damned with the consequences. It was worth it.* Once inside, he looked around the dark room, seeing only a pile of pillows, a bed, a table, and a hookah resting on top while thick smoke constricted his breath. Bent over in the tent's corner, Turneroth was on his knees, sticking his finger down his throat as far as he dared, eliciting a reaction where his body curled in on itself, forcing bile from his stomach to the ground in bitter yellow streams.

'I need your help, Bohan,' came his strangled cries. 'I don't know how long I can hold on to him.'

'You should've thought about that beforehand...my King. I fear there is not much we can do now.'

'But there *is* something? Right?' Turneroth crawled closer, the yellow strings hanging from his mouth and chin, but Bohan ignored the question. The king crawled even closer, dragging himself up on the hem of the wizard's robe. 'Is the boy all right?'

'He is shaken, especially now that he knows you're not his father, but he will be fine. I guess the rumours are true, then? That he is the son of that sorceress. Stolen from her while she was imprisoned, and you raised him as your own. For what, may I ask? Leverage? Or did you do it as an act of kindness to the boy?' His voice was condescending and disgusted.

'At first, yes. I thought he could be a great asset to us one day. Make him a bonded. But I came to love that boy, more so than my actual son, I dare say.'

Bohan grunted and sighed, shaking his head, then kicked the king off his robe and sat in the chair, waiting for Turneroth to pull himself to the other. He knew there was a way, but with his inferior use of magic, he had not the talent for it, especially if the subject was to survive the ordeal. 'Only the Gatekeepers know the way. Your only hope lies in finishing this battle and going home to the Gatekeeper. He might save you.' *If he's still alive...*

The king sagged in the chair and gripped his hair, wishing this was all over.

'Are we to ride out to their gates to discuss their terms of surrender?' asked the wizard.

Turneroth's head swivelled up, eyes bloodshot and hair dishevelled. 'No. We attack at first light. Bring me Xare and the other Kingsguard. This city must fall quickly.'

Chapter Fifteen

Trumpets sounded over a field of vociferation while soldiers stormed the wall. Rocks the size of wagons sailed through the air to crash into the city's defences, but the walls held. The thrums of bowstrings sounded and arrows raced from murder holes in the wall, killing remorselessly while dragons raced overhead, fire billowing from their mouths. Under the streaming blazes flashing over the magical dome of the city, men scampered past the chanting wizards and warlocks spread throughout. Every scholar of Elvenandre fanned the magical dome to safeguard the city, taking shifts to ease the burden. Young to old, they would all do their part.

The night before, the queen had coldly informed the students who had refused to help that she would exile them from the city if they continued to deny their headmaster, leaving them to the tender mercies of Turneroth. Every single one had changed their minds.

'They aim to break our spirits fast! Don't let them!' shouted Captain Volar to the men around him. 'The dome will hold! Keep your eyes on the approaching soldiers! Push the ladders down!'

An enormous boulder sailed overhead, crashing in loud thunder against the magical dome, shattering to pieces and rolling down the sides. Men stood ready, fearful and panic-stricken, watching the dragons hover above the city. The beasts' eyes burned with hunger, impatiently waiting to devour those inside the walls.

The gigantic steel gate shook with the strike of a boulder, but the blacksmiths had done their jobs well. Singer had taken up a position next to an elf they had claimed was their best marksman, wanting to pit himself against such an opponent before the annual city games started. Now that elves would be allowed in the games, he needed to know what he might be up against. He leaned on the wall and nocked a new arrow from the hundreds of stands placed along the wall. 'Did you really hit a cicada at five hundred feet?' he asked the elf as he stuck the arrowhead through a murder hole and let it fly, seeing a man drop to the ground with the arrow through his skull.

The elf grinned and loosed his arrow. It bucked and weaved, racing for its target further away to slice through a man's carotid, severing the soft flesh, and then piercing through another man's throat, dropping both to the ground. 'How far was that? Three hundred feet? I would say that was the size of a cicada, wouldn't you?'

Singer swallowed hard. *Seems my competition just got a lot better.* 'You can call me Singer. How about a friendly competition for the day? Anyone can shoot a bow and arrow, but few can do it with style.' He loosed an arrow high in the air, following it through the sky as it plummeted down, cutting the tensioned rope of a loaded trebuchet in the distance. The construction's ropes snapped and the arm spun wildly, hurling the boulder to roll recklessly over the fields, killing dozens of the enemy.

The elf nodded with brows raised and said, 'That was a fine shot indeed. I will concede that point with grace. I'm Yharl Mheladinth.' He changed his stance and nocked two arrows at once, letting them fly to kill two nearing men, both arrows jutting from their heads.

'Ooooh, this is going to be fun.' Singer leaned over the open cast-iron stairs, looking down, and shouted, 'Bring up more arrows!'

Below in the courtyard, Kehlos wiped the muck from his dark face and pushed his way through the deluge of soldiers, shouting to two who appeared on his right. 'Brookley, I want you and Rhoden protecting Abe at all times. He's our main defence against those things. I'll be at the queen's side. She's on her way to the gates with King Elyon.'

'Yessir!' they shouted, and dashed into the wall and up the stairs. Two steps at a time, they ran up the inside of the wall, gripping the sides as boulders rocked the world. Soldiers — men, women, young, and old — streamed up and down constantly in their duties, making the climb laborious and time-consuming. Ellàthean hung on Rhoden's belt for quick access, cocked and ready to be fired, the silver of its wings glinting in the sun as they reached the top of the wall. He had got so annoyed with the old military crossbows. Their clunky, heavy nature was a frustrating hindrance, but the worst was that you couldn't load one and leave it hanging on your side. You could try, but as soon as you'd want to use it, the bolt would be lying in the dirt next to you, making you look like a fool. Ellàthean had a simple and elegant catch, holding the bolt in place no matter how the bow swung and knocked on his hip. He would be forever grateful to the Elven weaponsmith for this gift.

Up on the wall, so close to the monstrous dragons, Rhoden felt his heart stop for a moment when he looked into one's eyes as it grabbed on to the side of the wall, spewing fire between the parapet and the protective dome, biting with its huge fangs into the magic and mortar, its loud screech echoing through the city. Men and elves alike jumped back from the flames, loosing arrows into its gaping maw and striking its flicking tongue, pinning it in place to look like a giant pincushion. One man, set ablaze, dropped to the ground rolling, while others slapped at his clothes to extinguish the flames as the beast took off, flying back to the enemy's camp. Plenty more circled the city, just waiting for a chance to strike. 'Stand ready! It was a diversion!'

Up above, between the thunder of dragons, a few flew in with enemy soldiers on their backs and in their claws, dropping them on the magical dome to slide down to the wall and start the battle proper. Rhoden grabbed Ellàthean at his side, lifting it just high enough, not even unhooking it before he pulled the trigger. It made a satisfying thrum, the strong, short bolt sinking into an enemy soldier's eye socket and scrambling his brains. The man dropped to the ground as though his feet were cut out from under him before he could reach Abe, who continued chanting and nodded his thanks to Rhoden. Many more dropped from the sky, sliding down to clash with New Runswick steel. The Terenorans were pushing to get to the mages when a party of elves, agile and fast, jumped into the fray, slicing left and right, turning with pirouettes and lancing out to stab their targets. It was a supreme show of grace, seeing them move like water over stones in a river, unencumbered by any resistance.

Rhoden ran to clash with a Terenoran, tackling the woman off her feet and knocking her dagger out of her hands as she hit the ground. Fists swinging, she cut Rhoden's right eyebrow open with a blow, tearing the skin wide. He had not expected her to hit that hard, and brought up his hands to protect his face, but a barrage of blows landed on the side of his head. Brutally fast, she jumped to her feet and reached for his sword. Rhoden grabbed the blade below the hilt, slicing his palm open, and kicked her in the stomach, loosening her hands from the hilt to draw it himself. He blocked her blows and stabbed out with his blade, but she dodged it with ease, slapping the weapon away with her palms. A ladder crashed against the side of the wall near him, and he could hear men storming up, but this woman had him on the ropes. He wished now he'd charged the other warrior and left her to Brookley, who had already stepped over the body of his Terenoran to meet the next. She ran at him, teeth bared and dagger swinging. *Where did she get the dagger?* He stepped to the side and grabbed her chain mail shirt, spinning her round to gain momentum, releasing her at the perfect time to crash into the ladder, tipping it over with her riding the top step to the ground. 'Ha! I won't die that easily!' he shouted after her as she plummeted to the ground, giving him the finger all the way down before falling on the hundreds of soldiers beneath, tucking and rolling to get away. 'Crazy bitch!'

'If you're done flirting, Rhoden, I would appreciate a little help here!' Brookley was under the blade of another Terenoran, using his own to stave off the nearing edge. The Terenoran jerked the blade, and a drop of blood dripped on Brookley's face, followed by a steady stream from the soldier's mouth, a bolt sticking sideways through his throat. The Terenoran staggered back, grabbing aimlessly at the bolt and fingering the feathers at its base before falling down the back of the wall, hitting the ground with a loud thud. Brookley stared at the man's bent and broken body and shuddered, a ripple of adrenalin shooting through him. 'Thanks, Rhod.'

'You sleeping on the job?' shouted an elf as he kicked a soldier from the wall, looking at Brookley.

'Might as well take a nap and leave you a few. Don't want you feeling left out, Valheim.'

'Knock it off, the both of you!' shouted Volar. 'Here comes a fresh squad being dropped in by those fire-spitting pelicans.' A small silver ball fell onto the wall and rolled a few feet away. 'What's that?'

'Get down!' shouted Ganda'har, running towards them just before the explosion shook the walkway, limbs flying up in tatters and red mist. Screams of pain and alarm echoed as more silver balls rolled from the dome, a cacophony of deafening blasts and howls of the dying accompanying the flashes of fire. The magical dome covering their city flickered and faded, retracing from the west and leaving a wide opening for the enemy. 'Archers! Aim for those bastards down there with the big packs! Use fire arrows!'

Burning arrows flew from the wall in volleys, trailed by multiple explosions on the ground so loud he feared they might have torn holes in the world. Gigantic craters pocked the ranks of the advancing army, burning and blackened, cleared of enemy soldiers but surrounded by the wounded lying a few feet from their centres, some crawling away on their arms, legs torn to shreds, most not moving at all. War was a nasty business, and it was only going to get nastier still. 'Stretcher bearers! Get the bearers up here now!' Ganda'har shouted, waving to the men down below. 'On me, boys! Let's hold these bastards back, to give the bearers a chance at getting to the injured!'

Untara and Stentor were in the lead, clearing the path for the rest of them like a runaway wagon barrelling towards a chosen target. Talgar and Blanka grabbed those Terenorans who hadn't been thrown off the wall, dealing with them swiftly: Talgar stabbing and cutting with his dual daggers with tremendous ferocity, lunging at enemy soldiers before they even knew what was going on, severing tendons and throats quickly and efficiently; while Blanka used his sharp dragon talons to slash faces and rip out organs.

The blasts had caused severe damage. Mages and soldiers lay scattered over the wall, some crawling away in pain where the city's shield had failed. A yellow beast dived from up high, racing towards the breach, fire serenading the wall. Magnus gripped Anavi's arm and shouted, 'We'll hold them before the stairs!' Ganda'har nodded and ran to his men.

'Magnus, you shouldn't be up here! Your leg is not fully healed,' growled Anavi.

'I ain't leaving youse alone up here! Where youse go, I go!' stormed the barkeep.

'Stubborn!' She spun low to the ground, her blade flashing, severing a man's legs at the knees, 'thick-headed,' and twisted round, disembowelling another, 'stiff-necked,' then stabbed over her head backwards, piercing a Terenoran's chest and yanking out the blade, 'mulish lover of mine! I can take care of myself!'

Magnus cracked a Terenoran soldier's neck, dropping him to the ground, and spat on the body. 'I can see that,' he tapped his head as he walked past her. 'Like a steel vault, very thick!' They both turned and saw Belgarr crash into the yellow dragon, both dropping to the grounds inside the city, tearing scales and flesh.

Before more dragons could make it through the breach, the magi filled the gaps, bringing it back just in time. A deep crack tore through the stones of the wall; the structure was taking a beating. Ganda'har got to the injured men, leaning over one as another dragon fiercely clawed and chewed at the dome and wall, reaching through the gaps with its talons and blowing fire to get to them. A ballista bolt fired from close range, drilling deep into the dragon's neck. It dropped from the wall, floundering in the air back to its camp.

Ganda'har pulled the fallen soldier's helmet aside and could scarcely recognise the disfigured man. Half of him was a swollen, bleeding mess, fine pieces of metal stuck in his face, neck, and chest.

From his right, he heard the stretcher bearers struggle with an injured soldier. Brookley reached out, crawling on his left arm as he mumbled, 'No! No! It was supposed to be me! Why did he do that? Captain? Wake up!' Face bleeding, his mouth torn on one side, right eye bloodshot and legs cut to shreds, Brookley pulled himself closer to grab the unmoving man's hand.

'There's nothing you could've done!' stated Ganda'har, picking him up gently by his arm to sit him up.

Wild eyes gazed around searchingly, Brookley's voice coming in between stuttering breaths. 'He, he jumped on the device... Saved our lives.'

Ganda'har rolled Brookley over onto the stretcher and said, 'He'll join you soon down at the tents. Take him away.' More bearers came and hauled away the rest. A groan of pain sounded from the left, where Rhoden Bellfrey leaned up against the parapet, a smear of blood on the wall from his back. 'Bearer!' called Ganda'har.

'No! I'll be fine. Plenty more killing to do. Besides, they're flooded with people far worse off than I.' Rhoden pushed away from the wall and coughed up some blood, spitting it down the side. 'Bastards will have to do better than that.'

Ganda'har eyed the soldier sidelong. 'I bet your captain would beg to differ.'

Rhoden shied away. 'I might not have had the most love for the captain, but that's probably the bravest thing I've ever seen a man do. He jumped onto certain death without a thought to his own life, all to protect us. Didn't even blink,' Rhoden jerked to the left. 'Shit! What about Abe? He was here with us.' The fighting had lessened now, order restored somewhat.

'I'm still breathing, Rhoden. I don't know how, but I am...' came a strangled voice from around the corner of the stairwell's walls. Abe pushed himself up, using the wall behind him, and hobbled over, eyes flushed with grief and covered in soot, his robe torn by the shrapnel on the right, but with no bleeding. 'Volar was a good friend. For all my power and knowledge, I'm afraid healing is not one of my talents. I feel like such a fraud.'

'This section of the wall is clear, Cap'n,' growled the giant, Untara, standing at attention.

Ganda'har nodded and said, 'The day is not yet done, wizard. We have dented them, but they have many cards to play, and there will be plenty more bloodshed. I have seen their tactics first hand, and this is not the worst they offer. They call on dark elements, demons from the underworld, to do their bidding. Powerful creatures that should not exist. Go now and help your students. They're struggling on their own.' Loud shrieks came from below, where the two dragons clawed and tore at each other, chunks of flesh and scales hitting the stone wall.

The soldiers didn't know what to do. Should they help? Should they stay out of it? Even knowing that Belgarr fought for them, some couldn't help but be anxious about its existence, wondering if it might not be better to see it dead with the rest of them. Some leaned over the wall, cheering on Belgarr as a rogue spray of fire from the yellow beast set homes and buildings ablaze.

Belgarr drove his horns through the yellow's head, driving it into the wall and ripping out its heart in a display of power, feasting on the organ. Shouts and cheers sounded, the men's morale boosted with Blanka on their side.

* * *

'Congratulations. Ye beat an old man. Does that make you feel good? Wanker!' Malachai grumbled from his horse, picking his teeth with a huge knife and sucking at the bits coming loose.

'Oh, you're fit and strong enough to beat most men I know. I outplayed you at your own game. That's all there is to it. Besides, when are you going to let this go? It's been two days already, and you're still complaining.'

'I'll complain fer as long as I have this shiner you so graciously gave me. Just look at me... I look like a forlorn jester. You might as well put a fool's cap on me and march me to Karta's halls for entertainment. I'll sit on the king's lap and juggle knives, smiling like a fool with his black eye.'

Khanaseri chuckled. 'I didn't peg you for someone so dramatic. You look more the quiet, sombre soldier type. Do your duty and get on with things.'

Malachai glared at him. 'Yes, well. That's what two children will do to you. Kids these days... You can't lay a hand on them, or they run to their mother. So you have to use words...and I ain't good with words like most. How about you? You have a mother? Or did you suckle on your father?'

The warlock turned to him slowly with raised brows and said, 'My mother died when I was young. My father passed away a while ago now.'

A loud fart, long and percussive, came from the big farmer, who rose slightly from the saddle to give him some clearance. 'Whoo! That's gonna linger. It's good to be in the company of another man for a change, even if he's a fool. I can say and do what I want and the judgement is minimal. I've missed this.'

'Dear god, I've not...' mumbled Khanaseri.

'What was that?'

'Hm. I asked how far is it?'

'A few days' ride. Why are you in such a hurry? What are you not telling me?'

'Stop grilling me like I'm one of your children! I don't have to tell you everything.'

Malachai sneered at him, then laughed and said, 'Yer way too ugly to be my child.'

'Oh, shut up! I've seen your children... Where are we headin', anyway?'

'Oi, careful, those are the sprouts of my loins. We go to the Dhore Mountains to see an old friend.' Malachai smiled, turning to a pair of blue-green parrots nestling their heads against each other in a passing tree, chirping lovingly in the shining shafts of the morning sun piercing through the forest's trees to light up the surface below, where patches of green grew. He sighed, feeling lucky his life had turned out as it had, having a wonderful wife with children he adored. Even if he wanted to throttle them at times.

'Halt! In the name of Barlow Hill!'

Malachai jerked around and cursed that he had become so content in life. 'Barlow Hill? What does that shite want?' Ahead, more men appeared from the forest, with Barlow at the front, holding a big crossbow as he stepped closer.

'I might have...humiliated him a bit when I arrived in Millanthross,' replied Khanaseri, halting his horse in the middle of the road.

'Oh, come now, he must be used to humiliation.' Malachai cupped his hand over his mouth and shouted, 'Barlow, take yer ears and fly away. Maybe go gnaw on some cheese while yer at it.' The big farmer giggled and saw the disapproving look from Khanaseri. 'What? It's actually got nothing to do with his appearance. I just hate the snivellin' rat.'

Barlow Hill shouted back, 'We have no quarrel with you, Malachai. We have been waiting days for this interloper to pass this way. He doesn't belong here.'

'I agree with you on that, Barlow... See that you don't include me in...' he waved his hands about, 'whatever this is,' and turned his horse to a nearby rock to dismount and sat down, moving around to get the most comfortable seating.

'What are you doing?' asked Khanaseri from his horse, peering at the big farmer.

Big-eyed and ruefully perplexed, Malachai glanced between Khanaseri and Barlow Hill's men. 'I didn't want to be here. I have ugly children I need to think of, remember?'

'Oh, you know I was jesting!' Seven men closed around Khanaseri's horse, and he dismounted. 'At least let my horse stay with Malachai. He doesn't deserve to be injured in this petty squabble.' They let the horse through at the nod of Barlow, and quickly closed the circle again. 'I didn't come here to hurt anyone, but if you force me to, know that I've warned you. Whatever happens next is on your heads.' He jumped around, waiting for the first to strike.

Seven men: Barlow held a crossbow, two others had rusted swords, three carried small axes, and one had a spiked mace. Khanaseri slowly drew the enormous axe from his back, and wished he could use his magic, put these men to sleep and walk on by, but he was in no shape to try. Healing his arms and hands after the creation of those wyrm cages had taken it out of him, and if he pushed too hard, it could be even more detrimental to his health. No, he would need to fight to get out of this. Seven on one was no good, though, no matter how badly they fought or how well he did.

'There's only one of you. I don't think we have much to worry about,' said one man, creeping closer with his axe.

A shadow flashed over Khanaseri's head, and he raised the axe in both hands, using the haft to block the barrelling mace. The man in front sliced for his stomach, but missed as he jumped back, headbutting the mace-wielding man with the back of his head. He felt a tooth sink into his scalp where the man hit, burning like fire from the filth in his mouth. A boot crunched into his ribs, followed by a fist to the jaw and a knee to the thigh. Khanaseri hit the ground hard and heard Malachai wince in a distance, seeing him cringe at the blow. The hubbub of the men standing over him, kicking and screaming, did not stop, and he swung his axe to his right in an arc towards the ground. A scream exploded instantly, and the others jumped back, seeing the one's foot cut in half, the other half still stuck in the boot on the ground.

The bigger man with the mace picked Khanaseri up from the ground and clubbed him in the ribs, then kicked him in the chest, skidding him over the ground close to Malachai. The warlock looked up and coughed, spat blood. 'Are you still not helping?'

'This is yer mess. And a fine one at that.'

Strong hands grabbed his jacket and lifted him up. He swung his fist hard, cracking the mace-wielder on his jaw. Without a sound, the man dropped to the ground, eyes lolling around uncomprehendingly. He thrust the man back, knocking down two others who approached, and ran for his axe. The thrum of the crossbow string sounded, the bolt flying for his torso, and he jumped out of the way to fall into the arms of another wielding a sword, parrying wildly with his axe when he received a blow to the head.

'Barlow! Ya cocksucker! I told you to keep me out of it!' Malachai stormed towards the retreating weasel, holding his arm up, the crossbow bolt firmly wedged through his forearm. He grabbed the crossbow and snapped it in half, throwing it to the ground.

'It was an accident! Please, Malachai!' Barlow screamed in agony with the snap of his arm, and crashed into those harassing Khanaseri, knocking them to the ground.

'Get out of here before I plant his foot up yer arse!' Malachai pointed to the boot and foot on the ground next to the unconscious man. 'Take 'em with you. Don't want them stinkin' up the woods.' The men scrambled to their feet, looking to Barlow for answers, who had already decided that running was the better option, clutching his broken arm as he dashed down the road to where they'd left their horses.

Khanaseri moved his bruised jaw, wincing at the tender touch, and retrieved his axe before jumping on Flintlock's back. Malachai followed suit, and soon they set off, leaving their attackers to carry their half-footed comrade.

'You showed great restraint, not killing any of them. They would not have done you the same favour,' said Malachai, wiping some blood splatters from his beard. He rummaged through his pack and raised a flask from it, taking a big swig, then handed it to Khanaseri.

'Mpf, I didn't think you would see I was holding back.' The liquids ran down the warlock's throat, and soon after, a burning fire coursed back up to his mouth. He shook his head, blowing out a lungful of air, eyes tearing up, and wheezed, 'What is that?' He handed back the flask, and Malachai took another swig, grinning.

'A present from Old Bill. Finest grog there is.'

Khanaseri glared at him. 'Old Bill is a still? And you thought I'd want to steal that? I'm on a horse... How would I have carried it? On my back?'

'Hey, it ain't just any still...' Malachai mumbled.

'We should get that bolt out of you,' the warlock said, shaking his head.

Malachai turned his arm, gazing at the bolt. 'It's not the first time I've headed to the Dhore Mountains with a bolt stuck in me. One thing I learned was, don't remove the bolt. It's not bleeding now, but I'm sure it will if you pull it out. Ha. That's what she said.'

Khanaseri shook his head in defeat. 'What?'

'You know... If you pull it out... Oi, it's no fun if I have to explain it! Say, back in this Artokla. Did they circumcise your sense of humour?'

Sense of humour? I've had nothing to laugh about since my father died. The world's gone to shit and people are fighting for their lives. An army of dragons and men from the deep past are besieging the country, and death is the order of the day. Sense of humour? Yes... It would seem they did *circumcise my sense of humour.* Khanaseri didn't answer.

Malachai kept staring at him with his arm leaned up against the horse's mane. 'A world without laughter is not a world worth fighting for. Why do you fight? And don't give me some B.S. about how it's yer duty. Or it's the right thing to do. No, I'm talking about the real reason. Those dark reasons we keep hidden behind solid steel doors, the key on a chain around yer neck at all times. I saw it in your eyes. There's more to this story of just taking his bones than you'll say. You *need* his bones.'

Khanaseri closed his eyes, working his jaw muscles. 'There's a war going on, and I need—'

Malachai bleated like a goat. 'No. That's not the reason.'

'People are dying—'

Another bleating sound came from him. 'Nope. That's not it either. We fight because we like it, because there's something deep inside us that drives us towards it. We want to stop, but we can't. It will find you... It seeks you out, hunts you. We fight because something deep inside us broke a long time ago.'

'You know nothing of me. I could stop if I wanted to.'

'Then stop. Put down yer axe and walk away from this.'

'Is that what happened to you? You stopped fighting? You let the enemy win?'

'I've fought more battles than I can count, and each time, I was sure I was on the right side. But every single time you reflect, you realise you killed a son, a brother, a father, a mother, maybe even a daughter. And it haunts you every night. And every one of them thought they were on the right side...'

Khanaseri shook his head. 'So what? Just give up? That's what you're peddling?'

'No. Just pointing out that everyone thinks they're on the right side, until they aren't.'

* * *

A concatenation of explosions danced with flashes of light and debris arcing through the moonless night in trails of smoke, their damage untold at this distance as Dorgal and his men watched from afar through slits in the underground tunnels they'd dug. 'Oh great Yamlhieer, they are getting slaughtered up there,' said Bleak, bunching up his leather-and-wolf fur trapper hat in his hands, eyeing the devastation he could see only in his mind.

'So let's equal the numbers some,' Dorgal whispered, hefting his axe and checking the blade. 'Today, she will sing songs of red and white,' the rest of the men joined in, 'cutting through flesh and bone. We are dwarves. She will guide our arms and bring swift ends to those that oppose us. We are dwarves. Our blades run sharp and unblemished. We are dwarves. Except for the songs of red and white. We are dwarves.' He nodded to his men, and they set off, splitting up and running low down the maze of tunnels under the feet of the raging battlefield.

Dust and small stones fell on their heads, the drumming of feet and shouts racing over them as they waited. 'Wait for it, lads.' The ground gave way before them to an eruption of cries as men fell into a pit of spikes made from timber offcuts planted in the earth below. The pit filled up quickly, the spears disappearing in the avalanche of bodies. Now was the time to strike. From the darkness, dwarves jumped out at various points, dragging alive and confused men off the dying pile, their axes singing and adding to the flood of red and white. As quickly as they appeared, so they vanished into the maze.

More traps made themselves known and more bodies piled up;

more axes sang. Dorgal did not have to like the idea to agree that it was proving effective. It felt dishonest somehow, pulling the feet from under a man and sticking him full of holes... *Where's the fighting chance in that?* he wondered. *These bastards aren't playing fair either, Dorgal, having all these dragons and little exploding balls. Don't go softening up on them now. They brought this on themselves.* He shook his head as he yanked his axe from the ribs of a soldier and whistled twice, an ear-splitting skirl keening through the tunnels. The soldiers had figured out the traps and now filed down, trampling the bodies of those before them, searching for the dwarves.

The game of cat and mouse could never be won if the cat didn't know it was a game... Down the dark tunnels they sprinted, comfortably running where they knew the humans would struggle to keep up, being all bent and hunched. Galiban and Odus jumped up, using their hands and feet against the sides of the tunnel, creeping over a section, then waited. The silhouettes of the men appeared, moving steadily closer until the first one fell, crashing into more spikes and belting obscenities, crying for his mother. Dwarven arrow bolts thudded into the second and third man, dropping them on the first in the pit.

Bleak ran behind Dorgal, pushing himself to keep up with Dammelsfiere, when something caught his attention: a glimmer lining the side of the tunnel with every flash of explosion above shining through the holes in the ground. He stopped in his tracks and rubbed his eyes, then the wall, and leaned in to bite a rough protruding piece. His eyes lit up. *How did we miss this?* 'Dorgal, look at this! Gold!'

'What are you doing, Bleak? We don't have time for this!'

'But—'

'Bleak! Move it!'

Annoyed, Bleak rushed after Dorgal, looking over his shoulder at the glinting metals, when an onrush of heat filled the tunnels, followed by surging flames racing through the maze. 'Shit!' Dorgal and Bleak swung around and ran as fast as their stubby legs would allow, the flames on their heels. Dorgal put his fingers to his mouth, bouncing up and down on the uneven tunnel, trying to whistle.

Fire converged from all tunnels and they ran like dogs, dwarves sprinting from those same tunnels moments before the flames. In a burst of fire and heat, Dorgal launched himself from the exit of the tunnel, his men following closely, the flames bursting out after them, reaching out with its warm touch. Three dwarves rolled on the ground, quickly extinguishing their clothes. Soldiers' shouts of alarm sounded close, and they legged it to get away from the area and into the darkness. 'Our tunnels are blown, boys! Let's get back to the castle. They be waitin' for us at the southern wall, but we better climb quickly.'

* * *

Grappling hooks sailed up to latch against the parapet, digging into the mortar for grips as the ropes pulled taut. They'd left the main force behind, sneaking through the darkness of the forest to reach the wall where men awaited their arrival. The main attack was concentrated to the east, where the only gate stood; few enemies dwelled near the south.

They quickly made it to the top, helped over the parapet by the soldiers pulling them clear, and retrieved their hooks. Dorgal slid down on his backside, panting like a mutt. 'Is everyone here? Bleak, confirm, and report.' He got to his feet again, standing on his toes to see over the wall, but only managing to reach the peepholes when Bleak reappeared.

'Only thirteen, Dorgal. We lost Ughu!'

'What? Help me up on the wall, men!' shouted Dorgal, but before they managed, he heard the angry, coarse voice of the dwarf down below.

'Ya beardless tool-snatching shit-for-brains leaving me for dead? Throw a rope down! I lost me hook.'

Dorgal laughed and said, 'Get him up, Bleak.' Fires raged at the front, where a couple of houses burned, the sound of steel clashing spanning the distance, and he saw the fighting men look the size of ants from where he stood. A horrifying shriek came from up ahead to his left, racing closer, fire rolling over the wall and dome above. 'No!' he ran and jumped to the top of the wall, pulling himself up, and saw Ughu struggling on the rope nearly halfway to the top, the beast drawing near.

'He's not gonna make it! Ughu, drop and run!'

'I'll make it!'

Dwarves and men shouted for him to drop, but he did not relent. 'Drop, Ughu, you stubborn mule!'

'I can make it!'

Dorgal jumped down and grabbed the rope, pulling with all his might. All the dwarves jumped in with the help of the soldiers, screaming as they pulled. 'Heave, ya bastards! Heave!'

The roaring flames raced through. The rope snapped and sent them to the arses, the inferno scorching the flagstones like a fanned flame. Everyone took cover, shielding their faces from the blast. Only the burning fibres of the rope's end appeared over the parapet. 'Ughu!' The dwarves ran to the wall, covering their faces from the heat. They tried to climb onto the wall, but their hands got singed, the wall still scorching. Soldiers peered down, shaking their heads.

Out of sympathy, the soldiers blocked the dwarves from the wall, pushing them away when Dorgal shouted, 'Get out of my way before ya taste my blade, lads!' The soldiers backed away reluctantly, apologising as they did. Fires raged up against the side of the wall and into the forest, trees and fields burning high, the smoke constricting breath and burning eyes. They saw no movement in or near the flames, no sign of Ughu having survived. Dorgal sighed and shook his head. Just the fall could have been enough to kill him. 'Come, boys. Let's join the fight at the front. Grimmel...'

'Yes, Dorg?'

'Go tell the others what's happened. They'd want to know. Then come find us at the front.'

'Yes, Dorg.' The dwarf ran for a stairwell while the rest marched over the wall towards the fighting.

Chapter Sixteen

'How much further?' begged Khanaseri, hoping it would be close. The constant complaining about Malachai's arse hurting and arm throbbing and balls sweating was getting to be a lot to handle.

Malachai slowed his horse, following the winding road with his eyes as he mumbled, 'Not much longer now.' The rock face to his left seemed too familiar still, the forest on the right as foreboding as it was all those years ago. He drifted back in time...

The road leading up to the monastery felt much longer than he remembered it to be, the gravel crunching louder than usual. They had passed the finger rock to the side of the mountain a while back, and he could now smell the scent of old, burnt wood drifting on the wind. His heart skipped a beat as he heard voices coming from the monastery, and the massive wolf, Baldrake, dug his claws into the dirt, speeding away from the group in haste.

'Baldrake! Wait for us!' Gordon shouted from his right, but the wolf did not stop. They pushed their heels into the horses' flanks, kicking up gravel and dust to catch up with the wolf. Rounding the bend to the outer garden wall, they saw people milling about, carting off debris and fixing what they could, their desperate faces lifting from their work momentarily, streaked with tears as they heard the footfalls of the horses drawing near. A terrifying growl erupted from the front steps of the burnt-down monastery, and fear gripped him. They pushed their mounts to get there quickly.

A priest stood cornered by the colossal wolf, fearing for his life, while it growled at him with lips trembling over deadly fangs. Malachai jumped from his horse as he reined in and stepped in front of Baldrake, who growled at the frightened man, 'Where is he?'

'Calm down, Baldrake! Let me handle this!' Malachai held out his arms to stop the wolf from advancing, his heart racing wildly.

The wolf was anxious, its heart thudding heavily in its chest. Unable to wait for an answer, Baldrake bounded around the monastery and disappeared from their view.

'I'll go find him,' Gordon said as he neared and ran in the direction the wolf took.

Malachai turned back, placing his hand on the man's shoulder. 'I remember you. You are one of the priests that saved me.' A horse whinnied, and Malachai glanced back to see Gweniviere dismount and move to his side.

'Yes, I was. I'm Magnus.'

The big man looked around and lowered his head. Doors hung off their hinges, walls were charred and smeared with blood. Shattered glass lay in the foyer, mixed with terracotta shards from the overturned planters, soil and plants scattered about. 'What happened here, Magnus?'

A long, deep howl went to the air just then, and Malachai could feel the hairs on his arms rise. His stomach churned, and he closed his eyes for a moment, feeling weak in the knees.

Magnus lay his hand on the big man's shoulder and said, 'Follow me.' They quickly made their way through the rubble-strewn corridors, and Malachai dreaded what they would find as he saw the old blood splatters on the white walls. Up the stairs, they followed the priest, the howling getting louder with every footstep. They passed through the doors leading out and as they went under the archway, he saw Gordon sitting on his haunches next to the black, howling wolf, before a great tombstone with a wolf's head carved into it. Although they had prepared for this, Malachai felt his heart break as he neared the wolf and saw two more tombstones to his right, with no plaques or carvings. He walked over to the railing, gripping it tight, his knuckles whitening from the pressure, and saw burial mounds with crosses sticking from the ground in the field below. Beginning at one end, he counted, '...ten, eleven, twelve...' but when he got to *twenty-five, he turned around, shaking with grief.*

Now, here he was, riding back to the same old feeling. The farmer took a deep breath, shaking the memory from his head, and mumbled again. 'Not far at all.' The old stone wall around the outer garden still looked as battered as it had all those years back; the long red dusty road still neatly swept. They turned onto a narrow path wide enough for a wagon, with trees lining the side all the way to the monastery. People with shaved heads and long, loose white robes worked the fields on either side, carting off seeds for planting and the fruit they harvested. Here and there, one would rise from his work and wave at the pair with a smile. He thought of his memory again, and released a long breath.

'Who's that?' asked Khanaseri, pointing to a man in a robe waving in the wind, waiting for them on the steps.

'That would be the abbot. He's the master of this house. Try not to insult him too.' The old man's smile was contagious and warm, the glittering chain and golden earrings lengthening his lobes, his skin tanned and wrinkled.

'Why is it you only come here when you are injured?' mocked the old man.

'Ha! Or do I get injured just to come here? You know I can't stay away from your food.' Malachai dropped from his horse and walked up the steps with arms stretched out. 'Magnus, you old geezer, it's been too long.'

'Run-in with another bolt, I see. Come, we'll sort you out fast.'

'Magnus, this is Khanaseri. Khanaseri, Magnus.'

'Well met. Come in. Let's eat and have some wine. I'm sure there's a story here somewhere.'

Khanaseri dropped from his horse and watched as one of the white-robed men shuffled closer to grab the reins. 'Hey!'

Magnus swung around and said, 'Oh, don't worry. Flintlock will be looked after very well. Come.'

Wait, how'd he know Flint's name? I don't like this... He glared at the old man waving for him to join, and crept up the steps cautiously, scanning every corner for someone lying in wait, but there was no one.

'Relax, Khanaseri. No one is out to get you here,' mocked Malachai over his shoulder, leaning on the rails of the stairs as he scratched his behind before walking up to the second floor, where the priest waited on the landing.

'Wait here, and they will bring food up for your enjoyment while I tend to this wound. We shouldn't be long.'

Something gnawed at his stomach, and Khanaseri was not about to be taken for a fool. 'I'll come with you.'

Malachai and Magnus jerked their heads to him, and the priest exclaimed, 'There's no need—'

'I insist,' Khanaseri growled.

'Well, if he insists...' Malachai mocked again. 'We can't stop him now. Just don't interrupt the priests while they work, ya hear? I want to keep my arm attached to my body. I insist...' The big farmer leaned over to Magnus and whispered, 'Are the pups here?'

'They have yet to arrive.'

'Good.' He glanced over his shoulder at the interloper and said, 'Not very trusting, are you?'

'You haven't given me any reason to be.'

'Ow!' roared Malachai, catching the bolt on Magnus' robe as they walked down the white-walled corridor to the healing room. 'Blasted donkey balls! What do you mean, I haven't given you any reason? I've not lied. I've not betrayed, and now I have brought you to the place you requested.'

Khanaseri did not respond. He just kept staring at the ornate decorations around them, the hangings in various colours, vases and items of unique importance and value seeming so dull to him. Anxiety grabbed hold of him suddenly. He flung his pack around and rummaged through it, searching for the Balamuth. At the bottom of the pack, his fingers wrapped around the cloth with the sphere inside and he opened it a crack to see, watching the whirling white and blue swirls cast from within.

Magnus swung around and glared at him. 'What seems to be the problem?'

The warlock slung the pack over his shoulder again and said, 'Thought I might have lost something very important.'

* * *

The procedure didn't take long at all. Magnus pushed and prodded the flesh around the bolt, and yanked it from Malachai's arm with little sympathy given as the farmer screamed. The old abbot inspected the wound and bobbed his head up and down, then said, 'It looks like it missed the major arteries...little bleeding, and no sign of infection. We will stitch you up and you will be fine.'

'Wait, what? No,' Malachai turned his arm, staring through the big hole, and waved his hands in front of his face, moving them up and down. 'No magic healing for me? Come on, Gwen will notice it...'

'No magical healing for you today, my friend. That is reserved for urgent matters.'

'Argh! Fine.'

They followed the shuffling priest back to the dining hall in relative silence. Khanaseri was sure he was doing the right thing, yet here, now, between this farmer and the priest, his confidence was fading fast. He stared around suspiciously for some kind of trickery, yet found none as they sat on the long benches, the room decorated with murals of old men in prayer.

'They are a redrawing of the antecedent abbots, all my predecessors. No doubt you'll notice only the last one's face differs from the others... We had a fire a long time ago that destroyed almost everything. He was the last before the fire then. The others are just a show of respect, an acknowledgement of their service.'

'That is a sad story, but I fail to see why you recount it to me,' said Khanaseri, glancing between the murals.

Malachai grumbled, 'Because it was Anukke's fault that these fires raged. That's why he tells it.'

Priests entered the room from a door swinging on its hinges, trays of silver platters in their hands, an intoxicating aroma wafting through the air coming from the kitchen, and Khanaseri pondered if there might be something more toxic being disguised. He eyed the plates placed before Malachai and Magnus, then to his own, resisting the urge to surge into the meat and stuff himself with the potatoes.

Malachai gestured him to hand over his plate, and exchanged it with his, then said, 'I would never poison my enemies. And I'm not even sure I can call you that. If I came for you, you'd know it.' He took Khanaseri's plate and tore the steak with his teeth, gulping down big chunks at a time. 'So good,' he said, the juices running down his chin and into his beard.

Halfway through their meal, Malachai mumbled, 'Our friend here would like to take Anukke's body away. What do you think about that?'

Magnus choked on his food at the shock of the statement, coughing violently until Malachai slapped him on the back so hard it felt like his lungs would come flying from his mouth. His voice squeaked out, 'I think it foolish, that's for sure.'

'Aye, I've tried to make him see reason. But he's as stubborn as a mule.'

Khanaseri stayed quiet. He didn't feel the need to explain himself if not asked, and even then he might not. He took another bite of the meat, wondering how things were going back home. Time was running out, he knew that for sure. 'Thank you for the food, abbot. Can you take me to his remains immediately? I would like to leave as soon as possible.'

'See, I told you. A mule, or maybe Pheistus. Not sure who's worse,' mumbled Malachai, stuffing another tomato in his mouth, the red juices and pips splashing over the table as he bit into it.

Magnus rolled some wine in his cheeks, swallowed hard to wash down the last bits and clear his throat. 'I'm not sure she will be happy about this.'

'Aye, not at all, I gather.'

'Who are you talking about?' asked Khanaseri, quaffing the glass of wine, enjoying the fruity flavours dancing on his tongue.

Malachai rose, skidding the chair back with a screech on the marble floor. He wiped his mouth with a serviette and dropped it on the table, belching loudly. 'It's time to introduce you to his keeper. Magnus, show us the way.'

They took lanterns from the wall and followed the abbot down the stairs to a door leading into a cellar. 'This year's harvest has been very good, and the wines are absolutely divine, wouldn't you say?' mumbled the abbot from the front over his shoulder. 'That was our brand you drank upstairs. Home-made. Nothing better.'

Khanaseri nodded his approval, but he was never one for small talk. 'It was, yes.' They walked through the gloomy cellar past all the empty bottles waiting to be used and barrels filled with the pungent wines to a small private library at the end. The room was encased with books of all kinds on shelves from floor to ceiling; some bound in thick leather with pressed print, while others barely held together anymore, written by hand. Once the door closed behind Khanaseri, he could not tell where the door began and where it ended, as it vanished behind a flurry of books. The other two did not seem distressed at all, turning right to stand before a bookshelf. One by one, in a very specific order, Magnus pulled books slightly from the shelf until a soft click was heard and the wall swung open, revealing dark stairs beyond, leading down. 'Nearly twenty years ago, when all considered him dead, Rose brought him to us, begging for our help. At first we refused, for he is a sadistic creature, after all. But she wore us down, reminding us we were a house of peace. We do not turn away those who seek help. With the land in turmoil and the hatred for Anukke, we built a secret room for them where she has cared for him all these years. If the people found out we harbour him still, I fear they would burn this place to the ground. He is in a deep sleep, one she has tried to wake him from for a long time.'

'So he lives? That's terrific news.' Khanaseri's journey was almost at an end. He could soon go home to see an end to the madness that had plagued his world.

'Don't be a fool! How are you going to carry him across the seas? Leave him be in her care, and forget about him. What worth is he to you, anyway?' growled Malachai. Thick, tall stone pillars propped up the foundation of the monastery above, hiding from the world this vast chamber with glimmering lights magically burning to create a peaceful environment, the air unnaturally calm. Not too hot, not too cold, with fresh air wafting in through vents on the sides leading up and out.

'Oh, I have a use for him.' It surprised Khanaseri how huge the chamber was, thinking it must span the entire monastery and its fields. A fire crackled in the distance, tongues licking above the rim of the pit with no one in sight, just an empty bed and an empty couch resting in the gloom. He didn't see Anukke's body anywhere. 'What is this? There's no one here.'

'Don't wet yer trousers... Ye will soon see.' Malachai walked on, lantern burning brightly in his big hand, swinging back and forth to cast hideous shadows against the walls, sounds echoing with every footfall, with every shifting stone. They walked through a shimmer, the gloomy cavern falling away to a beautiful home with many rooms, the walls oiled red cedar with portraits and lanterns on both sides.

Floorboards creaked underfoot; it all looked so real. Khanaseri struggled with what he was seeing, shaking his head in disbelief. *How could you maintain this magic?* They turned down a corridor where the left wall was a pane of glass with water rushing over it to drop in a groove at the bottom and vanish. He stared out of the window and raised his hand against the glass, feeling the cold on the other side where stood the peak of a mountain high above the clouds and valley far below, pockets of green flashing through the white-purple puffs. 'This is incredible,' he muttered, seeing the smirk on Malachai's face. He had used his magic for survival, never for pleasure. Though being fair, survival had been his game since he received his gift. For the first time, he saw what could be. He shook his head, shunting the ideas from his mind; he was a warlock, not a wizard who led a life of studies and glamour. No, they needed him to win battles and wars, to fight enemies until his last breath left his body, just like his Da.

A squeal of delight sounded from down the corridor, giving Khanaseri a fright, followed by quick footsteps on the wooden floor as a woman rushed forward, curly hair bouncing wildly to throw herself at Malachai, hugging him fiercely with her head pressed to his chest.

'Malachai?' she shouted, gripping his head while the big farmer laughed. 'It's been years! What brings you here, and how'd you know? Did Magnus finally break and tell you my secret?'

He pulled away and said, 'Oh, I knew from the start. A body doesn't just vanish like that without a trace. I figured you had it under control. Magnus has been sending me updates every few months.'

'I'm sorry I didn't tell you. You know me, always leaving something out... I honestly don't know why I do that... Who do we have here?'

The farmer chuckled, 'This is Khanaseri. I think we better sit down to have this conversation.'

'Sounds serious... What's going on?' she asked, glancing between them before walking down the corridor to the lounge area, gesturing them to sit on luxurious couches stitched with the finest hides.

'I see you kept the theme of the house.'

'I liked it. Why change it?'

Magnus struggled to get down to the low couch and preferred to stand, his hands clasped together in front of him. 'Rose, you have tried for years to wake Anukke and failed. He is not in there anymore. We ourselves have ventured into his mind, and we saw nothing but darkness. This man has come from across the seas to take him away from us for good. You need to move on. What you are doing is not healthy.'

'What?' stormed the woman, her hair bouncing as a wave of power formed over her.

'Calm down, Rose. We told him you wouldn't allow this. But he wouldn't listen,' Magnus stated.

Rose swung to Khanaseri, brows bunched and angry looking. 'You came here just for this? I want you to leave! All of you!'

'All right, all right,' acknowledged Malachai, already rising from the couch and moving away slowly. 'I told you it would be a waste to try. So much for it, then... Come on, leave her in peace.'

'I can wake him.'

Everyone fell silent and stared at Khanaseri.

Malachai bunched his fists. 'You didn't just say that.'

'I can wake him,' he repeated to the shocked Rose, ignoring the fuming giant. 'All I need is a little time.'

'No! That wasn't the deal! You take his body away, not wake him up! You don't know what you want to unleash.'

'I have no choice, Malachai! For my world and possibly yours, if this isn't done, far worse things can happen. Heck, they're already happening! I know, because my world is the one it's happening to right now.'

'And you think *he* will save us? Ha! He will betray you! It is his nature! He will stab you in the back and smile while doing it!' Malachai had Khanaseri by the throat, pushing him up against the wall. From the corner of his eye, he saw Rose move away from him, hurt by his words. He knew she loved him still, but she knew what he was. 'Go back home and forget about this foolishness! I will not ask again!'

The axe flashed past, twirling over the warlock's hands to break his bond, and Malachai dropped him to the ground, wincing at the blood dripping from a cut on his left arm. It was a shallow cut, done as a warning to back off.

'I did not ask your permission, Malachai. This needs to happen. I won't be as forgiving with the next cut. Stay out of this.'

Magnus backed away from them, worried he might be caught in a brawl between the brutes. 'Can we not talk this out?'

'The time for talk is at an end, abbot,' answered Khanaseri, keeping his eyes on Malachai, who unslung his hammer and placed it on the ground to spit in his hands.

'Yes, the time for talking is at an end indeed.' Magnus scurried from the room.

Khanaseri charged, his head rocked by a vicious blow a heartbeat before driving his shoulder into the farmer's chest and pushing him against the wall with a loud crash, splitting the timbers. Malachai elbowed him in the back, then kneed him in the stomach. The axe clattered to the floor, and he rolled back, avoiding a swing from the hammer. As he got to his feet, he dived to his right, seeing the hammer flying towards him, spinning in the air to thunder into the wall behind, tearing a gaping hole into the wood.

'You will not destroy my home!' shouted Rose, and the structure vanished, dropping them from a few feet above the stone surface. She ran to where the fire burned in the pit, mumbling her magical language for a veil of illusion to drop and reveal the sleeping bastard, the bed standing close to the pit for warmth. 'Malachai, stop this, please,' she begged, but he ignored her wholly.

Unarmed fists cut the air, landing blows and breaking ribs, cutting faces and bruising limbs. Khanaseri jumped and swung his right, spinning the farmer dizzily on his feet with a blow to his face, dropping him for a moment. 'I don't want to hurt you! Stop this!'

'Hurt me? Boy, I've broken vegetables bigger than you!' Malachai growled, spitting out a molar. 'And you hit like a girl.' *If I can't take you down, you little shit, I will take away what you came for,* Malachai thought. He turned to the sleeping Anukke and grabbed his hammer from the ground.

Khanaseri tackled him from the side, wrestling the hammer from his hands and getting pummelled by the farmer's left hand and knee to the ribs. He swung down his right hand and felt hard bone crack against his knuckles. A hand reached for his face, fingers searching for holes and finding his nose, pushing up hard. 'Argh!' he shouted before he bent over from a vicious kick and hit the ground, holding his fruits while he rolled on the floor. Malachai ran for Anukke, but suddenly flew back past him, and skidded over the ground to hit a pillar, the wind knocked out of him from waves of magic.

'I will not let you hurt him!' Rose shrieked, holding her sceptre at the ready.

'You know what he's capable of,' came Malachai's pained voice, his hair dishevelled and his face bloody. 'You helped us stop him once... Do so again.'

Khanaseri stumbled as he got to his feet and said, 'My father was just like you. Too stubborn to listen. He died for his beliefs. Are you willing to do the same?'

'Was he right, though? At the end, was he right?' Malachai groaned from against the pillar, clutching his ribs as he pushed himself up.

Doubts settled into Khanaseri's mind. *Maybe he was, maybe he wasn't. I'll never know. Maybe if Beuneth never got Blanka back, she wouldn't have released the dragons and maybe all of this could have been avoided, or maybe she would have found another way and we'd have ended up in the same place.* Fate, destiny — call it what you will — has a habit of getting what it wants no matter what you do. 'We're here now, and this is what's needed.'

'And you have your answer.' Terrifying growls and barks echoed through the chamber and bounced off the walls, hiding their origin. 'Oh dear!' chuckled Malachai. 'It seems you have more trouble on your hands now. These pups will obey my command to leave you alive if you just listen to me! But if you kill one... Then there's no stopping them.'

Khanaseri backed away towards Rose, holding his axe ready while searching for these pups. 'What are they? They don't sound like pups to me. Then again, Malachai has a habit of making everything seem small.'

'Gar hounds!' shouted Rose from the back, pointing to a fast-moving pack of fur in the dark. 'We cannot fight them!'

In the distance, they did not seem as threatening, but as they drew closer at terrifying speeds, Khanaseri's eyes grew wide and he took a step back, then another and another, until he was in a full sprint, running towards Rose. 'Can you slow them?' One wolf was close behind, its enormous paws drumming on the stones beneath, its panting breath in his ears. He risked a glance back to the beast, its head level with his, its mouth pulled in a snarl, revealing a jagged line of teeth and fangs large enough to make bears look like pups... *Pups*, he thought, *what a ridiculous thing to call them.* Khanaseri spun around as it lunged for his back, striking it in the face with the flat of the axe, using all his strength. The yelp and crash sounded as one when it hit the ground, and he kept on running, more on his heels.

Six more were at his back and Rose shouted, 'I can try!'

Pain lanced through his calf, with the giant wolf's claws tearing skin and flesh as it stepped on him moments before its head knocked into his back, flinging him into a pillar already weakened by time. Cracks and groans reverberated through the chamber and the pillar split with a shudder, debris falling from up high. Stones the size of fists hit the nearing wolf, making it jump away. A ripple of power raced through the vast cavern, and the wolves were stuck in motion. The warlock got to his feet, hobbling closer to the wolf, watching its eyes still locked to his, but unable to move forward. Incongruous fractal movements, slow and barely noticeable, tortured their bodies while the roof plummeted stones from up high, smashing down around them, shards and splinters scattering over the floor. He saw Malachai a few feet from them, also caught in the same trance, and wished this could have ended differently. Folding his hands together, Khanaseri chanted and focused on another pillar to his right, snapping his hand shut to see it explode in absolute glory, a burst of rock flying out before the stone blocks collapsed to the ground. 'Let them go!'

Instantly, the wolves and Malachai came out of the trance, confusedly looking around at the collapsing ceiling. 'Go, while there's time. I know you understand me,' said the warlock, staring into the eyes of the grey wolf. 'Leave before you're trapped down here forever.' The wolves spun around and ran from the chamber. 'You too, Malachai! Go now! Your children need you. Gwen needs you.'

Weighing his options, Malachai considered running through the falling rocks to get to him, then cursed. 'Argh! Bastard! He better not come back here!' Gigantic rocks crashed down behind him as he ran for the stairs leading to the monastery.

'Quick! I can't hold these forever!' shouted Rose, holding back the collapsing roof with her magic. Khanaseri joined her side and rummaged through his pack, pulling out the cloth-covered sphere with care. 'What is that?' she demanded.

'This is what will bring him back, I think.'

'You think? We destroyed this entire place on a "you think"?'

'Yes, well... It doesn't really come with instructions. Hold him down.'

'Why? He ain't moving!' Rose exclaimed, struggling under the weight of the rocks pressing them from above, her magical shield their only protector. 'And I'm a little busy here.'

Khanaseri placed the sphere on Anukke's chest and clasped the sleeping man's hands over it. He called out, 'I implore you, Yidrog, Lord of Ice, to gauge the heart of this man and form the bond.'

The Balamuth fell apart through Anukke's hands like a clump of snow, then drifted into his pores until it vanished. Rose frowned at him. 'Now we wait,' said Khanaseri.

* * *

Deep in the darkness where no light ever touched, Anukke walked with a presence next to him, a presence he knew was always there but never seen. In a field of silence, they sauntered over the imaginary boardwalks of the harbour, breathing in the imagined sea breeze, listening to the imagined birds chirp, to the people around them buying and selling the fish from the blackened fishing vessels, the barnacles reaching up the hull to climb out of the water. The dried corn kernels he popped into his mouth tasted salty and crunchy, lingering on his tongue while he chewed and swallowed. A woman shouted for her boy to get out of the muddy street, not to dirty his clothes before going to the temple for prayer, slapping his bum as a wail echoed over the scene. The voice grumbled next to him.

'I am surprised you haven't asked how long you need to be here still.'

'Oh, it isn't so bad here. I can do what I want and go where I want. No one bothers me. I fear you have rubbed off on me, yet I don't know who you are or what you look like.'

'You see it as I've held you captive. But I believe I saved you, guarded you for the right time. You wanted a power unlike any other, and I will give it to you. It will come at a cost, though.'

'Why me?'

'You remember nothing of your birth? Your family?'

Anukke shook his head. 'Get on with it... You *tried* to teach me patience, but I was never a good student.'

'You are one of few remaining Darvath in the world, and I have chosen you to be my vessel. Until now I couldn't show myself, for I have also been imprisoned; but finally now, we can both be free if you choose to bond with me.'

'Dar what now?'

'Darvath. An old race we respected for their abilities. Millennia ago, the first Darvath lay with a human female, and soon more followed, bringing forth with the age of man those able to touch the Source. Magi of all kinds. But in this, the thinning of the bloodlines started for the Darvath. Your bloodline, however, remained pure through the ages, keeping to the old beliefs. That Darvath are gods among men. To be revered. Not to spill their seed with humans. Most bloodlines are now lost completely. You, I sought to protect.'

Anukke stopped chewing the kernels and saw everyone around him — the imagined he believed he was controlling — turn to him, staring at him with dull eyes. The presence next to him emerged, growing less transparent, a daunting cold wave flowing from the white scales that formed before his very eyes. Retreating slowly, he watched as the colossal dragon fully emerged from the air around him, formed from the darkness by falling snow so white against the utter black. Everything had disappeared now: the people, the harbour, the noise, the kernels in his hands, and the sea breeze, except for the dragon before him with its yellow eyes, its front legs joined with the wings, massive talons at the end and more talons at the knees. A crown of black horns adorned its head, nostrils flaring with puffs of white, jagged, filthy fangs flashing beneath a vicious snarl.

'Do you accept?' roared its voice, eyes gleaming at his.

Laughter, harsh and discordant, burst from Anukke, his hands clutched together over his mouth as he bent over. 'Do you accept...? Classic. This was a good one, thank you. I needed that. Good work. I could even feel the cold coming from that illusion. Well done indeed. Oh, and the Darvath story — brilliant.' He turned around and walked away, eating his kernels again.

'Look at me!' roared the beast, a stream of cold rushing from its mouth. 'This is no illusion! Do you accept the joining?'

More tests and tricks. Anukke swung back to the beast, spreading his hands, and said, 'Yeah, sure. I accept. There's nothing else to do here.' He turned, laughing as he walked away until a force pulled at him, stopping him in his tracks. A powerful gust forced him off his feet, and the vast blackness spun around him. Everything looked the same: up, down, left, right, his only point of reference, the blurring white of the tremendous beast crawling towards him. The floor came out of nowhere in a rush, his head bouncing off the soundless stage of black ink. Brows knitted and breathless, Anukke tried to crawl forward, but slid backwards instead, the force only growing stronger, drawing him back to the dragon like a violent tornado, ripping him across the black nothingness on his stomach. He grabbed at everything and nothing. It would not make a difference.

'Do not fight me!' echoed the dragon's roar.

No matter how hard he tried, he could not get away. The dragon towered over him and broke apart one flake at a time. It melted away into a storm of fine, white mist once more, flowing like snowflakes dancing on the winds to seep into Anukke's pores, lifting him to the air, and drowning him with its memories and feelings: a wealth of information collected over centuries. He saw the world bloom from an age when animals were king and humans were virtually non-existent, a time when the only threat was another dragon seeking to assert its dominance in your domain. Time sped by, seasons changing in the blink of an eye, years vanishing swiftly as Yidrog watched the birth of new creatures from his cave up high in the mountains. Small, impotent things called man. He never thought with their rise, would come the dragons' fall, their numbers dwindling dangerously. Anukke's senses reeled at the touch of the beast. His sight turned sharp and focused, the sensation paining his head. A certain power crawled up his spine, making the hairs on his back stand on end and the slightest smell curled his lip. Not to mention the carnivorous hunger that plagued him so utterly. He craved for raw meat and blood to flow down his throat. The dragon settled into its new host, and Anukke dropped to the ground on his one knee, catching his tired self, puffing long breaths as he whispered, 'Yidrog, Lord of Ice. I see you now. We are one!'

* * *

Anukke opened his eyes to a world of chaos, debris crashing down all over from above with Rose and the horribly scarred warrior struggling under a weight of rocks pushing them down, magically held back but gaining ground with every breath. All around them, the room had collapsed. He groaned as he sat up, clutching his head, the world spinning and making him want to gag. It felt like every muscle in his body would tear from the smallest movement, and when he tried to speak, his voice squeaked, frail and soft. 'Can we get out of this dump?'

Rose nearly lost her focus on the rocks and smiled at him. 'I can't believe you're awake.'

'You hold the rocks back, Rose. I'll get us out of here,' said the warlock, helping Anukke from the bed and supporting his weakened body with one arm.

Anukke pulled his face into a sneer, smelling the warlock's pits. 'Gods, I thought I was the dead one, yet you have the reek of a thousand stillborn.'

'You get used to it,' grumbled Khanaseri, and a portal flashed open close by. He folded his free arm around Rose's back. 'We jump together, on my mark.' Loud cracks and shudders vibrated through the ground, the rocks shifting dangerously closer. 'Now!' They jumped for the portal, vanishing as the rocks plummeted to the ground in a hail of dust.

* * *

Bright light blinded Anukke as he stepped onto the red sand. 'Water. Do you have water?' he croaked, scratching at his parched throat. Khanaseri handed him the waterskin, and he yanked the stopper out, flushing his mouth and drinking deep.

'Slowly, now!' said the warlock, eyeing him sidelong.

'Anukke?' Rose moved closer, her voice trembling in confusion, being stern and loving at the same time. For so long she had cared for him, knowing what he'd done, not just to her, but to the lands of Kraydenia. Now that he was awake again, she was unsure if the caring and love were justified.

'Rose,' he said, ragged breaths assaulting his body as he lowered the waterskin. 'So it *was* you who manifested those flowers. I never thought you would want to see me again, let alone save me after what I did to you. Thank you.' He twisted away, groaning with clenched teeth, and bent over to vomit, feeling a strenuous pull on his consciousness, a continuous, mind-numbing screech echoing between his ears. Palms pressing over his ears to silence the skirl, a voice filtered through, riding the hissing waves, commanding his presence while hammering on the walls of his sanity.

Yidrog revolted against the orders, roaring out its defiance in his mind. *'Belroc commands our presence! He will never stop.'*

'Anukke! Are you okay?' Rose called as she rushed forward, reaching out to him with her mouth agape, her eyes stretched wide.

'I will be,' he muttered, and took her hand, drawing her near for a moment. They stood a good distance away from the monastery, watching the building collapse with the priests kneeling in the dirt all around, crying and praying for a miracle to save their home. More priests ran closer from where they laboured in the barley field, soil covered hands rubbing their cleanly shaven heads while Gar hounds howled deep and long, their heads lifted to the clear blue sky above. To the right of the despondent gathering, Malachai stood with his hands on his hips, shaking his head in disappointment and anger.

'It seems there's something I must do before I can be completely free,' Anukke said to Rose, squeezing her hands, then turned to Khanaseri. 'I reckon that's why you woke me, why you brought Yidrog to me.'

'Nothing for nothing,' said the warlock.

'Wait, what? Who is this Yidrog?' Rose stood, perplexed, frowning at them.

'He's the one who woke me, the one who now dwells within me; and I owe him a debt, my love. A debt I fear that cannot go unpaid. Do not worry, for I will be back, and I will find you.' He looked towards the destruction in the distance and continued with a sigh, 'It seems I am the cause of more hatred even before you woke me. We leave soon, warlock. I want to get this over with.' Anukke sauntered closer to the crying priests, risking the wrath of the gigantic wolves and Malachai, uttering words of power while the warlock dashed away to get Flintlock from the stables.

Waves of magic pulsed from Anukke, and the roar of the collapsing building stopped with a groan, the hanging dust hiding its descending fate. The wolves jumped around, growling and snarling at his approaching footsteps, and Malachai readied his hammer. Anukke grinned and pointed to the building, lifting his hands gradually.

'The monastery! It's coming back!' shouted a priest. They all watched the building crawl out from the mountain grave to settle in place, a little worse for wear, but not lost to the depths below.

Puzzled glances flashed from Malachai, and Anukke smirked, enjoying the discomfort his presence brought, then said, 'I take no pride in the role I played here. We were a team once, for a short while at least... Can we not be so again?'

'Anukke, ye piece o' shite. I should smash yer languid, pale face against the rocks and be done with ye.'

'But alas, you are too weak...as always,' came Anukke's sinisterly calm voice. 'I will always be a few dozen steps ahead of you. But I'm not here to fight.' He watched the wolves scrape the earth with their gigantic paws, barking and growling at him with gleaming fangs. 'Today, wolves, you are not enough to stop me, so shut it!' He waited for them to quiet down, then continued talking over the low, rumbling growls in their throats. 'I have done terrible things in the past, but they are the past, and I finally have what I've wanted for so long.'

'Meaning?' asked Malachai as he stepped closer.

'Do not hunt for me, and I will not hunt you... I bid you all farewell. I'm sure Rose will help fix the monastery.' A mist formed around him as Khanaseri neared with Flintlock at his back, the reins pulled taut in his hands. The horse was becoming skittish, pulling on the lead as the colossal white beast emerged from the fog. A terrifying cry escaped the dragon, its yellow eyes watching the falling priests retreat, the wolves tucking their tails between their legs with petrified yelps. But the farmer did not move. Malachai stood defiantly against it, the great hammer resting in his hands.

The beast took to the sky in a piercing shriek, its wings straining to lift its colossal body. It hovered for a moment above them, peppering them with small stones and dust, then turned and flew higher, quickly growing smaller until it became impossible to see.

Khanaseri walked up to Malachai, who shook his head at him, a look of disgust radiating from the farmer. He stopped a few feet away and said, 'I know you think I did the wrong thing. But this was the only way. Believe me.'

Malachai placed his hammer on the ground. 'You don't know what you've started. Leave Kraydenia. Leave with your life before I change my mind. And you, Rose? Are you happy now? Look at what this bastard has turned him into! Now the exterior finally matches the interior.'

She could not bear to look at him, nor was she able to answer, glancing away and scratching the back of her left hand anxiously. Her mouth parted slightly with a trembling lower lip, wanting to say something, but then swung away, closing her eyes and clenching her jaws. She knew there was nothing she could say that would change anything.

Khanaseri walked away, and a portal burst into life, swallowing the warlock and Flintlock with its cold intent. The rift snapped shut, with flakes of snow and fog left drifting in the air.

Chapter Seventeen

Demons with burning bone-blades at the end of their wrists, as long and sharp as broadswords, climbed up the side of the wall, liquefying the rocks with their intense heat while soldiers poured buckets of water down the side, slowing their ascent and burn, sticking them full of arrows only to watch the wooden shafts catch fire. Talgar had his dagger in the head of a demon that climbed over the wall, its arms flailing wildly as the man forced it to the ground, its quenched heat threatening to come alive again. A massive block of stone dropped onto the creature's chest, crushing its ribcage, and Talgar rolled back, dragging the red-hot dagger from its head. 'Oi! That was way too close to my head!'

Untara shrugged and said, 'You have a small head!'

'Argh! Just watch out next time!' Numerous enemy soldiers and dark creatures made it up the wall, the fighting intensifying ever more with the raging beasts still hovering above. The city felt like a furnace ready to cook its inhabitants. 'Magnus! To your left!'

The barkeep struck a man square in the face and dropped to the stones at the sound of Talgar's warning, feeling a blade cut into his leathers on his back. He jumped up and grabbed the man, hurling him from the wall. 'Thanks, Talgar! I owe youse one. Can ya see our friends yet? Have they returned from their mission?'

Talgar leaned over the parapet, squinting to the southeast. 'Nothing as yet. I'm sure they're fine. Let's worry about our own arses for now, eh?'

Magnus didn't want to worry about his own life; he wanted to worry about Anavi. He also never wanted to fight again, yet here he was, swinging his fists and killing people. Arrows whizzed past, thudding into a demon's head and chest, dropping it to the ground as a soft voice spoke.

'Magnus? Is that really you?'

'Little busy here, Princess!' A soldier swung his mace, and Magnus jumped back. He spun past the next blow and backhanded the soldier, snapping the man's jaw, then grabbed his arm, yanking it down hard, dislocating it. He pulled a cleaver from a pouch at his side and buried it in the man's skull, wrenching it out and dropping him to the ground. 'Would youse look at that? Seems we have a reason to fight after all,' he added, pointing to her stomach. 'What are youse doing up here? Ya should be resting in the castle.'

Ladriana lowered her bow and rubbed her stomach. 'Yes, isn't it wonderful?' Magnus joined her, clasping her by the arms with a big smile on his face.

'I'm sorry I haven't come to say hello. Since we got here, it has been chaos, as youse know.'

'Yes, we've definitely had better days.' Ladriana bit her lip and continued, 'Come, I need to talk with you.' She dragged him away to a quiet corner with her escort slashing and fighting to protect them. Glancing around to make sure they were fine for the moment, Ladriana said, 'I gather you've heard the rumours of Garidan?'

'Sadly, yes. Broke my heart is what it did... But I still have some hope. As I understand, there was never any proof.'

'None.'

'There it is, then. Hope.'

She let fly another arrow, impaling a man who broke through her guards' defence. Hope... A word she'd almost forgotten, one that held no meaning for her anymore...or did it? She couldn't tell anymore if the reason she was still fighting was hope, or one born from a promise.

Wanting to change the subject, she said, 'You look amazing, Magnus.'

'Yeah, I couldn't stay out of the fight any longer. They destroyed the bar...'

'Watch out!' Ladriana pushed him out of the way and loosed two arrows, killing two men and grazing a third, who swung his sword at Magnus.

The barkeep cursed as the blade bit into his back, and he slapped the man off his feet. He grabbed a bundle of arrows from Ladriana's quiver in one hand and plunged them into the Terenoran's side with a growl. 'Bastard!' Magnus sagged to the ground on one knee, his left arm hanging down to the stones, blood pooling quickly under it.

'We need to stop the bleeding; come, I'll take you to the healer.' Ladriana grabbed his arm and helped him up. 'Make a path!' she shouted to her men.

'Leave another gap like that and I'll gut you myself!' shouted the dark-skinned man Magnus had come to know as Kehlos. 'Close up! An arm's length apart, no more!' Backing away, side by side, a wall of shields, they escorted the queen and Magnus from the wall to the healers down below.

To their left, Abe chanted continuously, watching all the students and magi on the wall, doing what they could to protect their families. Tired, sore, and dirty, he wished he'd left when he had the chance, but it was a fleeting wish, one quickly replaced by a wish to save everyone as he saw a soldier stabbed to death a few feet from him. Maintaining the dome took all his focus; he could not be there for everyone. He wiped his forehead with his robe's sleeve, wincing at the sting of blood that flowed into his eyes, and turned to his left, seeing the world's fabric torn open as a portal flashed into being a distance from the wall on the enemy's left. A big man, scarred and battle-weary astride his horse, emerged from the fold. The man slid off the horse and doubled over onto his hands and knees, coughing and puking red to the stones under his feet. *Who are you supposed to be? Friend or foe?* Abe pondered. 'Whoever you are, you should stop using portals... They will be the death of you.'

The man rolled over onto his back, wiping his mouth with the back of his hand, and lay there for a moment to catch his breath.

* * *

Ears ringing and jaw hurting, Khanaseri's eyes felt like they were popping from their sockets, like metal shavings were making their way to the backs of his eyes, scraping and sticking into the sclera. The world spun and his head felt like mush, his mind unable to form complete thoughts and ideas. Panting heavily, he lay on his back, waiting for the pulsing in his head to stop before sitting up. *I haven't felt this bad since my very first portal creation with Beuneth.* Eyes burning, he rubbed them with his thumb and index finger, and cursed at Flintlock, who nudged him and neighed loudly for the warlock to rise. 'Oh, hush, Flint. What are you complaining about?' He got to his feet. 'Blackened balls of Kelcai! Why didn't you warn me? I should make sausages of you!' Flintlock shook his head, bit at his arm in frustration. 'Oi! Not now!' Khanaseri stood near the forest, with an entire wing of Turneroth's men blocking his path to the wall. They hadn't noticed his appearance, being too occupied with the battle at hand.

'Don't just stand there! Come on.' He pulled himself up to the horse's back, and Flint bucked, nearly throwing the warlock. 'Oi! No need for that!' They pushed hard for the walls of New Runswick, Flintlock grunting loudly as he raced forward.

A shift in the weather saw dark clouds forming above, and a soft rain started to fall, rapidly gaining momentum.

Hooves thundering down the slope and through the fields, they surged past a rushing horde of soldiers, seeing the bewildered looks on their faces, knowing they were ignored out of pure confusion. Why would the enemy behind the wall suddenly be riding through them? It was only when a soldier shouted and pointed at him that the rest turned from the wall to give chase. Arrows flashed by, and he drove his heels into the horse's flanks. There was little he could do now; he lacked the strength to fight them. Ransacked homes and farms stood bare, providing some cover between him and the chasing soldiers, the drumming of their feet and their shouts labouring across the fields as he smelled the fresh scent of petrichor with the falling rain, washing away the stench of the dead. The earthly smell brightened his mood.

They ran at a full gallop through a farmstead with multiple buildings and barns, kicking up mud and stones before two men jumped from the roof of a house, blocking his path with spears stabbing at Flintlock. Khanaseri dragged on the reins and swung right, heading down a narrow path between the buildings, when a soldier appeared from a hidden alley. Flintlock kicked out, snapping the soldier's neck and crushing his skull, skidding the body over the slippery mud and into another who came running, cartwheeling the second to the ground and impaling him on his own sword as he hit the dirt.

A blade sang through the drops in the air, scything from his left, dangerously close. Khanaseri yanked on the reins, and Flintlock swung to the left, throwing up mud. Arrows missed his head by pure luck, hissing by to break against the stone wall of the building he raced past. He urged the horse on, heading for a wagon with its nose dug into the dirt, the house with a flat roof beyond. A soldier flew to the ground, diving out of the way as Flintlock leapt over him, using the wagon for leverage and jumping to the roof. There was no time to think. He needed to commit as the edge of the roof drew close, fast. Flintlock pushed off with his hind legs, neighing as he did, sailing over multiple soldiers screaming in anger from below. It felt like they were flying, soaring through the air on great wings. Time slowed. Flint's hooves pushed into the softened ground and he raced on. 'That's a good horse!'

Khanaseri laughed hysterically, seeing the black, tar-like creatures struggling up the side of the walls in the rain, their sinewy frames bending and snapping as rocks showered them from above. 'Argh! They've warded the walls against magic! Clever bastards! How am I going to get in? Flint, you're just full of bright ideas today. Where are they now?' A single snort from the beast beneath him was all he got. 'Ah, the silent treatment! I've heard of this tactic before. Guess I'll take the lead.' A portal flashed open a few feet from the wall as he neared, and he reined in, wondering what trap this could be.

'Run, you damned buffoon!' came a shout from the top of the wall.

Flintlock sped forward, and they jumped through the portal, emerging on the other side of the wall before it snapped shut behind them. Hundreds of men surrounded them with weapons drawn, their backs forced against the wall.

'Easy, Flint,' he whispered, patting the horse's trembling neck. Khanaseri slipped down and raised his hands, slowly setting down the axe on the ground. 'I'm not on their side!'

'But are you on ours?' Ladriana emerged from behind the group of soldiers, making her way closer as they separated for her to pass through. No rain fell in the city; the dome saw to it. Ladriana moved closer and said, 'I remember you. Your wounds have healed much since I saw you last.'

'Aye, and my hair's nice too,' he said with a grin, sweeping back the short, wet hairs that had grown on the unburnt areas of his head.

'Yeah, and you're still a bit of a dick...' she laughed and turned to her men. 'Lower your weapons. He's with us.' The soldiers lowered their weapons in unison, pitting the spears' butts against the ground and sliding swords into their scabbards.

'Look who finally showed up. Ganda'har and Blanka will be happy to see youse.' Magnus came in from behind Ladriana, working his stitched shoulder to see if the sutures would hold in a fight.

'Magnus? Have they not been feeding you? Where's the rest of you?'

'Left it on the wayside...'

Turning serious, Khanaseri said, 'I'm glad to see your spirits are still high.' He looked up to the dome, watching the dragons circle above. 'We need to hold them off for a little while longer. We have allies coming.'

* * *

Early morning as the winds howled, rocking trees and pelting down rain, Blanka, Ganda'har, Anavi, and Stentor snuck into the enemy camp while the battle raged in the distance. They'd come from the forest's side, sneaking through when the patrol turned their backs on them. Few guards walked around in the rain; most others kept dry, staying out of the wet unless absolutely necessary. Blanka hadn't thought it would be this easy.

Keeping as low a profile as they dared, Blanka stole a cuirass from a rack outside a tent and quickly donned it, the yellow paint splattered with blood he knew came from their side. To his right, behind a tent, he saw a soldier pulled from his feet, and Anavi appeared soon after, crouched low, with daggers in hand, slick with blood. Her yellow catlike eyes flashed to his, sending a shiver down his spine. *That woman doesn't mess around, does she? Wouldn't want to be on her bad side.*

'Hey, you three! Why aren't you on the front lines? Thinking of running away, are you?' shouted a soldier from the left, stomping towards them angrily.

Ganda'har spun to the man and said, 'Not at all, sir. We,' he pointed to Stentor, 'were sent to guard the prisoners. The king wants to ensure they don't escape again.'

'And they sent me to relieve whoever is guarding the king's son. Can't have him getting into trouble, now can we?' stated Blanka.

The soldier's thick jaw worked back and forth as he thought, glaring at them suspiciously through narrow, slitted eyes, and blinked the rain from them. 'The cages are in that direction. You're on the wrong side of the camp...not to mention it's those dragons' job to guard them.' He pulled a metal whistle hanging around his neck and set it to his lips.

'Dragons can't call for shit if there's trouble. The king wants us there. We just came to fetch some wood for a fire during the shift,' grumbled Stentor, seeing a pile of wood near a tent in the distance. 'I'm sure the rain will stop soon, then we can dry our clothes. You're welcome to join us.'

The man followed her gaze. 'That's Lieutenant Kalfa's wood. He'd be most displeased if infantry stole it. So don't let me keep you.' The thickset soldier walked past Ganda'har and slapped Stentor on the arse, laughing harshly. 'You are one *big* woman. That snivelling Kalfa can go to bed cold tonight. But maybe I won't.' His eyebrows jumped up and down, eyes glinting at her. He had to shout now to be heard over the bombarding rain.

Stentor's fists bunched up. She wanted to lay him out on the ground and beat him senseless. He looked as though he could take a beating or two, and seemed like he already had, his face marred on one side by cuts and old scars. *I'm not big... I'm strong, you impotent anus. Did your mother never teach you how to talk to women?* Ganda'har shook his head at her. A shiver of disgust rippled over her back, making her skin crawl. 'I should bed you now, just for the fun of it. The only problem is, whose cock are you going to borrow?' she heard herself say.

The soldier's face was flush with anger and humiliation. He glanced between them and stormed, 'Fucking infantry! Get back to your duties!' He slipped in the mud as he stomped away, catching himself just in the nick of time, and threw an angry look over his shoulder.

'That was completely unnecessary, Stentor! Are you trying to get us killed?' roared Ganda'har, teeth gritted to muffle the shout.

'But it felt so good, Cap'n. It was that, or my axe to his chest. I think this was better.'

'Argh. Come on! Let's go before more men stop us.'

Anavi hadn't been seen yet. She snuck around a tepee and stopped, spying the two guards outside the king's tent, carefully looking around at the few soldiers walking about. Smoke trailed from a tent down the path. *The cooks must be preparing food,* thought Anavi. *Shit!* As she rounded the corner of a gathering of tents to her left, a big tent with a large open front appeared on her right. Men ran around inside, fighting with injured soldiers to get them to lie still on the low beds, rags of blood and shouts of horror filing through the drumming rain. She waited for Captain Ganda'har to talk with the guards outside the king's quarters on the other side, and slipped past, making her way to the back.

'You are relieved of duty. We're taking over for a while,' demanded Ganda'har as they approached.

'On whose orders?' asked the men.

A moment of silence followed before she heard his voice again. 'The king's.'

'Master Bohan has restricted any of the king's men without his word. You'll need to leave.'

'Come on, fellas. Do you really want us to go back to the king and tell him two irrelevant guards have defied his orders?'

Anavi snuck around, leaning close to the tent, and drew her dagger when she saw the nearest guard's back turned to her. *That armour won't do much to stop this blade,* she thought. *I just need to get under the ribs. There's little protection there.* Quick as a striking viper, she jumped up and slid her steel between the armour's shackles, twisting the blade and ripping it out, her other hand clasped over the man's mouth. She saw the other guard fall in the mud, head rolling a distance away. Stentor had taken a more direct approach, her axe doing the brutal work for her. 'Subtle.'

'Always,' whispered Stentor, her loud voice still travelling, even in the heavy rain. Blanka and Ganda'har quickly ducked into the tent, while Stentor and Anavi moved the bodies away before they got discovered.

Inside the king's lodging, Blanka sneaked through the folds of material used as curtain walls to divide areas of the tent, brushing them aside slowly and carefully. A man's voice drifted softly, his voice calm and gentle. Ganda'har moved to the right, checking for more men. Blanka poked his head through the curtain wall and whispered, 'Master Bohan wants to see you right now.' He saw the boy lying on his stomach on a pile of pillows, reading from a thick book laid bare before him. Restraining himself, he quickly pulled his head away before the boy could see his face. 'The boy stays,' he said, hearing the pillows rustle as the man got up.

Blanka closed his trembling hands. He was so close now. They couldn't afford a mistake. The man barely left the room and was grabbed by the arms and pulled to the ground swiftly. Blanka wrapped his hand over the man's mouth and whispered, 'What are you doing here? You do not look like one of them... Whisper, or you die.' He removed his hand.

'I'm not. Forgive me, sir. I was captured a while back in a village southwest of here. My name is Balin. Master Bohan has been kind to me, gave me a duty to care for the boy. I was ready to give up after I stepped on a snake, but he saved my life.'

Blanka released his grip on the man. 'That boy in there is my son! They stole him from me when he was but a babe. You will tell him he needs to leave with us. Got that?'

'You're not with these soldiers?'

'No, we fight for New Runswick.'

The man's eyes lit up, his mouth quivering as he cried, 'Take me with you, please, sir. The boy will come with me with less suspicion.'

Blanka looked around and sighed. He remembered what the boy's eyes looked like the last time he had seen him. The man was right; the boy would listen to him. 'We have to move fast. Do what we say at all times. Got it?'

Balin brought up his finger and said, 'I know what to do. Give me a moment.' Blanka let him up and watched him crawl to the boy, taking out a vial filled with a strange-coloured substance from next to the pillows. He spoke briefly to the boy, and the child opened his mouth so Balin could drip a few drops down his throat.

'What was that?' Blanka stormed from the darkness beyond the boy's sight, but the man only brought his hand up then rose to meet him.

'A sedative is all. He's been having night terrors for a while. We don't want a screaming child on our hands while we make a break for it.'

It didn't take long before the sedative kicked in, Moseroth's head lolling around and his eyes drifting wildly, lids heavy and closing involuntarily. Ganda'har joined his side and said, 'We have to leave! What's taking so long?'

'He's coming with. The child will be more at ease.' The vestigial flicker of anger in Ganda'har's eyes did not sway his decision, even if he agreed it was not a good idea.

Thunderous explosions cracked through the air and earth, rattling the tent and its furnishings, and Ganda'har ran outside to investigate with a growl. Moseroth's dazed eyes opened in alarm briefly before closing again and Blanka grumbled, 'I'll take him! If he gets unruly, I will hand him to you, so stay close by.' He picked the boy up, and the sleepy child hugged Blanka's chest, his head resting on his shoulder as they ran outside.

Cheers of celebration sounded from the Terenorans as massive explosions billowed smoke from the walls' tops, craters blasted at every corner where the dwarven magical amplifiers were. The dome collapsed steadily, its golden vale over the city retracting to leave its inhabitants unguarded. 'The city is done for! We can't go back there!' mumbled Blanka.

'Give Khanaseri a chance! He must be doing something to bring aid. He wouldn't just vanish and leave us like this.'

'He's dead, Ganda'har! I'm sorry, but he's not coming back.'

'No! He's not! He can't be!' shouted Ganda'har, grabbing him by the shoulders. 'This is where it ends, Blanka! If Turneroth goes back to your time or not, he will live on. He needs to be stopped. He needs to die.' Trumpets blew from the north, blue banners waving in the slowing rain from men on horseback. Armoured and ready for battle, thousands raced over the hills to do battle with the foot soldiers of Terenore. 'Gods above! There must be ten thousand of them! Where did they come from?'

'I don't know, but they're not enough.' Blanka wanted to run, take his son and leave this godforsaken, war-torn lands and head south, back to his crater, but the beast in him awoke, creeping into his thoughts.

Belgarr spoke to Blanka's mind, *'If we leave now, your son will never be safe.'*

'We'll be torn to pieces. What will the two of us do against the might of all those dragons?'

'Whatever you decide, do it quick!' shouted Stentor, seeing men exit their tents and turn to them. 'We've been discovered!'

Blanka growled and ran after them, clasping Moseroth to his chest.

* * *

The bugle of the horns sounded as they ran, and soldiers stormed from their tents, confusedly searching for the threat until spying the five dashing through the camp, and gave chase. Blanka pressed the boy against his chest, legs dangling at his back, flopping around with every footfall sloshing through the mud. An arrow whistled past his left, missing him by a few inches to disappear into the soft ground, and shouts of anger rose at the back to stay their bows in fear of hitting the boy. Anavi and Stentor ran on his right, Ganda'har to his left, guarding his flanks, while Balin was just behind, trying to keep up. 'Anavi!' he shouted, seeing a man dive at her, but his concern was unnecessary. She'd seen the guard come a mile away and had her daggers ready, flashing menacingly fast before the man could even touch her, slicing in under his armpit and stabbing like a thing possessed. Anavi hefted the man over her head in a roll with her legs, using her momentum to throw him off of her, the blade coming away bloody, but cleaned quickly in the falling rain.

For a big woman, Stentor was fast, her great strides looking slow but gaining quick ground, even with her heavy armour and that axe. More enemy soldiers spilled from tents around them, and Stentor looked over her shoulder, keeping them in her sight when she stepped into a hole and twisted her ankle, the pain shooting up her leg. The ground rushed at her, and her breath exploded with the impact. *Watch where you're going, Alvogara! Always the klutz!* she remembered her brother say to her, though she was smaller back then. She doubted he would say it to her face now.

'Get up, soldier!' shouted Ganda'har, and saw her struggle to her feet, limping with her left ankle swollen and bruised. A man came at her with a sword, cleaving left and right, the first strike ringing off the steel plate over her chest, denting the metal and rocking her hard. The second strike she dodged, jumping forward to sprawl in the mud. The man towered over her and brought down his sword, but was taken off his feet by the captain, tackled to the ground and beaten senseless by the power of the beast inside. He grabbed the heaving Stentor and dragged her through the grounds to the low spiked wall that made up the camp's perimeter, her feet scraping mud. They did not have far to go, but men were filing out of the camp behind them. They only needed to make it to the wall, where archers would send volleys into their pursuers while they made the climb up to safety. 'Blanka, we need your help!' shouted Ganda'har, falling behind with the enemy drawing near.

Blanka and Anavi spun around, and he said, 'Take him, please. Get him to safety on the wall. I'll join you there.'

'No! You take him. I'll go back for them.' The conversation was over. She didn't wait for his reply and ran back, using the trees as cover.

He stared after her for a moment, then set off for the wall again.

'Where's that bastard going? Is he leaving us for dead to save his own skin? And that, after we helped him get his son? If we don't die, I'm killing him!' Ganda'har fumed, dragging Stentor's heavy load through the woods.

'You should go, Cap'n, leave me behind. I can make it back on my own. They need you in the fight.'

'Nonsense! Now shut up and start running!'

Two men crashed through the brush with mace and sword, and Ganda'har shoved Stentor out of the way. She went to the ground dismally, dragging herself over the terrain to pull herself up against a nearby tree as she heard Ganda'har engage in the fight with one. A blow rocked her, spinning her around, her breastplate mangled by a mace. It felt like her ribs had snapped. She couldn't breathe. Stentor ripped the mangled plates from her body and glared into the eyes of the flat-faced guard she'd insulted in the camp. 'You found that cock yet?' she asked with a sneer, and the man charged, swinging the dreadful weapon at her head in a shout of anger. Bark and wood splinters flew as she dropped to the ground, the mace connecting with the tree at her back. The mace swung from her left, tearing the plates on her arm, cutting a deep gash above her wrist, and she pushed off with her injured foot. The pain was excruciating, but that was better than the alternative. Her shoulder crushed his nose, a stream of blood covering her back as it gushed out from the man. The soldier dropped the weapon and grabbed her by the throat, squeezing as she clawed at his face, her hands seeking something to hurt.

Stentor heard more men drawing near, and more fighting, but she couldn't worry about that. Not now. She brought her arm over both of his, curling it around and hammered down with her other arm, breaking his hold before crashing her head into his. Both spat blood from the impact, her mouth cut open and nose bleeding. A thunderous right from the flat-faced soldier saw her bent over and grabbing at a branch as she reeled, but it snapped in her hands. Her vision was failing her, but she felt the heavy wood in her palms. The solid feel. *This will hurt.* She jumped up, swinging the branch, and felt it connect with his face, splintering the timber. Stentor sagged to the ground as the man dropped, the other half of the wooden club pinned into his head by a broken side-branch. Air wheezed through her teeth, and she coughed raggedly, then saw two men on the ground next to Anavi, while Ganda'har crawled out from under another.

Anavi grabbed her arm, while the angry Ganda'har grabbed the other, and they ran for the wall. 'I told him to go. He wanted me to take his boy. Don't be angry with him.'

Ganda'har didn't look back at her or answer. They just kept running.

* * *

The rain intensified, and thunder flashed in the skies, lashing out at large trees and the walls' tops. Sparks flew with every strike, men jumping to take cover from the frightening blue and purple bolts. Blanka dashed through the streets of New Runswick, with Balin next to him, the boy flopping around in his blissful ignorance.

Balin shouted as he ran, 'Millie! Millie Tole! Synthia Tole! Millie!' Rolling fire raced down the street at them, burning everything in its path as a dragon flew overhead.

'Take cover!' shouted Blanka, and ran to the corner of a building, leaning against the wet wall with the boy. The gloomy city lit up as flames rolled through the streets, until pouring rain extinguished them. More dragons flew over, crashing into buildings, toppling walls, and destroying homes. A red blur ploughed into another dragon that was headed for them, taking it out before it reached them. 'Thank you, Captain.' Blanka knew Ganda'har could not last out there alone; the other dragons would band together and tear him to pieces.

'Millie! Synthia Tole!' Balin shouted, leaning out from behind a wall to look down the street. They ran again, jumping over the burnt bodies of soldiers, the smell, something they would never forget.

'Balin!' came a voice from behind, and they spun around to see a woman step out from a door leading down into the basement below the surface of a building.

'Synthia!' Balin shouted and ran to her, embracing her and the little girl who emerged.

'Papa!'

Blanka looked around, noting the dark stone temple with white mortar at the end of the street, and handed the sleeping boy to Balin. 'Protect him and your family! I *will* be back.' He turned to leave and glanced back over his shoulder. 'If not, take good care of him.' Balin nodded and herded his wife and daughter down the stairs, pulling the door shut above them and latching it in place as Blanka veered and took to the sky, the black of his scales glistening in the rain.

It was a show of chaos as ballista bolts searched for the beasts, the gigantic arrows ripping through everything in their paths, the men working frantically to load and release the enormous contraptions from the walls and streets. Streams of dark magic snaked from Abe's hands, racing out from the top of the wall to the roving beasts, touching their psyches and suppressing the call of the Alpha. His mind was being torn, shared between the dozens of dragons near him, bending them to his will. He could feel the link break momentarily, their minds lashing out at the call. Abe felt the anger of Belroc reach into his brain. '*Who are you to challenge my authority? You are a speck of dust in a sea of sand,*' the deep voice roared, the walls of his mind crumbling under its rage.

'I am no one, but I shall defy you! I am no one, but I shall stand against you! You will not be the last thing this city sees!' Fire consumed Abe's thoughts then, his mind burning from the bitterness of the beast. A loud collision sounded to his right as Belroc threw its weight against the steel gate, crushing the metal with its claws and melting it down with terrible fire racing out of its maw. The Alpha grabbed hold of the twisted gate and flapped its wings, tearing the hinges from the stone and mortar in a vulgar display of power, tossing it to the ground, the metal keening and groaning as it bent and broke, snapping struts and beams. Men ran back, forming a wall of shields as Turneroth's soldiers stormed over the fallen gates, bracing for the fight to come.

The gigantic dragon crawled over the wall to stand before Abe, dripping fire from its mouth. *'You seem to believe yourself powerful. How do you feel in my presence now, wizard? Do you shudder at my every word? Do your insides want to escape your fleshy cage, every fibre of you begging to flee?'*

Taking a step back grudgingly, Abe was sure he could see the lizard smirk, regretting his actions instantly. 'You can think what you will. You're still just a snake with legs.'

Belroc roared as two dragons struck him from the side, tearing at his thick scales as they rolled into the buildings. Abe ran from the wall, hoping to keep hidden while he disrupted the Alpha's call, when four dragons – the Kingsguard – swooped by at speed, heading for Belgarr and Ganda'har.

Driven from the Alpha, Belgarr was in trouble. Back against the wall, three Kingsguard harassed him, snapping at him with their enormous fangs, their leathery wings cutting through the raindrops, until Khanaseri jumped from the wall above, axe gleaming. He brought the axe down on a dragon's head, shouting, *'Belavos, et siliate!'* A tremendous wave of energy followed an explosion, rocking trees and houses, throwing men to the ground and clearing the area of rain for a few heartbeats, the force ballooning outwards. The warlock wrenched the weapon from the dragon's head and saw its brain through a mighty crack in its skull. It still breathed, but barely; the Kingsguard, unable to transform back to his body or move away, lay there as the warlock plunged his hand through the crack and into the grey matter, pushing through until he felt the brain stem, and grabbed hold. A mighty yank, and the screaming beast's eyes flared wide before closing for good.

Ganda'har swooped in, streaming fire from its maw, and locked its jaws over the neck of a dragon tearing at Belgarr's leg, shaking the reptile away. Khanaseri wheezed and saw another dead dragon — heart ripped from its chest — from where Ganda'har came, but the yellow beast was gone. Fire rolled towards him and he leapt from the dead dragon's head, barrelling down a building's collapsed roof to fall into the streets below, rolling forward to break his fall, then ran to where he saw the queen of New Runswick fighting.

Creatures of the underworld burrowed up from the dirt, wreaking havoc on the soldiers protecting Ladriana, while Magnus and Anavi stood back-to-back in the fray. Men fell from the walls to their deaths in scores on both sides, unwilling to admit defeat. Ladriana grabbed Elyon's hand and shouted, 'Marry me!' as she stabbed a man in the chest with an arrow when he jumped over her front line of defence.

'What?' asked the elf king dubiously, slashing down with his sword to hack a man's arm off when an enormous creature with four arms broke through the line and backhanded him, throwing him off his feet. Immediately, more elves jumped in between them, with Valheim at the lead, pushing the beast back tirelessly, piling on him as they stabbed and kicked.

'Elyon!' she shouted, and ran to his side, helping the coughing elf up and seeing the blood seep from a cut below his eyes. 'Are you okay?'

'Mhaelenal guides me still,' he said, pushing himself up to his unsteady feet.

'We need to unite the humans and elves. This is the only way!'

'This is not the time to dwell on such matters. You are an exquisite creature, Ladriana, but let's talk if we survive this mess.' His voice was as calm as always, and soothing, his manner elegant. Her heart raced.

The creature surged up, throwing the pile of elves overhead, and ran for the queen.

'Fire, ya scallywags!' came a shout from the far left of the gate moments before an array of flashes and thunderous claps sounded. Attacking creatures and Turneroth's men felt the full force of cannonballs tearing limbs off and blasting holes in chests. Inhuman screams echoed as soldiers milled around, carrying their severed arms and legs with mania in their eyes. 'Fire! Bring those bastards to the ground!' shouted Captain Bellof, walking behind the cannons, swinging his girth with every step. Those solid balls ripped holes into buildings after cutting through a field of bodies. It was carnage. More fired up to the air, striking dragons out of the sky as soon as they came close to the ground. One beast fell on a building, collapsing it, and suddenly all dragons shook free from Abe's intervention, assaulted again by the Alpha's command. Abe lay in the street unmoving, his head bleeding and a piece of mortar next to him.

'Kehlos! Protect Abe!' shouted Ladriana, seeing men run in his direction. Kehlos nodded and ran for the wizard, cutting left and right.

* * *

Hysterical laughter came from Turneroth as he veered and retreated from the fight, watching the chaos unfold, and for a moment, he forgot what he was fighting for, why he was attacking the city. A lust for blood seeped into his mind, a craze that wanted nothing less than the taste of human flesh. The city would soon be theirs, or what was left of it. Belroc pounded on the walls of his sanity, a constant barrage in his head, and the walls were getting paper-thin.

The king walked to the mage standing alone between the bodies of men, women, and boys, all pierced with arrows and missing limbs, a reign of fire their fate. He looked over the field with disgust and said, 'This is a tragedy... If our men were better fighters, most would be alive still.' Bohan kept quiet. He just kept eyeing the king, his hands behind his back. The rain eased, and the wind had stopped its rampant howling, allowing the stench of the dead to take over. Turneroth pulled his face into a sneer as the stench hit him, trying to work the smell from his nose, but it didn't work. He had to live with it. 'Are you ready for the trip home? I need to know I can count on you, wizard.' He pointed to the wizard's waterskin and gestured for him to hand it over, taking a big swig from it and tossing it back.

'Indeed, my King. This is a tragedy, and yes. I am prepared for the way home.'

'Good.' Turneroth groaned and twisted to the left, his facial structure changing and scaling over, horns pushing out of his head and retracting again, his eyes flickering with madness.

Bohan moved back cautiously, and asked, 'Are you well, my King? It seems these assaults are getting stronger and more frequent.'

King Turneroth stood with his hands on his knees and spat out some blood. 'I'll be fine. We just need to get back home to the Gatekeeper, fast.'

'Keep your anger in check, my King. The beast feeds off it.'

A soldier ran across the field towards them at great speed, falling twice as he slipped on the wet soil. 'What is this dolt doing?' sneered Turneroth, doing his best not to look like he was falling apart at the seams. Only then did he hear the shouts of alarm coming from their camp. The messenger skidded to a stop, covered in mud. 'My King!'

Turneroth sneered and glanced at the man sidelong. 'Yes, yes, what's going on in the camp?'

The messenger was a young man with stubble barely growing on his chin, thin as a reed. *No wonder so many have died... Just look at this excuse of a soldier. Pathetic.* 'Speak! We have a battle to win!' The thousands of horsemen with their blue banners, whoever they were, were getting closer, making a mess from the back lines of his forces. He could hear the shouts from the back now.

'It's your son, sire,' the man whispered. 'They *stole* him. Snatched him from the camp. He could be anywhere in the city.'

'What?' stormed Turneroth, chest heaving suddenly, the air racing from his lips.

Bohan moved further away from Turneroth and the messenger.

Turneroth stared at the ground, squeezing his eyes shut and opening them, shaking his head and doing it again. A terrible ringing in his ears drowned out the messenger's voice, his vision shaking, the world contracting inward and constricting his throat. It felt as if the earth beneath his feet was moving, shaking and bouncing him up and down for some comical torment in this time of despair. *It was that Blanka; he must've figured out he's the father.* A burning rage took over then, and his heart gave way to the monster beneath the surface, opening up to it. His face expanded and his teeth fell out one by one, replaced by fangs pushing through the bleeding gum line. Turneroth screamed as his eyes bulged and bled, popping out of his head to be replaced by a new pair, slitted and large, growing as his skin tore from his body, scales slow to form over the visible muscle fibres. Bohan ran from the area, not looking back.

The messenger was in Turneroth's hands now as his fingernails peeled back, talons growing over and stretching out the hand, forming a dragon's claw. Hot blood spilled over his fingers, and the messenger's head came off, dropping to the ground. His back arched, his spine breaking in a thousand places, morphing into Belroc's. Bones snapped in loud succession, becoming deformed and reptilian beneath the scaled sack. The beast grew and fire illuminated the sky in a bright, billowing stream. Turneroth was no more. Belroc turned his gaze to the closest humans, reborn. *Yes, I am death to all.*

Chapter Eighteen

Garidan walked the grounds of the imperial gardens, shocked at how different The Old Country was to Abru Noxel. Marvelous greenery blanketed the lands, and an abundance of fruit grew on trees everywhere. Great sums of water flowed in ravines, cascading down the declivous lands to form a river at its base. Everything just seemed better. He could not see hardship here, but nor could he see the other races enjoying it as the Ageians did. A very few select Tarks had the privilege of calling Velafrey their home. *A very sought-after blacksmith, for example, could surely be on the list,* he thought. *Would they still want to go back with me, now that this world might change for the better?* There was little doubt in his mind... Once it was decided, he knew they would stick to their plan.

He twisted his neck, cracking sounds emanating from within, breathed deeply and exhaled, releasing the built-up tension, relaxing his muscles. Since he'd left New Runswick all those months ago, stress had been piled on him, increasing day by day. He wanted to leave, go back home and be with his wife, but he was so close now, and they needed the allies. *I hope the city still stands,* he thought, as images of fire invaded his mind; the sight of bodies lying unmoving in the streets, a blaze of eternal damnation burning around them. An onrush of anxiety and tension assaulted him again; his breath caught in his throat. He could feel the familiar nausea creeping up from his stomach, the taste of cold iron on his tongue, a sensation he dearly did not want returned to him.

Garidan paused in his stride and bent over, a yellow-green bile spurting from his mouth, covering the pink flower petals with its misery. Those walking around him scurried away, not wanting to get close, their lips curled in disgust.

'Are you well, Garidan?' Tulvar asked as he approached, and patted the regurgitating man on the back.

Snorting and coughing, Garidan spat the remaining bile from his mouth and took a drink from the offered waterskin, swirling the contents around before spitting it all out. He took another big sip and rested his hands on his knees, waiting for his heart to calm. 'Tulvar, where did you come from?' It annoyed him that someone who had just lost a son — a son whose death Garidan was partially to blame for — was showing any kind of sympathy towards him.

'I was taking the long route back to the Library of Cabinet. Now that I've been reinstated, I have full rights to most sections, and there is so much I would like to go through before heading back to Norvaldmire. They have organised a seat in a cabin carrier for me. I will ride in style all the way to the city, with little fear of being murdered or robbed.'

'Cabin carrier?' The look on Garidan's face made Tulvar chuckle.

'You must have seen them. They are colossal pieces of metal using tracks to guide their way, large plumes of smoke billowing from a chimney at the front-most cart we call the charge.'

Garidan remembered seeing the machine when he first arrived in Norvaldmire. 'They're strange contraptions, but I can see their benefits. I'll walk with you to the Library.'

Tulvar pursed his lips and, thinking about the words he'd use, said, 'Don't take this the wrong way. I will be forever grateful for what you've done for our world, but I cannot let go of what happened to my son. Although I don't blame you, I...uh...' Tulvar glanced away. 'They have assured me you will get what they promised to you. But I will not be here to see it. I can't stay here any longer. My failure haunts me terribly. I am leaving tomorrow.'

Garidan couldn't blame the old khaliq. 'I understand—'

A startling scream erupted from the Library's direction, followed by many more joining in. 'I don't like the sound of that,' said Garidan, and both men ran in the direction whence it came, with Tulvar quickly falling behind the sprinting human.

The Library of Cabinet was just on the other side of the wall to the imperial gardens, but he needed to thread through the labyrinth of paths, walkways, and small bridges running over the narrow rivers. He pushed through the throng of excitement that was the midday rush as they turned to search for the sound. 'Excuse me! Move! Out of the way!' he shouted, and knocked a man to the ground. 'Sorry!' he shouted over his shoulder, his tunic flapping in the wind as he kept running.

'Watch where you're going!' the man shouted back in Ageian.

Skirting a hedge of thorny bushes with big yellow and white flowers in his dash for the wall, he heard the fabric tear as he felt the thorns reach out and grab him. The gravel underfoot crunched loudly, the sound grating in his mind and setting his nerves on edge. There was little time to think about trivial matters now. The wall approached fast, and he jumped, crashing into the solid structure. For a moment, he thought he had broken his hip with the impact; the pain putting him into a dizzying spin, but he held on to the top of the wall, pulling himself over. *You idiot! You can't fight if you're bedridden! Control yourself!*

The ground rushed towards him and knocked the breath from his lungs, his feet stinging from the impact. Ageians ran around, scampering for cover while soldiers approached from the right. A terrible shriek sounded from near the wyrm's cage, and he saw the bottom half of an Ageian flung through the air, entrails whipping behind. *Shit! It must have broken free! Why weren't the Djak-tas here to stop this?* Then he saw the flutter of wings and the roving feelers. Bladed legs sliced a warrior's arm off in a clean swoop. Massive pincers and bug-like eyes scanned the area, while more soldiers stormed at it. Its exoskeleton made for difficult piercing. Swords bounced off with little damage, and arrows broke against the thick plates. It grabbed a soldier and stuffed him in its mouth, crunching down on the Ageian with little trouble, snapping bones with revolting sounds. The creature had lost much of its size and had only six legs now, although it was still the size of two elephants and much fiercer than the wyrms, much faster.

Borka was already there, nearing from the left with his poleaxe, carefully gauging the creature's movement. 'Move!' he shouted to an Ageian woman standing too close to the creature's back leg. Before he could reach her, spurs on its hind legs speared her through the chest and dragged her body along as it writhed and kicked at its attackers.

Borka hacked at a leg with his poleaxe, hoping it was as fragile as the wraethers'. The legs were thicker than his arms, and didn't break with the first blow, but Borka swung again, and again, and the leg shattered, the black blades cracking and splitting before snapping at the joints, oozing a green ichor. Soldiers on the other side did the same, while others chopped at the buzzing wings, immobilising the creature before using a hammer to drive a sword through its hard skull. Its squeals and snaps of the pincers echoed throughout the city, its birth announced to the world in a gruesome display of hunger and instinct.

Oh no! There are thousands of them in the mountain. If they break free, it will be carnage! Garidan drew near, too late to take part in the victory of killing the creature, as the Ageians hugged and congratulated the surviving soldiers. He knelt before the creature, gazing at those glistening eyes. A slimy effluence dripped to the ground from the sword still stuck in its head, the smell of brimstone in the air. He watched as a weed covered by the slime cindered, a trail of smoke appearing before it shrivelled up and smouldered until it fell apart as ash in the wind. His eyes went wide, and he shouted to those around him, 'Take off your clothes and armour! Now!'

Soldiers stared at him, frowning, and Borka glanced down at the splashes of green over his dirty black gambeson. 'That seems an odd thing to do in public, don't you think?' Borka asked, perplexed, scratching his arm profusely; and soon others joined in, scratching where the slime had splashed over them.

'Take it off now! It's burning you!' Mocking laughter sounded from a few, thinking it was a jest until one screamed, his hair singing and his scalp burning, skin turning black as smoke trailed. Instantly, all the soldiers threw their clothes on the ground and ran for a nearby well, pouring buckets of water over their heads while standing buck naked before the gathering citizens, getting a fierce applause from some rowdy Ageians.

Tulvar eventually made it to Garidan's side, huffing and puffing with eyes wide. 'This is the Kahu?'

Garidan's head came up fast. 'You know this creature?'

'We've seen it once, yes, and called it such. Though we didn't know where it came from. It killed many citizens in Norvaldmire before we brought it down. This isn't good. There are so many of them.'

'Yes, I was thinking the same thing. I have a plan, but I need you to speak with the Cabinet and get them to order the troops they promised me. We need to go to the mountain right away. If all goes according to plan, I'll leave with them from there.'

'What are you going to do?'

Garidan smirked. 'I'm gonna dance with the devil. Come with and you'll see.'

'Oh, your devious tricks to tempt me will not work. But I appreciate the effort,' Tulvar said with a smile.

* * *

Ten thousand soldiers stood ready, their gear polished and packs hanging from their backs, bits of armour glinting on the cloudless day. A host of excited citizens droned around to see them off, more wanting to see the monolith function than saying farewell to the poor soldiers who might never return. It was an act of bravery Garidan knew few had the courage to attain; not knowing where they would end up, or if they would ever see their loved ones again. He stood next to the monolith in the park, gazing over the soldiers, when a heavy hand gripped his shoulder and spun him around. 'We are still coming with you,' stated Arundhàbu, removing a pack from his shoulder and placing it on the ground.

'I was wondering if you'd show up.' He bowed slightly with his hand to his chest and a big grin. 'I would be honoured to have you join me, but I must mention that I don't know what we'll walk into. There might be a battle.'

'You *should* be honoured. We did not come to this decision lightly,' Naghita chimed in, arms crossed and glaring at him defiantly.

Garidan nodded his understanding, knowing that he would need to make good on his promise. That they would live free from the constant down-talking and humiliation, not be persecuted as they were here for being Tarks.

'If what we see is worth fighting for, we'll help,' Arundhàbu said.

'Then it's settled. We're about to get going. Do you know if Borka will join?'

'Ha! Did you really think I would miss out on this new quest?' The big Tark pushed through the lines of soldiers, ignoring the angry glances as the Ageian soldiers moved out of their ordered rows for him to pass, a quick hubbub of growls and comments cast his way. 'Besides, you need to show me more methods to uh...' he showed something with his hands, 'you know, er...carve wood. I've been practising a lot.'

'It's called whittling, you fool!' snorted Naghita mockingly, holding her stomach to emphasise her delight and cause him more embarrassment. 'Even I know that, and I'm not even interested in that waste of time. But that's what you can expect from a gladiator, brains all mushed up from too many knocks on—'

'Why do you do this?' growled Arundhàbu. 'You two will need to settle your differences, and soon! I will not live out my days with you two bickering like old housewives over a dirty cloth.' Borka was about to say something, his mouth hanging slightly ajar, his eyes narrow as his hand reached for his poleaxe. He turned away from her, his torso swelling and waning as he breathed to calm himself.

'Of course I will, my friend,' said Garidan. 'You will all live in my castle until we find suitable homes for you. There will be plenty of time for some wood carving.'

Borka smiled sullenly to the ground. 'Thank you.'

'Oh, you're no fun!' stormed Naghita, grabbing her pack and

approaching the monolith.

A great throng forced their way closer, the streets lined with people everywhere, held back by guards with shields and batons. They overcrowded the roofs of surrounding buildings to the point where it became dangerous, with people barely able to stand or sit on the edge of the structures. Loud, roving cheers followed their fist-pumps to the air, a resounding drumming stamped into the earth with their feet.

'Look who we have here... I see you are back to your old stature, Khaliq Tulvar,' mumbled Borka, eyeing the approaching Ageian.

Flanked on either side by guards and dressed in a fine silvery-white robe, his hands cupped in his sleeves, Tulvar acknowledged the statement with a curt bow and said, 'I have come to bid you farewell, astute warriors of Norvaldmire. You have done our world a great service. We will forever be in your debt. If you ever decide to come back to our humble city, we will welcome you with open arms.'

'Humble, eh?' snorted Arundhàbu, 'That's a little imperious, Tulvar.'

The two guards flanking the Ageian stepped forward in unison, pointing their halberds at the blacksmith. But Tulvar stopped them, holding out his hand, and said, 'There's no need. Step back. In fact, go wait over there by the fountain where I don't have to see you.'

The two guards glanced around, unsure, not knowing if this was some kind of test, for their duty was to be at his side and protect him when out in the open. Tulvar turned to them, his wrinkled old face stretching as he flared his eyes and raised his brows. 'I said go. Shoo, shoo!' He waved them away and turned back to the group. 'They are a terrible bother, but they have their uses. There will be many changes going forward, and one of them will be the tenured positions of khaliqs. Information will get shared and schools will be opened. The khaliqs will hold conferences, sharing their knowledge with the world and vice versa.'

'Sounds like more Ageian false promises to me, but I hope it happens,' grumbled Naghita from the monolith. 'It's time. All the soldiers are ready. We need to go.'

'Farewell, Tulvar, and good luck with everything,' Garidan said, and reached out his hand, gripping the old Ageian's.

'Get over here,' Borka embraced the khaliq, squeezing and lifting him from the ground with a smile, and continued, 'Thank you for everything. Take care, ya old buzzard.'

Tulvar gasped as his feet found solid ground, the red disappearing from his face as he straightened his robe. 'You too, Borka.' Arundhàbu nodded his goodbye before walking to join Naghita at the monolith, who waved an offhanded salute to the khaliq and turned away.

The buzz of the crowd drowned out the noise of the monolith, its metal rings spinning faster and faster, a brilliant light beaming outwards from the device, gradually growing brighter still. Soldiers stood before them, shifting nervously, unsure of what to expect. Louder and louder it got, the humming intensifying while Garidan clutched the device with both hands, screaming as words stretched up his arms, burning into his skin. He dearly wished that he was near the Spring of Ananathia to be healed from this garish experience, but he knew there was no respite forthcoming. He had to push through, knowing the worst was yet to come: moving all these soldiers to New Runswick. Ageians everywhere shielded their eyes and crowed in awe at the use of the monolith, as the world swallowed all those in the park in a bright light.

Garidan held on to the device, feeling the grips of his Tark companions slipping from his arm as soldiers screamed in the distance over the lightning strikes arcing all around them in the ephemeral plain. It felt like they were moving at incredible speed, the forces on their bodies pulling them left and right, their minds breaking under the strain. Soldiers grabbed at the air, trying futilely to hold on to something that wasn't there. The world opened up to them in a flash of glowing red, and suddenly it was intensely hot, the air extremely volatile. A soldier's screams did not echo long as he slid down the steep banks in the vast open chamber, and burst into flames halfway down, before melting in the boiling magma at its base. They had appeared inside the mountain, too close to the edge of the magma pools, and soldiers pushed to get away, sending more of their fellow warriors down into the deadly liquid.

Arundhàbu looked up and saw the cages waning, their magic depleting as Kahu burst from their cocoons to spread their wings. He pointed and shouted, 'Get down!' Buzzing like gigantic, monstrous dragonflies, the creatures flew at them, scooping up soldiers and stuffing them in their maws, ripping them apart with ease. Soldiers ran, hunting for cover that did not exist. The flying creatures could reach them anywhere. Arundhàbu turned at the shouts of Borka and Naghita, seeing Garidan slumped over the monolith.

'He's not breathing. I think this trip knocked the breath from him.' They dragged him away from the main group of soldiers being harassed by the creatures, and Borka poured water over Garidan's face. When nothing happened, Naghita slapped him hard, his face rocking side to side from the hit. His eyes popped open, and he winced at his burning jaw.

'Ow!' Garidan shook his head and looked around, working his jaw back and forth. 'Did we make it?'

'If by *make it* you mean, did we land in a stinking pile of shit? Then yes, we made it. Get up!' yelled Borka, pulling his poleaxe from his back and swinging it just in time to cleave the blade into a Kahu's face, tearing the skin and snapping off a pincer. It crashed on the ground, wriggling and thrashing with its deadly legs.

Garidan gazed up at the roof through the dust and rock falling from up high, seeing the creatures bash against the stone. *They're trying to get out... If they do, thousands will be killed, and more wyrms will be born. The cycle will never stop. It needs to end here.* 'Everyone! Get on a Kahu!'

'Are you insane?' shouted Arundhàbu.

'Trust me. It'll be like riding a horse.' Garidan did not look back as he ran for the monolith.

* * *

The rain had ceased and their forces were scattered, but they fought like demons to protect the city and its inhabitants, unwilling to go silently into the night. They roared their defiance and beat their chests, putting on a grandiose display of bravery. Lightning arced from mages' fingertips, scorching dragons, while fire destroyed so much more. Flames licked high into the sky, with thick black smoke its prize, swirls of air creating vortexes through the billowing mass. Magnus ran past Abe and his students, seeing streams of black funnel from the mage's body, the magic snaking out to grab hold of a demon, forcing it to the ground and crushing it utterly. Men died in scores around the wizards, with Abe protecting them as best he could.

'Anavi!' shouted Magnus, searching the appalling views of the street and its bloody contents. They had become separated after the fall of the gate, with all the soldiers streaming in. At first he'd thought that was the worst of it, but then Belroc flew in, the colossal beast killing everything in its path – including Turneroth's own men, and any dragon that fell in its way. 'Anavi!' Covered in soot and nursing a bleeding arm, Magnus clobbered a man on the nose, snapping his neck quickly. A woman came at him with a pitchfork, running through the smoke and screaming at the top of her voice; then a roar sounded behind him. 'Wait, no!' It was getting hot... He dived to the side of the road, hunkering down in a sewer filled with excrement. It stunk to high hell, but at least it wasn't as hot. A turbulent hail of fire wreaked havoc from above, the roar of its existence astounding.

Struggling to get out with his bleeding arm, he clambered up steadily and looked around, not seeing the beast that caused the flames; nor did he see the pitchfork woman alive anymore. She lay in the middle of the street, her clothes melted into her dripping flesh, her eyelids burnt away with her lips and hair. He watched her die as the fire continued to incinerate her. 'Argh!' he shouted, and kept running. 'Anavi!'

A group of men were locked in battle to his left, their swords and axes clanging together, a demon and its hound ripping into another group on the right. He desperately wanted to continue and leave them to fend for themselves, wanting to get to Anavi. The screams of the dying tore through him. Magnus took a few strides further and slowed, stopping before a dead man with a large gash that opened his back, and bent down to pick up a morning-star mace, working it out from the unfortunate man's clutching hand.

The demon grabbed a soldier at the back of the neck, twisted and pulled off his head, spine dragging out of its cavity in loud cracks to hang in its hand while it celebrated the death. A thick silver spike collided with the creature of the underworld, sinking into its temple as the weight of the mace crushed its skull, collapsing the left side of its already mauled face. It staggered and careened to the right, struggling to find its footing when its ragged-haired hound turned on Magnus, charging with those angry, dead eyes and rotten fangs. Magnus dragged the morning-star from the demon's head and kept swinging as the hound jumped for his throat, feeling the solid mass of the steel drive into the creature's neck. He stepped away and the hound hit the ground, but it was fast on its feet again and leapt at him. Magnus dropped the mace and grabbed the hound's head, holding off the brutal fangs with everything he had, pushed back by its ferociousness. On one knee, he rotated and snapped down his arm, wrestling the hound to the ground, when he saw the soldiers fighting with the demon again. At least they were buying him some time to finish the dog. He planted his enormous foot on the hound's upper jaw and grabbed the lower part, pulling it up with all his power. The hound snapped its jaws, the bite nearly taking his fingers, and he worked them open again. Squealing and growling now, the beast knew it was in trouble. Shouting as he pulled, he heard the beast yelp underneath him, then a loud crack, and the jaw came off, ripping a part of its throat out with it.

The demon lurched forward and groaned in pain, a short arrow bolt protruding from the back of its mangled head. Magnus swung around and saw a soldier with a small crossbow limping closer, snapping a handle down and pulling the trigger, snapping a handle down and pulling the trigger until he was only a foot away from the demon. 'I've got this. You carry on. I think I saw her down that road.' Magnus nodded and continued running, searching for Anavi.

Eyes burning like acid had been poured into them, Magnus struggled through the smoke of the street he'd turned into, snot dripping from his nose, his sinuses in turmoil. A mighty sneeze rocked him as he ran and he collided with something solid, fell back, and planted on his arse, the morning-star skidding over the ground a foot away. He knew the sun was shining somewhere above, but this infernal smoke made it impossible to see even an arm's length away. He'd run into a statue of some old king. 'What a shite place to put a statue.'

The roar of rushing fire came from ahead, the smoke changing colour to a deep orange for a moment. He quickly got to his feet and picked up the mace, creeping closer. Men shouted orders, and a dragon's growl drowned them out before the smoke cleared some. A big, dark-green dragon toyed with the soldiers, stepping on the leg of one who fell, crushing it utterly. A deep laughter resonated from the beast then, its face a portrait of enjoyment. Magnus saw Anavi and the dwarves huddled behind a wall and pillars, biding their time, choosing when to strike carefully. 'Hey! Flea-ridden cave-rat! Why don't youse fight me like a man? Or are youse afraid?'

'Magnus! No! It'll kill you!' Anavi shouted, a stream of fire cutting her off from him.

The dragon sneered and glanced between the two, then veered to stand before them as a man and said, 'I am a bonded! A Kingsguard. No mere man can stand against me!'

'Oh, I won't be standing against youse for long. Youse will be dead soon enough,' Magnus said, letting the morning-star slip down his hand until he gripped the handle.

The Kingsguard ran at him, his face pulled into a snarl, talons on the ends of his hands slicing through smoke and air, missing Magnus' throat by a hair's breadth as he jumped back. The barkeep brought up the mace, clobbering the Kingsguard on the back of the shoulder, tearing flesh and skin away from the man. A scream of pain sounded from the Kingsguard as he fell, floundering on the ground to get up steadily before rolling his shoulder, blood running down the torn flesh. Again, they came at each other, mace and talons swinging and swiping. The Kingsguard leapt through the air, pouncing on Magnus from a great distance and knocking him from his feet.

Magnus staved off the Kingsguard's swiping talons, using the mace to push him away, but he was losing ground fast. Leaning over, the Kingsguard pushed down on the haft, laughing through gritted teeth, his sweat dripping from his chin to splash over Magnus' face. It was becoming difficult to breathe with the haft choking him, his windpipe close to being crushed. Air wheezed through his parted mouth, his lips becoming numb, a tingling sensation crawling up his face. Fists bounced off his cheeks and nose, each punch feeling like it would tear his head clean off. His vision swam in a red mist, and his hacked-off ear rung deep inside his head, screaming for it all to end.

'No!' Anavi shouted from the sidelines, and ran in with her sword, but quickly sailed back to fall on her backside, a smear of blood on her face from cuts on her cheek. *How did he move so fast?* she wondered, dragging herself away and wiping her face on the back of her dirty arm. *I didn't even see him come up.* Her cheek was bruised and sore to the touch. It felt like a metal gauntlet had crashed into her face. Rocks sailed over her head and the shouts of dwarfs came from behind. The four dwarves spread out around the Kingsguard and peppered him with stones, drawing his attention away from Magnus. It annoyed him more than anything, but that's all they needed to do.

The Kingsguard laughed cynically at them and turned around to finish the job of killing Magnus, but his head rocked back suddenly, streaming blood. Magnus' enormous fist crashed into the Kingsguard's face, snapping his head around and dropping him to the ground. Visibly shaken at the power of the blow, the Kingsguard scrambled to his feet and tried to veer, but was not fast enough. Magnus grabbed him at the back of the head and hit him with his forehead over and over, roaring as he crushed the Kingsguard's nose and orbital bones. The barkeep staggered back dazedly and dropped to the ground next to the mace, his hand closing on the weapon's haft. He jumped up with it, thrashing the Kingsguard's jaw, and swung it down to get stuck in the man's head. The Kingsguard collapsed spasmodically, pulling the weapon from Magnus' hand. It had been a long time since he'd felt this anger, this hatred towards anyone, and he didn't like it, but it was an all-consuming thing.

A hand pulled on his shoulder and he swung around, fists ready, eyes red, growling in anger.

'It's me, Magnus! Snap out of it!' Anavi shouted, jumping back at the sight of his fury.

'Ye a'right there, lad?' asked a dwarf, stepping slowly closer with arms raised.

Magnus shook his head, panting, squeezing his eyes shut to rid himself of the fog clouding his mind. 'Yes, I'm fine. Anavi, are youse okay?'

'Are ye sure? Cause ye just crushed a dragon's face with your own... I don't think ye should be fine,' stated the dwarf, drawing near.

'Positive. I have a thick skull.'

Belroc shrieked to their right and settled over a building a few blocks away, blowing fire through its windows and hatches, stone and mortar exploding from the incredible heat. They ran in that direction, knowing they would be needed.

* * *

Ladriana loosed arrow after arrow, and ran as fast as she could with the pillow bouncing up and down. There was no time to worry about how she looked. She jumped across a fissure torn in the wall and sliced with her sword, opening the throat of a soldier before sprinting ahead, not waiting for her screaming escorts who were trying to catch up with her. 'Khanaseri!' she shouted. 'Where are these allies you mentioned? We're getting slaughtered out here, and I see no end to it!'

'They'll be here!' The warlock kicked a demon in the head as it clambered up from the wall, watching it fall back down.

'They sure are taking their time getting here! Tiam's cavalry has driven them up the streets and caused ruin to their back lines. They're making good progress, but the dragons and the demons are too much.'

'We have to get you to safety, Queen Ladriana!' stormed Kehlos, arriving with King Elyon and several guards to take her to the castle.

'I'm not going anywhere. This is my fight as much as anyone out here. Look! The city is burning. I will *not* sit back like a damsel in distress, cowering behind walls that will crumble once that thing gets to it!'

'This coming from the woman who wanted me to stay in the castle...' sneered Elyon.

'What are you two doing?' Khanaseri asked, drawing their attention. But he gazed in the distance at two dragons: a red and a charcoal-black swerved through the maelstrom of beasts to collide with Belroc again, the gargantuan beast clinging to the side of a building. Debris fell from the building as it shuddered and groaned, collapsing the top section to the ground below in a storm of dust and fire. He could hear the screams of those trapped inside, and saw in his mind's eye how they were crushed by the collapse. Everywhere they looked, dragons soared, burning rows of houses to the ground, their shrieks a constant reminder of their new reality. 'I have to help them! They're only two in a flood of enemies.' He ran past Ladriana towards the stairwell and was thrown from his feet by an explosion of power from above, the blue sky cracking and tearing, folding in on itself as ripples of sparkling amber-like dust drifted down. A flicker of another world appeared, and again, before a portal ripped open, forcefully pushing the clouds away around it, a loud buzzing coming from the other side.

Soldiers stopped their fighting and looked to the sky, pointing and waiting to see what was about to happen. A plethora of enormous insect-like creatures sped through the rift in the sky, heading straight for the dragons. Soldiers straddled the creatures, looks of terror in their eyes, and he heard one shout in the Tark tongue as he flew over, 'This is nothing like a horse!' Khanaseri looked back up and saw dark specks falling from the breach towards the ground far below. 'They are falling!' He jumped to his feet and chanted, his voice drifting over the winds as he moved his arms about, weaving a magical cushion and slowing their descent to the ground. For some time, they poured through, until the portal snapped shut with a mighty *crack*.

Like a swarm guided by a natural instinct, the insect-creatures latched on to the dragons, biting through the hard scales of the beasts to get to the softer bits. Tall soldiers jumped from their backs, joining the fight on the ground.

'Whoo hoo! Oh, Garidan, I wish you were here!' Ladriana shouted, and swung her fist up.

'He is.'

Ladriana nodded, touching her chest, and said, 'You are right. He will always be here.'

Khanaseri turned to her, frowning as he asked, 'What nonsense do you speak?'

'I thought you knew... He died trying to bring us allies.' Ladriana glanced at King Elyon and took his hand.

'Uh...no he didn't. That's all his doing up there. He's undoubtedly somewhere in this mess,' grumbled the warlock, waving towards nowhere in particular.

'What? If this is your idea of a joke, it's *not* funny.'

He shook his head, searching for Garidan, then saw a bright light flicker on the sand in the distance beyond the gates. 'You really thought he was dead, eh? Look for yourself.'

She could not see clearly at this distance, the light of the device obscuring the surrounding people, and she shouted, her voice trembling and teeming with emotion, 'Garidan?' She wanted so badly for it to be true. Her mind sped forth, thinking rapidly of the possibilities that could have been, that would have been, and she raced from the wall, skipping steps to get to the bottom, fighting with men along the way. Kehlos and King Elyon were close behind, with a host of soldiers falling in to guard their flanks.

Khanaseri looked towards the brawl between Belroc and his friends, then to the running queen racing through the torn gates and the confused Ageians and Tarks in the distance. 'Argh! Bastard!' He knew conflict would quickly arise if the Ageians, or worse, the Tarks, were near Garidan, unable to speak the queen's language. He ran after Ladriana, cussing under his breath. It surprised the warlock just how fast the queen was moving, with that enormous stomach bouncing around like that. *I'm glad I'm not that kid,* he thought, jumping past a sword lancing for his ribs, snatching out his axe, and cleaving a man sideways in the face.

The only consolation he had was knowing the dragons were too occupied with the swarming creatures from the other world to help Belroc. Khanaseri searched the skies, hoping Yidrog would arrive soon. Time was running out for the city. He couldn't see those creatures lasting long against the dragons, even in their swarm... *They might kill one or two, maybe even ten, but it wouldn't be enough. Where are you, Anukke?*

The queen was already there. He could hear the shouts in different languages, and when he arrived, he saw Garidan unmoving in the arms of the blacksmith. Kehlos was shouting for them to put him down. King Elyon had his sword out, and the guards all shouted at the two Tarks, brandishing their swords in anger and fear. He pushed in between the nearing groups and shouted, 'Put down your weapons! Lower your weapons!' He glanced at the Tarks and continued, 'Arun! I'm glad you made it. You can lower your weapons. We are all allies here.' Naghita glared at him, then to all around with her massive, jagged daggers, ready to open throats. He motioned for Ladriana to put hers down as well, seeing the arrow tremble on the string of the bow. 'Ladriana. Put it down. They're not the enemy! I know them. This is Arundhàbu, and that's Naghita.'

Ladriana waited for Naghita to sheath her weapons first, then lowered her bow. The tension was still high, and she glanced at the warlock, seeing him nod. Arundhàbu backed away slowly from Garidan as she approached, but the queen was not one to wait. She rushed forward and grabbed her husband's head, tears flowing uncontrollably as she shouted, 'Wake up, Garidan! Wake up! You're home!' His lips parted slightly, his trembling hand coming up to stroke her face. 'Warlock, take us to the castle,' Ladriana demanded, and looked around at her soldiers. 'Spread the word to all of our men. These foreigners are not our enemy. Don't treat them as such.'

Before Khanaseri turned away, Garidan grabbed his arm and whispered, the words struggling to leave his mouth, 'Do not...let any of those things...escape. The dragons...need to kill them all. Beware of their blood...it burns.'

The warlock nodded and opened a portal as Garidan lost consciousness again.

* * *

The portal opened in the castle's courtyard, and Khanaseri was the first to step through, followed by Kehlos carrying Garidan, then Ladriana, King Elyon, and a host of guards following the two Tarks, their hands resting on the hilts of their weapons at all times. Men were fighting all around them, the castle's guards doing their best to keep the advancing enemy out. From above, a shout of urgency sounded, yet only the Tarks and Khanaseri seemed to understand. The warlock twisted around and shouted, 'Get down!' Everyone dropped as the bug-like creature wildly spun out of control towards them, just clearing their heads to crash into the earth, quaking the grounds and scraping a thick trench into the soil until it hit the castle walls. The castle guards drew their weapons and rushed forth to protect their queen. 'No! He's an ally!' shouted the warlock, and ran to the fallen Kahu with Arundhàbu and Naghita close by, seeing its broken limbs and burns all over, half its head missing as it lay pressed up against the castle walls. A groan came from its right, and Borka sat up, dragging his leg behind him. Arundhàbu draped his arm around his body for support, and together they all ran for the castle doors, seeing more men and dragons heading towards them.

'Quite the entrance, Borka!' said Khanaseri with a grin, and the gladiator chuckled.

'Like a horse my arse...'

'We need to get Garidan to safety before we can fight with these!' said Ladriana, storming through the doors and hearing the latch fall in place behind them. Up the stairs they ran, feeling the castle shake with a hit.

'Highness. I'm ready to fight,' came a voice from a room to her right, and Thelanor stumbled out, holding on weakly to his sword, his face pale and clammy. She looked at him with worry in her eyes. 'I will be fine once I fight. Besides, I would rather die fighting than in bed.'

'Very well. Fall in,' she said, and was about to run when Khanaseri spoke.

'Ladriana, I have to get back to the fight. These men can protect you. Trust them.' Khanaseri turned to the Tarks and nodded, then opened a portal to step through.

Men jumped through the windows and crashed through the door. More stormed through before the castle shook again, and part of a giant claw broke through the shutters of a nearby window, clawing and scratching, unable to reach, followed by a roar that shattered the heart of courage. Roof tiles fell from up high as the beast clambered over the castle, searching for a way in when more Kahu attacked it.

Borka drew his poleaxe and pushed the blacksmith away. 'Time to fight. No time to be soft.' The first of the enemy reached them, and Borka jumped with a vicious battle cry, cleaving the man's head in two, and swung right, shattering the arm and ribs of another, cutting halfway through to the man's sternum. An enemy swung his hammer at the Tark and it bounced off his thick chest, angering the gladiator, who now glared at the man. Borka grabbed him as he tried to run, twisted his head in his hands until a loud snap was heard, then dropped him to the ground. He looked back at the astonished guards and queen, and smirked before jumping at another man.

Arundhàbu pushed one of the guards forward, pointing to the brawl taking place, and shoved him again when the man didn't move. He grunted and glared at the terrified soldier, shaking his head before elbowing him out of the way to stand beside Borka, breaking a man's face with a swing of his fist. Naghita jumped in when another swung his axe at Arundhàbu, grabbing him by the neck and throwing him across the room.

'Charge!' shouted Ladriana, and ran in, sword held high, cutting left and right as she entered the fray, her guards right beside her.

Kehlos stood holding Garidan in his arms, watching the battle take place. *Great! What do I do now?* His eyes caught a hallway closet and thought, *No, surely I couldn't... I mean, I shouldn't. Oh, hell. He'll understand.* He ran over to the closet and lay Garidan down in the corner, piling blankets and pillows on the man before closing the door. 'Apologies, my King.'

* * *

The sky bled orange from the grey clouds above, the fire serenading the air in streams of anger while the Kahu attacked the dragons, their burning wings and fat bodies leaving a strong smell of churned butter become rancid. Anavi danced through the throng of enemies, slicing with her blades like a thing of beauty, her dance sensual and exquisite in its own right, something to behold and rarely told. Magnus could not keep up with her grace of movement, struggling through, bashing heads and throwing people out of the way. To her left, Anavi saw a figure waving his arms about, dressed in a dark blue robe and unnaturally clean for someone standing in the centre of all this death. Then she saw another demon burrowing up from the ground. She ran at the figure, his eyes flaring in fear as she leapt with her sword, slicing to decapitate him; but he bent unnaturally backwards in a way that should have snapped his spine. Stabbing and slicing, she reversed her blade, smacking the pommel against the mage's nose, cracking it open. She jumped backwards in a pirouette, avoiding a dagger that flashed from the mage's robe, knocking it to the ground with a clatter, and rolled over her shoulder to break her fall, flashing her steel out in a blur. The mage dropped to the ground, hands clasped around the blade piercing his chest. To her right, the demon collapsed back into the hole as if dragged down, the ground filling in around it.

Magnus finally appeared, out of breath and wheezing, puffs of red mist evaporating from his mouth with every breath. 'I forgot how fast youse are.'

'I'm not that fast. You're just that slow,' she said with a wink, and retrieved her sword from the dead mage, pressing him down with her foot and yanking the weapon from his chest.

Magnus smirked and chuckled. 'No wonder Lexiphene likes youse so much. She has the same dour joviality as youse.'

'Same dour what now?' she asked, raising her brow as they ran down the street.

'Move!' he shouted, and tackled her out of the way as a gigantic black tail tore up the street with its spikes before the enormous body crashed into a building on their right, snapping wood and stone pillars, collapsing walls. Anavi pushed him off her, groaning at his weight. Even though he was considerably thinner, Magnus was still a big man. 'Youse a'right?' he asked, looking at her.

'Yes. Get off me!' She coughed and rose, and saw the charcoal beast's tail hanging from the building. 'Is that Blanka?'

Belgarr veered and disappeared from their sight.

Magnus pushed himself up and ran across the road, entering the ruins, jumping over large pieces of demolished wall. He climbed over a heap of debris obstructing the stairs and ran up through the wreckage, shouting, 'Blanka!' He heard coughing to his right, where a small bed stood laden with a pile of grey stones and mortar, its feet reduced to mangled metal under the weight. Further away, he saw a broken piece of fallen wall and ran closer, trying to lift it. The mortar scraped his fingers bloody, digging under the nails of his bruised hand. Anavi joined his side, and they lifted the wall over to fall away from them. Blanka coughed ragged streams of blood from his mouth, struggling for air through the liquid pooling in his lungs. 'He needs to get to a healer... Can youse take him?'

'I'm not strong enough! You take him,' Anavi said, shaking her head at him.

Magnus weighed his options, knowing that where she would go would be dangerous, but she was right. She could not carry Blanka. 'Argh! Fine, I'll take him, then. But youse don't get too close to that thing, youse got that?'

She jumped up and hugged Magnus, kissing him fervently before running from the building and down the street. Anavi rounded the corner, bracing as a thick lightning bolt flashed from up high, snapping and cracking with thunderous anger. Belroc careened from the strike, a shriek leaving its maw, followed by a gust of fire so intense it melted the metal it came in contact with: bins, lampposts, weapons, all bending and changing their shapes before cooling down. She ran into a park to hide behind the foot of a fallen statue. Ganda'har swooped in from above, wings stretched out, spraying fire over the Alpha, and Abe chanted from the side. The wizard's eyes had turned black; the dark veins on his face marbled his features. His booming voice was a cacophonous garble, while his toes scraped the dirt as the force pulled him on. Soldiers were loosing arrows and throwing spears at the beast from everywhere in the park.

Belroc lashed out, and trees toppled before it headed straight for Abe, its rotten fangs snapping with thunderous claps as it tore a man in two. Fire bouldered over the wizard moments before the monstrous mouth closed over him; the sound of metal screeching reverberated as it bit into a protective shield around the wizard. Furious, it thrashed around, unable to move or penetrate the magic sphere.

A deep, dark force clawed at Abe's heart and mind, wanting to attain complete control of the vessel, but the wizard knew the game well. Give a little, get a little. Negotiate and compromise and bluff the hell out of it. He felt the build-up of power in him as the beast raged over him, the teeth piercing the magic shield like a glass bauble, splintering the magic slowly. The reek of the beast's rotten breath changed suddenly, becoming noxious and foul, and then he saw two glands spurt out liquids, one on either side of the mouth, mixing to form instant fire, burning purple and violent. Through the cracks in the shield, the fire blazed, hunting for him, the world shaking within. He let out the power in him...

The fire ceased instantly, choking Belroc as black plumes of magic entered its maw, and Khanaseri shouted a battle cry to run for the beast with Untara and Stentor next to him. As the beast thrashed to rid himself of the dark magic, they clambered up its scaled hide, chopping at the scales to remove them. Ganda'har ripped into its back, talons scything and fangs tearing. A burst of fire ripped from Ganda'har's mouth, blackening the scales and infuriating Belroc. Lightning roiled and arced from above, a storm of electric fire.

Abe's magical shield shuddered, weakened by the pull of the Source.

The wizard chanted while Ganda'har tore grooves into Belroc's skin. An old grey building decorated with flowers and fairies painted on the outside — its windows stained with tales of wonder — toppled with a violent swing of the Alpha's spiked tail; a heart-breaking destruction for a building so old. Again the tail swung, snapping a tree from its roots and flinging it aside like a rag, nearly killing Anavi, the stump crashing into the fallen statue and flipping over her. The tail swung by her at great speed, a forceful gust of wind pulling her from her feet, hitting Abe's magic bauble with a wonderful expulsion of the Source, shattering the protective sphere.

'Abe!' Anavi shouted, and ran to him as he desperately crawled on the ground to get out of danger, the tail flicking overhead and ripping out dirt around them as it tore into the earth. She grabbed him and hauled him up, half dragging him away to get behind a broken wall. Hands trembling from adrenalin, she floundered, cutting a gash in Abe's arm with her knife while trying to cut off the sleeves to see the damage, the blood making the robe stick.

'Ow! Should I rather take my chances with the dragon?' he growled, clutching his bleeding shoulder.

'You're welcome to!' Anavi retorted, pointing the knife at him. 'Now sit still!' She set to work bandaging the hole in his shoulder to stop the bleeding, when a blast of flames rolled over them, the heat fierce and unrelenting. *This is how we die? Engulfed in a flame born from this miserable lizard?* She did not even realise she had dived over Abe to protect him until the flames died around them. Anavi's head came up, and she saw Abe's weak arm drop to the ground, the shield of magic disappearing around them. *Thank you, Abe...*

She knew she could not stay with him. The danger was still very real. All around, men still fought on both sides, getting closer to them. Anavi ducked under a swing from a Terenoran soldier and stabbed out with her sword, skewering the man and spinning around to parry a blow from another. She reversed her cut and sliced deep into another soldier's chest. Behind her, a woman was dragged to the ground with vicious growls and snapping fangs, and Anavi spun around to see her white wolf companion tearing at her assailant. 'Bogar! You beautiful thing!' She patted his head and pointed to Abe as she demanded, 'Protect him.' Anavi ran up the side of the destroyed building, past the crumbling wall, and went low, cutting off the feet of another soldier heading for Abe, then glanced at the two dragons. *Here is where I make my last stand. I will protect the wizard. If all else fails, we will need him. Good luck, Captain.*

Ganda'har slammed its fangs over Belroc's wing, biting down hard, splashes of blood dropping to the ground with a hail of shrieks. The Alpha flapped its wings, pushing off from the ground, and purposely crashed the clinging Ganda'har into a building, throwing all from him as they rolled over the top, collapsing the structure and blowing fire over the vicinity. After the hit, the earth quaked for a while, the concatenation of blasts and rumblings felt in the chest. Gauging each other, the two beasts roared as the Alpha towered over Ganda'har. They charged, flying low to collide in a tremendous clash, and with its overbearing weight, Belroc drove the red dragon to the ground, ripping into its chest.

Khanaseri dashed across the field of debris. 'No! Fucking cave-rat! Take me!' he shouted at the beast to pull its attention, bringing lightning down upon its head with little effect. Chunks of the red dragon flew from the tearing beast. 'Anukke! Where are you, you bastard?'

The world suddenly grew cold.

A stream of white mist frosted the land; a thin layer, freezing plants, water, men, and animals alike, quenching the city from the terrible heat it had been subjected to. Dark grey clouds shimmered and rumbled, verging on green as the thunderous medium built to a perfect storm. Great cannonballs of rock-hard ice descended upon the city in a sudden hell-storm, destroying buildings and killing anyone in their way. Dragons and Kahu took severe beatings, scattering to get out of its path. The gargantuan hailstones hurtled into Belroc with great force, tearing off plates of armoured scales, and the beast swung around to billow fire, melting the ice into harmless drops of water.

Icy stones crashed down around Khanaseri as he ran towards the beast and he saw, in between the falling stones, a gigantic form concealed within, heading straight for Belroc. It hit the world unlike anything he had ever felt, throwing him off his feet. He was sure it formed a crater in the earth, quaking the world a ripple at a time, spreading outwards to lift the earth in mounds, toppling structures all around it. The hail stopped thundering down, and Khanaseri rose to his feet, seeing the two beasts tear at each other while they lifted into the air, and he ran to Ganda'har's side.

The world shuddered, reverberating underfoot as Yidrog dropped on homes with Belroc on top of him, streams of fire and ice fighting to be the victor. Talgar ran next to the warlock and shouted, 'We need to get them closer to the ballistae over there!' He pointed to a section of the wall that still had two weapons left standing, Untara and Stentor already in place, working them to aim for Belroc. The warlock looked back from the wall and nodded.

'Can we trust this, Yidrog?' Talgar asked.

'We'll find out soon enough.' Khanaseri opened a portal, and they ran through, coming out on the other side of the brawling beasts near to where the captain was last seen. 'Ganda'har!' shouted Khanaseri, scanning the debris. 'Ganda'har!'

'Khan...' came Talgar's voice from around a mountain of rubble, and Khanaseri skidded around the corner, falling over the debris.

They found the captain perched up against the wall, his skin grey and his eyes open, sticky blood dragging long threads as it dripped from his mouth, his chest ripped asunder. The warlock sagged to the ground, his knees not strong enough to hold his weight. '*How many more do we need to lose? How much more do we need to endure?*' He didn't realise he was shouting. He crawled over to the captain and grabbed the man's head, pressing it to his, screaming and shaking.

Talgar closed the captain's eyes, and lay his hand upon the snowy head, mumbling a prayer under his breath. His heart ached at losing his friend, but there was still a dragon to kill and a city to save. He pulled Khanaseri from the ground and said, 'He wouldn't want us to give up now.' Invigorated shouts came from the direction of the fallen gate, getting closer. 'What is that?' asked Talgar, dropping the stricken warlock, then saw men running down the street, and he recognised one. 'Obediah?' A group of nearly fifty mages caused havoc as they made their way closer, lifting soldiers and throwing them to the wayside, manifesting weapons and hurling them at their enemies. Then he saw another in the distance that he knew, but barely recognised. The man had thinned to nothing, but he still fought with everything he had. 'Geolas?'

The man at the front made a hand gesture to the others not to kill Talgar and Khanaseri. 'This man I know, but you,' he pointed to Talgar, 'I don't. How did you come by my name?'

'We're the ones that rescued Khanaseri. We saw you taken prisoner as well, but there was little we could do.'

Obediah nodded. 'Do you have a plan?'

'I have ballistae on the wall there with men waiting...'

Obediah thought for a moment, staring at the silent and despondent Khanaseri and to the body of Ganda'har, and said, 'They will be seen to. I will take care of that.'

'Talgar!' Geolas shouted, making his way to them, and threw his frail arms around the soldier. 'I can't believe I am finally free.'

'What happened to you?'

Geolas glanced over to the fallen captain, his mood suddenly sombre again. 'Turneroth took me captive and left near to death. Obediah looked after me.'

Khanaseri pulled himself up and lay his trembling hand on his friend's head, kissing his forehead, and spoke, his lips trembling with rage. 'Time to kill this fuckin' thing.' He ran for the beasts, drawing his axe as he chanted, focusing on nothing else.

Yidrog lay under the ripping claws of Belroc, feeling the hot talons slice into its side, and sprayed a thick stream of liquid from glands in its throat that was so cold it froze everything instantly, turning Belroc's right claw into an icy mess. Yidrog's neck snaked out, and it snapped its jaws over Belroc's front limb, shaking violently and shattering the leg into shards of ice, flesh, and bone. Belroc reared up from the pain, the iced limb thrashing about bloodlessly, pieces of meat dangling from the wound like cold cuts.

Suddenly, a great mist enveloped the area, spreading fast and growing thick. Belroc burst through the fog in a glorious blaze, and flew after Yidrog, heading for a wall of smoke in the distance, crashing into buildings, struggling to fly with its torn-off limb, the wing unable to open completely. Belroc pushed himself off the ground, snapping at the swishing tail of the white dragon ahead. The wall of smoke drew near, rising high into the sky, a towering, thick wave billowing over the city.

*　*　*

'Do you think they can see us?' shouted Untara, leaning to his left with his hands cupped over his mouth.

Stentor glanced at him, the wind pushing at her back, then turned to the two dragons speeding towards them. She removed her helmet and dropped it to the stone floor, hearing it clatter at her feet. Wetted by sweat, her red hair was streaked and glistening. A faded wall of smoke rose high before them, concealing them from the dragons. 'I sure hope so,' she whispered.

Untara scowled and turned back to the beasts, setting his feet firmly on the ground while taking hold of the massive bow's handles, straining his muscles to move the ballista in the grooves on the floor to line up his shot, groaning as he did. 'Do you need me to help you move it? Untara wouldn't mind, you know, showing you how to use his weapon,' he said with a smirk, but Stentor was unusually quiet, focused on the dragons coming in at great speed. She grabbed the handles of her ballista and lifted it to change aim, glaring at him sidelong. Untara raised his brows at the strong-willed warrior woman, feeling a warmth in his pants, and he shook his head as he whispered, 'Witch...'

Leaning in, Untara waited for the ice dragon, thrumming the thick string of the ballista to check that it was taut. Yidrog came at them head on, its gigantic body nearly equal to Belroc's, but the black beast's outline overshadowed it still. They burst through the wall of smoke and reared up against the soldiers so close Untara thought he could touch them. Belroc snaked its head forward to wrap its jaws around Yidrog's neck, but air was all it got at the snap of its fangs. The illusion vanished with the smoke. Untara found the mark he was waiting for: the area where he'd chopped off some scales, seeing the raw pink flesh underneath, and let loose, the thick bow rope twanging loudly in his ears. The gigantic spear-like arrow struck deep, and fire burst forth from the beast's maw, exploding the ballista into a ball of flame.

'Untara!' Another spear hit Belroc's side, burying itself moments before the real Yidrog swooped in from behind and latched on to the Alpha's neck with its gigantic fangs, ripping and forcefully shaking with all its might. Stentor ran to where she saw Untara go over the parapet, searching for him as Khanaseri dashed up the stairs to her left, coming out on the wall near the entangled beasts with Talgar on his heels.

Dark blood sprayed from Belroc's neck, Yidrog's fangs doing their work well. 'Here!' Talgar shouted, and tossed him one of those silver balls that caused so much destruction. Khanaseri nervously grabbed it from the air, a sigh of relief escaping him when it did not explode. 'Got them from a dead soldier on our way here.' He showed he had another, and they ran towards the writhing beasts to throw the balls, watching them explode gloriously in flames of blue and red against the black dragon's scales.

Fragments of the balls lanced into the dragon's skin, taking more scales off the beast in a shriek of pain, and Khanaseri readied himself, dragging his axe from his back. He ran straight for Belroc, leaping from the wall with the axe held high, followed by Talgar and his daggers. More shrieks sounded from Belroc as the axe bit into its flesh, dragging a long cut down its chest until it came to a rest. Clutching on to the scales, Khanaseri beat the weapon into Belroc like a madman, splashing dragon's blood all over himself and screaming in anger and hatred until he felt the butt of the ballista arrow in the beast, and hammered it, driving it deeper still. A spray of fire warmed his back, the beast swinging its head from side to side.

A loud crack sounded with a final swing of the axe to the ballista bolt, and Belroc's pupils grew large as it lurched to the right, a sorrowful groan escaping its maw. It staggered, and Yidrog was instantly on top of the beast, tearing out chunks from its chest as it dropped to the ground in a hail of debris and dust. A roar so loud as to awaken the dead echoed over the city. Yidrog stepped on Belroc's body and tore out its heart, feasting on it before blowing streams of ice up into the air.

'Untara!' came Stentor's shouts as she looked down the wall, then saw him clamber back over the parapet, dropping to the stone floor a few feet away.

'If I knew you cared...' he muttered as he lay on the stone floor, his chest heaving up and down as he breathed.

'Oh, shut up. I was just worried I would be the only strong one left in the unit. Then I'd have to do all the work.'

'Ha! I ran when I saw its mouth open up, jumped over and held on for my life! Damn lucky I did,' he said, searching for the ballista, finding naught but charred remains burning on the wall.

Cheers sounded throughout the city as they heard the death cries of Belroc echo over them and saw the beast fall. Instantly, the remaining dragons snapped out of their deathly trance and flew away. Khanaseri had ridden the beast to the ground, falling and rolling between the wreckage and gore. He slowly rose, coughing up blood as he got to his feet and saw the last Kahu flutter its broken wings to get away. Hands trembling, he reached out to it as he chanted, snapping his fist shut, and the creature fell from the sky in a shriek. It hit the ground some distance to his right, tearing limbs and wings and splitting its skull in a spray of fluids against the rubble on the ground. *We did it, Ganda'har; we did it!* Khanaseri dropped to his knees, exhausted.

Turneroth's men lay down their arms as word spread of their king's demise, and were quickly placed under arrest and herded into lines, their weapons stripped from them. Cheers sounded all over the city, and soon people made their way out from under the rubble of their homes and cellars.

* * *

'The beast is dead! The beast is dead!' shouted a messenger, banging on the doors of the castle. 'They've surrendered!' The doors opened to a bloody display beyond, where lay dozens of bodies scattered around while Thelanor hammered his fists into the face of an enemy soldier near the entrance. Elves, Tarks, dwarves, and Ageians all fought with Terenore's soldiers. Thelanor drove the man to the ground with the punch, and kicked his leg from under him, snapping the limb at the knee. A howl of pain grew as the man sprawled on the ground. 'The beast is dead!' shouted the messenger again. 'Turneroth is dead!'

Terenore's men stopped fighting, the shock on their faces a thing of beauty to the rest.

'You lie!' shouted one Terenoran in the sudden silence of the room, limping to the door with his bruised and cut face, wanting to gut the messenger.

'Listen to the cheers of celebration! Your king is dead! Lay down your arms!'

The man reached the door, and the messenger jumped back to get away. 'No! This can't be! We're stuck here forever!' he shouted, dropping his sword to the ground in a clatter as he stared up at the white dragon standing triumphantly over Belroc, spewing up blasts of ice. All around, the fighting had ceased, the Terenorans sagging to the ground with their hands in the air, begging to be spared as weapons dropped in surrender.

From the back of the hall, a scream of pain sounded suddenly, a woman's voice ringing out loud, and everyone turned to see Ladriana sag to the ground, a knife sticking from her fat stomach, her face a mask of horror. Men dashed over to her, Kehlos, Thelanor, and Elyon in the lead, to reach her side. Thelanor winked and chanted, and a stream of blood flowed from her wound. 'Get Ehrhard and the healer here, quick!' Kehlos shouted. 'And get these prisoners out of here. We'll deal with them later!'

Elyon reached out to her stomach, wanting to heal her, but Thelanor quickly picked her up, and said, 'I've got this, King Elyon,' and carried her to a nearby room with Kehlos close behind to pull the doors shut.

The elf king stood perplexed, palming the door to get in and help them, but the door remained locked to him. Valheim appeared from around the corner of the castle's door, nearly running into the wall as he skid to a halt and stormed through. 'My son! You're alive!'

'Father!'

They embraced, holding each other for a moment before letting go, and Elyon drew back, clasping the young elf's shoulders to look at him, pride swelling in his chest.

'What's going on here? Why is everyone so dour?' asked Valheim.

Elyon was about to speak when a scream sounded from the room next to them. 'Ladriana's been stabbed in the stomach. It's a grave wound, not just for the babe, but for her as well. Her mage is with her now.'

'You're the best healer here! Why aren't you in there with them?' stormed the elf prince, readying to break down the door.

Elyon shook his head and said, 'Thelanor is confident he is enough. They will call for me if not, I'm sure of it. We need to have faith in others.'

The door swung open, and Thelanor stepped out, quickly closing it behind him again, his face a pale sheen of grey. All eyes were upon him, waiting for him to speak. A pregnant moment of silence lingered. 'The queen is safe; she will be fine.' Everyone relaxed, smiles crossing their faces before he continued, 'But we couldn't save the babe. It was a mortal wound. The child was dead before we could even start the healing.' A buzz of comments and voices filled the castle from all over. 'She asks to be left alone while she mourns her loss. I will go to the king and convey the message. Even though he is still recovering from his ordeal, he would want to know.'

Epilogue

The roar of the crowd was insatiable. The houses still smouldered, and the dead were still being carted off, but the people had gathered in the rubble of their city, waiting for the king to make an appearance. They lined the main road of the city, standing wherever there was a cleared spot on the street. The remaining forces of New Runswick stood proudly with Tiam's cavalry next to them, ordered in neat rows and blocks. Behind them, thousands of Ageian soldiers stood silently, waiting to be sent back home, their duty completed, their debt repaid.

The king once thought dead, limped up the blackened steps of the park, staring out over his people, clutching his side. Garidan searched through the sombre face before him, and said, 'Fellow citizens of New Runswick — we have endured. Endured not only a terrible onslaught of epic proportions, but endured as a nation. We stood together, not just as humans, but as a nation united! Elves! Dwarves! Humans! And not just people from this world, but beyond! Ageians, we thank you for your service and sacrifices. I promise I will get you back to your world. My Tark friends,' he stared at them off to the right, 'Arundhàbu, Naghita, Borka, you are now a part of this great nation. You protected the queen in these dire times. For your reward, I will grant you homes and land to do with as you please. Call Elmohria your home and start anew with us. We thank you for your service.'

Garidan translated it for them, then continued, 'We were beaten to the ground, yet we are stronger than ever. Let your voices be heard, brothers and sisters of Elmohria.' The crowds burst out with more deafening cheers and applause. He waited for them to grow quiet, letting them voice their defiance. Garidan sighed deeply and said, 'It is unfortunately true that the queen was stabbed during the battle. And it is with great sadness that I bring this news.' He paused for a moment, letting the words sink in. 'My unborn son died before I had a chance to even meet him, but the gods have spared her life. The queen is resting and in good health.

'Stand with me in a moment of silence to honour all those who gave their lives for us to live.' Heads bowed, the city fell silent. Wind rushing through the alleys and some trees, leaves rustling gently, were the only sounds made. A babe's cries broke the silence from somewhere down the street, and Garidan lifted his head. 'Now, as I stand here, I beg of you all, let us not have the divide of race in this nation. Let us work hand in hand and use each other's strengths. Let us pull together as we did in this battle. For we can conquer all.'

Again the crowd erupted, and Ehrhard shuffled closer, embracing the king with flowing tears and a blooming smile. 'Atwood would have been so happy to see you return, King Garidan.'

'Yes, it broke my heart to hear what had happened in my absence. It's something I'll have to live with for the rest of my days. Thank you, Ehrhard, for filling in wherever you could.'

'It was my pleasure, Highness.' They walked from the stage, heading back to the castle to plan the rebuilding of the city.

* * *

'I still can't believe you held the seat of power by faking a pregnancy,' Garidan laughed. 'Nor that you were ready to marry King Elyon to strengthen the rule and keep it.'

'Hey! I did it all for you, you know... I wanted to leave. Without you, this place isn't for me. Besides, it's not like I lost my fingers or nearly died from a spider bite. You were presumed dead, and looked it when I saw you, by the way. Next time, don't take so long to get back!'

'Next time?' Garidan jerked to her. 'There will be no next time, ever... I hope.'

'Is that so?' mocked Ladriana, her horse tugging on the reins and neighing as it walked on, wanting to stop and feed on the tall green grass next to the road.

'Yes, it is. I will live out my days inundated with the horde of children we will have, pestering me night and day to play with them while I need to deal with state business.'

Ladriana laughed. 'Oh, wow. You think I want children now, suddenly? To ruin this body, for you to get fat and let yourself go?'

Garidan sighed, seemingly enjoying the scenario she had painted. 'Best times...' His smile turned to a frown then, as he thought about the days that had passed since the fall of Turneroth. The lands were still bleeding from the devastation left in the dead king's wake. Good friends lay on rows of pyres, their smoke trails a cold reminder of the fires that had ravaged their city not long before. *So many died,* he thought. *Could we have done anything differently?* But many new friends had been made as well. Garidan had asked the dwarves what they wanted as a show of gratitude for their aid, but they wanted nothing except an invitation to a feast in the near future. After long goodbyes and lots of heartache, Dorgal and his dwarves had returned to Dorgandul with the gift bestowed by Abe.

King Elyon's elves returned to Rolldemere to rebuild, escorted by a host of men to help them in their endeavours. Garidan was still unsure if this was a favour for the elves or for the humans. Either way, both were happy about it.

Tiam's forces returned home a great deal richer, their bond to the crown strengthened more than ever.

He remembered seeing Khanaseri walk from Ganda'har's pyre the morning of The Great Burn, as it would come to be known, when thousands of pyres were lit – a day of remembrance for those who lost their lives defending New Runswick. The warlock had walked from one mourning site to the next, paying his respects to the fallen. Then made his way to one of the healers' halls, to sit beside Blanka's bed, waiting for the man to wake up. Garidan had walked down to join him every day to see how things progressed, and talked at length with Khanaseri, hoping to console the man somewhat. They waited and talked at the foot of his friend's bed, but even with the dragon inside him, Blanka did not look good; his chances were slim, and they worried he might not pull through. As a friend, he wanted to stay, but as king, he had duties to fulfil, and one of those duties was ensuring their safety.

For days, he tried to convince Magnus and Anavi to stay in New Runswick, but he could not persuade them. 'There's too much history here, too much death,' Magnus had said. 'We can't be part of it. I will go back to Kobo and rebuild The Flying Squirrel. There I can grow old and enjoy my last days. Here, I will never forget...' he had turned away then, slinging his pack over his shoulder. He could not remember a time ever seeing Magnus in such good shape. And all this talk about growing old and living out his last days seemed a tad far-fetched, to be honest, but that was what his friend wanted, and more so, deserved.

A thread tugged at his mind, and instantly a world of ash desecrated his well-being. The world burned beneath his feet, the rocky floor sharp and hot. Waves of hot air rippled over the burning, blackened plain, filled with streams of boiling red lava.

'Ah, my pet. You have come to speak with me? To beg for your release yet again?'

Garidan stopped and regarded the woman. Cross-legged, she sat before a spinning dagger on the dark stone, scraping rock as its tip dug into the hard surface. She eyed him with cold intent, spinning the blade, her dark eyes unwavering, and wispy dark hair fluttering over her face, concealing it from time to time. 'Who are you?' Garidan asked. 'And how did I get here?' She cocked her head. 'Speak!' he stormed, grabbing at an empty scabbard.

'Careful, now. I have broken you before... Don't make me break you again.'

A cold sweat bathed his forehead. 'You're the one from my dream?'

'Was it, though?'

'What? Why?' he started forward again, fists bunched.

'You have done me a great service, and for that, I will answer you. I am Dresra, and I needed a deeper connection with you to cross over.'

'Cross over?'

Her eerie voice, sounding sinister, a tone of laughter always present as she said, 'To this world. You built a bridge for me to walk over. There is so much potential in this world for me...'

'Garidan! Garidan!' He heard Ladriana say after the snap of her fingers brought him back. 'Kehlos is speaking to you. Where did you drift off to?'

'Yes, Kehlos? Apologies.'

'We're almost there, sire. I think it's time for you two to get in the coach.'

They reined in to dismount, and Garidan spoke to Ladriana as she took her seat. 'Do you think the Tarks will be fine while we're away?'

'Arundhàbu seems very at ease wherever he is, and Borka doesn't care too much where he is, as long as he can whittle. It seems you've done him a great favour. Only Naghita seems a bit of a puzzle, as if something haunts her. But it might just be my imagination. A whole new world and all that must make you think about things. I've left strict instructions that they're to be catered to as royal guests. I'm sure they'll be fine.'

Another man entered the coach, and Ladriana smiled. 'Thelanor. You've been unusually quiet. I'm glad you stayed on, even if it isn't as court mage. We can still use your skill in times like this when Abe isn't available.'

'I have been humbled, my Queen. There are few times in one's life that I think could alter one's course ultimately, and I bore witness to one such. I cannot be the same person I once was.' He chanted and sat back, keeping his focus on his work as they rode into Deresford.

Garidan held Ladriana's hand and said, 'I'm sorry for what you went through with this Baron. He'll soon be just another memory, just like Turneroth.'

*   *   *

Veranay opened her eyes slowly, smelling a sharp and unwelcome scent forced into her nose. Confused, head pounding, she blinked a couple of times to focus on an old man with grey hair and a beard hovering over her, a small vial of red liquid in his hands, which he quickly stowed in his pocket. Her breath caught in her throat and she scampered back, feeling the softness of a bed under her, her back now against an icy wall. 'Yallrick!' she screamed. Instantly, the items in the little home drifted into the air, and the old man's face changed to one of wonder.

'I'm here, girl! Don't fret. Yallrick's here,' said the dwarf on her right, where he sat on the bed, stroking her head with his hard hands.

Her heart calmed, and she pulled away from the calloused fingers, groaning as one scratched her cheek and the items dropped to the floor. 'What's going on here? Last thing I remember was the dragon, and then... Oh no...' She jumped up from the bed, her eyes wide, hands trembling. 'Yallrick? What did I do?'

Yallrick lowered his head. 'Ain't nothin' you did, girl. If anything, ye saved the rest of us.'

'Who did we lose?' she asked, her lips quivering.

'Veranay, it is not good—'

'Tell me who we lost!' Her scream was louder than she'd meant for it to be, a shrill cry leaving her cracked and scabbed over lips while she heaved breaths in loud rasps.

'Mpf. We lost Yantore, Hestith, Yogel, Blaskor, and Yanush. Vedalbore is not out of the woods yet. He is fighting for his life.'

Tears rolled down her face as she squeezed her eyes shut and dropped onto the bed. 'What about Skrug? I didn't see Skrug at the end.'

The dwarf limped into the room, squeezing his cap as he moved past the old man and said, 'Few new scratches, dear. But I'll be a'right. Glad to see you up, girl.'

She jumped up and hugged the dwarf. 'You too, Skrug.' She turned back to the quiet old man, watching him stare at her thoughtfully. 'Why is he here?'

Yallrick cleared his throat and said, 'You remember those men a while back asking you all those questions? Captain Gandi'har and his friend. This man is a friend to theirs.'

'Ganda'har, master dwarf. Let's show some respect to those who died for the rest of us to live.'

'My apologies, friend, I didn't know. We only want to help ye, lass. Ye know, get ye to someone that knows this sort of thing. We dwarves can't understand this mumbo jumbo. Give us a hammer and some iron and we'll forge the world for ye, but magic...tapping into the Source and that sort of thing...we know very little of. Anyway, this gentleman is—'

'Named Abe, but I have a feeling you were closing in on that already, weren't you?' Abe interrupted. Veranay looked around the room, unsure of what to say. 'It's okay, Veranay. You don't have to fear me. Captain Ganda'har told me about you, about your gifts, and your struggle to control them. I was naturally curious and wanted to see for myself.'

'Yes, you were giving me that vibe. An Abelore vibe...' She looked at the dwarves, embarrassed at the use of her words. 'What? I've always been good at guessing names.'

'An Abelore vibe...' jested the old man, and winced as his shoulder touched the back of the chair. 'Very impressive. But it is not a vibe, as you so casually put it, nor a guess. It is a sense very few have. Not even I possess the skill. You are born with it, or not.' Her stomach growled, and Abe sat back. 'How rude of us! You must be starving, girl. Goodness me. Yallrick, do you mind if we take this up while she eats something?'

Only now, with the talk of food, did Veranay smell the delicious aroma wafting through the home, but she ignored her stomach's pleas. 'No. What is it you want? I'll eat afterwards.'

Halfway between sitting and standing, Abe paused, glanced back at her, and sat back down. 'Very well. I am the headmaster at Elvenandre, in New Runswick—'

'New Runswick?' she whispered, clutching her knees. 'That's where the wicked men are.'

Abe sighed, seeing her mind reel at the thought. 'The fighting is done, Veranay. Those men have lost. Their king is dead.'

'Dead?' Her eyes came up fast, begging for it to be true.

'Yes, dear. It was a horrible battle, but we were victorious. Now, where was I? Oh yes, I am also the court mage there. For years, I have roamed and served, never having an ally by my side to share ideas with, or a meal on the dark roads. It is time I found myself an apprentice, my dear. You seemed like an ideal candidate to fill the void. There are few things in life more frustrating than to have a gift and not be able to use it to its full potential, wouldn't you say?'

'I guess...' she drawled.

'Good. You will learn from me directly, then, but mainly from books. It will be hard work, but a rewarding life. You will travel and walk by the side of royalty. Just don't get in their way; they don't like that. I speak from personal experience.'

Sombre stares followed her as she shifted on the bed, the dwarves keeping quiet and waiting for her to speak. She had come to love the dwarves. They were the only ones she could trust since her father's murder. They had shown her great kindness and a world she didn't know existed, having saved her life twice. But although they would never say it, she knew she was a hindrance to them. 'Can they come with me?'

She had caught the dwarf and Abe unawares, and both stammered before Abe said, 'Of course they can, my dear, but they won't. They have family here, Veranay.' She looked at the downcast dwarf, his face creased with deep lines of sorrow.

'Can I come and visit the dwarves whenever I want, and can they come visit me whenever they want?'

'Ah, we are negotiating. This is good. I will give you ten days a year to do with as you please and go anywhere you want. And yes, they can come visit you any time they want.'

'Make it fifteen days a year with coin, and I'll agree to your terms.'

'You drive a hard bargain, missy. Remind me to take you to the emporium with me,' Abe stated, biting his lower lip in thought. 'Excellent! We have an accord! Tonight we eat, and tomorrow we leave for New Runswick.'

Yallrick smiled happily, his eyes wet. 'I'll open a new cask. Oh, before I forget. We thought you might want this.' The dwarf revealed the dual poleaxe her father had held when he came to rescue her, and lay it on the bed. 'We went back and found it near the cage. I don't know how it survived, and the metal is something I have never seen before.'

Veranay watched her reflection in its shine and glided her finger over it. 'Thank you, Yallrick. This is the last thing I have of him now.'

* * *

The sun was high and the sky a deep blue, almost unnaturally so. Dorgal watched the rim of the world in the distance, where the blue of the sky melded with the blue of the sea. To the far right, the land stretched far into the dark waters, reaching for the rim but not quite able to make it, falling short with a long, curved bend of strand. He blinked a tear from his eye, thinking of the brothers they'd lost, and wondered how he would tell their families. *For all they know, we just went to deliver the weapons, nothing else. My brothers, one day I will join you at the Great Table and we shall feast until our bellies swell and our minds grow dim.*

He whipped the oxen, and the wagon lurched forward, rocking some of the sleeping men awake, a few snorts sounding as they swallowed their snores. The rickety wagon creaked and groaned, going over the ruts and rocks in the road. They were in no hurry to get back, but here on the summit of the mountain, where he could see far and wide, he could also see Dorgandul waiting for them, its great hammer resting wistfully in its place before the entrance. He looked back at his men. Despondently, they hugged their knees with little in the way of conversation. He knew not the words to cheer them up.

The slope down the rocky mountain path jostled them all awake, and Galiban climbed over the seat rest to join Dorgal. 'Seems we have a greeting party.'

'Aye, and Rochar seems none too happy.'

'He's just been worried, I'm sure.'

'Tell that to his face...'

'Dorgal Dammelsfiere! Where have you been?' Arms crossed and chest pushed out, Rochar stood in front of hundreds of dwarves who had gathered to see what was going on, their normal jovial customs hampered by Rochar's anger.

'First son of Yonas! The day is long, and the sun burns our backs.'

Rochar dropped his arms instantly, knowing something was wrong. Dorgal hadn't used his father's name since the day his mother died. He'd been out hunting for wild boar that fateful morning, and returned with the swine bleeding out over his shoulder as he walked into Dorgandul, proud of his catch. He had sauntered towards the great hammer where Dorgal had been waiting for him. That was the last time his brother called him by his titled name. A nasty pit in his stomach churned suddenly, and he could feel the blood drain from his face. 'What happened, brother?'

The wagon came to a stop a few feet from Rochar and dwarves moved past, leaving space for Dorgal to climb down and walk to his brother. 'The dragon army cut us off. We could not come back home. So we fought, like dwarves do. We stood with the humans and elves, and we killed those bastards.' Dorgal trembled, his eyes glistening and arms shaking with grief. His breaths came quickly, and spittle flew from his mouth. He wanted to remain strong for them all, but his heart grew heavy and his knees weak, his voice breaking with every word. 'We fought, brother...' Dorgal shook his head. 'With everything we had, we fought and made the names of the dwarves stand proud.' Dorgal dropped to the ground on his knees before Rochar, who grabbed him by the elbows to carry his weight. 'But we lost so many. On all sides...men, elves, dwarves. We stood as one and we defeated the bastards at a terrible cost.'

Rochar looked at the remaining dwarves, their clothes in tatters and their faces bruised and scarred. Odus limped off the wagon, followed by Galiban. Altogether, he counted seven dwarves, then looked back at Dorgal, worry in his eyes. 'Where's Bleak? Grimmel? Where's Brulle? Where're the rest?'

Dorgal pushed himself up with great effort, his legs shaking, pulling on Rochar's arms, and said, 'I'm sorry, brother. They know peace forever now.'

Those around Rochar couldn't believe what they were hearing. Thirteen dwarves snuffed out of existence! All gone, to be carved as statues in the Halls of Axeos. Their wails filled the air. 'We gave them their last honour and a good send-off, brother.'

Unable to comprehend the amount of loss and grief, Rochar shook his head in disbelief, wanting this day to start over. It felt like the great hammer of Dorgandul lay on his chest, his rapid breathing struggling to ease his need for air. 'Thirteen, brother... Thirteen that we'll never see again. Never be able to drink ale with again. Bleak, a dwarf I grew up causing mischief with. A dwarf who always had my back, now gone forever, and so many more. I need to sit down.' Rochar collapsed to a stone, hands covering his face.

And so he sat for the rest of the day, watching the dwarf women wail the news of their husbands' deaths, the children not comprehending the loss they had suffered. He sat there outside Dorgandul until the wagons moved off and the dwarves filed away to lock themselves behind doors to grieve. He sat alone until the sun disappeared and the stars came out. Until the cold became too much to bear, still he sat. He was a dwarf who didn't feel like celebrating.

At last, Rochar rose from the rock and walked to the hall, hearing the soft buzz of dwarves talking inside. He pushed open the doors, and all fell silent, staring at him as he dragged his feet to his chair and asked, 'What is this? What's going on here?'

'There's something else, Rochar,' stated Dorgal, and gestured to Galiban to fetch the wooden box. Galiban ran to the back of the hall, grunting as he lifted the box and brought it forward. He placed it before Rochar, nodding as he turned away. Old and worn, the box had seen better years. The hinges were loose and rusted from time spent in damp areas. *It's heavy, then, Galiban ain't no lightweight.* The box was the size of his bedside table. *Gold? Silver?* He frowned at Dorgal and sneered, 'What is this? Payment for our services?'

'A gift from the court mage of New Runswick.'

'That doesn't say what it is.'

'Open it.' Dorgal watched Rochar unclip the latch and slowly open the box, then said, 'Remember the tales of Uglëbahn? What was the saying again?'

'Whosoever wields the Rolägahr will gain entry to Uglëbahn, the City of the Forgotten,' read Rochar from a plaque inside the box, a shimmer reflected on his face from the item inside. 'Impossible! It's a myth! Said to be lost for generations! It can't be!' Gasps of awe sounded from the dwarves around them as they pushed to peer inside the box.

'There's only one way to find out, brother. We find Uglëbahn...'

*   *   *

Ale, warm as a hot summer's day, sloshed around in his mouth. It tasted bitter and flat, the bubbles all gone.

'How can you drink that hot piss?' he could hear Ol' Slip ask, and he looked up, then lowered his eyes to the table again, remembering Ol' Slip was no more. He took another swig, and swirled the liquid around in his mouth.

Ragian was right... We were never going back home. I shoulda listened to him. Now look at us, stranded here in a time not our own with nothing but the guilt of murdering all those people. I shoulda listened to you, my friend. He remembered how the men had died in the ditches those dwarves had dug, running in the darkness and falling into those spikes. *Brutal.* Then came that mage's sorcery, tearing at man and beast with those tendrils of dark magic, breaking their psyches and bodies for good. *Diabolical.* But standing on that hill, watching Turneroth lose complete control to the beast within to kill his own men, feasting on their bones like they were caviar. *Unimaginable.*

'Snap out of it, Xare! You can't keep going back there,' said a woman's voice from the other side of the table. His head came up slowly, and he removed his hood.

'And where should I go, Fen? All we have is each other now, and you're more drunk than sober. Hell, you were probably drunk during the battle.'

'Weren't you? I thought that's how we stayed alive. I know that's how I stayed alive when I fought with that bastard on the wall. Rode a ladder down to the ground from the top of the wall, breaking no bones. Try doin' that sober...'

He shook his head, working his temples with his thumbs, then chewed on a wet cigar.

'Look, I might be drunk most of the time. Doesn't mean I ain't ready for anything. We've got to find our own way now. At least here, in this time, I don't have to worry about that godawful sister of mine. Nag, nag, nag all the time. No wonder I drink so much... I've been trying to drown her out for years.'

Xare wasn't listening anymore. He was staring at another table on the far side of the inn. 'Oi! Talking to you! Rude bastard,' Fen snapped.

'Shh! Can you keep quiet? Or are you completely incapable?'

'I guess I'm capable. I just don't wanna. What you looking at, anyway?' She followed his gaze, but didn't see what he was looking at.

'Come on, Fen. Let's go say hi to someone.' He grabbed his mug of hot ale and rose from the table.

'I was just gettin' comfortable,' she mumbled, her feet crossed over on the table as she leaned back, the mug of ale resting on her stomach. Annoyed, she dragged her feet down, nearly flipping the flimsy bench with a start, and glanced around, daring anyone to say anything with her cold stare. 'Wait, I'm comin'. Hold on, don't move so fast.' She swerved past the other tables, the patrons staring at her silently as her ale sloshed all over, and she bumped into Xare from behind. 'Oops! Why'd you make me spill my drink?' she said, and slapped him on the arse.

'Sit down, Fen! You're attracting attention.'

As she lowered herself to the chair, and placed her feet back on the table with a kerfuffle, her eyes went wide and she said, 'Bohan? I thought you're dead.'

'Shh! Not so loud!' scowled the mage. Content no one was paying them any heed, he continued, 'I ran when I saw Belroc emerge. I knew the fight was over. Do you two have any plans on what to do next?'

'I was hoping *you* had...' said Xare, taking a seat next to the mage.

Bohan shook his head. 'I'm still running through a few ideas. No doubt they are hunting all the Terenorans who escaped. I guess it might not be a bad idea to stick together for now.' Xare and Fen nodded, taking small sips of the hot ale.

* * *

'Hey! Hey! Khan! Wake up, you dolt!'

Khanaseri snorted as his head dropped from his hand, his neck whipping back fast and his eyes shooting open. His heart raced in his chest, the drumming a spectacular display of his mortality as the lurid dreams were snatched from him. He coughed and spat in a bucket near the end of the bed, then ran his hands over his pate, feeling the bristling hairs grow out. 'Blanka? You're awake! How are you not dead? The healers said your lungs aren't functioning properly. The hit collapsed them or punctured a hole in one. I can't remember. They sedated me when I picked up one of the healers by the throat,' the warlock said, grinning wide.

'That's only because you have few friends. You don't want to lose any of them.' Blanka chuckled, but saw his words strike true. 'What's wrong?'

'They're only getting fewer... Ganda'har's dead. Belroc tore him apart after you got injured.'

'What? No, that can't be...he's Ganda'har. He's Captain Ganda'har. He's unbreakable.'

'Well, Belroc broke him.'

'I'm so sorry, my friend. I know you two were close.'

'Aye. Thank you.'

'I was lucky. Being bonded with a dragon as strong as Belgarr has its perks. He has healed me a lot. What happened? I can't remember anything after crashing into that building.'

'We won the—'

'Yes, with my help!' crowed a man from the bed next to Blanka in the long hall of injured people that surrounded them, diaphanous veils covering the beds to keep the insects out. The man rolled to his side, lost in wonder as he pulled up one side of his lip and said, 'I was astounding...'

'Who are you?' Blanka sneered, air wheezing from his mouth, puffs of red mist spraying up. 'Khan, who is this nitwit?'

The warlock sighed, dropping his head back. 'Don't you mean Yidrog? You were merely a host. An annoyance he had to deal with while he fought.'

'Wait, you're Anukke?' Blanka asked, flabbergasted.

'The one and only.'

Blanka frowned. 'Why can't I sense Yidrog in you?'

'I will it so. You're welcome, by the way.'

'*Welcome?*' stormed the warlock, his gruff voice loud and deep. 'You nearly left us for dead. Why did it take you so long to get here? How many lives could have been spared if you'd come in haste?'

'Just remember, I could've not come at all.' Anukke lay back on the bed, folding his legs on top of each other. The hustle of the healers got louder, and as a group moved closer, he cursed and turned away from them. *You do bad things, and you don't get rewarded, you do good things, and you still don't get rewarded... At least doing bad things is fun. Maybe I should stick with that.* Anukke threw open the veil covering his bed, groaning as the stitches pulled in his chest. 'I don't care, I'm leaving.' Limping from his bed, he grabbed on to the railing of nearby beds and tables, anything to steady his sway, and saw the cold drift from his fingers, spreading out and freezing drops of condensation on the warm metals, making them slick and icy to the touch.

'You're leaving already?' Khanaseri asked, and rose to follow him.

Anukke pushed open the door, and sunlight bathed him fully, blinding him until he cupped his hand over his eyes, his wispy white hair flicking and waving in the wind. An annoying voice, shrill and droning, came from his right.

'Lord Anukke! Lord Anukke! I'm so glad you are well.' A pot-bellied man with black hair curling from under the rim of a dazzling red beret ran towards him, and, with his shouting, more citizens turned to regard him, clapping and chanting his name. 'Lord Anukke! I am Cecil Von

Rhose. The king and queen have sent me to liken your appearance so they can erect a statue in honour of the great Anukke. I have a few ideas that I'd love to run by you... That is, if milord has the time.'

A man dropped to his knees before Anukke, kissing his grimy shoes as he gave honour. 'Thank you, Lord Anukke! You saved my family! How can I ever repay you? How can any of us?'

A glimmer came to life in Anukke's eyes. *I think I can live with this for a while after all. Now, what can I ask him to do for me? Mmm. Ah, I have it.* 'Prepare me a proper feast. Not this garbage they give me here. And you! Find me a tailor to fix my clothing. And you, Cecil Von Rhose, better have something good for me. I don't want to seem weak. Or greedy.'

'Too late for that...' whispered Khanaseri loud enough for Anukke to hear, but not the rest of the crowd.

'Don't test me, warlock. I'm grateful for you saving me from my prison, but you are not my equal.'

Anukke limped away, giving orders to the folks of New Runswick, when Blanka appeared from the door, pushing a healer away, his breath rasping. Khanaseri turned in time to catch the collapsing man and said, 'Whoa, Blanka. You need to rest. What are you doing out of bed?'

It took a while for the bonded to speak, his face turning various shades of purple and red, his eyes deep-sunken. 'My son,' he wheezed. 'I need to find my son...'

'He can't leave! He will die! Do you want your friend to die?' roared the healer.

'If my friend wants to go find his son, I'll carry him,' replied the warlock sincerely.

'I am the physician here! Not you! I am the esteemed Belikane Rouge! You, sir, are a verpus! You know nothing of healing... Don't come knocking on this door when he stops breathing!' The healer spun around and stormed back into the hall, slamming the door shut behind him.

Khanaseri shook his head in disbelief, jaw hanging slack. 'Did he really just call me a cock?' Blanka laughed and coughed, struggling for breath again as he choked on the constant blood in his lungs. The warlock creased his forehead, brows raised high, and asked, 'Are you sure you'll be okay, my friend?'

'Positive. Pick me up.'

Moaning as he came upright with Blanka in his arms, Khanaseri said, 'I know where they are. I searched for them while you slept. It's not far.'

The End

AFTERWORD

Thank you for reading Warlock's Path. I really hope you enjoyed this novel. If you have a moment, please leave a review on your preferred store as this will allow me the opportunity to write more books such as this. I would really appreciate it. Reviews are especially critical in today's world. Help other fantasy readers and tell them why you enjoyed this book. Thank you!

* Leave a Review by scanning this:

Want to stay updated with news about my books?
* Join my mailing list at:
https://www.mariushvisser.com/contact
* Like me on Facebook:
https://www.facebook.com/mariushvisserbooks
* Follow me on Instagram:
https://www.instagram.com/mariushvisser
Thank you again, reader. I hope we meet again soon amidst the battles to come in a new adventure.

* If you haven't read The Call of Jonas Creed, there's an excerpt on the next page.

The Call of Jonas Creed

Bereaved, Jonas Creed stared over the mound of dirt before him. A wreath of white and yellow flowers hung over a rough-edged marble headstone that glared back at him, accosting him with his failures as a father and husband. There was no one else, just him and the awful silence screaming in his ears. In terrible anguish, he pulled at the heavy black and grey beard that covered his blotched face - a gift from many years of felling trees in harsh weather. Tears streamed down his cheeks, wetting his beard as he forced a smile and remembered a time before his son became a man. A time when Jorin was but a boy playing with sticks instead of swords. A time when his wife was still alive, not lying before him under a heap of dirt in the deathly chills of the vacant cemetery.

There had been many wonderful days in his life since the birth of his son, but none were better than that very day sixteen years ago. With all the stress that day had brought, it had been burned into his memory forever. The day had started off just like any other during the previous few months, with him waking in a pool of sweat, breathing heavily, and glancing around the dark room, searching, listening, and gripping the sheets tight. But then he heard the groans of his wife next to him and saw her turn in her sleep, a gigantic belly lifting and pulling at the sheets. His heart slowed, and he wiped the sweat from his face, knowing he'd just had another nightmare. Jonas threw the sheets aside and swung his legs off the bed, yawning, stretching, and forcing his eyes wide to wake himself and get ready for the day. He quickly dressed and then tiptoed across the room to Ayla's side of the bed. He lifted the blanket, smiling as he rubbed the big mound where her flat stomach used to be, and kissed it.

'Where are you off to so early in the morning, mister?' he heard her ask with a groggy voice, gentle and soft. 'No kisses for me today?' she mocked. The sun was barely up, its orange rays creeping through the wooden slats over the windows, the thin beams of light giving life to the gloom as a cool breeze accompanied it.

'Aye, only because if I start, I won't stop,' Jonas said all serious, brows knitted with deep creases between his eyes as he felt her warm hand slip into his.

'Don't you dare leave me begging for a kiss. You will have to contain yourself.' She chuckled. 'Don't work too late today. The little one has been kicking me all night long. I fear the time is drawing close.' She didn't know just how right she was.

He leaned over Ayla and kissed her, squeezing her warm arms with his cold hands and felt goosebumps come alive over her body.

'You're cold!' she snapped and yanked the blankets over her arms.

'Hey, you wanted a kiss. I merely live to please you.' He laughed at her scowl and slipped from the room, hearing her call to him as he closed the door.

'Get the midwives to come and see me this afternoon, just to be safe.'

'Yes, dear.'

'And bring some bread home with you.'

'Alright, dear.'

'Ooh, and some cold meats.'

He rolled his eyes, sighing in the dark, and picked up the feller's axe that leaned on the wall. 'Of course, Ayla.'

'What happened to dear?' he heard her growl and chuckled as he quickly sneaked from their home, knowing he would pay for his insubordination later. 'Jonas!' Her voice followed him down the narrow footpath of his garden but was already growing faint by the time he reached the gate, where he smiled at the crooked metal arms of some structure his wife had been toiling with. 'You doubt me, but it will be beautiful. You just wait and see,' she had told him a few days back when she had started the project.

Dew darkened the red sandy roads, a layer of wet covering the surface of everything left out in the open. He made his way down the street. 'Agh!' Jonas cried and nearly fell because of the slippery mud, arms swinging wildly for balance as his boots gathered clumps of clay. He stopped at a dry patch of grass under the awning of Kelvar's bakery and stamped his feet to rid them of the muddy parasites. All around him, doors creaked open and closed with a caring touch so as not to wake the entire village; men and women groaned and yawned, readying for the day.

Jonas hoisted his axe over his shoulder and walked past a building of grey stones packed with red clay, which sealed it from the cool draughts that came ever so frequently during the winter seasons. Angelica and Toly, the village's midwives, shared a home out of convenience, for neither had children nor a husband to concern themselves with. He would need to come back later to get them, but for now, he needed to head west.

The walk up to the forest in the mountains didn't feel particularly bothersome today. Jonas felt light, his spirits high and his mood jaunty. With a big smile on his face, he joined the other fellers already chopping down trees, stripping them of their branches by running their axes along the trunks, cleaving through the wood like butter.

'What ya smilin' at, ya big lug? Get to work! Your plums have done their job. Now you do yours!' called a man with a great ragged head of brown hair and a short, crooked nose that leaned to the right.

Jonas couldn't help but laugh even more. 'Oh, Yurgassun. Life's too short to be angry all the time. Today, you won't get me to join you. And I have to leave early to get the midwives—'

'And if you don't start working pretty soon, this day will never end. Just wonderful. I got the happy one today... I swear, there's always got to be one every day. Brison needs a partner to trim the skinnies at the back. Lend him a hand for the day. At least there you won't be missed when you run off again. This baby of yours is already makin' the rest o' us work twice as hard.'

'Can you imagine how I feel then?' Jonas chuckled and saw the grin on Yurgassun's broad face.

'Good. Maybe we can make a feller out of him yet.'

Jonas slapped him on the shoulder and said, 'We don't even know if it's a boy or a girl yet.'

'Does it matter?'

'I'll not have my daughter lugging logs around with the likes of you bunch hot on her heels.'

'I'm her godfather. She won't be safer anywhere else.' Yurgassun laughed as Jonas strode past him and climbed over a fallen tree. 'I just hope she looks like Ayla.'

'Still don't know if it's a boy or a girl...'

'Uncle Jonas!' came a high-pitched wail from the woods over the rise. 'Uncle Jonas!'

He turned around, searching the woods for movement, and called back, 'Over here!' Through the darkness of the forest, he saw a figure running toward them, its short, thin legs buckling from exhaustion. Then a boy darted into the clearing, stumbling forward and breathing heavily. 'Here, boy! What is it?'

Men turned from their work and gathered as the boy drew close, huffing and wheezing air with terrible rasps from his throat. 'It's time! Ayla...' The boy sucked in some air. 'The baby's coming.'

Eyes wide, Jonas tensed up, his heart racing crazily. 'Did you call the midwives, boy?' he shouted. 'Are they on their way?'

Bent over with his thin, frail arms resting on his knees, the boy glanced up and wiped the snot dripping from his nose with his rolled-up sleeve. 'They left when it was still dark out for a birth in Yuronia. We have no one.'

Shit. His axe dropped to the ground as he sprinted from the clearing with some of his feller friends following close behind.

* * *

'Ayla!' Jonas burst through the door, heart pounding in his chest, and heard a humming chant echo from down the hall, followed by a shriek. 'I'm here!' The world spun, eyes darting, legs moving on their own. He could not remember giving them the orders to run. The weathered, grey boards of the corridor walls rushed at him, and his hands shot up instinctively in front of him; the impact to the slats was too much for the wall, splitting the timbers with his weight as one arm went straight through, burying him up to the shoulder. He yanked it out, tearing the skin from his arm, and spun around, running for the room to his right. Stopping in the doorway, he watched a long-robed man of greying years who was holding Ayla's hand, mumbling a prayer over and over.

'No offence, Arlon, but I don't want whoever you are praying to here in this house.' Ayla screamed again, and he rushed forward, grabbing her other hand. She lay in a tub with her legs propped over the sides, the rusty, worn edges cutting into her calf under her knee, a thin trickle of red leaking to the floor. Her white gown was soaked from the water as she thrashed about, sticking to her naked body, her hair plastered to her face in a sheen of sweat. It all looked very undignified, but there was nothing for it. She had to push through this and more so. The lukewarm water sloshed over the sides of the tub, splashing over Jonas and making the wooden floor slippery. He glanced back to the priest, who had fallen silent. 'Thank you for lighting the fire under the water heater.'

Arlon inclined his head and whispered, 'I thought it could bring her some comfort.'

'What do we do now?' he begged, and leaned closer to his wife.

'I'm no midwife, Jonas,' Arlon mumbled, spreading his hands. 'I only bless and pray for good health.'

Another scream tore through the home, and Ayla's hand shot up, grabbing Jonas' ear to pull it down against her wet breast. 'I don't care who you are or what you can or cannot do, but get this baby out of me!' She let go, and Jonas dropped to the floor, rubbing his burning ear, surprised at her strength.

'Okay. Arlon, bring me some sheets and thread,' he said and rolled up his sleeves, kneeling over the end of the bath to get close. 'You will have to push, dear. I know it hurts, but there is no other way.'

'You know nothing, bastard! Fuck!' her head careened backward, and she let out another scream, veins bulging on her forehead and neck as her face turned red.

Jonas couldn't think of a time he had ever heard her swear and tried to calm her, rubbing her leg as he nervously muttered, 'It a... It's going to be okay, dear.'

'Oh, shut up, you prick! You did this to me!' Jonas cleared his throat and slipped back, away from her wrath.

'Push!' he shouted, glancing at the priest who had run into the room with a basket full of brown and white sheets. Ayla grabbed Jonas' hand and squeezed, trembling from pain and cold, sobbing utterly as she screamed and pushed. 'I feel something! Breathe, Ayla. Now push!' Jonas felt the thin hairs, then the side of the head. 'Push!' The bathwater turned red, and he wanted to scream to the priest for help but saw the man's wide eyes and feared for the worst. She was in it now. There was no turning back. 'Breathe, Ayla! Push!'

'Cocksucker!' she shouted, gritting her teeth.

He felt a tiny ear and nearly wept. 'Push!' A shoulder. 'Push!' An arm, chest. 'Push!' A soft bum, and Ayla screamed, clutching the sides of the bath, bending the metal with the adrenaline rushing through her. 'Nearly there! Push!' A leg, then feet, and he raised it from the water quickly and grabbed the umbilical cord between his teeth, tearing it in two. 'Tie it off, priest,' he said, spitting blood onto the floor.

'It's not breathing! Give it here!' roared Arlon and held out his hands, taking the baby as the mother wailed and the father stood with eyes wide, lips parted to release a scream of utter helplessness. He turned the baby over, tapping it on the back a few times, the silence in the air an overwhelming horror. Only the whimpering of the stressed parents filled the room. Jonas stood with his hands in his hair, tearing at it as snot and tears streamed down his face. He was slowly backing away to the door, feeling the urge to run and never stop, to never turn back. A soft wail was born at first, growing louder and louder, then tiny arms and legs were suddenly kicking the air.

The child breathed, and Jonas sagged to the floor, a sensation he had never felt before sweeping over him, a feeling of desperate relief. He wailed and crawled over the wet floor to his wife in the tub, grasping her hand and kissing it dearly while she also cried with joy.

Arlon wrapped the baby in a sheet and handed it to Ayla. 'Congratulations, it's a boy!'

Jonas leaned over her, staring at the tiny, frail boy with his black eyes and the few hairs on his head. He kissed her forehead, then the boy, and rose, feeling her hand clutch his still.

'Where are you going?' Ayla asked, exhausted and in pain.

'I'll be right back, dear. Just got to tell the boys the good news is all. They ran down with me, and I'm sure Yurgassun wants to know what's happening.'

Jonas remembered that day clearly. How he had walked out of his house and given the news to those who waited outside. How they had clapped and laughed, raised him over their heads, and congratulated him. It was the happiest day of his life.

And now. Now he stood in this solitary place on the worst day of his life, burying his beloved Ayla, and knowing not how to handle it.

The Call of Jonas Creed is available for purchase right now OR get it free when you join my mailing list and get all updated information of my novels: https://BookHip.com/FFQRGVS.

Heroes may be forged in fire...

Legends speak of a shadow realm that echoes our own, called the Void, where gods and demons roam the very paths we mortals tread, hidden from our sight and touch, judging us at our worst moments, laughing at our woes.

The Void is inaccessible to all still living save those blessed, or perhaps cursed, with the means to cross between realms. The lands of the gods are not to be trespassed lightly, but the rewards...

Deep in the heart of Yahrska, past the beautiful Brokar Valley, lies Barren Hollows: a small and peaceful village where all Jonas Creed wanted was to leave his past behind and become the loving husband and father he swore he always would be.

But fate leaves none unscathed. Someone is looking for the Voidwalker, and will stop at nothing to get what they want.

...but Legends are born in blood.

The Call of Jonas Creed is an epic fantasy short story that is the prequel of the new up and coming series to be released next year, by Marius H. Visser.

A professionally trained Information Technology Specialist Marius H. Visser spent the better part of a decade honing his writing skills and pushing the bounds of imagination after his début fantasy novel Mercury Dagger - A Tale From Kraydenia. When Marius H. Visser is not off exploring the wilds of Australia, he is dreaming up new adventures and monsters to cause chaos in a fantastical world filled with twists, loyalty, honour and great and terrible battles.

www.ingramcontent.com/pod-product-compliance
Lightning Source LLC
Chambersburg PA
CBHW050111120726
47904CB00004B/1304